DISGRACED

JAYNE GREEN

CONTENT NOTICE

BEWARE: CONTENT NOTICES ARE SPOILERS

It is a thriller, meaning difficult circumstances are its bread and butter. Of concern to some readers might be: a one-sentence description of a deepfake porn video (suggestive only), a memory of a rape (minimal detail), extreme physical violence (with minimal description of gore), attempted suicide, an abduction, and a controlling, abusive relationship.

DAY ONE

1

____

The university security guard postured in the doorway, hand on the walkie talkie hanging off his belt as if it were a gun. Martin bristled, jerking open the last drawer of his metal desk and tearing into a pile of unclaimed student papers.

He guessed Bernard had insisted on him being watched while he emptied his office. Bernard did not have a grey metal desk from the seventies. Bernard had a beautiful oak desk and an office with stained glass windows and used the old college mystique to groom female students.

Yet Martin was the one who had been terminated. His union lawyer had done what she could, but tenure was no protection. And he knew that Bernard had arranged it all. Martin dug out the papers and dropped them into the recycling box.

He eyed the guard. "You willing to take that out to the bin for me?"

The man only moved his hand from the deadly walkie talkie to cross his arms in that way meatheads do to push out their biceps.

Martin picked up the full box, making a show of its weight with an Oscar-worthy grunt, then waited for the guard to stand aside, which he did, slowly. Past him and into the hall, Martin shifted the box to a more comfortable position.

There was a perverse satisfaction in giving those who humiliate others exactly what they want, knowing their day would come. Martin was a triple black belt in Tae Kwon Do and could take the guard down before he knew what had happened to him, but did not look it. A gay man hiding lean muscle under baggy flannel shirts, a worn fleece jacket, and tree-hugger hiking boots, Martin did not mind seeming harmless, especially to those who relished every bit of petty power they got into their hands. Maybe he would be there for their downfall. Maybe he would not. But their day would come.

In the past, he had exposed abusive systems of power within the government and their corrupted relationships with big business, especially in the financial sector. Bloodsuckers of the poor, all of them. His colleagues and pundits could call him a crypto-communist all they liked, but the numbers in the data he produced did not lie. They had tried to link him to foreign governments. China, Iran, Russia, whoever was the favoured boogeyman of the news cycle. That was all done now. Position lost. He could no longer have that kind of influence.

One office door after another was shut. His colleagues knew he was moving out this morning and decided goodbyes were not in order. No surprise there. But as Martin turned through the hall, he saw a sliver of light cutting into the stained industrial carpeting. Bernard had left his door ajar.

"Martin, is that you?"

A few of the papers fell off the top of the box, and he left them there. "Fuck him," Martin said under his breath by way of reply. "Let him pick them up."

In the alcove with the printer and bins, he opened the recycling lid with his free hand, inadvertently slamming it against the wall. Wincing, he expected Bernard to come around the corner to taunt him and held his breath for a moment. Then, pissed at himself for caring, he dumped in the paper and let the top fall noisily. "Let him gloat," he said, walking away.

This time, Bernard's door was shut. Martin rubbed his closely shorn head, considering whether to knock and have one last word, but kept going.

At his office, the guard was still performing his masculinity, but Martin no longer hid himself, walking past him with the relaxed stance of a man who can kill with his hands. The guard flinched. A bit of his pride restored, he packed the last of his things. Digging into a drawer, he grabbed a handful of pens and pencils and threw them into a cardboard box.

"Stealing pens?" Bernard appeared, leaning in the doorway. "Why not? Why limit yourself to stealing a graduate student's research?"

Martin turned on him, saying through gritted teeth, "In for a penny, in for a pound."

But Bernard simply chuckled, leaning more comfortably into the frame. His lanky body was draped in trousers and a tweed jacket, and his affected long silver hair drooped over one eye. The man was only short a pipe for all his pretensions. It did not matter that his sallow face would not have inspired any of those students to turn their head if they passed him on the street. Bernard was like a greasy-haired boy with a guitar when he stood in front of the lectern, postulating grand themes. A zero made a ten merely by standing on the stage.

"If screwing students were a terminating offence, Bernard, this would be you."

"Alas, it is not. That right has yet to be taken from us. But you can add denying students their sexual autonomy to your crimes." He gestured with a flourish. "Martin Monaghan, you are hereby cancelled for not affirming sexual positivity inside the student body."

The guard laughed, but Bernard did not acknowledge him. Instead, he watched Martin with the benevolence of a criminal priest as he continued to throw odds and ends into the box.

Martin put the rest into the nearby red canvas wagon, slung his bursting backpack over one shoulder, and gave one last look at his office.

He said goodbye to his days alone at his desk; the door shut and window open, crisp breezes winding in with the scent of freshly mown grass, warm sun spilling onto open books piled on top of other books, their marked-up pages outstretched to catch the light. The sound of students chatting outside his door and laughing on the lawn at the joy of term's end, all promising long days of writing in solitude.

Now, the desk was barren and the shelves against the wall held nothing but scraps of paper, and the odd push pin or paperclip. Two hard orange-seated chairs were stacked against the dingy wall, a few yellowing political cartoons taped overhead. The stained armchair, where students had cast themselves down, struggling to understand, or leaned in, eager to debate, sagged lonesomely.

Martin stooped to grasp the wagon handle and the backpack shifted around in front of him, making the whole damn thing even more awkward. Putting the backpack firmly on his shoulder, he left his sanctuary behind.

"That's it?" Bernard said as he stepped to the side, then directed his attention to the guard. "He hasn't stolen anything other than a few pens?"

"Who paid for the books?" The guard asked.

It was a good question and Martin wondered if he would move up out of this job and into the police, thinking of new ways to harass innocent victims over his donut and double-double each day. It would not be a walkie talkie in his hand then, and Martin had no doubt he would use it whenever he got the chance, and exactly on whom.

Bernard appraised the guard. "Paid for out of his books allowance. He's entitled."

For no good reason, the exchange broke him. The control Martin had on his resentment slipped, and with it his pride, as he stormed past the two men, dragging the bright red wagon behind him, banging it on every obstacle, and fully intending to throw onto the road every box he had so carefully packed in his car downstairs. There was nothing left to salvage from this life.

He punched the ancient elevator's button, but there was no movement. Someone had it on hold. He stood, breathing shaggily, waiting for whoever still had a career to release it.

Yes, he had done it. He had stolen Parisa's work. But she had insisted that he not cite her. Not even as an anonymous source. They would come looking for the author of the data that could bring down one of Canada's most influential families. Offices for the Wellingtons' payday loan company were in every small town and low income neighbourhood. Their political influence was wide and deep. There was a reason for her to be afraid. So Martin shielded her in his work. Everyone in the department knew it and why. No one had approached him or warned him, not even Bernard, the chair. Then suddenly, the dean demanded a review of his work. As the victim, Parisa's name had been kept out of it. Then on the last day of the tribunal, when his termination was handed down, Bernard let it slip and Parisa and her son disappeared.

One text.

> We're on the road don't come after us it's not safe.

He had tried to call, but the phone was dead. Parisa knew her phone could track her. In her teens, she had been an activist in the democratic movement in Iran and that had taught her hard lessons about state powers of control. She must have thrown out the SIM card.

After the tribunal, he rushed to her basement apartment all the same. Martin ran around to the back of the house and down the stairs. The door was wide open. It had been turned upside down. The red canvas wagon she used to haul books and groceries was on its side, near the door. He righted it, then searched for mementos, things she would miss once she was safe. Maybe he could get them to her.

Then he saw it. Arash's stuffed rabbit. His heart tore open. Imagining her son sobbing for the blue-eared bunny, worn thin and lumpy from a child's love, Martin sank to the floor, clutching it, blaming himself for not having protected them. Finally, he got up, wiping his face on his sleeve and gathered what he could into the wagon and left.

The elevator doors finally heaved open. Martin manoeuvred

Parisa's wagon in and pressed the button for the ground floor. Clanging and sighing, the elevator descended the three floors and finally opened.

"Martin."

And there stood his brother in his bespoke three-piece suit, looking like all the money in the world, but with his heart on his sleeve. Conor put a firm hand on Martin's shoulder and drew him in. He dropped the handle of the wagon and fell into his brother's embrace.

2

"This is where the magic happens?"

Nick smiled privately as he watched Bea tug at her jean skirt in the reflection of one of the massive computer displays.

Her lower lip trembled with the pleasure of being the first of his women to be invited into his inner sanctum. Bea had made it through a year of small requests to please him, one little thing here, a yes, a no, a not that, a please this, now come, now go, until she lost what she wanted navigating the territory of his desires. At first, Bea had balked as the gifts, flirtatious and flattering texts, phone calls, and expensive dates came one after another, objecting, "You're love-bombing me!" But she had said it all with a vulnerable turn to that beautiful mouth, and he knew he had her.

That night at the club, she and her friends stared at him over their drinks, tottering on their expensive high heels, sucking on straws, advertising their skills. Rich girls like this, looking to snag richer men, securing a future. Her friends were haughty and wild, but Bea's eyes darted among them, checking to see if she was doing it right. Her lips. Her chin. Perfect.

Nick gave her his boyish smile, softening his eyes for a touch of broken-winged bird. Then he walked over slowly, letting her see the power of his body, and took her hand. The lights flashed around them. The music thumped through their flesh. He led her away from her friends into the VIP section without looking back. She must have, though, her eyes wide, expectantly mouthing to her friends, "Oh my God!"

"Mr Barnes." The guard held open the velvet rope for them to pass. His booth was there, ready whenever he needed it. Nick was a perfect gentleman, not touching her except to make sure she was seated comfortably where the cameras could get a shot.

The pair would be hashtagged within minutes. Photos posted on every social media platform. Her Instagram account would be scoured for the details about the beautiful young woman sitting with Nick Barnes, the founder of the rising star in internet security, Cristo Solutions. He would set his team to deepening that online conversation tomorrow. Beyond the company's security work, he managed a cyber revenge hit team for the special client's needs. The goal would be to draw Bea in closer. They would comment on posts and share pictures of her with gushing compliments about her beauty and how he was smitten. They would leak the budding relationship to the gossip sites and move the news through there.

On cue, the cameras flashed and she turned and hid, letting her thick blond curls fall across her face. The team could get those AI corrected and up within the hour.

"What's your name?"

"Beatrice Young," she said, blue eyes shining, her bow-shaped mouth and sharp chin caught in a stunned smile.

"Bea," he corrected her, speaking loudly enough to be heard over the music.

"No one's called me Bea, since, well, my grannie!" She said, tumbling into a giggle at her rhyme, then swallowed her laughter just as quickly, worried she said the wrong thing.

The server opened a bottle of Moet and poured two flutes of champagne. He used to have them bring out Goût de Diamants, but these wealthy girls were not wealthy enough to know it, so he preferred to offer them Moet and an apology.

He held up the glass for a toast, "In honour of your grannie."

She blushed, acquiescing to his naming her, and the first chip in her dignity had fallen. As she babbled on about herself, he noted the changes he would make. The blond would be dyed the required shade of auburn, and if the curls were natural, they would be straightened.

"What a strange night. I'm never out with them." She glanced at her friends quickly. "I walked out on my family, on that life, a few years ago. But I ran into Hannah at the dog-park and one thing led to another." She looked down at herself. "I even had to borrow this dress."

"What happened with your family?"

"A long story," she replied reluctantly, "but bad enough I ended up on the street."

He gestured toward her friends. "None of them took you in?"

Sorrow deepened so sweetly in her beautiful eyes, he wished he could taste it. "I stayed with the hippies out in the woods at Cherry Beach. I was out there for weeks, just drumming, getting high, dumpster diving at the grocery stores on Leslie."

"Looking at you now, it's hard to believe."

"I got lucky. Days I'd walk over to the other side of the beach, you know, where the dog-park is, and I fell in with the dog walkers. I picked up walks when one of them was sick or injured and moved in with two friends. Eventually, I got a license myself."

He leaned in, frowning with empathy. "What did you want for yourself before you left?"

"For myself? I haven't wanted anything for myself since I was little."

"And you have no contact with your family?"

"My mom comes to see me on my birthday, but keeps it from my father."

He suspected the father had abused her. This one was different from the others and he nearly let her go, but then she said, "You understand. You know what it is not to fit in."

Nick wanted to confide in her what she already knew, as if it were a revelation for her alone. Articles had long covered the story of his mother's work cleaning homes, his after school hours emptying garbage and mopping floors at fast-food restaurants barely covering the rent, and finally, his mother's tragic death right before he graduated from high school. Bea would have read how he taught himself to hack, how he had been rejected by the computer science program at Simcoe University, the Harvard of the North, and how he had snuck into their courses, finding he did not need them after all.

He leaned in, shaping his body to match hers, allowing his expression of a workingman's pride to be touched by shame, and her body moved with perfect empathy. It was the oddest tug on him, being understood. He sat back, considering her. The two of them. So similar. Decided, he made plans to create a place for her, a place where she fit in and could never leave.

This time, he would get it right. No escapes. No small rebellions leading to privileged families swooping in to rescue their kidnapped daughters. There were whispers about him, going after girls with particular looks of particular backgrounds, taking over their lives, but only that. His non-disclosure agreements were legendary. But always with these girls, there was money, connections, always someone to show up and solve their problems. The advantage of Bea, he wagered, was that no one would show up for her.

Despite her isolation, Bea's submission had not been animalistic and cowering like the others. As arousing as that was, he found something unanticipated with her in their first months together. They had fallen in love. She cared about people like his mother, the cleaners, the dog walkers, the gig workers, people who were one cash payout away from being on the street. Bea used his money to serve the poor. And the yoke he placed on her shoulders became a burden she carried willingly out of devotion.

She was more than another Patricia Wellington to destroy.

Inviting her to join him now and exposing his work to her was a risk perhaps, but what was the point of any of this if the woman he loved could not see it?

Cristo Solutions took up a whole floor of the Markham building downtown. His public office sat at the centre of open cubicles of deep ocean blue spiralling out to matte black walls. Pinpoint lights illuminated paths leading to a restaurant, a playroom, and a meditation space. A bank of glassed-in offices for the highest level team clung to the exterior wall. But his private office lay undetectable behind a wide bar of black glass.

Behind that impenetrable glass was a secret room of warmth. The inner sanctum. There was hardwood flooring and a couch upholstered in a textured weave with pillowy arms for long naps. A maple rocking chair with one broken spine sat in front of a low but wide bookcase under the window. His childhood books were lined up, most stolen from the library—their catalogue marks taped to the spines—others, precious gifts like the set of *Encyclopedia Brown* mysteries his mother gave to him one Christmas.

He observed Bea in the computer displays, tugging again on her skirt, waiting for him to tell her what she wanted.

"Pick out a throw and some pillows for the couch. Bring down your magazines, stay with me sometimes. I need you."

Bea approached the couch, then jumped on it, lying down on her side, smiling. Her eye caught a fading cross stitch hanging over the bank of displays. She got up and came to him, her gentle hand on his shoulder.

"My mother made it."

"What is it?"

"A crest from *The Count of Monte Cristo*."

Except, over the mountain, instead of a Christian cross, she had put two pistols and the loving words, "Gun For Hire."

Her fingers had worked the thread using the last cells not eaten by early onset dementia and driven by the pride she had in him for humiliating the payday loan company that had ruined the end of her life. "I'll hire you to do that hacking," she said. "Whatever it is you do in there. Don't tell me. I don't want to know. But I'll pay you." Her eyes were incandescent with rage as she slid a five-dollar bill across the kitchen counter. "Give back to them what they took from us."

He took to skipping school, hiding in the thick cedars growing through the fence surrounding the Wellingtons' faux Mediterranean mansion. Nick was patient. The family came and went. The father. The mother. The two daughters. The help. He settled in with a backpack full of Red Bulls and beef jerky and sleeping in fits, jerking awake when the gate would rumble and their cream Jaguar or the van for the help would come and go. He watched the windows. He took note. But mainly, he kept an eye out for the red Porsche and the state of its driver. Waiting for the uncontrollable sixteen-year-old, Patricia Wellington, to show up drunk.

In the full light of the third morning, the red Porsche pulled up, swerving and jerking to a stop. Patricia stumbled out. Her long, straight auburn hair covered her face until she stood—half-drunk, full-drunk, he did not know—hanging onto the roof of the car to steady herself with one hand. She pushed her hair back with the other to show her face. Bow lips. Pointy chin. Heartbroken blue eyes.

Soon she was leaning over the hood, directly in view, vomiting. He clicked and cranked the disposable camera. The front door to the mansion opened. A middle-aged servant looked around frantically before rushing to her. The sister, maybe thirteen or fourteen, ran out. Nick clicked and cranked. Then he pulled out another disposable camera, taking pictures all the way until Patricia was safely, they thought, within.

The pictures sold to the tabloids. Not as much as he hoped, but more than he and his mother had ever had in their hands. They finally paid off their debt. The rest went to his mother's home care, all except for several throwaway computers to stalk Patricia Wellington.

Bots did their part, but he relished the handcraft of creating dozens of accounts and false identities through which he orchestrated her decline, spending his nights commenting cruelly and, he thought, hilariously, on gossip websites, blogs, her Facebook account and those of her friends and their friends. His accounts commented on each other, shared each other's insults, defending her there, taking her down here. When real people joined in, he came at them with even more accounts, stalking them to find out what would make them angry or what would give them guilty pleasure, and exploited it until Patricia was surrounded on all sides.

From the computers Patricia Wellington paid for, he shared the pictures of her red Porsche wrapped around a tree. Her bloody body on a board, covered with a sheet, then placed onto a stretcher.

Nick had just as good as killed her, but he was not done ruining the family that had ruined his mother's last days.

The first time he read *The Count of Monte Cristo*, when he got to Dante's regret, he scoffed, throwing the book across the room. It had been a perfect novel until that one moment. He tore those pages out and began again. What regret was necessary in revenge?

"Stay," he said to Bea, putting a hand over hers on his shoulder.

She kissed his cheek, as he liked, letting her breath stroke his ear.

He almost hated to do it, worrying she would take it the wrong way, as if he did not trust her, as if their love were not guarantee enough.

"Look there." He tapped the keyboard, and one of the displays came to life.

It was her. Bea. He had tweaked it just enough to bring out her resemblance to Patricia Wellington, but it was Bea. Bea's face on another woman's naked body, moaning as a man took her from behind.

Bea stumbled back onto the couch, hand to her throat.

"I didn't even use a recording of you. It's a deepfake. I can do whatever I like from here." Nick swung his chair around. "Where the magic happens."

3

<hr>

Conor Monaghan left his brother at his sprawling Scandinavian home in the care of his Irish housekeeper, Oonagh. He had sent Tom, his gardener, in a taxi to retrieve Martin's car from the university. When Conor shut the door behind him, Martin was resting on the long leather couch. He was confident that Oonagh would pour tea down his brother and stuff him with potatoes and meat and butter until he fell asleep under the sheer weight of it. Conor slid into his Polestar and pulled out onto the road, setting aside what would come next until he returned from work. In the meantime, he would leave it to the Lord's wisdom and pray for an opening.

The door to Wake Financial opened without a touch. Marta was on her way out. "Did you get your brother home all right?"

"He's at my house. I'll just clear a few things up and get back to him."

"There's not much for you to do. Miss Henson has been muttering, but you know how she is."

"She's always been an odd soul, but she is our odd soul."

"We take good care of her."

"You do, mainly. Without you, where would I be?"

Marta smiled. "Cover the front desk for me, then. I'll be right back."

The price of entry to have Conor Monaghan manage your money at Wake Financial began at ten million. He had not picked the starting investment, the old man had. The old man was not his father, but was as good as. The famed Harold Bailey. A multi-millionaire who lived simply in a bungalow in East York. No wife. No children. Never even updated the kitchen. He valued thrift and he valued an inscrutable quality he saw in some people.

And he saw it in Conor, even though he and his friends ran through the neighbourhood making trouble. As Mr. Bailey told it, Conor was always the one holding them back from doing worse. Despite keeping Martin out of it, Conor did not remember things that way. His mother was off at St. Brigid's church praying for his father's soul while Mr. Bailey protected them, talking to corner shop owners again and again after he and his friends had stolen a few bags of chips and cans of pop.

"It would have been worse," Mr. Bailey insisted, "if not for you. I knew you would take my offer. Not like the other boys. They would not recognize an opportunity."

The offer came as Conor was riding by on his bike. Mr. Bailey called him over to the chain-link fence. One hand was on the aluminum post, the other held out a long piece of paper with a list of figures on it. "You want to see what I've got here?"

Conor stopped cold, mouth open, more afraid than anything else. Mr. Bailey was a good man. Everyone knew it. You could go to him for a small loan when you got stuck and he would offer it, no interest, on whatever terms you could manage. If your kid got in trouble, Mr. Bailey's lawyer could make some phone calls. More than that sometimes, but only if he saw that inscrutable quality in a person that inspired his trust. He had helped many in the neigh-bourhood start a business, buy new equipment they could never afford, or lay down a new roof when theirs had become chipped, mossy, and leaking. And he advised one and all to use credit unions, not banks. He would holler, "Never trust a bank!" The neighbourhood thought he was crazy. A good man, but crazy, and with the power to make their lives better or worse. And that kind of goodness was intimidating. He felt like Mr. Bailey could see right through him.

"It's a tabulation of everything you and the boys have stolen from the corner stores."

Conor panicked, looking up and down the street, wondering if the cops were coming and how his mother was going to beat him raw for bringing police to her door.

"Oh now, son, don't be like that. I've paid for it. You're in no trouble." He winked. "We will not have to bother your mother. She is a good Christian woman and knows all about the prodigal son, but she need not know he is living in her own house."

"The who?" Conor wished he had listened more in Sunday school to know what kind of trouble he was in.

"The one who knows he's done wrong, comes home, and makes up for it."

"How?" He stammered, "H-How can I?"

Mr. Bailey pointed to the push lawnmower and the weedy grass in his small yard. "That will do it. You come here every week, or after a good rain and we've had a burst of growth, and mow my lawn."

He nodded eagerly, wondering if this was all it would take. "And you won't tell my mother?"

"If you and the boys stay out of the stores. That is, unless you have money to pay."

A chill came over him despite being sticky with sweat from the July sun. "We will. I mean, we won't steal again. I'll make sure of it."

As it was, he could not stop the other boys. He tried, even following when they planned to shoplift again and begging them.

That last time, Jamal ordered him to quit whining. "You're our lookout, then. There's a new guy running the Milkmart."

Fists shoved in empty pockets, he followed them inside, the old bell clanged as the door behind them shut. If he had any money, he could just pay. For a bare moment, he cursed Mr. Bailey for making him mow his lawn without giving him a cent. Surely, he had long paid off their debt. But just as quickly, he banished the thought, fearing the old man could hear him.

Conor moved to the side, keeping an eye on the shopkeeper, but it was no use. It was as if he had been waiting for them. Conor's voice caught in his throat. A stand of garden seeds was in front of him and he thought to throw it to the ground, make a scene, do something that would be a distraction, and make his friends run. But the shop-keeper came around the counter, grabbing Jamal as he and the rest of the boys escaped.

Conor ran home, but circled back on his bike, watching from a distance. A police car was parked in front of the shop. Jamal was in the back seat, looking down. Across the road, he saw Mr. Bailey observing. He expected the old man to step in, but, like him, he just stood there, able to do something yet doing nothing. Jamal was taken to the station, remanded home, and the Youth Court judge gave the twelve-year-old probation. Conor's awe of Mr. Bailey turned into genuine fear of what would happen if the old man stopped seeing whatever it was he saw in him.

But he never did. Conor came back to mow as instructed, and Mr. Bailey would sit on the stoop and talk. He could not half hear him over the clicking and whirring of the push mower. But over time Conor heard enough, and he kept mowing straight through to the first frost because Mr. Bailey was giving him an education in how to make money from other people's money. And Mr. Bailey was all he had left.

It did not take long for the neighbourhood to take sides. Those to whom Mr. Bailey would not lend money made no excuses for him not stepping in for Jamal, and none for Conor and his family siding with him. The families loyal to Mr. Bailey said Jamal had to learn his lesson and used it as a cautionary tale to their own children.

Despite the lesson learned, his mother took hold of him, and Martin watched, helplessly, from behind the kitchen door as she beat Conor with a wooden spoon. "God protect your dead father from seeing your shame from heaven!"

The tone of the street changed. Jamal's punishment and his family's suffering struck fear into every one of them.

Jamal and his friends passed him in the hallways at school, giving him dirty looks and shooting insults for not warning them. Conor sat alone at lunch and avoided them in the field. Soon, the shame was too much and he withdrew to the empty gym. Sometimes Martin would come to sit beside him; but mainly, he ate alone. He knew he could have acted and wished he had said something to Mr. Bailey. Out of loyalty to Jamal, he should have walked away from the old man. If he had any courage, he would have told Mr. Bailey to call the cops on him, too.

If Martin blamed him for the changes on the street and at home, he never said. But his mother made sure Martin fell in line behind Conor as far as Mr. Bailey was concerned. No more television on the weekdays. They were both forced to wear khakis and button-downs like the kids in Catholic schools. Jeans and t-shirts were on the weekend only. And no hoodies, Mr. Bailey had made that clear.

From then on out, Conor "apprenticed" at Wake Financial. Twelve years old, he had not understood a thing, but he was always by Mr. Bailey's side. Martin had to come along, too. His mother insisted on it. No Martin, no Conor.

After school, the two did their homework under the watchful eye of the strange Miss Henson in the outer office. Each day, she would put out snacks and juice in her eccentric pattern for them to consume at a specific time and in the order she instructed. First the crackers, then the cheese, then washed down with the juice. Sometimes the opposite. But stubborn Martin ate as he liked. Her face would turn red, and she would stomp out of the room. Conor begged Martin not to taunt her, but there was no stopping him. Later, Mr. Bailey would come to collect Conor, stern but kind, assuring him not to worry about Miss Henson but giving Martin a look that said he would beat him if he could.

Once they were alone, Mr. Bailey would ask first, "What did you learn at church on Sunday?"

Conor knew to have an answer. Mr. Bailey made it clear that he guided his business by Christian values and Conor would do the same.

"There are faster ways of making money," he had said, "but it's harder for a camel to pass through the eye of a needle, than a rich man to get into heaven."

"But you're rich, aren't you, sir?" Conor had asked timidly.

"I am poor in spirit and I never invest my clients' money in companies known for dirty dealing."

He never saw Mr. Bailey in church himself. On Wednesday evenings he went to his meeting, but he did not talk about it, and Conor did not ask. In later years, he assumed he went to Alcoholics Anonymous and never broached the subject.

When Conor graduated high school, he was admitted into the Economics program at Simcoe University. His way was paid for and his admission guaranteed by Mr. Bailey. After that, he completed the Master of Finance and became a full partner by twenty-six years old. But no matter his successes, no matter their partnership, no matter coming to love Mr. Bailey like a father over the years, he never lost his fear of him. "Yes, sir." "No, sir." These were the best replies.

It was not until Mr. Bailey had died and left the business to him alone did he find out his secret. The will stipulated Conor could have it all, but on one condition: he must agree to never miss a Wednesday meeting and to live by the precept of The Cluster. If he could not accept the brotherhood and their principles, the firm's clients would be dispersed to other advisors and the office closed.

"The Cluster?" Conor had asked, looking up from the will at Mr. Bailey's lawyer across the desk. "I thought he was in AA."

Vincent Allen chuckled, the old man's laugh lines crinkling more deeply. "Not quite."

"Are you one of them?"

He smiled kindly, but something creepy was behind it, as if an elderly Mr. Rogers were playing a part in a horror movie. "I would not have been entrusted with these instructions for you if I were not."

"What are you? I don't—"

"That's not how we do things," Allen said, sliding a card across the desk. On it was an Orthodox Christian cross, but with mushroom caps at the ends of the bars. Conor had to hold back the impulse to scoff at the silliness of it. He turned it over. An address was handwritten on the back.

"You come to the first meeting. We will explain to you our mission and vision. If you agree to take the next step, we will invite you into the Ritual. Then you will be informed if you are one of us"—he paused almost comically—"or not."

"Informed?" He tucked his head back, holding back a laugh. "You mean agree or not?"

"It is not for you to agree or disagree. The Ritual chooses you or rejects you."

Conor broke the news to Martin over breakfast at The Bagel House. Martin told him not to go. He had enough money invested to walk away and never work again. And if Conor wanted to work, any firm would take him on. But for all his talk of only going to satisfy his curiosity, agreeing or disagreeing on his own terms, he felt like he had no choice at all. His brother saw it, threw his bagel down, stood, nearly knocking over the tiny table, and told everyone in the shop Conor was a "fucking child." He let Martin leave, knowing when his temper cooled, he would come back to him, not agreeing, but always his brother.

That Wednesday, Conor stood before the double doors of a one-story office building. The exterior paint was stained from years of rain dripping through rotted leaves in the broken eavestrough. He had to tug the doors open, thinking first they were locked, and nearly turned away, taking it as a sign that he should leave Mr. Bailey's secret alone and let the business go, when one flew open with a crack and he nearly lost his footing.

Fluorescent tube lights flickered, turning the grey paint on the chipped walls a sickening blue. There was a reception office ahead, with a sliding glass window, and a long hallway to the right. It must have been a medical clinic once. He could barely imagine it bright and sterile, instead seeing it as a place where children had to be dragged by their feet to get their shots by a cruel nurse. He shivered and nearly left again. But when your life is taken out of your hands at the age of twelve and all you know and have is bound up in the legacy of one man's work, it is hard to turn around.

"Conor, is that you?" Vincent Allen called to him from down the hall. "We're just in the last room. Lock that door behind you, please."

Conor threw the bolt, then went ahead, following the voice to a meeting room and that night, the Ritual chose him.

4

____

It had been three days at different motels. Only paying cash and refusing to show identification, the front-desk clerks had not let Parisa stay more than one night. They had taken pity on her, assuming she was escaping a violent man, but also they did not want any trouble. The dream of Cyrus beckoned again, and she took a chance.

After the call telling her to run, Parisa had called Arash's school to say he would be out for a week, texted her sister in Iran saying she would be out of touch, then Dr. Monaghan, taken the SIM card out of her phone, turned off the Wi-Fi and Bluetooth, then grabbed what she could carry, rushing with Arash to the subway. Heading east to the end of the line, she watched the other riders out of the corner of her eye, hoping no one had followed.

"It's like hide 'n' seek," she told Arash. "We've got to be sneaky." But no explanations would assuage him. She had left his stuffed rabbit behind and that they could not go back meant this was no game.

Now, heading to Cyrus's home, she kept one hand on her sleeping son, the other on her backpack containing a thick envelope of cash. She feared someone could track her to the motels. So she had taken a taxi further east, deeper into Scarborough, to a random address on Eglinton Avenue. Laden with a tote over her shoulder, the backpack, and Arash clinging to her waist, she crossed the street to hail another cab to take her north to Little Persia.

There, she walked through a strip mall arcade plastered with posters in Farsi, advertising dentures, legal services, and restaurants. Parisa saw a handmade sign on the window of a tiny grocery store advertising delivery and slipped inside. Arash was exhausted and clutching at her through the narrow aisles. A young man was seated on a plastic lawn chair, one leg thrown over the other, his black hair slicked back, chatting with a man stocking boxes of cookies from cardboard boxes nearby. Parisa steeled herself, a hundred-dollar bill in her hand, not rudely sticking out, but visible. She said in Farsi, "I need a ride, no questions asked. I can pay."

One look at her and her son and he rose, blinking yes and waved off the cash. "It's nothing."

She tried again, insisting on paying, then again, but he continued to resist, so she let it go, but put her hand on her heart with deep gratitude for showing them kindness in a moment when she felt alone.

The young man grabbed his things, but first took a pack of cookies from the box with a nod to the other man, and led them out. Once in the car, he gave the cookies to her, along with a bottle of water.

The streets rushed past. Arash, finally quiet after eating cookies by the fistful, lay his head in her lap. She settled back into the seat, thinking of Cyrus.

They had met only once. Parisa was in San Antonio for a conference, Cyrus for a business meeting. The very first paper she had given had gone well, presented before a room full of other graduate students, future colleagues, and several "old boys" in the field. She had been terrified and she had done it. Dr. Monaghan had praised her to all and used the short time afterwards to help her network with the colleagues who could make or break her career. But the precision she had to maintain to field the sometimes hostile questions had left her frantically exhausted. She slumped into one of the lobby armchairs set around a central low table, wishing again she had the habit of drinking. It was not religion. The leaders of Iran had rid her of any love she might have carried for it. Alcohol simply did not suit her. Then, a man she had not noticed sitting nearby spoke. It took a moment to register that he was speaking to her, and in Farsi.

"You look like you've had a long day," he said, and pushed over his untouched pot of tea and cup. "Bagged mint, not badranjboye, but you might enjoy it."

Drawn into awareness, she took him in. Generous lips. Eyebrows perfectly arched over wide-set brown eyes framed by long eyelashes. A noble nose and soft cheeks. Thick black hair swept up off his forehead, perfectly barbered with a clear side part. She nearly exclaimed "joon" at the sight of a man who so uncannily resembled the pietistic portraits of the heroic men of the Prophet Muhammad's family. She had joked once to a friend that she would like to know the man who had sat for these paintings, and realized she had just met his stunningly handsome descendant wearing an expensive suit tailored for his athletic body.

He asked about her work, listening to her recount the paper she had given, prompting a conversation about Iran. They told stories about the neighbourhoods they loved, how fruits and vegetables here did not taste the same, and poetry. Cyrus kept returning to poetry, reciting lines here and there from his declared beloved, Forugh Farrokhzad.

The surrounding crowds thinned and the silence of the hotel lobby forced a question that she knew he would be too gentlemanly to ask, and that she would not hint at for fear of spoiling it all. She moved to go, hand over her heart.

In reply, he recited a line of Rumi's poetry with a playful smile. *"How long will you turn away?"*

She answered with the next line, *"Come, come closer. Do not cover yourself,"* but stood, ready to leave.

Then, he offered his cell number, even his home address, scrawling it on the back of his business card. But in all the hours they talked, he had shared no details of his present life and she had not once mentioned her son. Their conversation had ranged through dreams and love of Iran, not this world, and she refused to bring it down to earth. So she left him, hiding the card without looking at it in an inner sleeve of her wallet to treasure the memory.

On the final night at the final motel, trying to sleep, she wished herself and her son into his care and came fully awake. No one could trace her to him. It was a desperate and foolish thing to think. But Parisa sat up, reaching for her backpack. She assumed he lived in the United States. They had their Canadian passports. They could cross the border, then she could pay cash for train tickets, bus, whatever it took, to wherever he lived. She turned on the light. The card had been waiting all that time in that sleeve of her wallet.

Cyrus Dadashi.
Imports of Fine Dried Fruits and Nuts.
Lawrence Avenue, North York

She read it again, not believing he was here, based in Toronto. Parisa turned the card over. A private number and his home address. In Etobicoke. She nearly left the room to use the phone at the front desk to ask if he would welcome her. But she did not want to take the chance. What if he had not thought of her every night, just before dreaming, as she had all this time, drifting away, holding onto a perfect love in a lonely world? She begged the universe that he remembered her. That he was as she imagined him to be. That he might be home. That he even still lived there.

The delivery driver pulled into a cul-de-sac of split-level homes that spoke of wealth with no need for ostentation. She touched Arash's cheek. "We're here, azizam." His eyes fluttered open, and he reached for his stuffed rabbit. "We'll go back for him," she lied. Then added another, the kind of lie all mothers tell their suffering children. "I asked Barbara next door to get him. He's snuggly safe." Arash nodded reluctantly and slid out of the back seat as she thanked the driver for his kindness.

They stood at the end of the driveway under the stark cast of the street lamps for only a moment. There was nothing to do but go ahead. The house was brightly lit. Music was playing within, some kind of popular rhythm and blues, something she should have recognized had she not had her head in books for the past few years. She pressed the bell and knocked, worried Cyrus, or whoever was within, could not hear. But then someone was running to the door. She heard a laugh and muffled words, a woman's voice, and the door pulled open.

"So soon, we only just ordered!"

A beautiful East Asian woman stood in the doorway, slim and statuesque, her long hair pulled up in a messy bun, and wearing loose, yet flattering sweats, the kind of thing only women of grace can pull off. She was much younger than Cyrus, at most in her mid-twenties, but it made sense; he was a beautiful man. Parisa felt sick, grieving that the man she had only spoken to one night had not waited for her.

"I'm sorry! I thought you were food delivery."

"I'm a friend of Cyrus. Does he live here? It's been over a year since we spoke."

"Ah!" This time the young woman looked her up and down, appraising, even giving Arash a quick examination. Parisa imagined she was looking for any sign of Cyrus on him. She called for Cyrus over her shoulder, seemingly satisfied with Parisa's average looks and her son's parentage.

Cyrus came down the stairs from the main floor and stopped short. Then she saw it, recognition followed by the memory of what they had shared. His expression opened with wonder and she imagined she saw hope and maybe love there. "Parisa." Then he gave a flustered look at the young woman. "Tomoko, I met Parisa maybe over a year ago at a conference in Texas. I gave her my address and number." Then to Parisa. "This is a surprise. Please, come in."

The young woman stood aside. "And who is this?"

"Arash, my son." They kicked off their shoes and she directed Arash ahead of her up the stairs, but he squirmed unhappily under her hand.

The main floor was a long room dominated by an open kitchen at the back, a family-sized dining table in the centre, and a living room with two deep-brown leather couches, comfortable armchairs upholstered in fabric of tiny repeating patterns, and leather poufs. A large glass coffee table held bowls of pistachios and dried fruits. A pot of tea was out and two small glasses. She recognized its scent immediately. Badranjboye, the mint tea he wished he could have given her that night at the hotel, and she felt suddenly tired.

"Sit, please," he gestured to one of the couches.

She pulled Arash down with her, holding him tight. "I won't waste your time." Parisa glanced at her son, hoping for their understanding of what she could not say in front of him. "We're having a bit of trouble, but nothing that can't be solved."

Tomoko returned from the kitchen, put another tea glass on the table with a clink and a glass of orange juice in front of Arash, along with a few cookies on a small plate. "Trouble?"

Parisa glared at her. "We need a place to sleep tonight."

"Is it safe to help you?" Tomoko asked, looking at her sideways.

"They are welcome guests." Cyrus's tone implied they were welcome, especially if they were not safe. He tipped his chin at Arash, saying to Tomoko, "The walls have mice and the mice have ears."

Tomoko raised an eyebrow, but she seemed to grasp, finally, that Arash was listening.

"Drink your juice," Parisa said to him, but saw his eyes were heavy. He would be asleep soon. "May I put my son down in another room?"

"Of course." Cyrus got up and led her past the dining area. A large stencil of one line of Rumi's poetry stretched along the far wall. The line he had recited to her a year ago.

How long will you turn away?

She finished it silently.

Come, come closer.

Do not cover yourself.
Come, come back to the truth.
You have seen the poison, now see the remedy.
Come, come back to the remedy.
At long last, come.
Come back to the root of your true self.

Cyrus looked back as he directed her into the hall to the bedrooms, caught her glance at the stencil and blushed, sending its heat through her and she nearly wept in relief. She had not imagined what they had felt that night.

The guest room was crammed with two single beds and a double.

"My nephews are here often. You might find some pyjamas for Arash in the dresser." The air was thick between them as he pointed to the closet. "Maybe something for you, too? My sister keeps some things here. It doesn't look like you brought much with you."

He left her to care for her son, but she did not change Arash, just in case they had to run. Instead, she nestled him between the covers of the double bed. He turned over, complaining only for a moment, then was fast asleep.

Back in the living room, Cyrus and Tomoko were whispering, then turned when she arrived and gave her their attention. She saw his feeling for Tomoko, then, and the problem she was by simply being there.

"I am sorry for this. We'll leave first thing in the morning."

"Sit down and tell us." Tomoko's tone had changed. He had allayed her concerns about them. "You shouldn't be alone."

Cyrus seemed relieved. "Please, Parisa. Tell us."

And so she told them, not everything, but enough. She began with Dr. Monaghan's tribunal and termination, working backwards to the day she received a package in the mail, a USB drive with the data proving that Wellington Payday Loans was defrauding its clients by charging pennies in hidden fees, pennies that added up to millions of dollars on a national scale. "The fees are invisible. If a client asks about their balance, the clerk pretends to be confused and corrects it."

"If there is no complaint?" Tomoko asked.

"We have proof showing the fees remain."

"How can they get away with that?" Cyrus exclaimed.

"How can they get away with their legal loans?" Tomoko's colour was high. "The government permits it, robbing people who cannot make it from inadequate pay check to inadequate pay check, instead of legislating a living wage."

Parisa welcomed her anger, and added, "The worst of it is that you have to be responsible to qualify for one of these loans. But if you fall behind, the effects are worse than not paying your credit card in full each month. In Ontario, it amounts to a 391% annual rate, more elsewhere."

Tomoko looked straight at Cyrus.

He held up his hands in submission. "I pay generous salaries. Do not look at me."

"It's the entire system," Tomoko said. "The banks are the same. Overdraft protection, credit cards, fees, interest, compound interest. Who even understands how compound interest works? Paying interest on the interest? But who can pay their credit card off all at once? Only the people who use credit for convenience, not necessity."

"Lines of credit are better," Parisa said. "But it only works as long as you can afford to borrow money you do not have."

"I'm not arguing any of this with you two." He chuckled uncomfortably. "Especially not this one, the communist."

"As you can see, Cyrus and I do not talk capitalism to keep the peace," Tomoko joked.

Parisa could not enjoy the easy intimacy between them.

"And your academic advisor, Dr. Monaghan?" Cyrus prompted.

"Somehow, the Wellington family forced his termination. They found out about the data I was given. But it wasn't my work. My research is on democratic movements in Iran."

Cyrus's eyes lit up, remembering their conversation after her conference paper.

She withheld a smile.

"I want to know more about how you got that data," Tomoko said.

"Like I said, I got sent a USB to my university mailbox."

"And you didn't think that was strange?"

"I looked through it, got a sense of what was going on and brought it to Monaghan. We both assumed it was a whistleblower."

"Why you?" Tomoko's voice had taken on an uncomfortable edge.

Cyrus glanced at her with concern.

She sounded like a cop, but Parisa guessed a journalist was more likely. "Are you a writer?"

Her eyes lit up. "An analyst. For *The Spanner*."

There were some good investigative articles in it, but also opinion pieces that made a lot out of nothing to serve the political ends of the far-left journal. She had enough of political extremes in Iran and wondered what Tomoko's contribution had been.

Parisa continued, "I gave Dr. Monaghan the data. He asked me to do the initial pass. I shared my analysis with him and he became involved. We both dug into it. We did interviews with clients. We even took out loans ourselves and saw it being done. Once we were certain, Dr. Monaghan spoke about the research to colleagues. That's when the intimidation began."

Cyrus said, "Oh, Parisa."

"Intimidation?" Tomoko asked with a glance at him, cutting off his concern.

"Anonymous threats to ruin Dr. Monaghan's career. He didn't take it seriously for himself. I mean, it's not the first time his research has threatened the powerful."

"Right!" Tomoko turned to Cyrus. "Martin Monaghan. He was the one who broke the WBSN scandal."

"Gunnar Armitage was forced to resign from Parliament over that!" Cyrus exclaimed.

"Yes, and more. So, you see, he was worried about how the threats would affect my career. He had tenure and assumed he was safe. It's the responsibility of those with tenure to take the risks, he said."

"And the credit," Tomoko said plainly.

She wondered what Tomoko knew, but did not ask, instead saying, "After the threats, I told Dr. Monaghan not to cite me. I left the project and returned to doing my own research. Everyone in my department knew I had worked on it and the risks to me, but my name came into it all the same. The tribunal was called and the chair insisted on naming me, saying it was my original research and Monaghan had plagiarized it. I couldn't deny it. It did not exist except through me, and I had done a lot of the analysis."

"You were exposed at the tribunal?" Cyrus asked.

"Not at first. I was 'Graduate Student 1'. But on the last day, the chair said my name, right into the record."

Tomoko remarked cynically, "White professors get censured for plagiarism. Why was Monaghan terminated?"

It was true, and Parisa shared her ire. "The grad students. We all thought there would be a reprieve at the last moment. Monaghan and the chair have fought for years. Maybe the chair was just trying to humiliate him, but the ax fell all the same."

"And you were threatened?" Cyrus asked.

"I received an anonymous call saying that my life and the life of my son were in danger."

"Have you called the police?" Cyrus asked.

"No," she said too quickly. Then added to put him off, "Not yet. Maybe soon."

Tomoko glanced harshly at Cyrus for the question, then turned to her. "Your phone?"

"I took out the SIM card, turned everything off, and left my computer behind. I came here using cash, money I had hidden away."

Cyrus nodded, understanding. Who back home did not hide money?

"Good," she said. "And how did you get here?"

Parisa recounted criss-crossing the city.

"Then you and your son are likely safe." She looked at Cyrus. "And us, too, at least for tonight."

DAY TWO

5

Nick stood before the glass walls of his penthouse, looking out over the stormy-blue water of the lake, trying to understand why Monaghan's research had not been published. What did his termination matter? What mattered was the data, data he had sent that graduate student, data she brought to Monaghan, data they corroborated. The data was good. The analysis was good. Fire Monaghan if necessary, but publish the findings. He glanced at his watch. The chair of Computer and Mathematical Sciences at Simcoe University, Hardeep Singh, would be over soon to secure more donations, but the price would be explaining to him what he needed to know about Monaghan's case.

He had been certain there was no better way to ruin the Wellingtons than going through Monaghan. The government was hardly going to take away their right to offer short-term loans in Canada by an internet smear campaign. Mysteriously sourced and unverified data dropped in the Office for the Superintendent of Financial Institution's mailbox could be easily mislaid by a government official committed to looking the other way. But maybe going through Monaghan had been a mistake? Maybe he should have sent the data to *The Sentinel* to let their investigative journalists do an exposé? But who could he be sure would not be influenced?

Looking out over the lake typically calmed him. Days off, his mother took him to the beach. She would buy him fries and a pop from the food truck, then they would walk past the sunbathers in the summer, or through the near-empty beach in the colder seasons, to the picnic tables close to the woods. The hot fries, just out of the oil, covered in salt and vinegar, burned his mouth and he would hold one fry, half in, half out of his mouth, panting. "Why don't you just wait until they cool?" she would ask him. But when had he ever liked waiting for anything?

Her friends would already be at the lone table by the water, making sure to get it before anyone else. Wild looking hippies would wander in from out of their camps in the woods, still tripping. The women would lovingly tease them, give them some food, and shoo them off. In winter, she and her friends would start a fire in a pit made from rocks and lake tumbled bricks. Thermos of coffee opened, they would begin sharing their complaints.

"They'd need two crews to clean that mini-mansion the way they want, but only want to pay Happy Maids for one of me."

"Oh, Sandra," one of them mocked a client's voice, "what would we do without you!"

The laughing would begin as they insulted the clients' habits and told their secrets. He stayed by her until he saw his mother sigh as she looked out over the water. Then he would wander along the beach, taking the quiet for himself to think about the code he was writing.

"Breakfast, sir," his private chef called to him.

Small white caps erupted, whipped up by the fall wind, and a cloud burst open with rain in the distance. He reluctantly turned away. There would be no quiet gazing at the lake now, not until this last stage of his plan to destroy the Wellingtons was in place.

Bea was already seated at the African blackwood table. He hugged her from behind and leaned his head over her shoulder. She turned her cheek into his kiss. The porridge was set out for them in his mother's bowls with a heaping spoon of brown sugar on top, just as she used to make. Étienne did not mind learning to prepare his mother's dishes just as Nick remembered them. He, like all those who worked for him, was paid more than enough not to mind, but when guests were invited, the chef served his own work, cuisine worthy of a Michelin star.

"Dr. Singh is coming soon. I'll meet him here instead of in the office downstairs." He ate a spoonful of porridge and its warmth soothed him. "I'll need you to make yourself scarce, Bea. Cash in the box. Why not go shopping?"

"Mmm." She nodded, mouth full of porridge. He could tell that she had already planned on it, but was acting as if it were his idea. Their love allowed these small freedoms.

"Go to Yorkville. I hate thinking of you wandering around the mall."

Her expression froze.

"What is it that you like about the Eaton Centre?"

"It feels like old times." Bea pushed away from the table. "I'll get ready now."

She disappeared past the wall of bookshelves into a hallway off the vast living room with its seating areas designed for parties, not comfort. The penthouse was impressively modern and cold. But Bea brought a warmth to it that he thought he would never feel again after his mother's death, and he did not want to crush her in his hold. She would go to Yorkville if he insisted, but since she did not openly disagree, he let it go.

Singh would be here in a moment. The man was never late, but who would be for the kinds of donations he gave to a program that had not admitted him? Étienne cleared the bowls and Nick returned to watch the storm coming in across the lake.

"I'm off!" Bea chirped from the door. Her long auburn hair was in a high ponytail and she had on faded skinny jeans, ratty sneakers, and a studiously nondescript, but very expensive, grey sweater, with a raincoat over her arm. He realized she was not going to the Eaton centre, after all, but the church next to it. It needed saying, so she knew he knew. "Off to sort clothes? They could hire people, given how much I donate to them."

"They do hire. From the encampment. I enjoy helping. Reverend Lee likes me to help. We know, you and I, most people are only a slip away from the street or jail."

He opened his mouth to speak, but she had turned away from him as she donned her coat.

"You saved me from that," she said, her back to him. "I want to help."

The admission was sincere. "Let me see your face."

She turned, smiling, eyes warm, making him feel like mornings in his mother's arms.

"Do you have your AirTag? I don't want to lose you."

She pulled it out of her purse and showed him, waving it playfully.

Of course he could track her phone, and, if he wanted, put invisible tags in everything she wore, but what good was invisible tracking to her attachment to him? She needed to see and feel that there were no secrets between them every day.

"Cash?"

Bea patted her purse, pouting her bow lips into a kiss goodbye.

"Make sure people see you giving it out."

The door opened behind her.

"Oh. My apologies, Ms. Young." His assistant Trang stood in the door. "Dr. Singh is here."

Bea ducked past the older woman into the hallway and was gone.

Trang opened the door wider and a small, trim man came through wearing pressed jeans and a hand tailored blue blazer over a black turtleneck, smiling broadly. "So good of you to invite me this morning."

Singh crossed the room to him as Étienne brought a tray of french press coffee and freshly baked croissants to a small seating area near the bookshelves. He poured the coffee into the white porcelain cups and disappeared.

"I must apologize," Nick said, gesturing him to sit. "I haven't asked you here about your recent donation request, although my team is going over the numbers. I need your help on another matter."

A hint of disappointment slipped behind an expression of respectful interest.

"I've been following the recent case of Dr. Martin Monaghan's termination," he said, sitting.

"Yes?" Singh asked, taking his place across from him.

"It seemed unusual to me."

"You mean, why was he terminated?"

"Yes, but more why the work itself must be terminated along with him?"

Singh took a sip of the coffee, then placed the cup carefully back into its saucer. "Monaghan plagiarized from his graduate student's work. Plagiarism in and of itself need not result in termination, but it was also a grave misuse of the trust between advisor and student. We were all shocked. He has the reputation of being a scrupulously ethical man. He is outspoken, but I like him and found it hard to believe. Yet, the evidence was conclusive."

"But what about the evidence of the data he was presenting?"

"It seems the findings will be put on hold." Singh's expression withdrew. He was holding something back.

"Tell me. I have an interest in this work."

"You?"

"Tell me."

He paused, considering, then considered wisely given the money he wanted, and said, "The graduate student, Parisa Soltani, has gone missing."

Nick started.

"No one can find her. Her phone is dead." He paused. "Her apartment seems to have been ransacked. The police were called, a report was made."

"Ransacked?" Nick touched the edge of his coffee cup.

"Seems. She could have pulled it apart in the rush to leave."

Nick scoffed. "She cannot be contacted and her apartment is turned over?"

"Then another student"—Singh held up a hand—"a graduate student said she got a call from her, shortly before her phone went dead, and so the police dropped it."

"What about this call?"

"She said the termination was upsetting and she was taking some time away to think over her next steps."

"That doesn't sound like she is missing."

"True. Perhaps I'm over-reaching. Only the data, if the source could be verified and the findings corroborated by other scholars, would be damning to a very powerful family, their entire business. And now, you inviting me here rather than in your office, I suspect I am not over-reaching at all."

"As I said, I have an interest."

"Then you should know she told the other student she would not be reprising the research. She was determined to give it up. There were even a few ill words for Monaghan himself for having wasted her time with it when she should be getting on with her dissertation, not to mention tainting her reputation going forward."

"But she can't!" Nick took in a sharp breath and looked out the window to settle himself.

"Perhaps you should tell me what's going on."

He stood. The in-house lawyers in the offices below could draw up a non-disclosure agreement in a moment if he asked. He turned toward the lake, then back again.

"Nick?"

Before he could do the wise thing and commit Singh legally to secrecy, he sat down hard and said it. "The data comes from me. I leaked it to Monaghan's graduate student. Monaghan had planned to present his findings at a conference next month. The press would have reported on it. Then it would have been published and confirmed by peer review."

"How?"

"A member of my team found it while working on a case for a client. I knew I could not simply bring it to OSFI. I could not guarantee confidentiality, but more likely it would be covered up,

corrected, maybe the practices ended, but there would be no account-
ability."

"If you brought it to them, with the knowledge of your minister of
parliament? Nick, you could pick up the phone and call the Prime
Minister's office."

"That's not how I wanted it done."

"But why don't you trust them?"

He lunged forward in his seat. "Thieves! All of them!"

Singh fell back against his chair from the force.

"I'm sorry," he said, recovering his composure, at least on the
surface. "You know about my childhood. We were poor. I don't trust
institutions."

"But you founded a firm that protects institutions from cyber
attacks."

"Which means I'm in a position to know how they work."

"What do you want from me?" Singh seemed afraid.

"Is there any way to get the research published now?"

"If you are determined to go this route, I would suggest
approaching another professor willing to take it on, but openly this
time. It will make it easier for the work to be verified and corroborated. I still do not understand why Martin was willing to work with
data the source of which he could not verify. Do it, but do it in the
open."

Singh should know better. He would never risk exposing a client;
it would be professional suicide. But that was not why. Nick looked
out again across the water. Someone might discover that he had
installed a virus in Wellington Payday Loans. A virus to steal from the
poor to disgrace the rich.

6

Tomoko held her cup of coffee in both hands, certain how to begin, but uncertain how Cyrus would respond. His briefly whispered explanation had put her at ease enough to know he had not seen this woman in a year, since well before they met, and that they had only spoken one night. But when she had tried to discuss it further, once alone in bed, he had begged off tired. Her own relationship with Cyrus had been a whirlwind, for her at least. Last night made her suspect that he fell in love a little too easily and that put her own feelings for him under examination. He had given her a key to his house, but had never hinted at more. She watched him sitting on the couch with a glass of hot black tea balanced between his fingers, sipping, and staring into the distance. Parisa and her son were asleep, but would be up soon enough. The conversation had to be now.

As she approached, he stood, took her hand, and sat next to her.

"This is serious," she said, half joking, half worried that there might be more to his feelings for Parisa than he let on.

"We had one night. Simply talking in the lobby of a hotel. I only knew her name because of her name badge." His eyes became tender in a way she recognized.

"Oh Cyrus, you fell in love."

He squeezed her hand. "Yes. Absurdly. I didn't know such things were possible."

"How did she find you here?"

"Her institution was also printed on the badge, so I knew she was in Toronto and when I gave her my card, I wrote my cell number and address on the back."

"And she never contacted you."

"No. I began to see it for what it was, a strange night, never to be repeated and ultimately unreal." He looked toward the hall to the bedrooms. "She never told me she had a child."

She took in a sharp breath, understanding. Cyrus did not want children. That had been an explicit discussion between them, a discussion initiated by her, as she had no interest in being a mother. Her work would always receive the kind of attention parents save for their children, that is, parents other than her own. Being a red-diaper baby meant the cause came first and she agreed with them. But a little companionable love was no harm, even if with this kind-hearted, and eminently beautiful, capitalist. She relaxed into the couch, relieved more at not having to feel jealous—an emotion she found wasteful—than knowing there was no threat to her relationship with Cyrus. She patted his hand. "It's done. Let's see what we can do for her."

"What do you think of her story?"

"I think *The Spanner* would be interested in it."

He grinned. "Did you have a particular journalist in mind?"

"I've never done primary investigative work before, just research and analysis for the journalists."

"Perfectly judged analysis."

"Even if you disagree," she teased, touching his soft cheek. Those lashes. She sighed, forgetting the chance of her first real story in the heat of the moment and wishing that woman and her son were not in the spare room.

The door opened and she shook herself free of the thought. Cyrus shot up, rearranging his face for Parisa, and she found herself irritated again.

"Morning." Cyrus was already up and over to them.

Maybe it was being on the run, but Parisa was not as beautiful as she should be to inspire a night's conversation as Cyrus had described. Her clothes were dumpy. She was short, utterly average, and had a big nose made bigger by her close cropped haircut. Expressive, dark eyes. But that was it. It must have been some conversation.

The three were in the kitchen, Cyrus and Parisa preparing food, acting cheerful for the boy, who was standing to the side like a limp doll.

"Arash," Tomoko said, coming towards him. "I happen to know that Cyrus has all the cartoon channels subscribed."

The boy's eyes lit up momentarily. She noticed they were blue, and that his hair was a good shade lighter than his mother's, but he had the same skin tone. The father had clearly been of the lighter variety and she wondered where he was when his son, and maybe, still, his wife, were in danger.

Arash dragged his feet to join her, Parisa shooing him on, promising breakfast in front of the television. "Wouldn't that be a treat!"

The television on, she got Arash settled. Tomoko had barely got the controller into his hand when he took over, knowing how to do it, and settled on something loud, bright, with talking cars rolling violently over things. Clearly a familiar treat. There were probably a lot of meals in front of the television while Parisa worked on her degree. Tomoko felt for her suddenly. If the husband were around, he did not help, and Tomoko wished she could give her the time she needed.

Parisa put a slice of barbari bread with butter and jam down in front of Arash and a glass of juice. "Some eggs, too?" As if she were preempting a complaint, she added, "There's no cereal or porridge." But the boy was in no state to complain.

"Come," she touched Parisa's arm and they went to the kitchen to join Cyrus.

"Coffee or tea?"

Parisa answered, "Coffee."

His expression sagged. Cyrus had also been disappointed when she refused morning tea. He had muttered something in surprise about her being Japanese, so she made a point to never talk tea with him in the future. Instead, she reminded him she was also half Jewish and took him out for a smoked meat sandwich on their second date instead of her hole in the wall noodle joint where she and her Marxist friends hung out.

"Who do you think warned you to run?" Cyrus asked as he placed a pod in an expensive coffee machine he reserved for guests with inexplicable taste.

"It was a woman's voice. She seemed older." Parisa looked at Tomoko. "Protective. It felt motherly, fierce. And before you ask, the number was unidentified."

Tomoko leaned back against the island. "*The Spanner* has a computer guy. A white hat hacker who can look into who called you."

"Can people do that?" Cyrus asked, shocked.

"Maybe." She addressed Parisa. "I've never covered a story from this angle before. I'm not one of their investigative journalists. I'm an analyst. So, I'm not entirely sure what Anthony can do, but it's worth asking. What about your computer?"

"I left it at my apartment."

"We should get it, and that USB drive, see if anything can be traced from the data back to its source."

Parisa glanced at Arash. "I'm not sure I should follow this up. The woman told me to run. I should listen."

"Your child's safety comes first," Cyrus said.

Tomoko wanted to jab him in the ribs. Did he want her to get this story or not? "But will he be safe, always on the run? If you expose them, this will end. How can they come after you when they've been ruined?" She pressed, "The safest thing to do is expose them and *The Spanner* can do it."

"We had so much optimism in Iran—that if we just got the truth out—but they crushed us. I was arrested along with so many others." A pall came over her face.

She knew better than to say, "This isn't Iran." Tomoko had seen what the Canadian government could do to people who interfered with big business. The Mounties' physical and cyber attacks on the Wet'suwet'en for protecting their land from oil pipelines, for one. If the government got involved in this, she could imagine them smearing Parisa as a spy for Iran, ending in deportation, and she told her just that. "The best defence is exposure."

"I will do whatever I can to protect you." Cyrus reached out to Parisa.

Stifling a huff at Cyrus's chivalry, Tomoko said forcefully, "We need the data. It may still be at your apartment."

Excited cries and a large crash came from the cartoon. Parisa jumped, then asked, more than a little fear in her voice, "How do I get back there safely? Won't someone be watching?"

"Wouldn't Monaghan have the data, too? Tomoko, why not try him? There's no reason to put her in danger for this."

She felt like a fool for not thinking of it. "I guess I can't reach him through the university. Parisa, can you give me his private email or number?"

"No," she said firmly.

"I don't understand." Cyrus said. "Do you feel you should protect him? He must take the risk of telling this story. Not you."

"I said no. I won't explain. But no."

Tomoko looked at Cyrus, who raised his eyebrows, seeming both confused and concerned.

"So you want to do this alone?" Tomoko asked, not sure she cared why as long as they could get the data and trace its owner.

"I must."

"First," Tomoko said to Cyrus, "I can move her to a hotel on the journal's dime. A safe house. She doesn't need to stay here."

She was talking out of her ass and desperately wanted to get out of the house and take a walk, call Frank James, *The Spanner*'s managing editor, to get some advice on how to proceed. But what would happen, then? The thought brought her up short. Of course, Frank would take the story from her. It was too big, he would argue. It was too big, but she could get it going, get the data, the outlines of the story. Then she realized, Amina. She trusted Amina. Amina would work on the story with her, not take it from her. Tomoko might get her first by-line: by Amina Warsame with research and reporting by Tomoko Abrams.

"No, they stay here," Cyrus insisted. "The neighbours will notice, though. What should I say?"

"Why do they need to know anything?" Her parents had never cared what a neighbour might say. They flew a Soviet flag every May Day and dealt with the glares and comments without trouble. Cyrus was a bit too concerned about what others thought of him, but she left it.

"You don't know my neighbours, especially Mrs. Aquino next door. She sees everything. I can guarantee you that she knows these two are here and that she has never seen them visiting."

"Maybe she should work for *The Spanner*?"

But Parisa did not laugh. "Tell her your cousin and her son are here from Iran. Be careful not to say anything online. In fact, stay offline."

Cyrus nodded. "I'm not even on Facebook, so no difficulty there."

"Where do you live?" Tomoko asked Parisa.

"A basement apartment in the Annex."

"Cyrus can drop us off at Kipling station. We have to assume people will be watching the apartment."

"Then let me go there alone, so they don't recognize you. Let's keep you out of the picture, then I can rely on you more."

But Tomoko wanted to be in that apartment. "No. You might miss something. Is there an alternative entrance?"

Parisa's eyes widened. "Yes. Better than that. We can go along the laneway and enter by a gate a few houses up. It doesn't look like it from the outside, but there's a fully fenced off walkway behind the laneway fences. If we go in from the north, we should be able to reach the house unobserved. The door to my apartment is in the rear. Come with me, then."

"We'll split up on the way back. I'll watch you. We'll head east first—"

"Yes. We'll switch cars, turn around, turn around again."

She had not noticed that Cyrus had left them. He was speaking with Arash. The boy nodded unhappily and went back to staring joylessly at his cartoon.

7

A few clicks and Nick was in the Wi-Fi at the house where Parisa rented her apartment. He had wasted time going through various internet providers to find her instead of checking first if she was on her landlord's account. Nice of them. He had her address, then their names, then their account, then in their Wi-Fi and into all the devices on the network. That was when he noticed the camera. He doubted her landlords were spying on her, or, rather, they might. It happens. But given the circumstances, it was more likely someone else and that would be Wellington Payday Loans. One camera, and only in her apartment. The feed showed an empty living room, turned upside down in a search. He put the live feed in the background and focused on her computer.

It was closed, but on, and connected to Wi-Fi, so he had no trouble getting in. There was next to nothing on it, just documents, all except the Wellington data which, if it had been there, was now securely wiped. He could not access her phone, but it had been connected to the cloud, so he was able to get into her photographs and videos through the computer.

They were similar to what he had found on Bea's devices. Superficially artistic shots of architecture around the city and clusters of friends. But Parisa also had hundreds of photos of Arash going back several years, the life of the phone. Arash walking down a trail. Arash playing soccer in a field with other children. A selfie of the two of them eating ice cream.

He clicked on a video of her with a friend. She had filmed them at a coffee shop, facing each other through a cavern of books piled on the table around them, laptops open, joking at the absurdity of it, calling each other "data sisters." He was entranced by her slight accent, charming, breathy e's scattered inexplicably throughout her sentences. Nick imagined himself at the centre of her affection. The camera turned and there was Parisa, hiding behind her laptop, then popping up with a crooked smile.

Nick continued through all the devices connected to the Wi-Fi until he found one with a security wall. He did not have to throw much at it to get in and take control. The desktop wallpaper made no effort to hide their identity. "Fort Security" and a logo referencing the military fort downtown where Canadians had held off the United States in the War of 1812.

It bothered him he had never heard of them and took a quick detour to look them up. They were a boutique firm for the rich, offering minimum security for maximum prices. Everything from fresh-faced bodyguards out of the local dojo to overcharging for virus scanners. They were smart enough not to network that computer to the rest of the company, but he had access to the video files. He copied them to his system and poked around to see what else was there. It was dedicated to this one job.

They had only been filming her for a week or so. She paced her apartment, worried, watching over her son. She was on her computer a lot. When she was seated in the one reading chair, he could see her screen. He paused, blowing up the frame, but not getting much other than blurry suggestions of spreadsheets and news sites. Fort had to be in her computer, too, and did not need to squint sideways to guess what she was doing.

The television was on as a distraction for the boy, and he wondered where his father was in all this. Nick paused the videos and tracked him down to rental records. Andy Van Slyke from Red Deer, Alberta. He worked in internet marketing and was, at present, unemployed. There would be no child support coming her way. He dug into that for a moment and confirmed. They had divorced through a mediator before Arash was born. The records had him signing away his parental rights in return for no financial responsibility. His LinkedIn profile was entirely unimpressive, his photo pathetic, and he was glad Parisa was rid of him, but was sorry the boy was stuck with the television for a babysitter. His own mother had struggled to supply him with Meccano engineering sets by that age.

From there, he checked Instagram. Her profile was open, and he wondered if she was with another man now. But all he found was a selection of the architecture photos from her phone. It put him at ease, especially that she did not expose her son's image online. He went through her followers. She did not restrict them. There were a number of scam accounts, supposedly single dads looking for love, and, as soon as the hook was in, money.

One caught his eye, a cowboy in all his Albertan glory. He got through the password in a moment to the email. Unsurprisingly, it was Andy Van Slyke, using another man's image and actively liking her every post. How could she not know it was him? He clicked back on the LinkedIn profile. Van Slyke himself was not what Nick would call handsome. Regular features, blue-eyed and red-faced, but his sun damaged skin might pass for the sort of ruggedness women like. A bit more digging and he had all of Andy's information, including a credit card, then popped it into a file to pass on to the dark web for others to exploit.

That done, he returned to the videos saved by Fort Security. They mainly consisted of Parisa trying to get her work done while caring for her son. In the last of those dated before the tribunal, Arash was sitting in front of the television holding his stuffed rabbit, while Parisa graded blue books piled up next to her on the couch. His chest became tight with love. It could have been him in front of that television. It could have been his mother on the couch. Nick darkened his screens and pressed a button, raising the security blinds on the exterior windows, and looked out at the lake. He would protect her.

He closed the security blinds and started the video again. In this one, Arash was crying as Parisa grabbed their passports and other paperwork, a few file folders, then some of their clothes, stuffing them into a backpack and a tote. She spoke gently to him, saying everything would be all right. They would be home again soon. It was the cadence of mothers assuring their children when all was lost. She made a call, but he could not hear it, then texted. Right before she left, she pried her phone from its case and used a paperclip to remove the SIM card. Then, they rushed out of the house. Strangely, she left the computer behind, but so did she also leave Arash's stuffed bunny sitting up properly on the couch.

The video of the search infuriated him. The two young men barely talked, every so often looking up at the camera, aware they were being watched. One opened her computer, inserted a USB drive into it, and got her password. He took the thumb drives from the bowl and, one by one, inserted them into the computer, finally saying, "Got it." But he threw all the thumb drives into a backpack beside him, despite not needing them. He pulled out another from his pocket, made a few more keystrokes. After a few minutes, he removed the USB drive. "Got everything. It won't take long to wipe it. There's not much on here."

The other was busy turning things over, checking through papers. "Nothing printed out," he said at last. He got bored searching and sat on the couch. "Done?"

"Now." The man closed the computer.

The other nodded. He threw the bunny across the room and kicked over the red canvas wagon on his side on the way out.

Fast forwarding, Martin Monaghan came in next. He moaned and swore as he went through the apartment, picking up things Nick supposed Martin thought were important, but little of it made sense to him. Martin opened the computer and shut it, but did not take it. He took the bunny, but not before collapsing with it and sobbing his heart out. For the child, perhaps. But Nick suspected it was for himself.

Trang knocked on his door. Nick flinched, then pushed back from his desk, incensed at the interruption.

"Sorry, sir. Samuel needs you on the Tracey-Carlton account."

"It's so urgent you could not just ping me?"

Samuel came up behind her, carrying on at length, then handed him a sheet of paper.

He read it. Their lawyers were objecting to some of the finer details in their smear of an Arab-Canadian MP with manipulated evidence of foreign interference. It was solved easily enough and he shoved it back into Samuel's hands, tapping hard on one of the line items. "Just run it through the account of some businessman, not Arab, someone who has been in Saudi too much in the past few years."

8

Once on the subway, they hashed out their plan. Tomoko was excited despite the risk to Parisa. She knew it was wrong, but could not control it. Her stomach fluttered. Her nerves were tingling. Frank probably felt like this. He went at investigative journalism like a real cowboy and was not the example to follow, she told herself. It was Amina she admired. Amina had reported on Canadian mining companies in Mexico and government corruption in their relations with Indigenous communities with the gravity the stories deserved. Amina would not get excited about making plans to lose an imaginary tail, let alone forget the impact of the story on the people involved. The thought sobered her enough to attend to her obligation to Parisa. She was a woman with a child, a woman under threat, not a source to be exploited.

"We can turn back. Leave all this behind," Tomoko said. "There's got to be another way out of this. We haven't even considered the options."

But Parisa was determined. "What is there for me? Ship my son off to Alberta to live with his father and grandparents? People who have not given him one thought in all these years? Leave all my work behind? Live my life on the run?"

So the boy's father was out of the picture. She responded a little too eagerly, "Cyrus goes back and forth to Iran for his imports. You couldn't go just to wait this out?"

Parisa stared daggers at her.

"Okay. Let's assume this is not as bad as it seems. You let it go. The story is buried with Monaghan's termination. You don't take up the research. They forget about you."

"And the phone call?"

"Maybe it was just meant to scare you, keep you from going back to the data."

Parisa was quiet, then faced her. "That might be true. I have to hope that is true. We won't go, then. There's no need to get the computer, the USB drive. I'll take Arash and go away for a while. The department will give me a leave of absence. Then I return and go back to my work, never touch the payday data again."

They sat in silence for a moment. Tomoko readied herself to get off at the next station, so they could turn around, and tried to accept that the story needed to die for Parisa and Arash. But she also knew she could not do it. Too much was at stake. The victims of the loan scam. How could she ignore their interests over the fate of one woman and one child? There had to be a way to protect them all. She heard her father's quiet, but firm voice, and saw her mother's withering stare. Tomoko was raised to choose the needs of the people over the individual. While it was not for her to choose for Parisa and Arash, there might be a choice she could make without them.

"No," Parisa said.

Tomoko twitched. "What?"

"We carry on."

She took Parisa's hand in a burst of comradeship and the two sat leaning into each other as the car jolted back and forth, watching people come and go. Students with backpacks, joking with friends, ignoring in the moment the economic grind they would face despite their hard-earned degrees. Workers exhausted so early in the day searching for open seats, others swaying, holding onto the grab bar laden with bags. Most focused on their phones, eating what they could between one job and the next. It was for them she and Parisa had to find the data and expose the whole damn system.

They got off at Spadina station and she followed Parisa through the dingy orange-tiled tunnel leading a couple of blocks north. Tomoko looked around furtively, checking for anyone watching them. They emerged onto a quiet sidewalk and walked north until they reached an intersection, then walked several blocks east to Parisa's street. They passed it and turned south into the laneway. Thankfully, there was no one to take any notice, but if they did, she assured herself, there was nothing to notice about them. They were within walking distance from Simcoe University; she knew she fit into the neighbourhood with her vintage suede coat and Parisa had 'graduate student' written all over her.

Parisa indicated the gate in the long fence and opened it. In a moment, they were walking between the houses and the laneway on a path covered from view of both. They went through another gate and emerged onto a garden path, hurried through the small backyard and down the stairs to the apartment. Parisa unlocked the door and swore. It had been searched.

"Tell me you hid that USB drive where no one could find it."

"It was in that bowl on my desk with my other thumb drives."

The desk, just a square dining room table made for a tiny apartment, was set into a corner on the other side of the couch. The laptop was on it, but the bowl was empty. At least they did not take her computer. But why didn't they take her computer?

"They must not have believed I would just leave the drive out and did a search?"

Instead of crossing the room to her laptop, Parisa turned over a couch cushion, and then rushed into the small bedroom in the back, growing frantic. She came out and stopped, hand against the wall to hold her up. "They took Blue-Ears. What could they possibly want with a child's stuffed rabbit?"

"Maybe they thought the USB was hidden inside of it?"

"Animals."

Tomoko searched under the papers, books on the floor, then

under the couch. She picked up a framed photograph. Ten or more people were seated outside on a rug-covered platform, a picnic set out before them, a rushing stream in the background and surrounded by scrubby trees showering them with dappled light. It had to be her family in Iran. She thought about that look Parisa gave her when she suggested going back, now knowing not being able to return meant she would never see these people again, in that place, that way. Parisa stepped around the overturned chair and snatched the frame from her hands. Tomoko set to work looking for whatever else seemed important, leaving Parisa to the loss of her life as she knew it, again.

9

Nick shut the door on Trang and Samuel, furious with Samuel's lack of imagination, and got back to work. He touched his keyboard and the display came back to life. He checked the live feed. The apartment was still empty. Another video popped up on Fort Security's site, time stamped from just moments earlier.

He opened it. Parisa and an East Asian woman were searching the apartment. They had been in and out while fucking Samuel was making him handle a matter that could have fucking waited. He cursed himself for answering the door and then for not telling them to fuck off.

Nick watched with self-incriminating fury. The Asian woman seemed to know what she was doing, but did not think to check for a camera or even assume that one might have been installed. And he did not like how she was talking to Parisa. The woman's blaming comment, "Tell me you hid that USB drive where no one could find it," set him against her. But it told him that they were there to recover the data.

This time, Parisa thought to take her computer. He was glad he had got into it before they arrived. Parisa did not check any of the papers, but printouts of the data would have amounted to nearly a ream and he saw nothing like that. At her aggrieved complaint—"What could they possibly want with a child's stuffed rabbit?"—Nick yelled at the display that Martin had taken it.

He went back and forth in the video until he found a good shot of the Asian woman's face, despite the downward angle of the camera, screenshot it, then another of her profile and another of her full body. The usable face shot went through facial recognition software containing images gleaned from every possible source on the web and narrowed the search criteria to Toronto. Several likely candidates came up, but only one fit the full body and profile. Tomoko Abrams, an analyst for *The Spanner*.

Nick drew a breath, forcing his temper down. This was a break. Parisa was planning on taking the data public if she could find it again. That was simple enough. He only had to resend it. But not to Parisa this time. A bit more work and he got into Tomoko's email and located her phone number.

"Problem solved," he said aloud, wishing that Bea were here so he could share the good news.

A message pinged through from Trang. He almost deleted it without looking, not needing to hear another damn thing from her for a week. Then he saw it.

Agapov has asked for a meeting. Himself. Here. Day after tomorrow at 11AM.

Nick stood, gripping the edge of the desk.

Andrei Agapov of Panopticon Security. Forbes had listed Nick, along with a number of up-and-coming leaders, as "The Next Generation in Cyber Security." Cristo Solutions, in particular, was singled out as having the potential to become the next Panopticon. It was hyperbole. Agapov would never look over his shoulder at Nick. Panopticon was global, providing cyber security for small nations and advising greater ones. But Nick hoped the claim brought him to the attention of those who worked with Agapov and used it to put out feelers to the company. If he could build a relationship with Panopticon, Cristo would be on the move. The feelers had worked. But Agapov, himself, here? No one even knew what he looked like. It seemed impossible.

Yes. Confirmed.

He refrained from adding several exclamation marks. There was even more to tell Bea tonight at dinner.

Temper redirected, he returned to the situation at hand with a hungry grin. Everything was falling into place. Part of him wanted to call Singh and let him know that he no longer needed Monaghan's research to go through academic channels, but he had already exposed himself too much that morning at the penthouse. Singh would know soon enough when the data came out in the press. *The Spanner* prided itself on releasing the raw data and documents shared with them by whistleblowers. This would not simply be a summary account that could be immediately denied.

Then it hit him. There would be the expected claims that the data had been manipulated. If investigators were inclined to cover it up, they would have time to manipulate it themselves to make it seem so. And the Wellingtons could have the virus out of their system before anyone knew.

He bit his tongue, angry again, but now from the misery of his error. Why had he not put in a failsafe so if they tried to remove the virus, their entire system would collapse? They would have to choose between being destroyed publicly or privately.

He paced his office, thinking it through. And what if there were a leak at *The Spanner*? Forget that. Not even a leak. A teaser for an upcoming piece? He could not send Abrams the data before the failsafe was in. The Wellingtons could have the virus out before the story even hit.

It was going to be a long night. Nick opened his small refrigerator. Red Bull in hand, he went back to the computer, searching for

Abrams through her phone. Her SIM card was off, but her Bluetooth and Wi-Fi were connected and he found her at the home of Cyrus Dadashi in Etobicoke.

He typed in Dadashi's name. The man had no social media accounts, not even LinkedIn. His website showed an import business bringing in nuts and dried fruits from Iran. Nick found himself lingering on certain pages and almost clicked on "saffron and lime pistachios," and made a note to tell Étienne for when they entertained.

Nick tried his phone, but it was dead to him, then pushed his way into Dadashi's home Wi-Fi. There were no cameras, not in his television, or even a doorbell camera. The man did not have any home automation devices to listen through, not even a virtual assistant speaker to play music. Could anyone be this analog? He checked for computers on the Wi-Fi. If Dadashi had one, it was off, the same if Parisa's computer was there. He was only able to get into his television history. He seemed to watch lots of cartoons and historical dramas. Not much help there, but then he saw it. Cartoons played most recently. Maybe Arash was there? Or maybe he had a child himself?

Nick spent a bit more time combing the neighbourhood and found his way into a door bell camera across the street, but there was not a good view of the house. He could only assume that this was where Parisa was hiding. The man was Iranian. They must know each other already.

He went back to social media. Abrams had an Instagram account, but it was private. He got into that and found pictures of her with Dadashi. In these images, he saw just how stunningly beautiful she was, but she hung off his arm as if he were the catch. Dadashi was handsome, but there was no bite to him. He had none of the simmering danger that made a man a man. But there was no doubt they were a couple. If Parisa was there, Abrams took her to him.

Nick would get Abrams the data as soon as he could. Nothing was ever easy, but he knew that with a little imagination—imagination he possessed—he could tie up every loose thread. Tight. Too tight for the Wellingtons to escape. He pushed away from the desk. First upstairs to the penthouse. Have something to eat. Take a nap. Then he would write the failsafe. He gave himself a day, two at most. The code was already forming in his mind. Nick only hoped the truly unworthy Fort Security had not done anything to protect the system. He could not release the data to Abrams until that failsafe was in place.

10

"Do you really think that Bernard is behind this?"

Conor spooned more coffee into the cylinder, poured hot water over the grounds, then pressed coffee into Martin's cup.

"He's certainly behind the vehemence of that tribunal." Martin took the cup from Conor, holding the handleless matte-black cup awkwardly, wishing not everything had to suit his brother's minimalist style and make him feel as if even coffee cups were against him. "He could have intervened. The dean could have intervened. I could have been censured. I could have had my graduate students taken into the supervision of another advisor. There were options, but they wanted none of it."

"Why discount the Wellingtons?"

Martin put the cup down and shovelled more scrambled eggs in his mouth, swallowing hard. "Of course it was the Wellingtons!" He gulped the coffee down on top of it. "But universities can protect their faculty if they want to and they did not want to and Bernard made sure of it."

"Going after Bernard won't protect your graduate student. What is her name, again?"

"Parisa Soltani."

"Your place was not searched. If it was only her, she's the one they are after."

"Everyone in the department knew Parisa did that work, but her name was not read into the record until the tribunal. That's when the threats shifted to include her."

"You didn't let me in on any of this until it was too late."

"I didn't want your firm involved. The data had to be untainted by any interest."

"What interest do I have?"

"You have it in for people like them."

His voice rose in protest. "I merely do not invest my clients' funds in certain financial instruments and institutions."

"Hey. I like that you have it in for them."

"Martin, please." He put his hands on the gleaming white kitchen island and leaned in. "You should have told me. I'm your brother. Who else do you have now that—"

He put his hand up. "Stop. Don't mention Oliver."

"Why not? I like him. He's charming. And he makes the best coffee in your neighbourhood." Conor stepped back from the island. "Now I cannot even get the coffee I love anymore. I went there after he left you and he was so friendly I had to turn right around."

"So friendly? That made you turn around?"

"Oliver is so good. What did you do?"

"He's like the rest of them. They can't stand that the suffering of others matters more to me than whether or not they've had a bad day at work."

"There we have it."

"There you have it." Martin stood, glaring at his brother, too exhausted to think, his career lost, his graduate student and her son in danger, and all his brother can think about is his own petty feelings of not being included and whine again about him putting work before love, as if his celibate ass had anything to say in that regard. "I'm going home." Martin took a last bite of Oonagh's soda bread, picked up his backpack, and headed for the door.

"Call Oliver!" Conor yelled after him.

Out in the driveway, he stared at the beat-up CR-V, packed back to front with boxes. He turned the key in the door, pulling it open. "Shit." Tom had cleaned his car out of used coffee cups and bags of chips after driving it to Conor's for him, and he was embarrassed that the old man had seen the mess of his life. Worse, Tom had probably told Oonagh, who told Conor, and Conor would end up nagging him.

Oliver used to clean it for him, teasing, but he knew how that would play out. Before long, it would become a complaint. Just like how Oliver first admired Martin's work, his dedication to his students, reading their papers late into the night, making notes, preparing lectures, his research and the impact it made. Then he found out Martin did not really have summers off and that the vacation Oliver was planning would not work unless it was scheduled around a research agenda. All the men he got involved with were like that. They had seen him on television speaking out for the vulnerable and thought he was someone he was not. He was a selfish bastard when it came to work. And so, they all left in the end with some version of "arrogant prick" as parting words. He told them up front what it took to be him. Not his problem.

He barely saw the streets as he drove out of the wealth of Leaside to East York and the brick semi-detached of their childhood. The neighbourhood had changed since then. It was not working class anymore. When their parents died, their children ended up selling to young professionals. They pulled out the chain-link fences that allowed neighbours to talk yard to yard and pass over food from the grill or a cold beer, and put up high wooden barriers. He could hear kids playing, but no longer knew their names. Holdouts like him and Jamal's family were few and far between.

But there was a price to pay for that familiarity, and he was about to face it. As he had turned the corner, he found Jamal sitting on his stoop, brushing a speck off his beloved Japanese denim jeans. Martin sighed. "Not now."

Jamal stood as the car pulled up into the driveway.

He rolled down the window, keeping the car running before bringing it all the way to the back.

"Conor called me."

"Then you know I'm in no mood to talk."

"It's Allah's will. There's something better for you ahead."

"Don't Allah me, Jamal. I'm tired."

"This is how life is, man. 'You may hate a thing that is good for you and you may love a thing that is bad for you, but Allah knows best'."

Now he was quoting Quran at him when all he needed was to get inside his house and figure out where to go from here.

"I got arrested and it turned my life around," Jamal went on. "Your brother saved us. The monthly payments from his investments. My whole family. We were able to bring my grandparents over. My brother is in medical school. Your brother—"

"My brother can't live with the guilt that he didn't back you up in that shop, then with Bailey."

"Forgiveness belongs to God, but he doesn't owe us a thing. It's on me what I did back then. We pray for him every day."

"I'm sure he appreciates it," Martin said with the last bit of patience he had left, took his foot off the brake and eased the car through the narrow driveway.

Parked, he lifted the back gate of the SUV and began unloading boxes.

"Someone was around the house yesterday," Jamal called to him from the end of the driveway.

Martin shoved the box he was holding back in the car and walked straight to Jamal. "Who? What happened?"

"A woman knocked on the door and when you didn't answer, she went around back."

"Then what?"

"She left."

"In what? What kind of car?"

"An Uber. It was waiting for her."

"What did she look like?"

"Older white woman. She looked drunk or something."

"Drunk!"

"Just strange, something strange about her."

"Tall, short, what?"

"Average."

"Dress?"

"Average."

"Come on!"

Jamal stepped back.

"I'm sorry. It might have something to do with the research I did."

"The reason you lost your job?"

"Yes."

"She had grey hair, but was wearing a headscarf. Like the Greek widows, not us."

"Maybe she was just a Greek widow?"

"She wasn't wearing all black."

"Jamal. You noticed her clothes. You notice everyone's clothes, down to the designer."

"Yeah, sorry, just a brown skirt suit out of the eighties. She didn't go in, or I would've stopped her."

He dropped his head in apology. "I'm a mess. I appreciate you coming by."

His wife came up behind them, smiling. Her baby bump was showing under her long, asymmetric sweater and she was holding a bag filled with yogurt tubs. "You know who sending you know what."

Auntie Zeb had made biryani just for him and sent over more than he could eat. What had these people done but gone through hell because of his brother's silence and that slimy groomer Bailey, and they remained kind to him?

The two turned around with a wave, walking hand in hand to the house they shared with Jamal's mother across the street.

Martin went back to finish unloading the boxes and took the bag with the tubs. "Now," he asked himself, "who the hell was knocking on my door?"

Boxes finally stacked on the dining room table and on the floor beside it, he went to put the tubs into the fridge. Martin pulled it open with too much force and the bottles in the door crashed against each other.

He froze, the jangle of the bottles still in his ears. His laptop was inside, propped up by a six-pack of beer and a plastic container of a half-eaten rotisserie chicken. He put the tubs onto the counter behind him and retrieved the laptop.

Jamal said the woman had not entered. Someone might be in the house now. He took a breath, every muscle falling into place, his hearing sharpened for a creak upstairs. The uneven floors would give anyone away. He waited. Nothing. He got tired of waiting.

"I found the laptop," he yelled, leaving the kitchen to stand at the bottom of the stairs. "I can come up there and kick your ass or you can come down here and I can kick your ass. If you know so much about me to come here searching, then you know I can kick your ass."

He heard a creak, then another, and stopped, waiting. Nothing.

Only then it occurred to him they might have a gun. Instead of going upstairs, he opened the front door. "The door is open. You can make a run for it. I'll step back. I won't look."

Martin left the front hall and went through to the dining room, where he had a good view but could not be seen from the stairs. But through the front window, he saw Jamal and Fariha standing on their front porch, watching his house. He tried to gesture to them to get inside before they became witnesses and likely victims, but they did not see him.

Martin launched into a run through the living room and up the stairs, taking two steps at a time. "I'm coming up!"

No one was at the top. He ran into the first bedroom. Empty. The second. Empty. His office. No one. At least, not anymore. His office was trashed. Afraid they had gotten down to the street somehow and seen Jamal and his wife, Martin rushed down the stairs and out onto the stoop.

Jamal ran across to him, running around one parked car, then another. "What happened?"

Martin grabbed his arms. "Did anyone just come out my door?"

"No one."

"The woman. You say she didn't go in my house?"

"She was only back there for a minute."

Fariha joined them. "We heard her knock on the back door, then she came around."

"Someone was in my house."

"It wasn't the woman."

"You didn't see anyone else here?"

"No, but we've been out yesterday and today. I was at the barbershop and Fariha's been with my mother for her medical appointments."

Whoever was in his house had not been witnessed by Jamal and his family. Martin bent over, breathing hard. "Okay. Okay."

"Let's get you inside," Fariha said, going past him into the house. He heard the tap running.

"Come on, you heard her." Jamal held out a hand.

Martin waved him off. "I'm fine. Go home."

Jamal looked down the street, and Martin followed his glance.

"Fuck's sake. Did you call him?"

"I did. You shouldn't be alone."

Oliver was rushing toward them.

11

"No running around the pool!" Cassandra Wellington yelled.

Her sons stopped short, laughing and falling into each other. Henry threw Max in, taunting him and posing triumphantly.

"They'll hurt themselves," Cassandra said, preempting her father's criticism.

"Let them hurt themselves. How will they learn?" Her father shifted position in the lounge chair, bringing one knee up, letting it open slightly, and smiled. It was sickening. He was a large man, well-muscled and fit. His strong jaw and chin had yet to soften, and she knew he would pose like this to a dog if a bitch wandered past. But she did not know what this display of masculinity in his seventies was supposed to impress on her. She was not one of the women he kept on the side, for God's sake.

"He's right, honey." Her mother lay her novel down on one fit but age-wrinkled thigh. "We let you girls make your own mistakes."

"Like with Patricia?"

"Do not mention your sister's name with that tone," her mother said, then crossed herself as if she had ever gone to church except on the day of Patricia's funeral. Then she went in for the sting. "You should let your hair grow out. Unfortunately, you inherited my father's wide face. It requires a longer look."

Cassandra tucked her short bob behind her ear, further emphasizing her jawline, and turned back to watch her boys in the pool.

The humidity from the indoor pool was stifling. The high windows dripped with it. She wanted to leave, but would not allow the children to be alone in her parents' care. Henry circled around Max in the water. He was going to push him under. Max knew it, too, and looked to her for help. Cassandra tried to intervene, but her mother touched her arm to hold her back. She threw her mother's hand off, addressing the children. "Mrs. Barstow has ice cream for you upstairs."

The distraction was enough. Henry left Max behind and scrambled out of the pool. Max followed, dripping wet, running behind his big brother, all forgotten.

"Dry off first!"

"Let them go, Cassandra. Your mother will have them mop up the mess they made as their ice cream melts in their bowls."

She stood to follow the boys, intending to mop it herself when her parents were not looking.

"No, dear, stay," her mother said.

All her "sweets," "honeys," and "dears" could not obscure the tone. They wanted to talk business. She sat back down.

"Stone will be here soon."

"The job he does. I cannot accept that's his real name," Cassandra said, worried that the man who was supposed to be protecting them was doing no such thing. If she were in charge, none of this would be happening. The virus would have been removed immediately and reported to the appropriate authorities. The company needed to remain secure. Secure until she could sell the moment her parents were in their graves. But this she shared with no one, certainly not her husband. Maybe it was paranoia, but her parents would cut her out of the will if they found out, and Cassandra did not trust Brandt to keep her secret. One slip, and the business would be laid in trust for her children, out of her hands.

"What other profession could Stone choose when his father passed the name on to him?" Wellington chuckled.

On cue, Stone entered. Hitting the heat and humidity of the room, he shrugged out of his suit jacket and laid it over one well-muscled arm. She covered herself with a towel.

"You'll be pleased with the news." He pulled up a chair. "The graduate student has not left Toronto, but she's afraid and has no plans to reprise the research. In fact, she seems to resent Monaghan for getting her into this mess. The camera we installed in her apartment is giving us what we need. She returned with another woman we're presently tracking down."

Wellington asked, "The computers?"

"The data and all associated documents were wiped from the cloud, all hard drives, and we got the original thumb drive."

"Monaghan?"

"We sent a message for him to cool it."

"As if being terminated was not message enough," Mary remarked.

"We knew he would not go easily," Stone said. "But the divisions in the department were simple enough to exploit, especially with a well-placed anonymous donation."

"I hate anonymous donations," said Mary.

"She is still after me for a hospital wing," Wellington said to Stone with an indulgent smile.

Her mother touched his arm. "Soon."

Wellington slapped his thighs. "Any further action?"

"Not at this point, but we'll be keeping an eye on everyone."

Cassandra interjected, "Aren't you going to take the virus out of the system?"

Her mother smiled at her as if she were a child. "Why in the world?"

"It is illegal."

"Yes, but the program is running so beautifully."

"Tell them, Stone. Tell them they'll be caught."

Stone's face remained impassive. It was not for him to have an opinion. But for someone whose firm protected the worst people for a living, he probably agreed with her parents. In the end, he assured them, "We've added a new layer of security to the system. If the government comes snooping or the person who created the bug comes back, they won't find what they need. The virus is there unless we don't want it to be there."

Her father replied, "Good. We will leave it in place until we decide that the risk has outpaced its usefulness."

"They know!" she said. "Everyone at the university. They know what the data said. It's not a secret."

Stone responded, "Yes, but the evidence is gone. And we will know if and when anyone who is aware whispers in such a way that the governing bodies are forced to listen."

"Forced," she said. There would always be people in place to bury complaints.

"And, darling, if they do, we can announce, privately, that we have finally rooted out the virus, as well as those responsible for not informing us, and negotiate favourable terms to compensate those who have been harmed."

She said 'harmed' with such loathing that Cassandra felt sick.

"I hate to ask," her mother carried on, "but if the graduate student returns to the research, or Monaghan—"

"That one. No better than a street preacher," her father grumbled. "At least his brother keeps his prejudices limited to influencing his clients' accounts. I wish we could do more."

Her mother looked at her father harshly for cutting her off. "As I was saying, if they decide to carry on, what would come next?"

"We have small intimidations already in place. We will 'raise the volume', as it were, if those hints do not make the intended impression."

"What do you mean?"

"Meaning, sweetie," her mother said, "if the girl or Monaghan do not care about their own safety, we move on to intimidate the innocents in their lives."

"Sacrifice innocents!"

She responded, "You would never be so foolish as to be innocent, would you?"

Did her mother mean that? Was it a warning? Cassandra faced Stone, wanting to see if he was on their side, but the man actually shrugged. How could Agape have hired this firm for them? She trusted him.

"Business is business, Cassandra," her father said. "Your sister understood that."

"Business! Do you expect the support of the financial industry if this goes wrong?"

Her father's expression told she had admitted the inconvenient truth. Wellington Payday Loans was expendable. If exposed, other short-term lenders would calculate how little they would have to pay on the dollar to buy out their loans and offices. The big banks with their built-in systems to steal from customers through false overdraft fees were unlikely to help, or they would be exposed.

Cassandra did not back down, but would say no more. She would not allow her children to be tainted by this business. They die. She sells. She and Brandt would take that wealth and build a new life out of it. But for this plan to work, she was going to act as if she were on her parents' side. "I am merely suggesting there may be a resolution that would not put us in the line of sight of OSFI."

12

———

Miss Henson stopped Conor before he could sit down at his desk. "You have not answered Marlene Jordan's request."

He looked at her quizzically. "I emailed her, reminding her that this firm cannot invest in short-term lending concerns."

"You did," she said plainly, "but I assured her you would consider the matter further."

"You what?"

"You will reconsider."

This was not her typical strangeness. He wondered if her age was getting to her. She had seemed forgetful recently, wearing the same brown suit every day. Her wiry, grey hair was unkempt at times. Once, he suspected, she had forgotten to bathe. Conor changed his tone, explaining gently, "I know that I have expanded Mr. Bailey's directives somewhat by including municipal bonds, and that may have given you the wrong idea."

"He would have allowed it. The brother has been informed."

Did she imagine she was speaking to Mr. Bailey's spirit? "I am sorry, Miss Henson, but as you know, Mr. Bailey would not even allow for investment in well-established banks."

She simply tapped an envelope on his desk.

It was plain but made of high quality paper, and not their stock. Miss Henson had already placed Mr. Bailey's ivory handled stiletto beside it. Conor went behind the desk and used the sharp blade to slice open the top. Only one line was typewritten on it, requesting again the purchase of one million dollars in shares of Wellington Payday Loan stock for Marlene Jordan.

Despite her ignorance of the true reason for the firm's investment principles, Miss Henson knew better. His bid to include municipal bonds required a frustrating and contentious debate with the brothers of The Cluster who had fought him over loaning money long term at low interest to invest in the life of the city. Surely it was within the Lord's edicts for the city to house and feed its most vulnerable, to provide clean water, and public transportation? He knew better than to cite, "Render unto Caesar what is Caesar's." Paying taxes was also an uncomfortable point of tension. To loan money to the city and to be paid back by the taxes of its citizens? He would not raise the spectre of tribute to the men. In the end, they bent enough to allow the question to go to ritual affirmation, which was given, but it was close. And here she was suggesting they invest in usurious short-term loans, as if he could even make such a decision if he wanted.

"Miss Henson," he explained. "I cannot change our principles at their core."

"You will find those who matter are in agreement."

What could she possibly mean? He chose to placate her. Perhaps tomorrow she would be her old self. "Thank you. I'll take it from here."

"I'll stay while you purchase the stock."

Miss Henson would not move. His patience was wearing thin, and he answered her more sharply than he intended. "You were here when I came as a boy. You were Mr. Bailey's most trusted advisor, much more than a secretary. You have been the same to me, but this is out of order."

She cocked her head as if she were waiting for the twelve-year-old Conor to finish his excuses.

Feeling a child again, forced to eat his crackers and cheese in the order she demanded, his temper flared.

He recited the scripture of the Prophet Pliny to calm himself.

"The earth produces first a womb, the Mushroom in the womb, like a yolk inside an egg, and the child eats its coat as does the chick. The coat cracks when the child first forms, and the coat is absorbed into the body of the footstalk—"

As he recited, he felt the tendrils arise from the spores of the Lord's body and wind around him, reaching out from the womb of the earth to his heart, and he was calm. He took a deep breath, then said firmly, but he hoped kindly, "I am sorry, Miss Henson, the firm's boundaries are non-negotiable and our clients sign on in full knowledge."

Miss Henson waited a moment more, then spoke, arms crossed. "You will see you do not have a choice in this matter."

He gestured to direct her out. "Thank you, Miss Henson, that will be all."

But she would not be moved. Her expression transformed into a superior frown. "Tomorrow is Wednesday? Perhaps you will let the brothers explain the choice you are refusing."

The tendrils holding his heart shrank back into the earth as if a scorching sun were bearing down. She knows. The men of The Cluster had told him no one knew. Further, no woman could know. By the Mushroom and the Cross, as the sacred Womb and Staff are one in the Mushroom, they are distinct in human creation. And woman was the Womb and could not know!

"How," he stammered, "how do you know?"

The cast of her face changed completely. The frown expressed confusion. Her grey eyes darted around the room as if she had no idea how she had gotten there, let alone what she had said. Her wrinkled cheeks slackened, her mouth fell open. Perhaps she had overheard Mr. Bailey once and now in her elderly confusion it arose from a hidden place in her memory.

Conor took her by the elbow and led her to the couch. "Sit, Miss Henson."

She did as she was told, looking around the office like a lost child.

"I'll be right back. I'm going to get you a glass of water."

But she grabbed his arm, clawing a hold on him. "Don't leave me!"

He called out over his shoulder. "Marta!"

Marta came in. "Yes?" Then, seeing the state of the old woman on the couch, rushed to her side, exclaiming, "Miss Henson! What's wrong?"

"I think let's begin with a glass of water."

Marta turned around immediately.

But the moment she was gone, Miss Henson's face changed again, this time panicked. "Glans-Crowned Anointed One! The women bridle and he pulls the reins, but the brother knows all!" Then her hand thrust between his legs. He jumped away from her, falling back onto the floor and scrambled away. Her shining eyes were wild and she clambered after him like a hideous spider, mouth gaping toward his open legs.

Conor shot up and ran to the door. "Marta!" He bumped into her as she was coming through, sending the glass and water to the carpet.

"My God, what's happened to her!"

He did not look back, leaving her to Marta. "I'm calling for an ambulance."

At the front desk, he grasped the handle to the office phone, forgetting for a moment to press "911" then recovered, punching it, but missing the keys as one does in a dream. He tried again, this time making it.

"Police, Fire, or Ambulance?"

"Ambulance. A woman has collapsed in my office."

The line connected and rang through, no one picking up immediately. A voice finally answered, but Conor only heard it distantly. The phone was loose in his hand. Miss Henson was standing before him, perfectly fine, with Marta at her side.

"Mr. Monaghan, please, there is no need."

Her brown skirt suit was pulled straight and the white blouse underneath had been tucked in hastily. Only her hair showed any sign of the horror of her attack on him just a few moments before. She smoothed it with a hand.

"I only fainted. It's my low blood pressure." She laughed lightly at herself, addressing Marta. "I'm getting on and I forget to take my medication."

"Hello! What is your emergency?" The phone.

Conor raised the handset to speak. "No emergency. We've had a scare here, but everything is fine now. No need." He hung up the phone. His back was straight and tight. All he wanted was her out of the office. "Marta, can you help Miss Henson home? Make sure she takes her medication?"

Miss Henson nodded sheepishly, as if she were humiliated by the degradations of age. "I'll just go tidy up."

"Do not leave her side."

He tried to sound concerned, but Marta had heard the disgust and fear in his voice and retorted, "I wasn't going to."

He let them go and sat in Marta's chair. Miss Henson had acted like a woman possessed.

It had happened once before, and Conor feared what this might mean.

The men of The Cluster had gathered on a Wednesday as usual, but Pierre had joined them late, frantic and trembling. A masked woman had attacked him in the street. She had used the same words, repeating over and over, "Glans-Crowned Anointed One," and came after him, grasping at his genitals and ultimately knocking him down. Passersby had come to his rescue and pulled her off the elderly man, recovering his cane, setting him right, but the woman had escaped.

"She is possessed," Pierre said. "The time is coming. She knew the name. 'The Glans-Crowned Anointed One'."

Agape had stood before them, a bulwark against their fear, and directed them to listen as Pierre recited the verses of the Lord casting out the demons.

They crossed the sea into a new country. When the Lord emerged from the ship, a man with a demon rushed to him from the tombs. It was known that no man could hold him. They bound him with chains and fetters, but he had always plucked them asunder and broke his fetters into pieces. Night and day the untameable man wandered the mountains and through the tombs, cutting himself with stones.

When he saw the Lord from far away, he recognized him and ran to him, falling at his feet, crying out, "What have I to do with you, Lord? You are the child of the Womb alone. O Glans-Crowned-White-Flecked Lord, the Lord of Womb and Staff, have you come to torment me before the appointed time?"

The Lord said, "Demon, come out of that man!" Then he demanded, "What is your name?"

"My name is Legion, for we are many."

The demons were tormented in his presence. The demons saw a herd of swine feeding in the mountains and they begged him, many voices sounding as one, "Cast us into the swine."

The Lord cast them into the herd, thousands of them. The swine ran, twisting and squealing, tumbling over each other to a cliff and into the sea, where they choked in the turbulent waters.

And the man fell before the Lord, asking, "When is the appointed time?"

He answered, "The time of the Anointed One is coming. The Womb is opening. The herd of swine will return in the shape of woman. She will wander among the tombs and when she finds the apostles of The Glans-Crowned Anointed One, she will attack."

A snowstorm was brewing, making entering into the Ritual impossible. Instead, they shrank in on themselves in reflection as the wind howled around them. Sitting in a circle, each knee touched that of the one beside him, Pierre's fear flowing among them so that he did not carry its weight alone.

Conor now understood exactly how he felt and needed his brothers.

Miss Henson returned to the office, colour in her cheeks again, and speaking briskly to Marta just behind her. "I can certainly finish the day, maybe just a cup of sweetened tea. I'll sit by you, dear."

Conor shook his head at Marta, who nodded in understanding.

The old woman continued, "And you, Mr. Monaghan, have stock to purchase for Ms. Jordan." She broke off from Marta and walked purposefully into his office.

Conor came around the front desk. "Marta, get her things and drive her home."

He followed Miss Henson in to find her standing behind his desk, holding tightly onto the clasp of her purse.

"Marta is waiting to take you home."

"I will go if you promise to purchase the stock."

"I promise." He lied. What else could he do?

She walked past him, satisfied.

Conor shut the door firmly behind him and went to the desk, but there was nothing there. Not the envelope, nor Mr. Bailey's ivory letter opener. Had she taken them? He searched his drawers and found the letter, but not the opener. It was sharp enough to slice open one's finger. Was she planning on hurting herself or Marta? He ran out of the office toward the elevators, but they had already gone. He went to the front desk phone and called Marta's cell.

"Yes?"

"She may have taken Mr. Bailey's letter opener, you know the one. I'm afraid she might try to hurt herself or you."

There was a fumbling sound from the phone as if Marta had placed the mic against her clothes, muffling her voice. Then the sound returned and he heard the two women giggling, obviously at his expense. Marta answered him, "She says you mislaid it."

He had not, but Miss Henson may have. Conor urged Marta to be careful all the same and hung up, tapping another number immediately.

"Vincent Allen, please." Bailey's lawyer picked up immediately. "It's Miss Henson. She attacked me. Just like the woman who attacked Pierre."

DAY THREE

13

Yesterday, Martin had been grateful to have Oliver nearby as he opened his laptop, expecting the worst and getting it. Then Oliver had followed him upstairs to his home office to stand as a witness to the aftermath of the search. His books had been thrown to the floor in great heaps. His filing cabinet emptied and scattered. The desktop computer was wiped to factory settings, just like the laptop. Martin cursed. It was not just the payday data; all his work and personal files were gone. His research data and drafts of his articles and books. All the scanned family photographs and digitized video. Music transferred from cassettes and CDs. The hard-drive backups were gone, too. No doubt, Parisa's computer had suffered the same.

Martin had never loaded the payday data and analysis on his work computer, considering their network insufficiently secure. He had even taken it to a local place to print out on their dated machines rather than use the Wi-Fi connected ones on campus. But he had two sets of printouts. One had been stored in a box beside his desk at home. They had found those and taken them. The other box he had stored at his office and brought home with him when he cleaned it out. It was downstairs, mixed in among the rest. They had not got that, but suspecting bugs or cameras, he did not say so aloud to Oliver.

"It's all gone, then?" Oliver did not wait for an answer, but pulled him into an embrace.

Martin tensed in his arms, his anger unwilling to be soothed, and shrugged him off to head back downstairs and unplug the modem.

If anything linked into his Wi-Fi, that would take care of it until he could log onto his internet account, check for connected devices, and change the modem name and password. He dug around his electronics drawer, pulling out cords and wires for devices he no longer possessed, and finally found his radio frequency detector.

"What's that you have"—Oliver appeared behind him, looking over Martin's shoulder—"a wee tape recorder for all yer dirty secrets, is it?"

Where Oliver's embrace found resistance, his tease, said in that delectable Irish brogue, broke through Martin's furious grief. His every nerve on fire lit into wanting his hands on the man. But he and Oliver would not end up on the living room floor for the benefit of anyone watching them, and he had to shake himself like a dog to get the desire off.

"It's for hidden listening devices and cameras." He turned the detector on. Batteries were fine.

The two of them went from room to room, sweeping for devices, keeping the bedroom for last.

Later, they stood half-dressed in front of the fridge. Martin opened the tubs sent by Jamal's mother. "Biryani. You know where the bowls are."

"We're to eat it cold?"

"Microwave. Just don't tell Jamal. His mother will never feed me again."

He turned the Wi-Fi back on and logged into his internet provider and saw there were two unknown networked devices, but he knew that already from the sweep. Martin saw no reason to scare Oliver and had dismissed the blips when he had expressed concern. One was in the office, the other in the living room. He changed the modem password. That should cover them until Oliver left and he could dig them out.

They ate in front of the television and spent the rest of the night watching a ridiculous thriller. They laughed with delight at one whiplash turn of events after another, right up until a scene in which a woman finds out she's being watched online. Martin shivered and found his way into Oliver's arms.

After Oliver left early for work, Martin dug out the two cameras. They were no wider than his pinkie and had been shoved in corners where the ceiling met the walls. Right where the winter spiders make their homes and easily ignored, at least in his house. Still, he wondered at the amateurish attempt at surveillance. He snapped the transmitting wires and put them in his jeans pocket, blaming Bernard.

After enough coffee to fuel a jet, Martin dressed, ready to confront him. He needed to get there early, before Bernard left for campus. Martin pulled on his usual flannel shirt and fleece jacket, rehearsing what he would say. He brushed his teeth, imagining Bernard's objections. He put on his boots, devising a way to counter them.

Martin was thick in his thoughts and halfway out the door when he realized he had left his wallet and keys on the kitchen counter. Back inside, he grabbed them and stopped cold. A camera, exactly like the two he found, was just under the Vitamix. In his mind's eye, he recalled Oliver leaning against the counter, hand near the blender. A fist pressed up against his chest.

How had it all began, him and Oliver? He slid down onto the floor, trying to remember, suspecting everything.

"Whaty're having today?" Oliver had called out as Martin walked through the door that first time.

The shop had been promising to open for a while. Whenever he went to see Jamal at Castries for his buzz cut, he would look in the window. No tables and chairs were in yet, but a commercial espresso machine was in place and the far wall had been painted a dark royal blue and the words "Coffee and Craic" written in chalk in one section.

But that day, it was open. Oliver was tall, broad-chested, and warmly handsome with brown eyes so kind, he wondered how often he got his heart broken. He had quickly introduced Martin to the other patrons in the small cafe and soon they were all talking about a novel he had never read but was now considering. Martin settled in, stealing glances at Oliver, while feeling as if the neighbourhood he had lost to tall fences had been restored to him.

Martin examined those early days. Who was the eager one? Had Oliver manipulated him into a relationship? But as Martin remembered it, he was the one who asked Oliver to go for a walk after work. Oliver had even declined, saying he was flattered but made a joke about drama in his business. Martin pressed on despite it, dropping by the cafe nearly every day. The openness of the man's heart to all his customers. How could he not keep trying?

Eventually, Oliver gave in and regretted it. Their relationship had only lasted a few months. It had been intense, loving, and emotional. Martin rested in that big heart of his, finding a quiet that was impossible when he was alone. But in the end, Oliver walked out on him like everyone else had. Walked out on him because the data that Parisa had brought to him, the chance to take down Wellington Payday Loans, had come first.

Sitting on the kitchen floor, Martin tried to convince himself. "He left you. Oliver couldn't be involved or there never would have been a breakup. He would have stayed through it all, wouldn't he?"

14

———————

Martin drove downtown to Bernard's to get the truth out of him. But with every pause in traffic, his doubts about Oliver resurfaced, and he repeated to himself that it was more reasonable that whoever had put in the cameras was simply sloppy. It was not Oliver. If anyone he knew was behind it, it was Bernard. It was hard to believe that Bernard would have intended Parisa, and now him, to be under threat. But sure as shit, Bernard had set it in motion and Martin would get an admission out of him.

He pulled up in front of Bernard's house. How many department parties had been held there? Bernard holding court in his manicured backyard. Everything just so. Wine and small batch brewery beer were paired appropriately with fancy appetizers like canapés and smoked salmon on tiny crackers. The old guard did not mind that his wife was so much younger than him and a former student. She carried trays, was barefoot, and wore flowing dresses. The department had one gathering at Martin's house and he had set out camp chairs in the backyard with a cooler of cheap beer and delivery pizza. It was the last time.

The brick house was typical of the Victorian mansions in the Annex. Like Martin, Bernard had inherited the family home, only

Bernard's was of much higher value. Martin followed the slate path to the oak door, but before he could slam the knocker, it opened.

Bernard's teenaged son nearly pushed him off the stoop going past.

"Mike, is your dad home?"

He spun around, his backpack over one shoulder, walking backwards for a moment before he carried on. "You think he wants to talk to you?"

"Little shit," Martin grumbled as he walked through the open door into the foyer, then yelled, "Bernard! It's your favourite former colleague!"

Bernard came through from the kitchen in the back, barefoot, wearing nothing but jeans and a t-shirt even though the windows were open to the fall chill. He slung the tea towel in his hand over his shoulder. "What else could there be left to say, Martin?"

Martin looked into the living room, furnished in that studiously shabby British Museum style. A worn brown leather couch with brass tacks hammered into the arms and mismatched armchairs sat on an aging Persian carpet. All that was missing was an antique print of the Elgin Marbles hanging on the wall. He asked, "Sitting or standing?"

"Standing, I think. And don't bother closing the door, so you won't have any trouble leaving."

"I can get you coming after me, but what you did, exposing Parisa. You put her life at risk. Did you know she's been threatened? She's on the run?" Martin watched his face for a guilty expression, but Bernard looked honestly surprised.

"On the run? For this?"

"Who pressed you to expose her?"

"Martin, if one of our graduate students is under threat, the university must know."

"Now you know."

"What evidence do you have?"

"She texted me." He pulled his phone out of his back pocket, flicked through to the message, and held it up to him.

Bernard approached, squinting at the screen. "My God." He gestured to the living room. "Sit, please."

But Martin stayed where he was, demanding, "Who got you to go after us?"

He went into the living room and sat, looking up at Martin. "Have you called the police?"

"Me? Call the police?"

"Now is not the time for your abolition talk. Parisa's life is in danger. I'm calling the dean." He got up and went back to the kitchen.

Martin strained to listen, but only heard Parisa's name mentioned.

Returning, he said, looking smug, "It seems she was trying to scare you with that text."

"What?"

"The dean said that her landlord called the police when they found her door unlocked and saw the mess she had made."

He took two steps forward. "She had made? It was searched. I saw it."

"That's your interpretation, not what the police said."

"Tell me."

"She let Karine know that the case had upset her and she was taking some time off. The dean said we should expect to grant her a leave of absence. Parisa also told Karine she blamed you."

"Blamed me?"

"She is not the first to complain."

"I, I don't understand."

Bernard gave him a satisfied smile. "Grumblings have made their way to my office. You believe you are championing your graduate students, but they feel taken advantage of, as if you aggrandize yourself through their research and successes."

His chest tightened. It must be a lie. No one had ever said anything like it to him. How could his promotion of their work take advantage? He burst out, "That's not who I am!"

"Oh, Martin."

Bernard was lying. Trying to destroy what bit of self-respect he had left after destroying his career. "I've had enough of you." Martin turned to leave.

"And," Bernard continued, "Parisa told Karine that she would not be reprising the research and finally get back to completing her degree."

He suddenly understood and spun around, attacking. "That's not news. She had already given it up. Don't you see? She left a message that would warn anyone off following her, intimating that she would be no threat. You know her past in Iran. She would react this way!"

"If that is what you believe, tell me why you involved her in work you suspected would invite dangerous scrutiny?"

"That's why I did not cite her! I told you all. But you outed Parisa to everyone at the tribunal. Why?"

"Leave it, Martin."

"My house was searched. My computers were wiped." He lied, "All the payday data, all the research, gone. I've got nothing."

Bernard's eyes widened. "All your work?"

"Every scrap of research. All my personal files, too. My taxes. My music."

He exclaimed sincerely, "The loss!"

"Do you see what you've done?"

Whatever he had felt for Martin a moment before, the accusation hardened him. "Consider it for the best. Your time doing this work may be over."

"And let them carry on stealing from the working poor? We're meant to stand by and do nothing because our lives are at risk, when hundreds of thousands of people are affected?"

"Stop tilting at windmills."

"You hate me. I get it. You've been looking for a way to bring me down for a long time. Who told you to go after me?"

His demeanour changed. "I'm going to have to stop you right now. I have a family. You may care nothing for your own life, or the safety of your former graduate student—and let me remind you, a graduate student who has already suffered enough for one lifetime—but I care about my family, my life, and our students."

"You've been threatened." Martin took a step towards him.

"You are correct," he said, arms crossed. "A brutal looking man came here by the name of Stone and suggested to me that as chair of the department, I should do everything I can to make sure the data was never taken up again."

"Do you know who he worked for?"

"The Wellingtons. He didn't try to hide it."

"All this. All this is on you." He shook his head at Bernard.

"Sad Martin. There will come a day when you see yourself in the mirror. Now, keep away from me and my family or I will have to get an order of protection."

Martin gladly left him. Outside, he called his brother. "Conor, you know how to get information on the rich. Can you get me the home address of the Wellingtons?"

15

"Brandt! You don't understand!" Cassandra followed her husband into his dressing room.

His dress shirts hung in a lighted closet and were organized according to colour. His fingers stopped at several shades of green, stopping at one in a vibrant chartreuse.

"This?"

"Can you stop for one moment and listen?"

"Yes, yes. You think the family is making a mistake not turning off the money-making bug. You think we will all be at risk. The authorities will take note."

"Then why are you not concerned? It's our wealth, too. This life." She stalked over to him. "This shirt!" She pulled it off the hanger and shoved it into his arms. "If you do not care about the future of our children, care about your damn shirts!"

"Cassandra, you do get overworked. Stone says everything is under control."

"Maybe Stone doesn't grasp the full picture."

"Agape referred Fort Security to us. The family friend. He whose advice you never doubt, even over your own husband."

How could she doubt Agape? When had he ever done her wrong?

Brandt tossed the now wrinkled shirt into the dirty laundry, then drew on one in a slightly paler shade. Buttoning, he said, "Don't react, but you sound very much like the last time you needed some time away to rest."

The accusation could not be defended. If she agreed, he was right. If she disagreed, he was right. She gave him her back, which he would take as conceding, but it was the only way for her to gain control over herself.

After a moment, she faced him. "My parents are greedy and narrow visioned people."

Brandt checked himself in the long mirror. "You've never minded spending their money."

The man was infuriating. "Was I supposed to walk away?"

"You've complained about them since I met you. How old were you when you first found these scruples?"

"What could I have done?" She retreated to their bedroom, sitting on the edge of the grey linen chaise.

"You were supposed to walk away," he called out to her from the dressing room.

She bit her tongue from saying that she nearly did. Agape had interrupted one of her teenaged crying jags as one of her parents' parties raged. She was leaning against his Corolla, her pink hair straggling in her face, sobbing and sucking at a bottle of beer she was four years from being old enough to drink.

"Now, now." He took the bottle out of her hand. "Tell me everything."

They had gone for a long drive and she had shared all her resentments with him. The impossibility of her sister's death. How her parents changed toward her. Before, everything had been focused on her sister. Afterwards, they turned to her. Finally showering her with the gifts and attention only Patricia had enjoyed.

"The pink hair," she had said to Agape, "it's for them, so they'll go back to ignoring me. But they won't. They're at me all the time."

It all seemed so childish now she understood the scope and capacity of the family business, including Agape's involvement in her parents' circles. Had she known, she would have been afraid to speak to him.

As he dropped her off back home, Agape asked her to trust him and she agreed. He came back a few weeks later for a dinner party and privately handed her a stuffed manilla envelope. The door to her room shut and locked, she opened it. Within were documents for a new identity. A passport. A social insurance card. A bank account with cards. And a very large balance, a million dollar balance, held in Wake Financial all under the name 'Marlene Jordan'. She could leave 'Cassandra' and this life behind.

But knowing she could leave gave her the freedom to stay, despite guessing there would come a day when she would be asked to return the favour. It never came and she had forgotten the price until this past week. Agape sent her a note asking her to request Wake Financial invest the principal million in Wellington Payday Loans.

"You were young." Brandt emerged in a perfectly draped suit, the pale chartreuse shirt, and a matching Hermès tie. "You could have worked"—he gazed at her, eyebrow cocked—"like most people in this world."

"Unlike you," she shot back. "You who have never worked."

"No. I've been blessed. You have been blessed, but you don't see it."

"Then our blessed children must have their blessing continue and we need to protect them."

He walked past her out into the gallery hall, where he called down the staircase. "Blessed boys, we'll be leaving soon!"

"I don't know why they believe the banking community will protect them if they are caught." She followed. "They would be made examples of, hung out to dry, so the rest of them can pronounce publicly that they would never do such things."

"You said the crucial word 'caught' and, again, Stone has assured us we are safe. Our lawyers have assured us we have a plan if the worst comes." He patted her on the arm. "Why don't you go to the spa today? Take some time for yourself."

Cassandra closed her eyes for a moment to keep from slapping him.

The boys mustered by the front door, half-asleep, their hair a mess, and backpacks slumped at their feet.

"And this"—she gestured to the boys—"you let them play video games all night, sleep in late. What will happen to them?"

He left her on the gallery, descending the stairs, and said over his shoulder, "Happen to them? They are blessed."

Clutching the railing, she watched them go, then returned to the bedroom and made a call.

"Has he acted on my request for investment?"

Miss Henson had answered, but seemed to have her hand over the mouthpiece and was whispering. "There have been some complications."

"He doesn't know it's me? That I'm Marlene Jordan?"

"Of course not," she hissed.

She did not want to hear about any complications. "Tell him I've changed my mind. I want him to sell it all. Sell everything I have and put it in cash. Hide it for me."

There was a moment of silence. Voices could be heard in the background. "Yes. Yes." Then she returned her attention to the call. "I do not think I could explain such a request to him at this time."

Her frustration with her parents, Brandt, and the crisis broke through. "That's your problem! Transfer the funds as I say! You know what is going on with my family. I need an escape plan for me and my boys. Cash in and move the funds to one of those off-shore accounts where rich people are always hiding their money."

She hung up before Miss Henson could respond.

There was nothing to do now but confront her parents. They would not listen, she knew, but she could be satisfied to have done what she could.

Once in her BMW i3, she cranked up the music. The sounds of

her disaffected youth pounded the car so that the windows were vibrating. She screamed along with the punk band *Fear*, "I don't care about you. Fuck you!" Cassandra pulled up short at a stoplight. The driver behind her honked. She opened the door, the music blasting for all to hear. People on the sidewalk watched in horror as she grabbed her breast, shook it at the man in the car just as the refrain began again, and sang at the top of her lungs, "I don't care about you! Fuck you!"

She was back in the car as the light changed, slammed down on the accelerator and was through in a shot, then through another, and another. The lights seemed to change just for her. The music blared and Cassandra wondered if this was finally her moment.

She was charged by the time she rolled through the gate to her parents' house. Seeing Stone's car, Cassandra was glad; she would force him to listen, too. She sat in the car for a moment longer, letting the sarcastic resentment of the music wash through her.

Slamming the door shut, she stood, hand on the roof of the car, and stared at the gate and the tall cedars—where someone had lain in wait to take pictures of her sister's collapse in the driveway and then sold them to the tabloids—remembering the morning that had changed their lives.

Then she saw movement in the trees. Fucking paparazzi. Her body quieted, relaxing into the extremes of the memory of the music in her body, and she opened the car door, pretending she had left something inside. Once perched on the front seat, hand stretched into the back, she looked through the rear window. There he was. Martin Monaghan. Hiding in their bushes on the other side of the fence, looking in her direction. She would have laughed if not for the real threat he posed. Cassandra got out of the car and walked to the house as if she had seen nothing.

The door opened for her.

"They are in the pool room."

"How do they stand it?"

But the old servant knew better than to answer. It was Francois who pulled Patricia back into the house all those years, cleaned up after her mess, and handed her over to Mrs. Barstow to deal with.

She threw open the dripping glass door to the pool area.

Stone and her parents turned to face her.

"Just when you assured us that everything was under control, Stone. Guess who is hiding in our cedars out front?"

16

____

It was a long walk from the streetcar to Anthony El Buhali's condo. The low building was visible at a distance. A wall of warehouse windows faced north, looking out over the industrial neighbourhood. Tomoko judged Anthony harshly before even meeting him. There was no getting around the charm of factory windows and exposed HVAC in converted warehouses. That is, if you did not think about the ruination of the worker class. She took the stairs two at a time and hammered her fist against the door. It was quiet inside, but she knew he wore headphones when he worked. The door opened swiftly. Anthony was wearing a thick down vest over his pyjamas, sheepskin slipper boots, and a wool hat over his braided hair. He was handsome despite looking like he just woke up at an expensive lakeside cottage, and it irritated her.

"No need to pound."

She pointed at her ear. "Headphones."

He pointed above the door—"Camera"—and retreated into the condo.

The space was vast. Thirteen, fourteen foot high ceilings. Polished concrete floors. Three long, armless couches upholstered in odd cuts of sapphire, ruby, and emerald velvet were set around a cream shag rug inset with several large embroidered black diamonds. Moroccan pillows were thrown casually against the couches. Bronze lanterns, possibly two metres high and one metre around, stood at perfectly chosen spots around the room. An Adrian Hayles portrait of an elder black man was spray painted on one long wall. Anthony's desk faced the windows. It was massive and looked like a kitchen table out of a French farmhouse. The three large displays were dark. An antique cabinet without doors stood beside the table, holding several large processors. How the hell did he afford this? She was told he donated his time to *The Spanner*. Unless there was a rich parent in this story, he was no white hat hacker, and she wondered if the journal knew.

The room became colder as she approached his desk. The original factory windows offered no insulation from the weather.

"What was this place before?" She asked, trying to bite back her scorn.

"Garment factory," he answered.

"They probably froze in the winter."

"Perfect for me." He gestured to the right and she became aware of a room off to the side, visible only from the desk. Industrial shelving held a bank of white boxes with whirring fans and cables neatly organized behind them.

"What is that?"

"Bitcoin mining."

So that explained it. Maybe he was white hat after all. Bitcoin was decentralized, at least, and she decided to give him another chance.

He pulled a chair out for her and sat down himself. "Frank didn't say you were coming. Is this for the journal?"

"A developing story."

"So Frank doesn't know yet."

"It's developing." She noticed his deep brown eyes, framed by long lashes, all set off by his warm, russet complexion. What is it with these long-lashed men?

"What do you need?"

She broke free from admiring his eyes and pulled Parisa's

computer out of her bag. "A whistleblower had data on this computer, but it seems to have been wiped."

"Cloud or hard drive?"

"Both," she replied, not knowing. He could find out.

"Phone? Your SIM card in?"

"No."

"Give it to me."

She held it out to him.

"Open it."

She brought it up to her face, then handed it over.

"Your Bluetooth and Wi-Fi are on. You could have been followed here and anyone could record us, just in case that matters to the people you are trying to protect."

Her heart pounded. Her gut roiled. Her whole body wanted to snatch back her phone and run.

Anthony turned them off and handed the phone back to her. "Don't worry about me. No one is getting into this machine and everyone knows I volunteer for the journal. Worry about your sources."

"I—" She stood and turned to leave, then shifted her footing.

"Sit back down. Tell me what it is."

"I don't think I had my phone with me when I went with my source to her apartment." She tried to remember exactly where she had it and when. "We weren't followed there or back. No one even knows I'm on this story. I only got involved yesterday."

He put a hand out to calm her. "That's good. The apartment? Where is it?"

She gave him the address. He touched the keyboard and the displays came alive. She had no idea what he was doing, but within a moment he said, "I'm in the house Wi-Fi." Then a window opened up to a video feed. A camera in Parisa's apartment. "This it? It's the only camera in the building connected to the Wi-Fi."

Tomoko gasped. They did not have to be followed. They had been filmed.

"I guess you didn't know about that. You want me to find out who has it set up?"

Did she even have to answer that question?

"What a joke."

"What?"

"The security firm who set up the camera. They're a joke. Fort Security. Local."

She opened her phone and made a note of it.

"I wouldn't worry about your phone. I don't think you are dealing with cyber masterminds here." He slapped the table with a laugh. "The school trips. Oh, man. 'Fort York'."

Tomoko shook her head.

"They named themselves after Fort York. The War of 1812? These guys are out there protecting the rich with digital muskets!"

"Yeah, well, my parents didn't let me go on the 'Nationalist Glorification of Militarization' field trips." She dug into her bag and pulled out the computer, placing it on the desk while he clicked through Fort Security's website. "Can you see if what we want is there?"

"Password?" he asked.

"Open it. It's on a post-it."

He snickered and opened the laptop.

His dismissiveness was making him less handsome by the minute and she sniped, "We just wrote that out. For you."

"Okay," he said, hand out at her tone. "What are we looking for?"

"Variations on 'Wellington Payday'." She felt worse. "Documents, spreadsheets. But the original file, the one we need, my source didn't remember. It was a bunch of numbers and letters."

"I assume you already searched it."

"Of course we did. Can you get it back?"

"If it was not completely erased from the cloud or the hard drive." He looked up at her. "You know deleting files doesn't delete them, right?"

"That's why we're here," she said, becoming impatient with his lessons. "We checked the temporarily deleted files in the cloud."

"Nothing there. Not by that name, anyway. Maybe it was renamed?"

She had not thought of that and should have asked Parisa, but then Parisa would have volunteered it if she had. "The hard drive?"

"I can maybe do something there." He poked around a bit more and said, "Oh, this has been cleanly wiped. None of the hajja in a computer that someone's been using regularly."

"Hajja? What the hell does that mean?"

"Technical term. Listen. Your whistleblower. They say anything other than the needed file is missing?"

"She didn't mention it."

"To me, it looks like someone transferred out her files, wiped the computer, then restored them from a backup. Probably all but the file you want." He thumbed her attention to his display, where he quickly moved through the video of the apartment. "Like by that guy."

A man was in front of the computer.

"Let me see that!"

They watched the search, then he played back all the recordings. Tomoko watched them with interest and more than a bit of humiliation. Parisa was working double-time, taking care of Arash and trying to get her work done, and she wished this world could care for women like her. At least she could tell Parisa that Martin had the rabbit and some of her things.

"Can you reach your whistleblower, see if she renamed the original file or mentions of Wellington inside it?" He tipped his head to the screen. "That guy knew what he was looking for, took it, then transferred the rest back. Maybe she was smart enough to rename it, something no one would check."

"There is another copy, but we don't have it."

"So, what are we doing this for?"

"We hoped you could find the file she has and trace it back to whoever sent it to her."

He handed back the laptop. "Get the other copy and bring it to me. But, look, I doubt if someone went to all this trouble, and all these people are after it, if the author of the file was stupid enough to include any traces pointing to its source. But you never know, maybe they are as dumb as Fort Security."

"Thanks." She stood to leave.

As they walked toward the door, his tone softened. "Don't worry about the mistakes you made. I've seen something like it with nearly everyone who comes to me. You won't make them again."

"But what if the mistakes matter?"

"Then you really won't make them again."

That much was true, but it did not make her feel any better.

At the door, she said goodbye, but he stopped her, looking concerned.

"Ask your source why there was so little on her computer. Everyone's computer is crammed with extra files, videos, screenshots of memes. Other than the hajja, I mean. Hers is basically empty. Ask her why."

The news took the edge off her self-recrimination and Tomoko replied with a cynical frown. So Parisa was wiping her computer on the regular. She would absolutely ask her what she was hiding and why she refused to get a copy of the data from Monaghan.

17

"Fuck!" Martin scrambled back out of the cedars to the street, thinking he should just get in his car and run. But he was sure Wellington's daughter had recognized him. They would send someone after him to his house, maybe after Jamal, maybe Oliver. At least they could not find Parisa. He had driven there in a fury and hid in the cedars, only to realize he had no idea what the hell he thought he could do once there. Now he was stuck. Stay or go, they were going to come after him.

He turned back into the trees and found one with thick enough branches to get a foothold, just enough to get himself to the top of the fence. Placing a foot in between the spikes, he jumped, not so much breaking through the trees, but tumbling clumsily, covered in sprays of cedar and tiny cones, and landing hard.

Wincing, he rolled over and up, ran to the side of the house, and flattened himself against the wall, away from the view of a window.

The front door opened. A man's voice called out. "Monaghan. Come on in. We'll talk."

Martin stayed put. There were only two options he could see. They offer him a bribe or threaten his life or the lives of those he cares about. But to do what? To walk away? Erasing the data from their computers and ruining him was not going to be enough, other-wise why get Bernard to expose Parisa? He did not know what they wanted. Whatever it was, it would not be good for him, Parisa, or anyone he loved and blamed himself for coming there without think-ing. "What the fuck am I doing?"

"Martin." The man was out on the driveway.

He glanced around the corner. The man was walking toward the cedars, gun in hand. High and tight buzz cut, maybe ex-military. He was built, but there was no way of knowing if he could fight. It did not matter. The gun trumped it all.

"Stone!" a woman called from within the house. "I saw him on the cameras. He's around the side."

Martin took off around the corner, ending up in a large backyard. A three-level flagstone patio extended from several wide arched door-ways to lush grass and a small evergreen wood beyond. He ran for the woods, hoping that there was no fence at the back or one he could jump over easily to get to another yard and away.

As he sprinted across the yard, he heard another man's voice. "There!"

Stone was right behind him. Martin ran straight for the back, hoping he would not shoot in this neighbourhood. The Bridle Path? Police would respond immediately. The outlines of an iron fence became visible through the trees.

"Stop!"

The fence came into view. It was too tall and there was nothing he could use to mount it. He stopped and turned around to face Stone, breathing hard, waiting for the shot. Everything slowed. The breeze whistling through the trees stilled. Choices opened up before him. The police would be called, but he was an intruder and the Crown would not lay charges against people like this protecting their own. He threw his shoulders back and opened himself up to whatever came. His brother knew he loved him and that was enough.

Stone walked slowly toward him, holding the gun out like a cop. "You want to die?"

"I've got no regrets."

"You should."

"I die with a clear conscience. How do you live?"

"Well. Thank you for asking." Stone took another step forward.

At the edge of the woods, Cassandra and Wellington were watching them from behind a tree. Stone slowly moved closer. It was the chance he needed. In a few steps, Martin could grab him, take control of the gun. If there were a distraction, he could do it. Martin slumped into the posture of a defeated man and yelled, hoping the neighbours could hear. "Wellington. You going to let Stone kill me? If he does, you pull the trigger, too!"

"You!" Wellington came out from behind the tree, but Cassandra pulled him back.

It was enough. Stone glanced behind him, lowering the gun slightly, and Martin moved. He had planned to grab the gun, but his foot had another idea. He became a bystander to the action as his crescent kick slapped into the firearm. Both hands on the gun, Stone held on, but the impact was enough to turn his torso to one side.

Martin planted his foot back on the ground as he turned forward, slamming his hips into Stone's groin while locking his arms around his outstretched arms, sliding his hands down, and taking hold of the gun.

Now there were four hands keeping the muzzle down and away as Martin stepped close to the front of Stone's legs. He leaned away, torqued, and Stone's feet left the ground, flying over top of Martin in a sloppy shoulder roll.

Stone slammed hard into the ground, his thigh striking a rock.

Martin scrambled to his feet, holding the gun.

Stone attempted to stand but stumbled, leaning into a tree to get up.

Gun in hand, Martin ran alongside the edge of the property through the trees, pointing it haphazardly at the Wellingtons as he headed back toward the front of the house.

Behind him, Wellington's voice. "What are you doing, Stone? After him!"

Martin got to the gate. It was shut and he jerked it helplessly. The trees grew on the other side of the fence and there was no way to climb over. He put his back to the gate. Cars were rushing by. He dropped the gun to his side so the drivers could not see.

Stone came around the corner, limping toward him. Wellington and Cassandra had gone through the house and now stood at the door.

"What are you doing here?" Stone looked at him like he was stupid.

He pointed at Wellington. "You put a young mother's life in danger. You ruined me and now it looks like you want me dead."

Cassandra moved back out of sight.

"What did you expect?" Wellington stepped outside the door like he was bulletproof.

The question hit him sideways. Every bit of work he had done so far had ended in the public shaming of those he had exposed and, more often than not, real consequences. But not one of them had come after him like this. There had been threats. Pressure from the university. One conservative politician outed him as if he were not already out. They called him a vassal of enemy nations. That was the worst of it. Until today, as far as he was concerned, they could do to him what they liked. What did he expect? Not this.

Stone became impatient. "So what now?"

"Leave her. Do whatever you want to me. But promise you'll back off of Parisa. She doesn't even want to do the work. I made her do some of the analysis for me, but that was it."

"Which you stole," Wellington said.

"Leave her alone. Promise me."

Stone took another limping step forward. "Where's the data?"

"You deleted it all. You must have got Parisa's, too. The USB. The print outs. Everything."

"How can we be sure?" Stone asked.

Martin finally understood. Stone did not want to kill him. His business was intimidation, cover-ups. He did not want a body on his hands, let alone the murder of a mother and child. Wellington? He probably wanted it, but doubted the man would do it himself.

"Parisa's on the run. You think she wants this? I don't want this."

"That's not what Oliver told me."

"Oliver?" Martin clenched, bracing himself.

Again, he saw Oliver's hand on the counter near where he had found the camera. He saw Oliver running to him after Jamal had called him. Why would Oliver leave the cafe during his busiest hours? After Oliver had walked out on him, they had not said one word since. Suddenly he's back? Fucking Oliver. Fuck. Fuck. Fuck. He had come to watch him, to see what he had found. Find out what he had hidden that Stone had not uncovered. The camera on the counter. It was him.

Stone looked satisfied and Martin knew everything he had been thinking was transparent on his face. He let him have it. "Okay. Oliver. I get it." He took a step toward Stone, arms out, gun limp in his hand. "You can always find a way to get at me. At least he was good in bed. I'm going to give you the gun back now." Then said to Wellington. "Open the gate. I'll leave. You all keep watch on us. You'll see. But you have my word. We're done."

"You don't mean that," Wellington said, his already deep voice becoming a low growl. He came out of the house, striding toward Martin with a power that surprised him.

Stone rushed to him. "Stop, sir. I have this!"

"Coward," he spat at him. "You won't do what needs doing."

But Stone was on him despite his limp, putting Wellington into a hold, nearly taking the old man off his feet.

The gate rumbled open behind Martin. He backed up toward it, then saw Cassandra in the doorway, mouthing, "Run!"

Martin ran to his car and tore out onto the road, nearly hitting a truck coming up behind him. He turned down one road and then another. Only then did he notice he was driving with the gun in his hand. He placed it carefully on the seat next to him and pulled over. No one was behind him. Maybe no one had seen the gun. He stared at it, not wanting to touch it, but had to put it some place. He opened the glove box and shoved it inside.

18

____

Parisa stared at the nearly empty refrigerator for something she could use to make lunch. The gleaming kitchen was kitted out for a chef, but there was little to cook in it beyond eggs. Cyrus had the essentials for Persian small plates: finger sized cucumbers, buttery Persian feta, and fresh herbs. The cabinets were filled with dried fruits and nuts from his import business and an array of jams impossible to get outside of Little Persia. But neither held interest for her son, who refused to eat anything other than plain sandwiches and goldfish crackers.

"You don't cook much, do you?" She peeked out from behind the open refrigerator door.

He looked up from the couch, where he sat with Arash under his arm, watching a cartoon. "I do when the family is over."

Arash had taken to him immediately. Cyrus crowed that he was the most beloved uncle in his family because he had devised all the children's favourite things and made sure they had them. But it was more than that. The gentleness that had held her in San Antonio had made her feel like she was the only woman in existence. Whoever he turned to was made to feel the world to him.

Cyrus gestured to Arash, whose head dropped against his chest. He gave her a look as if her son had offered him the greatest gift. And he had. Arash had given him his trust. He had slept badly last night again. She had, too, only ever half asleep, hearing his cries and worrying over his rabbit. She had held him like a baby, rocking him back to sleep. What had this boy known other than a regular life of neighbourhood friends, a school he loved, and a too-busy mother? She wanted to strangle whoever took Blue-Ears after she was done punishing herself for forgetting him.

Slipping out from under Arash, Cyrus lay the sleeping boy on the couch, covered him with a throw, then tiptoed to the kitchen. "Why didn't you tell me about him that night?"

She felt guilty and feared the truth would alienate him. What good mother does not mention her child? But she would not lie to him about this, about them. "My paper went well. I was accepted. The promise of it all. Everything that I had been working for, a good life for Arash and me, but also just for me. I mattered and I wanted to matter for me, alone. Then you found me. And I wanted you for me, alone, just that night. I wanted to be the scholar they thought I was. I wanted to be the woman I was in your eyes."

He began to speak, but she stopped him.

"I am not a brilliant woman. I am not a beautiful woman. Yet, for that short time, after my paper, then with you, I was those things."

He recited in Persian,

"'I speak from the depth of night
from the edges of darkness,
and I speak
of the depth of night.

If you come to my house, my dear, bring me a lamp
and a little door, for me
to see the crowds
in the joyful alley'."

Parisa pressed her hand against her heart, afraid it would break open from being understood.

"Your eyes, the brightness of your cheeks. You were proud of what you had done. I could see it. You were a flame I could not resist."

But he did not say she was beautiful, and she took a step back, needing this petty thing, even from this man who saw so much.

His expression said he knew he had done something wrong, but not what.

"Arash will be hungry when he gets up," she said, hoping to relieve him of the discomfort.

"Why don't I order something for us?"

"Delivery? Is it safe?"

"I'll go pick it up."

She agreed, but was worried about that, too, not wanting him to leave them alone. No doubt if someone threatened them, all he could do was bat those beautiful eyelashes; but his softness comforted her and made her feel safe. She was tired of men pretending to be killers and heroes.

"Maybe delivery is fine. Can we order from the grocery store, though?"

"Do you think you'll be here more than a day?"

The question was asked casually, but he could not hide his feeling, and the air became thick with what her answer might mean for them.

Parisa wished Tomoko out of her mind, but could not, and saw in his eyes that he could not either, nor should he. Instead of answering, "Every day, if you want us," she said, "Let's order those groceries."

Cyrus dutifully got out his laptop, placing it on the island between them, and turned it toward her so she could click on the things that Arash liked. In addition to goldfish crackers, milk, and cereal for her son, she added a chicken and a box of salad greens, taking care not to choose anything that would indicate they would be staying too long. At least she could make him a simple dinner before they left.

She watched his face as she turned the computer around and he saw how little she had ordered. There was a moment of hurt, then he said with false cheer, "Four PM."

To give him something, she asked, "Will you make me tea?"

"With pleasure." He bowed slightly as if he were welcoming her to dance.

She left the kitchen to check on Arash. He was finally sleeping deeply. His breath was even, his expression clear, and Parisa watched him for a moment, at a loss for the love she carried for him.

Prison had not prepared her for the weight of this kind of love. The spirit that had driven her into the streets of Tehran as a naïve eighteen-year-old had been inexorably drawn out of her after her arrest and imprisonment. She saw herself alone in her emptiness for the rest of her life, never experiencing this consuming, idolatrous love of another being.

She had been a favoured daughter in a favoured family within religious circles closely tied to the government. They did not know she was in the streets until they were informed of her arrest. Help was begged and negotiated. It took them two years to get her out and into Canada. But how does one begin again when there is nothing within oneself to hand? She had first stayed with distant cousins in Alberta. There she had met Andy with all his blue-eyed cowboy bluster. He had walked her into a marriage so awash with light, her prison-narrowed eyes could not see it for what it was. He left her when she told him about the pregnancy.

Then came her son. The soul of her soul, Arash.

How could she protect him? How would she carry the weight of this love in the face of the choices she had made?

"Your tea is ready."

She returned to Cyrus and the scent of roses. Her family garden in Tehran unfolded before her, then a field of roses seen from a moving car, then overflowing baskets of dried buds for sale in the markets, and her grandmother's hand on a delicate cup, rose buds floating on the surface of the tea. Cyrus passed her a tea glass so filled with them she doubted there was tea within except that the hot glass burned her fingertips and she wept.

"My beautiful Parisa, what will we do?" he asked, moving his hand closer to hers.

The word she needed was given to her, and so she said, "I was in prison."

He reached out. "I suspected it that first night."

"How?" She let him curl his fingers around hers.

"My aunt was in Evin prison during the days of the Shah. There were moments you reminded me of her."

"So then you know there is nothing we can do."

"I'll speak to Tomoko tonight. No matter what you choose."

She panicked. "No!"

"I will not lie to her," he said, turning her hand over in his.

"She won't help me if you do. There's more happening here. Maybe she can find out. If the story is in the press, what can they do to me?"

"What do you mean, more?"

Parisa deflected. "Do you trust Tomoko?"

Cyrus looked hurt.

She pulled her hand away and touched his cheek. "Of course you do."

"I understand. After all that's happened to you. I understand why you've been putting off calling the police, too. But—"

The front door opened and they jumped apart. He flushed and looked guiltily toward it.

Tomoko came up to the main floor. "I've got news!"

Arash woke up with a cry. Parisa ran to him, taking him in her arms.

"Oh, sorry!"

"It's fine. Don't worry."

"I've brought lunch?" She raised a bag.

"Fries?" Arash said, his mood shifting immediately. He stared at Tomoko with bright eyes and Parisa was struck by her love of her son again. Her little boy, only seven, had his first crush. "Thanks Tomoko!"

"Burgers and fries."

Cyrus brought over plates and cloth napkins.

"Oh, Cyrus!" Tomoko teased, taking a seat on one of two poufs at the coffee table. "Not plates, and cloth napkins?"

He half-smiled, seeming to make an effort, but his discomfort was obvious, unable to hide his feelings, even for her sake. "All I've got," he said, laying down the napkins, but returned the plates to the kitchen.

Tomoko looked at him strangely as she tore open the paper bag, emptying the fries on it, and scattered the packets of ketchup.

"Thanks." Parisa took a burger from her.

Cyrus came back, but did not eat, sitting in a chair at a distance.

Tomoko smirked and shook her head slowly.

It was done. Tomoko knew.

"I saw Anthony," she said. "The computer is wiped clean. Nothing in the cloud."

Parisa asked pointedly, "Are you still willing to work on the story with me?"

"Why wouldn't I?" She patted the leather pouf next to her. "Cyrus, babe, why are you all the way over there?"

He got up and moved beside her, but would not meet Parisa's eyes.

"Was there anything on the computer to be saved at all?"

"He thought you could have renamed the file. If so, it might be there."

The suggestion angered her. "I would have told you."

Cyrus got up and sat by Arash on the couch, playfully stealing a fry from him. "My nephew has an album of his Pokémon cards here. Finish that burger, and we'll get them out."

"Almosh done," he said, his voice muffled by a large bite, then gave Tomoko a sheepish glance.

Cyrus led him out of the living room, avoiding both women.

Tomoko ignored him, observing Parisa closely.

"So Anthony couldn't help me?"

"Not immediately. He had a couple more questions."

"Ask," Parisa sat forward on the couch.

"Monaghan has a copy of the data. Why won't you get it from him?"

"That's Anthony's question?"

"A question I should have asked."

"I won't. You'll have to accept that."

"I'm not sure I can."

"I'll give you his address." Parisa got up to get her phone, hoping the bluff would work and that she would not go after him.

Tomoko did not say one way or another, instead asking, "Why is your computer so uncluttered? Everyone has a computer filled with mess. Not yours. Just files for your graduate work. A lot of PDFs of academic books and articles. But nothing like the rest of us."

"You don't know my life. You don't know what's normal for me."

"Tell me, because I'm thinking there is more to you than I can see."

"Clearly." But as much as Parisa wanted to dislike her, she reminded her too much of herself when she was young, before prison, before life had challenged her and she thought she knew it all.

Cyrus came back into the living room, alone, and stood by the dining room table watching them warily.

"Tell her." Parisa stood abruptly. "Tell her why I do not keep extraneous files on my computer."

He sat on the couch across from Tomoko. "Parisa was a political prisoner in Iran. She's here now, yes. But you know there is no trusting any state after you've found yourself on the wrong side of it."

Tomoko's expression changed, considering Parisa in a new light. Cyrus, too. "Is that what you were discussing when I came back?"

"Yes," Cyrus answered.

Parisa settled her expression into a mask of passivity, waiting for Tomoko's response, hoping she knew about his aunt and would attribute the feeling she saw between herself and Cyrus to this connection.

"Alright," Tomoko responded, seemingly accepting the answer, but then she stood abruptly. "I forgot I have to take care of something across town." She gathered her things in a hurry and said to Parisa as she went to the door, "Give me Monaghan when you are ready."

Cyrus glanced at Parisa with a look of concern; but she kept her mask in place, relieved that Tomoko would carry on, as long as she could keep the worst from her.

19

———

Tomoko knew where to find her parents when they weren't home. She walked several blocks over to a small churchyard near Kensington Market. A cluster of elderly people was protesting in front of the encampment within. Much used signs declared, "RIGHTS FOR THE UNHOUSED" and "MAYOR IS THIS YOUR HOUSING PLAN?" She spotted her mother immediately. Short hair, spiked and dyed bright purple, wrapped up in hand-knitted woollens too warm for the fall day, she leaned into her walker as she yelled as passersby, all of whom were giving a wide berth to the woman with the burning eyes. Her father was within the encampment, chatting with residents, his homemade medical bag slung over his shoulder. He was long retired from nursing, but never slowed down.

She hung back for a moment and watched them, loving them for never giving up on anyone. They showed up for the vulnerable every day, believing the fight meant something—even if the revolution would never come—knowing they could, through small acts of resistance, make a difference. They raised her to learn what she could do and do it, and never fret about what was not in her hands. "Arrogance and frustration are wasteful emotions. Wasteful to the cause."

Their guidance had been a lesson that saved her a lot of grief, not just as an activist following their lifelong example, but in her personal relationships. She had little use for drama, exactly what Parisa's sudden appearance at Cyrus's doorstep had promised to deliver.

"Mom!"

Her mother hailed her over. "Bubala!"

"I saw dad. Either of you have time to talk?"

"That look. I know that look. We have time." She called out to a resident. "Brenda, will you get Isamu for me? Tell him our daughter is here and we need to go home for a bit."

"Sure thing."

In a moment, her father was striding toward her, tall and fit. Unlike her mother, he had barely aged. No one would ever know he was in his eighties. The only sign was his snow white hair kept long because her mother fancied it. They had never hid the fire of their love. Far from making her uncomfortable, she sought it out for herself without shame, finding plenty of fire wherever she liked, but less love. There was something there for Cyrus, but she did not know what to call it and she needed their counsel, needed to know if he was worth fighting for, especially given the story about the Wellingtons and the possibility of her first by-line.

In a moment, she was walking hand in hand with her father toward home, while their mother led the way, setting the pace with her walker.

"Any news?" she asked.

"The usual. Claiming the encampments are a fire hazard. There's an injunction going before a judge to tear it down."

"What are the chances?"

"There've been two fires already." He gave an incriminating glance at the gentrified row houses across the street from the churchyard. "There was no need to call the fire department in. Both were out in moments. The residents had it under control. But—"

She finished his sentence. "But it somehow became a three alarm fire with news crews called in to make a scene."

"Exactly."

"So now what?"

"The reverend is talking to them about letting go of some of their things. The more possessions built up around the tents, the more the case to evict them."

"But how do they give up the things that make them feel like human beings?"

"You know it goes."

"I do." She remembered breaking out of her father's hold as a child and running out in front of a backhoe to stop it from pulling down a cluster of tents under the Gardiner Expressway. Of course, the press was there. A photo was taken. She and her parents were questioned by social services. They were lucky. They had teachers, neighbours, and friends willing to speak in their defence. She supposed she should have been afraid, but her parents' confidence was all she needed. The photo now hung in pride of place on her parents' kitchen wall.

Once home, her mother handed the walker back to her while she hauled herself up the narrow stairs leading to the brick row house with its crumbling mortar. Her father moved past her to be behind her mother in case she needed help, but not close enough to make her feel like an invalid.

They went into the kitchen where her father turned on the kettle for tea. A much used round table took up most of the room. Every burn mark and stain told the story of nights filled with drunk comrades jabbing cigarettes at each other as they debated politics and organized actions. At its centre was a large, but delicate bowl her Jewish great grandparents had carried with them as they escaped the pogroms. Bamboo baskets from her grandmother's kitchen in Kyoto hung beside the sagging cabinets. One wall was crowded with framed photos of family, here and in Japan, snapshots from their activism over the years, old protest flyers, and the portrait of Marx she had painted in grade eight looking like a friendly, if earnest, uncle.

They settled down around the kitchen table, her mother easing herself into a chair, barely restraining a grimace.

"Amale, need meds?"

"Mmm," she answered.

Tomoko did not know how bad her nerve pain had become. Her mother resisted medication, never trusting the pharmaceutical industry despite her father's careful curation of what they should and should not take.

He handed her a small capsule, then, catching Tomoko's eye, said, "Gabapentin. Nothing special."

Swallowing the pill, her mother said, "No need to worry."

If they told her not to worry, then there was no need. They had never lied to her, even when she wished they would.

Her father set a small iron pot of tea on the table with three small cups.

"Gyokuro."

"Just for me? Cyrus would love it."

"Yet you never bring him," her father said.

"He's why I'm here."

"Oh?" Her mother watched the pot, waiting impatiently for the brew.

"There's another woman in the picture."

She felt her mother's ire before she said it. "I never liked him."

"Amale," her father scolded.

"You never liked him, either."

"That's true, and she knows that. But let her speak."

"We're on your side, Tomoko."

"I was at his house. The doorbell rings. A woman from his past is standing there with her son, needing help. She's there now."

Her father sat and poured the tea. They each took their cups, sipping carefully.

"I like this one," Tomoko said. "Wildflowers and honey."

Isamu grinned. "Our favourite at the moment."

"Cyrus doesn't know I know my tea."

"Why have you held that back?"

"He expected it. Did I tell you he took me to a $700 Omakase restaurant on our first date?"

Her mother snorted with laughter.

"Then why, Tomoko?" Her father repeated his question.

"You've seen his picture."

Her parents looked at each other knowingly.

"Cyrus is also very thoughtful." She blushed.

Her mother snorted again. "He would have to be for you to stay this long with a capitalist stooge. Do you want to know what I think?"

"I'm here for it." Whatever her mother said would be unpleasant, but usually right.

"They are forbidden fruit for you. These exotic bourgeoisie you keep dipping into."

As expected, she did not like it, and her mother was right. There was something delicious about them. But she had thought Cyrus was more.

Her father smiled indulgently and thumbed at the portrait of Marx. "What would Uncle Karl say?"

"Uncle Karl would yell, 'Free Love!' while running naked through a birch forest."

"So, what about the woman?"

"They had one night together, no sex—they say—talking for hours in a hotel lobby over a year ago. She never let on that she had a child. She never gave him her number. Cyrus gave her his card, with his home address and cell number on the back, hoping she would contact him once they were both back in Toronto. But she never did."

"I don't understand," Isamu said.

"He fell in love."

"And her?"

"I didn't think so at first, but now, yes, her too."

Amale rolled her eyes. "One night. True love. These bourgeois romantics."

"Come now, Amale! All those years ago, I fell in love with you in one moment. One moment of watching you hurl a Yiddish curse at a cop and I committed my life to yours."

"See!" She chuckled. "Exoticizing. He fell for the Yiddish, thinking it was some incantation drawn from our days in Babylonian exile when all I said was, 'May you get cancer'."

The two laughed softly, gazing at each other with deep affection. Cyrus had looked at her that way, like the world could be made right in her eyes, right up until Parisa walked through that door and she realized, watching them, she wanted him to keep feeling that way. She said bitterly, "He said he doesn't even want children. But here this woman shows up with her son and all of the sudden he starts auditioning for the part of the kid's father."

"The boy has no father?"

"In Alberta. No doubt some Nazi on a horse."

Amale asked, "And the woman, she a Nazi, too?"

"Maybe. Can Iranians be Nazis?"

"So they share that," Isamu said plainly.

"Yes."

Her mother said, "You haven't told us why she showed up with her son and moved into his house."

"She hasn't moved in. She's a guest."

"Why is she there?" her father asked.

Tomoko leaned forward. "This is the interesting part. You know Wellington Payday Loans?"

"Please don't tell me she's their CFO," Amale joked.

"No. She has data that could bring them down." Tomoko laid out the history of the case, as much as Parisa had let on. Her visit to Anthony with the computer, and, finally, her suspicions.

Isamu asked, "Can you be certain it's not jealousy leading you to suspect her?"

"Anthony raised those questions," she said defensively.

Her father reached out and took her hand across the table. "This could be a big story for you."

"It would be my first story."

"A by-line?" her mother asked.

"In *The Spanner*. Yes." A smile slowly broke across her face and her parents beamed.

"Bringing down the Wellingtons." Her father shook his head in amazement and pointed to the photo of her standing in front of the backhoe. "You were made for this."

"And the woman? Is she worth losing Cyrus over?"

"It seems I have to choose one over the other."

"It seems." Isamu said.

She put the choices in front of her and chose not to be wasteful. "I choose the cause."

Tomoko got up to refresh the pot of tea.

Amale raised her cup. "Death to capitalism!"

DAY FOUR

20

____

For nearly two days, Nick had closed himself up in his private office to write the failsafe virus that would keep Wellington Payday Loans from debugging their system. Bea had come down once to check on him the first day, but he pushed her out, telling her to stay close to home. He checked on her AirTag and phone every so often. She did as he asked and he figured she was spending her time binge-watching *Love Island* or one of the other dating reality shows she consumed like air. Trang and Samuel were told to put out any fires themselves, and they had left him alone. Only Étienne was allowed to knock at the door, bringing him food whenever he called for it. He only slept for a few hours at a time, but it was enough.

The failsafe was proving more difficult than it should have been. Fort Security was either better than it seemed or far worse. They had done something to the system that he could not get past. He suspected something incredibly stupid. Every attempt came with critical signs that their entire system would be wiped, and that could not be intentional.

A knock rattled his already frayed nerves. He pushed back angrily and threw the door open.

Trang blinked hard. "Mr. Barnes. Your meeting. A 'Mr. Agape' is waiting in your office."

Nick slammed the door in her face, grunted, then opened it again. "Wait there."

What the hell was wrong with him? He had muted his notifications. The meeting with Agapov. The founder of Panopticon. Back at the door again, he asked, demanding an explanation, "Agape, not Agapov?"

Trang, typically unmoved by his moods, stammered, "He said Agape. But sir, the secretary who called it in was clear. It was Agapov from Panopticon."

"Does it look like Agapov?" He knew the answer before the words were out of his mouth.

"Who has seen him?"

He slammed the door shut again. "Shit! Shit! Shit!"

It had to be Agapov out there. He probably used "Agape" to stay undercover.

Pressing a button, the electrochromic smart glass shifted to clear. Dozens of open cubicles spread out in a spiral from his central public office. Agapov was seated within, leaning back in an Eames chair.

He opened the door again. "Tell him I will be with him in a moment."

Nick shifted the window to opaque, ran his fingers through his hair and changed out of his rumpled khakis and t-shirt for a pair of black trousers, a black t-shirt and matching zippered cashmere cardigan. He added a pair of forest green suede Vans and hurried to his central office.

"Mr. Agapov," he said brightly.

The founder of Panopticon had a flat, brutal face. He was short but had a powerful presence, like a caber-throwing Scottish highlander. Nick would have enjoyed the thought of the most important man in cyber security with a tree trunk poised over his shoulder if he had been ready to meet him.

"Mr. Barnes." He stood and held out his hand.

Nick shook it. "Thank you so much for initiating a meeting. I've been looking forward to forging a relationship with Panopticon."

"I do not have much time." He gestured to the walls. "Can we have some privacy?"

Nick went behind his desk and tapped the screen, turning the walls opaque and putting the frequency jammers into play, then came around and gestured for him to sit again.

Agapov tapped his phone, then nodded, satisfied with the jamming.

"Cristo Solutions would be thrilled to—"

He cut Nick off with a wave of a hand. "I'm here to engage your services."

Nick sat across from him. "I'm honoured, but why would Panopticon need me?"

"Panopticon? I am not Panopticon."

"I'm sorry. I thought you were Andrei Agapov?"

The man barked out a laugh. "My name is Agape. Perhaps your assistant made an error?"

Indeed, Trang did make an error. Now he was stuck in a meeting with some little man named Agape when he needed to focus on getting the failsafe into the Wellingtons' system. "I'm sorry Mr. Agape. I am sure someone else in my office might be of assistance. If you tell me quickly what you need, I can direct you."

"I represent a private group who is interested in bringing down the short-term lending industry in Canada and we had an inkling your firm might be of use."

Nick froze, hoping this was a horrible coincidence, then found his way out. "I'm sorry, but there are at least four different criminal codes you would like me to break with that one request." He stood. "If you do not want me to report you, I am going to have to ask you to leave immediately."

But Agape did not move. He simply pulled out a business card, holding it out to Nick.

"I'm not touching your card." Nick went around to the desk and tapped the screen to clear the smart glass. He tapped again. His assistant answered. "Could you please escort Mr. Agape out of the office?"

Agape stood and laid the card down on the desk. "All your hard work, you must be disappointed with Professor Monaghan's termination. I would think you would be interested."

Who could have tracked him? He refused to think Panopticon or Canada's security services could link the virus to him. Who knew other than Bea? It took everything he had to remain in the chair and not go upstairs and shake the admission out of her.

The door opened behind him.

"My mistake, Trang. Shut the door." Nick pressed the glass to opaque.

"My brother is Agapov. Let's just say that we have different lives. He leans toward the glorification of the state's interests, mine, the Lord. But, every now and again, I ask him for a favour. It was Panopticon who tracked the data to you."

"Who else knows?" He gripped the edge of his desk, by turns humiliated for being caught out and terrified that he would be arrested, everything he built ruined, and the final revenge for the wrong done to his mother thwarted.

"No one at Panopticon speaks if they want to live. But perhaps you should worry more about me and the private group I represent."

Nick picked up the card. It was an Orthodox Christian cross but absurdly adorned with mushroom caps at the top, bottom, and the side bars. There was no name, just a phone number.

"No one will answer. Leave a message. Say your name and someone will call you back."

"What do you want?"

"I should not have opened with fear, but you forced my hand. Let us begin again. My brother, Andrei, would be interested in addressing some weaknesses in Cristo Solutions' approach should you agree to help us."

If that promise were true, he would not need threats to do what they wanted.

"I expect your complete trust. I may or may not answer further questions. We do not want your efforts to be wasted. In fact, we would like you to do the same with every payday loan company in Canada, Lord giving, opening up parliamentary hearings considering the abolishment of the service entirely. Panopticon will be happy to expand your capacities to handle it. My brother said that you were working alone on the project."

The humiliation doubled. They must be in his private computer. But there was no camera or microphone on it, and his phone was in a Faraday box when he was in the office. Security cameras did not have sight of the path from the penthouse. He hoped they did not know that Bea spent time with him there.

"First, let's focus on Wellington Payday Loans." Agape sat back down. "Explain why you chose to go through Monaghan."

"It seemed more likely to end in governmental oversight. I provided data untraceable—" he paused, correcting himself. "I provided Monaghan with data he could not trace, but more to the point, data he does not think to trace. He sees it as another exploitation to expose. The man thinks he is the lone voice in the wilderness. He's done this successfully before. Remember the WBSN scandal? I chose one of his graduate students and sent it on."

"How did you choose her?"

He immediately regretted mentioning her. There was no reason other than she was a woman, but the question made him fear they might go after Parisa. He said casually, "Random. I bet that any of his female graduate students would bring it to him and that he would take it from her. It's not the first time, apparently."

"Not quite. Nothing so crass as direct plagiarism. He gets the credit for the work they've done by being the mentor who moulded them and cites their research in a manner that steals their thunder. But you did not count on the graduate student refusing to be cited and the trouble that would cause."

Of course, he already knew it all, and certainly the name of "the graduate student." He feared for her, but answered cooly, "No. I did not."

"And here we are."

"Yes."

"What did you hope would happen?"

"I thought coming from Monaghan, no governmental bodies could ignore his work. The banking system would make an example of the Wellingtons."

"Do you mind if I ask why the Wellingtons?"

"I do."

"No matter." He tipped his chin at Nick. "What is your plan now?"

"I am installing a failsafe virus in the system so they cannot remove the bug until they are exposed. I'm worried they'll cover it up before I can prove it ever happened."

"How is that progressing?"

Nick wondered if he had the answer to that question already.

"Harder than I thought."

"It should not be difficult. Fort Security is hardly up to snuff."

"I'll get it done."

"Then I will leave it in your capable hands, for the time being. When the Wellington matter is completed, we will extend our efforts to all the payday loan companies." He stood, gesturing toward the card on the desk. "Keep us apprised."

Nick watched him leave the office, dumbfounded and too scared to move.

Trang came in, shocking him into awareness. "Anything I can do for you?"

"No," he replied brusquely and pushed past her, rushing back to his private office.

Once within, he leaned against the door, staring at his processors, knowing Panopticon was in them. He ripped the sweater and t-shirt off his head, stinking of nervous sweat, and threw them across the room. "Fuck!"

Pulling on another t-shirt, he turned on his displays and unmuted his notifications. There was a shower of pings. He half expected them to be taunts from Panopticon: "We're watching!" But they were office matters, all except one: a notice of a bcc email to Tomoko Abrams. Her mother had written to a woman named Sarah, mentioning Tomoko's pursuit of the data for an article in *The Spanner*. There was no time to wait for the failsafe to be put in place. He had to send the data to her now. A few keystrokes and the file was copied and sent via a secure anonymous email service to one Tomoko Abrams.

21

———

"Tomoko! Your phone is pinging!" Sky yelled from the kitchen.

She woke up out of a deep sleep and reached out for her phone lying on a wood crate she used for a bedside table, nearly knocking over a half-drunk mug of wine. The phone was not there. She pulled herself out of the mess of mismatched sheets and blankets and trudged to the kitchen.

"Where?" she asked, half asleep.

"On top of the microwave." Sky said, hands in the sink, washing dishes.

"Thanks." She picked it up. An anonymous email with a string of numbers for an address. A ping for that? It should have gone directly to junk. She jerked open a kitchen cabinet door. She needed coffee. Yesterday could only be called too much and the bottle of wine she drank alone late into the night to stop her head from spinning did not help. A chip of one of the hundreds of layers of landlord paint came off and fell to the counter. "No coffee?"

"Did you buy any?" Sky teased, pushing back a long strand of their pixie mullet with a soapy hand. "Mmm hmm. Too busy with your hottie to buy house coffee."

She gave Sky a conspiratorial smile. "Hot enough to forget to buy a lot of things. Did I tell you he keeps those expensive pods for me?"

Sky looked over, frowning with mock disgust. "Does he not know you boycott them?"

"No! Don't tell our friends."

"And here I thought you were ideologically pure."

"Let's get that on t-shirts."

"'I thought you were ideologically pure'?" Sky laughed.

"No. Just 'IDEOLOGICALLY PURE' all caps. Or maybe all lower-case. More hip."

"Oh please. Let's. Definitely lowercase."

"I'm going to break up with Cyrus, so I guess I'll be pure again soon."

Sky dried their hands and took Tomoko into an embrace, then held her back. "Oh sweetie. You really enjoyed him."

"He's in love with someone else."

"I don't understand."

"I didn't say. The one with the data, the one at the centre of the story about the payday loans I want to pitch to *The Spanner*."

"This is a lot of drama, Tomoko. It's not like you."

"That's why I'm breaking up with him. I want the story and I don't want to get into some emotional thing with him."

"Pity," Sky frowned comically. "He is so hot."

The laughter began slowly, until Tomoko bent over, heaving with laughter until the tears came and turned into sobs.

Sky put a hand on her back and pulled her in for another hug and she shuddered in her friend's arms. "Shh, girl."

Tomoko pushed away, whining, "But he's so hot."

The two broke out into laughter again.

Her phone pinged a second time.

Tomoko swiped. It was another email. The same email address of a string of numbers. "Why is this thing pinging?" She opened the email anyway and stopped cold.

THE RAW DATA YOU WANT. GET THEM FOR ME.

"Everything okay? Your mom?"

Tomoko held up the screen for them to see.

"Oh wow. You got it." They grinned. "You got it!"

Tomoko grabbed their hands and the two jumped around the kitchen together.

Breathless, Tomoko finally stopped, grasping what the message said. "Raw data." She turned to Sky. "How am I supposed to read raw data?"

"You're an analyst."

"Not that kind."

"Parisa?"

"I don't trust her."

"But she can help with the data."

"Listen. Who gets data like this and doesn't protect it? The USB just sitting in a bowl? No backups? She's lying, and I have to find out why."

"Still, maybe she can do it for you?"

"Sky, do you really think if she let the data get stolen, she would tell me the truth about what it says now I have it? Or maybe she would even corrupt it so I can't read it?"

"So what, then?"

"I need to bring in Amina."

Tomoko took the phone and wandered into their small living room, falling down onto the futon couch and a pile of pillows, wishing for a moment it were one of Anthony's gorgeous velvet couches. The phone only rang twice before Amina answered. Tomoko sat straight up. She expected to leave a message, not talk to her, and barrelled through before Amina could hang up on her. "Amina, salam. Listen. I think I have something for *The Spanner*. You know the story about Martin Monaghan being terminated for plagiarizing his graduate student? It's what he plagiarized."

Amina said to meet her at 2PM in Trinity Bellwoods Park by the greenhouse. Tomoko arrived early, walking slowly through the falling leaves, enjoying the bright yellow and orange, punctuated by fire red, imagining her name on a by-line and then the next story, and the next. As she reached the picnic area, her heart clenched. Amina was early, sitting at a table, glasses perched on her nose, scrolling through her phone. She popped against all that colour in her black slacks and sweater, with a deep brown Somali saash covering her hair and shoulders. As Tomoko approached, she removed her glasses, turned off her phone, and put it into her purse.

Embarrassed, Tomoko held up her phone. "Everything's off."

She gestured for her to sit down. "So, what did he plagiarize?"

"The analysis and data proving that Wellington Payday Loans skims pennies off client transactions amounting to millions. He was ready to present it when the case hit."

"Interesting!" She leaned in. "Plagiarism aside, why didn't he take the obvious route with it and send it to OSFI with copies to the appropriate ministers and the news?"

"Come on."

"No, Tomoko. You send it to enough people that it can't get swept under." She added ruefully, "Only to be swept over, buried under public debate, but it would be out there."

"He wanted the credit. But the graduate student, Parisa Soltani, didn't want to be cited."

"Why not?"

"Because the data is dangerous to the Wellingtons and they expected reprisal of some kind. But there's something she's not saying."

"Consider that they may be unreliable sources, even if the analysis and data are good. But the data alone will make a great story. You going to run with it?"

"If I can figure out how to read it. I don't have their analysis. Her place was turned upside down. Her computer was wiped and the original USB with the data was stolen. There are no printouts, either. That's what I've got from Parisa. I haven't approached Monaghan yet."

"I'm guessing you took her computer to Anthony, just in case."

"I did. Nothing's there."

"No hidden backups?"

"She claims."

"Unreliable source."

Tomoko nodded. "I don't trust her."

"Exciting, though. What about Monaghan?"

"She says he has the data, but she won't contact him."

"Why don't you contact him yourself?"

"I will," Tomoko said defensively. It had only been two days and she just got sent the data.

"She give a reason?"

"The threats. I figured because it wasn't safe. She says that she got a call warning her she was in danger. She went to my b—, my friend's house with her kid. She seems legitimately worried. Parisa was imprisoned in Iran for her activism, so she's got history."

She appreciated that Amina did not take up the slip of the tongue, saying instead, "Tell me more about the warning."

"Monaghan kept her name out, but it was exposed by the end of the tribunal. She got an anonymous call to run from what she said sounded like an older woman. This was on the day the tribunal decision came down. After that, her place was searched."

"More interesting."

"Anyway, that's why I figure she didn't want to contact him."

"What would the Wellingtons get out of her showing up dead or harmed? It's an obvious connection. Maybe the threat was only meant to scare her?"

"Well, she's scared."

"There may be another reason she didn't want to be cited and doesn't want to contact Monaghan. I'm not surprised she doesn't want her name associated with him."

Tomoko sat forward. "Why?"

"Monaghan holds the door open for a lot of people. Gets a lot done. But maybe so he gets the shine? You know Kara Adisa? She wrote that piece on the negotiations around the battery factory opening up in Oshawa? Happened to her. Maybe more than shine, there." She gave her a knowing look.

Tomoko started. "Did he assault her?"

"No. Not that. He used her analysis in his own work, cited her accurately, but he got the public praise for what she did. Her name disappeared from view because he was presenting it. But he made calls for her. Kara says she got her job at GreenPoint because of him, so she didn't want to complain." Amina leaned back. "Lots of stories like that. He probably doesn't even know what he's done. Probably cry if you let him know."

Tomoko snorted. "Okay. That explains why Parisa did not want to ask Monaghan for his copy of the data. But there's something about her I don't trust."

"Listen to that, then. Keep the evidence in front of you, but listen to what's going on in the back of your mind. It's made the connections you haven't yet here." She tapped her forehead.

"She may have made up the phone call?"

"Keep all your options open and follow the evidence."

"Are you interested in this story?"

"Your story? Yes!"

"No. Do you want to do it with me? Be the lead?"

Amina smiled. "Tomoko, you're not in over your head. But I'll be glad to mentor you on it."

Tomoko was so relieved she nearly let out a cry.

"Oh you. I remember my first story."

"I want you on it with me."

"Alright, but you send the pitch to Frank." She dug into her purse and pulled out a few sheets of paper. "This is an example of what you should send to him. You need all the points I listed there and in that order. I also did a bit of digging on the termination case before I got here. Names of the university board members and other interested parties. People who should be no more than rubber-stamps, but who get involved in controversial tenure cases or tribunals when they come up. There's almost always politics in these decisions, outside interference of one kind or another. I'd pay most attention to the other list." She pointed. "People in that circle, involved indirectly but who have a lot of influence and tend to keep their names out of the paper."

She looked at the names. Most were expected. Influential business people, a former ambassador. The others she did not know. One was highlighted in yellow. "Agape. Who is that?"

"Known associate of the Wellingtons. He could have put pressure on the tribunal."

"Got it. So what do I do with the data?"

"It has to be sourced and verified. Take it to Anthony to open. Don't touch it yourself."

She felt like a fool again. It had not occurred to her that there might be a virus in it.

"Once we know what's there. Let's all take a look at it."

"Frank, too?"

"Not Frank." Amina looked at her pointedly. "Send him the pitch. He'll jump on it."

Tomoko stood to leave, papers in hand. "Will do."

"I have to go pick up my daughters from school. Call and text me from Signal from now on. It's secure. I'll pick up if you call."

She wanted to hug Amina, but gave her a professional thanks and left, turning on her phone to text Cyrus.

> I'm staying at my place again. Writing my
> pitch for Frank. Going to send it to him
> tonight. Amina's behind me.

22

———

Conor stopped by Martin's house on the way to the medical building, but his brother was not home. He crossed the street and knocked on Jamal's door, but they had not seen him, either, saying the lights had not been on for two nights now. He walked to Oliver's afterwards, hoping he was there. But Oliver looked strained and hearing that Conor had not seen Martin, he knocked coffee grounds to the floor while making an espresso.

He left Oliver, promising to let him know as soon as he had any information, trying to sound cheerful. But it was unlike Martin not to call daily, let alone not answer his calls. Knowing his brother could take care of himself did nothing to ease his worry.

As he pulled up to the medical building, he tried Martin one more time, then reluctantly turned off his phone. He had called the meeting to discuss Miss Henson's attack himself, and could hardly cancel it.

The men were already seated in a circle when he arrived and clearly unhappy with him. Judgemental frowns pulled at their lined and sagging faces. Marcus rudely stuck his feet out.

He sat down warily, not understanding what he could have done wrong.

Ipe got to the point. "It is absurd to call a meeting because Miss Henson is acting strangely."

Conor was taken aback. Not once had he heard the men address each other dismissively when one called an emergency meeting. Certainly, they debated and had their tensions, but never when one of them had a concern that could not wait. Almost worse than Ipe's complaint and Marcus's glare, Vincent was looking at him indulgently, as if he were a foolish boy. Only Pierre understood, but he sat silently, avoiding Conor's eyes.

Conor challenged them. "None of you are concerned about Miss Henson's behaviour?"

The men looked at one another as if some private conversation was taking place.

Finally, Pierre spoke up. "You must tell him!"

"You were not to know, not yet," Vincent said, beginning carefully. "She was Mr. Bailey's assistant, but also ours."

Conor stood in shock at the news and secrets it implied. "Why didn't you trust me with this?"

"Please sit," Agape said.

"Answer my question," Conor said, still standing.

"It's not a matter of trust. You were not to know. When you were to know, we would have been informed."

They looked at him stubbornly, even Pierre.

Vincent said, "We did not anticipate ever having to tell you. Miss Henson has not worked for us for some time now, since long before you came to us. You see why. She is unreliable."

The answer did nothing to assuage the hurt of keeping it from him, worse it raised his suspicions. If they had done this, what else were they not telling him? He objected, not caring that he sounded like a child. "Even if there was no need to tell me she had been our assistant, you should have told me she is Legion." He turned to Pierre. "You remind them!"

"She spoke of the appointed time, brothers." Pierre looked among them. "Both those women. They called us 'Glans-Crowned Anointed One'. Conor is right, this must be addressed."

Marcus replied, scraping the floor as he pulled the waiting room chair forward. "Pierre, I can see why you are upset. But, please, call upon your training. You are a psychiatrist. I see it in my medical practice, you must in yours. In my opinion, she is suffering from dementia."

"Dementia would cause her to know that title?" Conor demanded.

Pierre took a shaggy breath, closed his eyes, seeming to look within himself, then spoke. "Yes. Marcus is right. As certain cells are reabsorbed into the divine-thinking-fungus, it can bring into contact cells that perceive this ordinary world with those that perceive the extraordinary."

"That makes sense to me," Benjamin said and the other men murmured their agreement.

Conor shivered as the fluorescent light flickered overhead.

But Pierre added defensively, "I am the Bearer of Exorcism. This is the knowledge I have been given. And I tell you that the woman who attacked me was a messenger from Legion."

Agape sat forward. "No one doubts you. The first woman was a messenger from Legion. But not Miss Henson. I must insist the time has not yet come and there is no need to worry."

"On what authority? You are the Bearer of Love, not prescience." Conor balked. "None of us has been given that."

"This is knowledge I have received in a vision for me, alone."

"We're just supposed to accept that?"

Pierre agreed, but articulated it with the intonation of a question. "No one has been given the gift of prescience?"

"All of us accept our own visions and those we report to each other." Agape looked at the men. "You, too, Pierre. Have any of us challenged you when you make a claim?"

"Exactly," Vincent said.

The wondrous things he had seen, and the extraordinary peace that came after, confirmed their mission, but each vision had been within his bearing. Conor had never supposed himself able to bear more than the Ritual had chosen for him, and that was exactly what Agape was doing now and what Vincent was defending.

The men carried on with each other, supporting Agape's right, drowning out Conor's attempts to interject. He gave up and retreated within himself, holding out the forming distrust to the Lord for an answer. He felt the tendrils arise from the spore of the Lord's body, then the familiar sway. He hardly needed the Ritual anymore to find his way into the visions. His body had become receptive to spontaneous communion and his mind drifted easily into an altered state and the memory of his first night when he walked through the doors of the medical building.

———

The men had welcomed him, but so eagerly he became afraid. They explained the nature of their brotherhood, spoke about sacred mushrooms, Jesus, the first religion, but were holding something back. Conor could not imagine what it might be given the strangeness of what they had already said, but they assured him, eyes bright, saying, "We hope you will see," or "If the Ritual chooses you, you will know," and "Bailey would not have chosen you, if you were not already chosen."

Benjamin left the circle to prepare the communion wine at a table set to the side of the room and the men chanted in words he did not understand. It was something out of a movie. A secret ritual held in a damp and dilapidated building. Vincent hovered over him, trying to whisper away his concerns, explaining it was only a decoction of *amanita muscaria*.

So this was the sacred mushroom? Fear flopped over into astonishment. He now saw it as ridiculous and bit his tongue to keep from laughing aloud, imagining the terrifying old man Bailey high on magic mushrooms. He took the cup, tasting its bitter, tannic communion for the first time and closed his eyes, waiting to see what Bailey's secret was about.

Sooner than expected, the hard seat underneath him disappeared as the men's guttural chanting carried him into a storm of ever-expanding Fibonacci spirals only to emerge, alone and naked, in a sunny field of wine-red, pulsating peonies from which he unfolded himself to stand. The field undulated, seemingly without horizon, until the walls of a massive temple appeared in the distance. He walked toward it, the velvet petals soft, yet firm underfoot, each step covering vast distances.

As he drew near, the imposing gates of the great stone temple opened, and a central building fronted by golden tipped columns came into view. There were sounds of a commotion within. He ran up the stone steps and through the gates with a crush of men chasing after the noise, while others pushed their way out, cursing. Jostled forward with the crowd, unseen hands pushed him to the front.

A beautiful brown-skinned man in simple robes pulled at the stakes of a kiosk shading a table that held several treasury caskets. The moneychangers begged for help, while others jeered. The man pulled at the stakes until the table itself turned over and the coins spilled out. The shower of clinking coins transformed into golden-flecked mushrooms tumbling over the stone courtyard. Onlookers scrambled to gather them, but Conor was transfixed by the man himself. He gazed at Conor. The pupils of the man's eyes dilated until his brown eyes became black and Conor could see starlight within them. He was a cosmos that enveloped them all. Conor fell into his arms and not a cell within him remained unforgiven. He wept, releasing the shame of his existence.

The man touched his cheek. "My child, will you join me? Will you bear the cleansing of the temple?"

"Yes." With that one word, he experienced an ecstasy beyond the bounds of the human body and awoke, his face wet with tears and his pants stained with semen.

The elderly men sat at his feet, their eyes gleaming, saying, "Brother."

He took their hands, understanding their earlier eagerness, vowed himself to chastity and to serve the Lord.

They explained how each bore a unique quality of the Lord's mission that inspired their work.

The Lord had said to Vincent, "I was in prison and you visited me," and directed Vincent to defend the poor. Pierre witnessed the casting of the demons into the swine, and the Lord asked him to care for those who suffered the tortures of the mind. Marcus sat spellbound as the Lord healed the sick and asked him to devote his life to public medicine. Benjamin stood in the doorway as Lazarus rose. The Lord asked him to bear the transition of the dying until they would rise again by establishing hospices for the indigent. The Lord guided Ipe to teach the children. On awakening, he pledged to found free private schools that produced ethical and creative children who would change the world.

Agape, though, had walked with the women. He spoke with awe as Mary Magdalene had taken his hand and given him his charge. The Lord stood behind her, his light infusing her. "Follow her," the Lord had said, "in secret." He abandoned his given-name for its Greek corollary, Agape, its meaning a sign. But he said it as if it were English, hiding in the mispronunciation that he was the bearer of the Lord's love.

Conor drove home that night a man drunk with adoration, one who hurries to bed after leaving his lover, eager to dream of her. But as the night wore on and he could not sleep, he shook, pulling the duvet over his head, begging, "Cover me. Cover me."

But the Lord did not come in his dreams. When he woke up the next day, he suspected they had fooled him, that what he had experienced was a drugged manipulation. Ashamed, he got up only to call in sick to work and ban Oonagh from the house. He crawled into bed and pulled the duvet over him again, and slept, waking to find the morning had become afternoon and the sunlight had turned to gold and the Lord standing before him, saying, "I am the light of the world."

Conor had told Martin what he could, leaving out the visions, explaining the needed celibacy and focusing on serving the path of the Lord, but Martin would not accept it, arguing with him any chance he got. Whether storming off or sulking, Martin refused to see the value of Conor's work at Wake Financial, and attributed conspiracies to his brotherhood, accusing Bailey of trapping him in a world of lies.

If it had not been for the confirming, spontaneous vision that morning, he would have agreed with his brother. But the visions of the Lord were perfect certainty. Having been held by him, how could he choose any worldly creature over the truth?

As the tendrils withdrew, he was certain of the answer to his suspicions. He trusted the Lord and their path as he trusted the air that he breathed, and must extend that trust to his brothers. But he found himself in a hostile room, all set against him.

Agape said with a note of irritation in his voice. "If you have returned from your reverie, we would like to address a more important subject. We are concerned about your brother, Martin."

"I don't understand." Conor shook his head clear, embarrassed, not knowing how long he had drifted. "Where does Martin fit into all of this?"

"Nothing to do with Miss Henson. His termination." Agape answered coldly.

Did they mean to console him? Agape's tone did not suggest it.

Pierre said, coughing for a moment before continuing, "It is a shame he lost his position, but does he believe the plagiarism was worth the end he sought?"

He felt cornered. "Yes, but it was not plagiarism. He did not cite the student to protect her. Lord witness! She instructed him not to cite her."

Agape said to the men, "None of you know, but Vincent and I have been involved in this situation." He turned back to Conor. "You should know."

His doubt thrust back to the surface.

"I have been close to the Wellington family for decades and Vincent has acted as their lawyer."

Conor asked, "Were you involved in Martin's dismissal?"

"By the Mushroom and the Cross, no," Agape said. "Although, as an associate of the university board, I was aware."

Vincent held out a hand. "I have directed the Wellingtons to call off Fort Security from following your brother or the graduate student. Our representation is limited and we are considering how to extricate ourselves from the relationship. But Agape suggested I hold on, if only to exert some influence."

"How could you represent them at all?"

"These are the clients who pay for our *pro bono* work, their filth transformed. From dirt to soil, we prepare them for the spore. You know this, Conor."

But he stood again, suspecting them of more. "This is my brother!"

"How can we help?" Benjamin got up, touching him, but Conor shrugged him off.

He stared at Vincent and Agape. "You are involved. You must protect him!"

Ipe got up. Then the other men, too. They stood around him, hemming him in.

"We will put it to the Ritual," Pierre offered, then dissolved into another fit of coughing and fell back to his chair. Marcus went to him, whispering in his ear. The coughing subsided after a moment.

"The Wellingtons had protectors in the university," Agape said. "I know that much."

"Is the graduate student safe?" Ipe asked him.

"She's disappeared," Agape answered.

Vincent asked, "Who was Martin's lawyer?"

"Union appointed," Conor answered. "I tried to offer him one, but this woman had a series of successes challenging university tribunals."

"You should have asked me."

"My brother had help."

Vincent took him into a smothering embrace. "I should have helped."

The men placed their hands on Conor, saying, "We should have helped," but their hands felt like restraints and he weakened under them.

Needing clarity, he begged, "Put this matter to the Ritual."

Agape agreed, bowing his head slightly. "We will set the Intention."

The men returned to their seats.

"And Legion?" Conor asked, now free of their hands. He had the sickening feeling it was all connected.

"That, too, must be put to the Ritual, but not today. For now, we must assume Miss Henson has simply broken through to the extraordinary because of her dementia. Today is for you, Conor, and your brother," Benjamin said as he got up to prepare the communion.

But he would not let it go. He saw Miss Henson crawling toward him, her mouth gaping to eat from his stalk. "Only Pierre understands. Tell them how serious this is."

Pierre agreed. "We must not explain it away."

"We will set the Intention for it another day," Agape said, closing the matter. "Today is for guidance, for all of us, especially those of us unfortunately associated with the Wellingtons."

He grasped at the peace that had only just assured him he should trust his brothers, but there was nothing there. Conor did the unthinkable. He set his own intention apart from them and asked the Ritual to expose them.

Benjamin drew out the wooden sacraments from their leather case and laid the bowl, the ladle, and the cups out on a small table, each in their places. He mixed the wine and mushroom powder into the hand-turned wooden bowl and whispered,

"Under the shade of the Mushroom Cap, we meet our Lord, Ukushtigila, The Key to the Kingdom. We eat our Lord. Ukushtigila, The Key to the Kingdom. We drink our Lord. Ukushtigila, The Key to the Kingdom. We serve our Lord."

Benjamin ladled the communion into the wooden cups, walked slowly around the circle, and handed each their cup. They held the cups out, saying as one,

"Under the shade of the Mushroom Cap, we meet our Lord, Ukushtigila, The Key to the Kingdom. We eat our Lord. Ukushtigila, The Key to the Kingdom. We drink our Lord. Ukushtigila, The Key to the Kingdom. We serve our Lord."

Then, they drank the communion as one.

Benjamin returned the now empty cups and they drew their chairs into a circle so that their knees were touching.

Each brought their hands together in prayer, fingers pointing toward each other instead of to the heavens, their hands taking the shape of a vulva, and recited together.

"The earth produces first a womb, the Mushroom in the womb."

Then they raised their hands to point to the heavens, curling the fingers of the left hand into the palm of the right, then laying the fingers of the right hand over it, hand over fist, into the shape of the glans-headed mushroom, and recited together.

"The earth produces first a womb, the Mushroom in the womb, like a yolk inside an egg, and the child eats its coat as does the chick. The coat cracks when the child first forms, and is absorbed into the footstalk, the stalk, like froth, grows substantial, like parchment, and the child is born of no father, a womb, a stalk, a glans-headed Lord, our Lord is One."

Conor felt the tendrils arise from the spore of the Lord's body again and was calmed, relieved as certainty dispelled his confusion. He could trust the Ritual. He would trust them. And he let it all go.

DAY FIVE

23

—————

"What are we going to do?" Cassandra peered from behind the heavy brocade curtains at the reporters crowding the gate to her parents' house. Her father was perched on the hideous French provincial couch, ready to attack. Brandt stood behind one of the high-backed matching armchairs. Turner, the lawyer Vincent had sent over from his firm, and a young public relations person named Celeste, were hovering but not speaking, while her mother wandered at the room's edges. They had sent the boys to their uncle's house, at least. Her brother-in-law promised to keep all the televisions off and the screens away from them, but she could not see how he would manage it for long.

Two vans with raised satellite dishes were pulled up onto the lawn on the other side of the fence. Reporters stood in front of cameras with microphones. But most were speaking into their phones.

"Don't underestimate those with the phones," Cassandra said. "That pig, Frank James, from *The Spanner* is out there."

"How the hell did they get the story?" Her father stared at Turner as if he had the answer. "And where is Stone?"

She nearly snapped, "You mean where is the ass who let his gun be taken off him by the man he was hired to intimidate? That Stone?" But she kept her mouth shut.

Her mother stopped by the credenza, her back to them, and stiffly fussed with the cut flowers. It was strange to see her in a dress, rather than her pool clothes, tennis gear, or cashmere sweats. She was just as lithe and elegant as the days when she would subtly flirt with the men at their never-ending parties. Her every gesture seemed a promise. Cassandra never understood why her father did not become jealous. Instead, he seemed to take pride that his wife could elicit such attention. But then Patricia died, Cassandra became a pink-haired problem, the parties ended, and her parents were left feeling the wrong child had died.

The lawyer interrupted her thoughts. "Vincent and I discussed it and, with Celeste's help, we have prepared a statement. At this point, we do not know what they have. They only published a teaser for the story, but it was suggestive enough."

Her mother swung around. "Suggestive? They have it!"

Turner straightened his back, but he was a twig facing down a storm and she doubted he could withstand his mother's onslaught, let alone her father. Cassandra asked him, intervening with an evenly intoned question, "Do we know how they got the data?"

"Stone let Monaghan leave here and he leaked it!" Wellington bellowed.

Turner held his hand out. "We do not know that, and I would suggest that you refrain from accusing him or Soltani at this point. We have no reason to assume they kept the data. Further, I have instructed Fort to withdraw from any contact with Monaghan, Soltani, and anyone else they suspect."

"Absurd," Wellington said. "We have more of a reason to pursue them now."

"We would be glad to find you new representation if you are unwilling to rely on our expertise, Mr. Wellington. There are firms who would pursue matters more aggressively and who are less concerned about keeping their clients within the boundaries of the law."

Turner looked very much like he wished he did not have to deal with her father. Vincent should have come. He could have easily maneuvered them into letting Monaghan and Parisa go. Cassandra sympathized with Turner, but her only concern now was protecting her children. The escape money Agape had set aside for her had grown, but not enough to set up a new life with the kids if this scandal destroyed the company. Brandt would not survive it. They would have to sell the house and move into an apartment. But Brandt would never work. She would have to carry them all. What could she even do? What skills did she have? "I told you this would happen," she spat out at her father. "You should have taken the virus out. But your greed!"

"Where is Stone?" Wellington demanded, again.

"Fort Security is investigating the source of the data. They are looking into *The Spanner*'s emails and phones, but they are having some difficulty."

"It's hard to believe that Agape would have suggested them," Brandt said. "It's as if he wanted us to be exposed."

"He's exposed." Cassandra said. "Agape's name was listed among those who put pressure on the tribunal to terminate Monaghan."

Turner put a hand out. "Fort is among the best. We have to expect that *The Spanner* would have superior security. They are not *People* magazine."

"What did you call Fort, mother?" Cassandra called out.

"Keystone Cops."

The young Celeste seemed puzzled.

"An old comedy routine," Cassandra explained, short tempered. "Cops like clowns."

Turner asked, "Mr. Wellington. The question is whether you would like to stand by me while I make the statement?"

Celeste said, "We think it would be best. You offer a concerned front, something that says 'getting to the bottom of it' and 'I take full responsibility'."

"Of course I will stand there!"

Celeste was unbothered by his outburst. "Then, if you will, please change out of your suit. We would prefer you to be in trousers with something more down to earth. A white shirt, under a sweater, sleeves rolled up. No tie."

Her father's ire rose for only a moment, then dissolved into a disgusting expression meant to invite her upstairs and help him change. Celeste responded with a knowing smile and playfully turned him around toward the stairs.

Sick of them all, Cassandra took Brandt's hand, pulling him away from Turner and Celeste to the far side of the room. "This may not work. What then?"

"The worst case scenario?" His eyes glinted with devious pleasure. "Do you know how long it will take for the company to be forced into bankruptcy and dismantled? Deal with civil suits?"

She shook her head.

"So long as to be meaningless for us. And most of the money is already hidden."

"What do you know?" She glanced quickly at the others, but they were not listening.

"I spoke to your father when we arrived. Whatever funds could be moved are already in Singapore. He is busy protecting the rest."

"Singapore?"

"Yes. He explained that Singapore banks are the go-to for financial privacy these days."

She should have known. Her father was ruthless.

"Is Agape handling this for him?"

"Of course. Who else?"

She sighed, relieved. Agape would protect them, and more importantly, her and her children. Cassandra tittered, suddenly feeling the fool.

Brandt touched her cheek. "What my sweet? You seem embarrassed."

"I was imagining myself working at Walmart. You at home taking care of the children. Us living in some high-rise apartment next to the highway."

He smiled gently, pulling her in. "But the views always seem so good in them."

She settled into his embrace. Here was the man she married. The gentle ski bum who was so unlike everyone in their circle, always watching their wealthy friends and families with an air of wry detachment.

"Remember when we first met?" She pulled away, but remained in his arms.

"January 24th, 2011 on the gondola at Whistler mountain. You were adorable. Red cheeks. Your hair in pigtails. Dressed like a skate punk in that plaid Burton's jacket. Holding your board like you were some tough young thing."

"I wasn't young, just acting it."

"It's why I loved you. You hated all this."

"What happened to us?" She stood apart.

He shrugged. "Nothing. We were always this way, only putting it off."

Cassandra broke away from Brandt. The sweetness turned to the sickening realization that he was right and there was no way back. More, that she was not sure that she wanted to, only wanting out of this damned business, not the money.

"Mr. Wellington. Yes. That's it." Celeste said, gliding towards him as he rejoined them.

She fussed with the cuffs, but it was more to seem as if she had a purpose. He looked exactly as he should. Attractive, powerful, trustworthy. The kind of man who need not have an age appropriate wife, but who would never stoop so low. The young Celeste with her blond blowout, high-waisted tan slacks, and tight dress shirt could have been his girlfriend. He gave her an inviting smile. Maybe she would be his girlfriend before long.

Cassandra met her mother and slipped her arm around her.

She slid out of Cassandra's embrace. "Please dear. This is serious."

Turner stood and handed out copies of the brief statement to everyone.

Cassandra took hers and returned to stand by Brandt, holding it up for both of them to read.

The Wellington Family had no knowledge of a virus in the Wellington Payday Loans system and has engaged a cyber security firm to confirm the claims made by *The Spanner*. They want to reassure their clients and the Canadian public that if such a virus does exist, they will remove it and Wellington Payday Loans will consider the next steps. They ask the government to step in and launch an investigation into the insertion of a virus into one of the most respected financial institutions in Canada. Certainly, it puts all our institutions at risk. Wellington Payday Loans takes these allegations seriously and hopes their swift response will allow them to remain a trustworthy source for short-term loans in Canada. We will have further statements to share with the public as we know more.

"Why are you inviting the government in!" His expression was cold at the betrayal. "I tried calling Davies, and he won't take my call. The man has always taken my calls. They've abandoned us."

"The government will get involved, whether you invite them or not," Celeste said soothingly. "Better for you to invite them publicly."

"Tylenol," her mother said. "The company accepted blame even though they were not at fault for the handful of bottles that had been laced with cyanide."

Celeste nodded appreciatively. "They became an even more trusted brand because they handled the crisis with transparency."

"But you are missing a crucial point," her father said. "They were not to blame."

Turner cut in. "Neither are you. Did you introduce the virus? No. Fort Security and, when the time comes, the government investigation will prove your innocence. Your only culpability would come if investigations prove you knew and did not act. Our efforts will be directed toward blaming the staff on that account."

"Good. Good." Her father seemed mollified.

"But," Turner continued, "we must remove the virus from the system for your defence to work."

Her father glared at the lawyer.

Brandt asked, "But won't *The Spanner* article portray it as native to our system?"

"Frank James said as much in the teaser," Turner said. "Any investigation will provide proof of incursion into your system and, hopefully, the government will track down who did it."

Cassandra whispered to her husband, "It looks as though we might come out of this."

"Yes, and if not"—he leaned in—"it is also not a serious matter. The loss of the company and the brand, but nothing else."

It was exactly what she wanted and her muscles unclenched for the first time since this nightmare began. Only one thing remained to feel at ease.

Turner was speaking, "As for Davies, or anyone else for that matter, he cannot take your calls. His office must seem impartial, but a message has come through back channels. Please, one thing at a time."

"Why didn't you say that in the first place, then?"

"I would rather not say it at all. And I am assuming no one in the room heard me say that."

Celeste gestured to the front door. "Shall we?"

Turner and Wellington went out. Cassandra moved to a window, watching as the reporters screamed questions over each other, then she retreated past the others to the dining room.

Cassandra pulled out her phone and called Agape.

He answered immediately. "My dear, I am watching it now."

"Am I safe?"

"I've taken care of everything."

24

Parisa left Arash waiting in the car with Cyrus outside her apartment. She went first to the kitchen for a dinner knife, pulled over a chair, got up, and used the knife to unscrew the heating vent, reached inside the duct, and retrieved a USB drive. She shoved it in the front pocket of her jeans. Then, reaching back inside, pulled out a burner phone and stuck that in her back pocket.

She turned to face the apartment and began restoring it to some order, setting aside the things that she and Arash would need. She wished she could get the rabbit from Monaghan, but to her it was gone for good. When she was finished, they were going straight to a toy store for Arash to pick out a new friend, then for a pancake brunch, and to see whatever movie he and Cyrus had chosen.

With the story out, the Wellingtons could hardly go after them. Any intimidation, let alone a physical attack or murder, would point to the family. But Cyrus wanted them to stay a few more nights to be certain, adding, "If the press makes the connection with Monaghan's case, you won't be able to leave your apartment."

Tomoko had texted she was not returning to Cyrus's yesterday to get the pitch in, but they had not anticipated a teaser for the story coming out immediately. Parisa had assumed nothing would be reported until the data was examined and the analysis completed, then they would publish, proof in hand. Tomoko had called Cyrus that morning, furious. Her name was mentioned. Amina's name, too. But it had Frank James's preening all over it. The man was a menace. Tomoko rightfully complained that she and Amina were now under enormous pressure to publish the complete story within days. The government was no doubt already stepping in with backroom calls and initial steps were being taken in what would be their own, lengthy investigation, giving Wellington Payday Loans all the time in the world to hide what they had done. If the story did not come out soon, the momentum would be lost and no one would have to answer the hard questions the piece would have posed.

Cyrus was supportive on the phone, not letting on that his feelings had changed. How could he tell Tomoko that their relationship had ended as she was preparing her first piece under intense pressure?

But once alone for the night, he admitted to Parisa that he looked her up on the university website after they met. He even had her email address. A thousand times, he conspired with himself to pursue an "errand" on campus near her building. But he would not do it. There would be no lies between them. There would be no false starts. He told himself that she had lost the card and he should email her. He answered that if she lost the card, she did not love him as he loved her. And so he went on with his life, silently waiting for her, hoping to run into her without pretence.

Then came Tomoko. As Cyrus had put it, "Tomoko is a joy, but she is not my love. I cannot imagine she thinks of me in any other way. But I must speak to her first, before we pursue this further." He looked at Parisa with those warm eyes, so filled with love, and said, "In the end, I trusted that if it were God's will, you would find your way to me."

Cyrus was careful not to do more than touch Parisa's cheek as they prepared their small dinner. Then his fingers brushed hers as the three sat on the couch watching *Transformers*. But each touch had set her on fire.

She retrieved a carryon suitcase out of the closet and rolled it into Arash's tiny room, packing it with what he would need for a few more days, but also dress pants and a nice sweater, what he wore for school pictures. Parisa imagined presenting him to Cyrus's family and wanted him looking his best. For her, she pulled out her bottle green wrap dress and laid it on the mess of her bed, then considered shoes. She picked past the platforms and found her good pair of low-heeled pumps. They were decorated with several large rhinestone jewels, the green stone matching the dress well enough.

Her backpack filled with the rest of what they needed and the suitcase packed tight, she checked the rooms, wondering if she had enough. It was more than she had with her when she left Iran, alone, sent off before those who had been influenced to let her go could change their minds.

Finally, she went to deal with the stink coming from the galley kitchen. The compost had long since turned ripe, and she tried not to breathe as she reached for the bin inside the sink cabinet. But the scent of decaying citrus hit her in that horrible way it did sometimes. She got up too quickly, becoming dizzy, and stumbled toward the living room, trying to get away before the flashback could consume her.

It was too late. The curtain descended, twisting her body up in memories. She slipped to the floor, knees up, shivering from the cold of her prison cell as the winter wind blew fumes from the garbage heaps through the leaky window of her cell. The guard's sweat mixed with the sweet stench of rotting bitter oranges. He forced her to undress, then pushed her down to the cold floor and thrust until she lay in ruins.

Parisa crawled out of the kitchen into the living room, shaking and moaning, trying to escape the vision, but found Andy waiting. He was standing over her, screaming, while she wrapped her arms around her belly to protect Arash within her.

She spread herself flat on the floor, forcing herself to feel the edge of the throw rug with her fingers and bring herself back into the apartment. She counted aloud until little by little she heard her own voice over the sounds of the prison guard's grunts and Andy's accusations. Lifting herself up, she crawled to the washroom, put her head over the toilet and vomited until she emptied herself of it.

Not long after she arrived in Toronto, she went to the Canadian Centre for Victims of Torture. She sat in the groups with the infant Arash strapped to her chest, saw the counsellor, and it helped. The world came to life around her. Her English was already nearly fluent; she only needed to complete the necessary adult high school credits to prove herself, then applied to Simcoe University. Parisa got a full ride, bursaries and grants that she did not have to repay, then an anonymous donor connected to her through the CCVT provided the rest. She even had daycare. There were afternoons lounging in atriums with reading groups for her classes that led to friendships with students of like politics that led to political groups and rallies. The rage she had carried transmuted into seeking justice for everyone but herself. For her, no justice would ever come.

Then one course with Monaghan and she was under his wing, soon graduating and into the master's program, then the doctoral program under his mentorship. She had not wanted to write about the democratic movement in Iran, but he insisted, suggesting she begin with one paper. The words came out of her like a bullet from a gun. The justice she wanted for herself was within reach, through words. Her stomach troubles abated. Her first public paper was the day she met Cyrus. She had been affirmed by senior scholars and her peers, then held in the sweetness of Cyrus's attention, all making her feel as if the safety she had known before her imprisonment could be restored to her.

Now here she was with her head in the toilet again.

As Parisa carried the compost bag out to the bins in the laneway, she glanced up over the door, suddenly remembering, and felt stripped bare.

She hurried back from the bins, picked up the knife again, dragged the chair to the front door, then said to the camera inset into the juncture with the ceiling, "You've seen enough," and dug it out with the knife. She snapped off the wire transmitter. Hopping down off the chair, she went straight to the kitchen, got a glass out of the cabinet, filled it with water, and dropped the camera inside. For good measure, she put the full glass back into the cabinet and shut the door.

Then she pulled out the burner phone, turned it on, and tried to remember Martin's number. Finally she got it. The line rang on the other end, then went directly to voicemail.

"I'm sure you've seen the news. Or maybe not. Maybe you are on the run, too? We're safe. But do not call me. Do not reach out. Not on this phone or the other."

Instead of closing the phone, she bent the screen backwards until the hinges broke, tossed the pieces into her backpack to throw away in a public bin, then rolled the suitcase to the door, hoping that Agape truly had everything under control.

25

———————

Afraid to go home, afraid to go to his brother, afraid to use his credit card, Martin had slept in his car at the end of the Cherry Beach parking lot for two nights. He dragged himself from underneath the ratty blanket he used to line the cargo area and squinted out the window. Every muscle hurt from the uneven surface and the twisting around, unable to sleep from the fucking drumming coming from the woods and thinking the cops would roust him at any minute, about how Parisa and Arash were in danger and all the ways he had been wronged and how Oliver had been a part of it all. Oliver. What a long game. He wondered how much Oliver had been paid and if it was worth it.

He saw the news when he was waiting in line at the food truck to buy a hot dog with the little cash he had on him. A man dressed for work was ahead of him, his terrier straining on the leash, tail wagging at the scent of grilled meat and fries. In the other hand, he was reading a story on his phone.

"That! Show me that headline!"

The man turned around, looking him up and down, and jammed the phone in his pocket.

"I know what I look like. I slept in my car, okay? Just hold it up so I can see the headline."

He jerked on his dog's leash, putting the squirming terrier between them, and held the phone out, but not within reach. Martin could hardly read it. But it was there.

WELLINGTON PAYDAY LOANS ACCUSED OF FRAUD

"You read it. What does it say?"

"*The Spanner* says it has data proving they defrauded their customers."

"*The Spanner*?"

"That's what I said."

The cook leaned out of the truck, handing down a cardboard container of poutine. The man pocketed his phone, took the poutine and hurried off, the terrier jumping beside him, waiting for a bite.

"What can I get you?"

"Hot dog," Martin answered as he fished for his phone. The news was out. Maybe they were safe. He pulled the case open carefully at the top and shook out his SIM card, popped it back into his phone, and turned it on. It pinged a number of times. Conor had called over and over and sent text messages, wanting to know why he was not responding. There were voicemails, probably all from Conor, a call from an unknown number, and one hello from Oliver with a string of cute emojis and a question mark. He frowned at it. "Stone gave you away."

He left Conor for later and went straight to *The Spanner*'s website. It was a teaser for an upcoming piece. It mentioned his case, but thankfully, Parisa's name did not come up. They had the data that proved the fraud and they had names of board members and their associates who may have pressured the tribunal to terminate him.

Martin felt a surge of justification. There had been a conspiracy to get rid of him! It was about much more than him not citing a graduate student, a graduate student who had asked him to keep her name out of it!

"Hot dog."

"Right, right." He put the phone in his pocket and handed over the cash. Hot dog in hand, he waved off the cook. "Keep the change." Then walked away, ripping into the hot dog with such large bites he barely swallowed.

"You get a pop with that!" The cook called out of the truck.

He ran back, grabbed a can of orange pop from the counter and stormed off again, heading straight to the edge of the water.

"They'll pay!" He yelled at a flock of ducks bobbing in the water and shoved the last bite of the hot dog in his mouth.

A German Shepherd walking off-leash ahead of an older woman approached, growling and baring its teeth. The woman came to attention, backed up, then turned and walked away. The dog remained until she was at a safe distance, then ran after her.

"Get in the car, you freak," he said to himself and stomped off down the beach, trying to shake off the thrill of it finally being exposed. He did not know what it meant for him. If they could prove it, maybe he would be reinstated. Certainly he could sue the fuckers. People were going down for this, and he hoped Bernard would be among them.

The Spanner had the data, but unless Parisa was helping them, they did not have the analysis nor the rest of the proof. Evidence of the loans they had taken out, the charges and the excuses made by the clerks and managers. It would take the journal months to build the case. But he had it all in a box sitting in his dining room. All he had to do was contact Frank James today and get it to him.

By the time he got to his car, he could think half straight. He opened his phone and navigated back to *The Spanner* website. There were two journalists on it. Amina Warsame and Tomoko Abrams. Warsame was well known, hard-hitting. Martin stopped. Maybe someone had sent *The Spanner* the data the same as they did Parisa? Warsame would not run with a story unless it was tied up. They must have been working on it for months already.

"Bring it to them anyway," he told himself. "The analysis may be useful."

Then, the language hit him. Data that possibly proved fraud and board members and their associates who possibly influenced his termination.

"Possibly."

Frank James didn't have shit.

They would need Martin's analysis.

He lowered the visor and looked in the mirror. There was grease all over his beard stubbled face and a fine layer of dirt on him from lying on the beach the night before. He reached into the glove box for a napkin and his fingers brushed against the barrel of the gun. His hand jerked back as if he had touched fire. How the hell did he forget the gun, and what the hell was he going to do with it? He shut the glove box and started the car. That, later. Now, home. Martin sniffed his armpits. He was a mess.

As he drove up the street to his house, Jamal's mother was coming up the opposite direction, her push trolley filled to the rim with groceries and waved to him. Martin slowed down and lowered the window. "Assalamu alaykum, Auntie! The biryani was delicious, thank you!"

"When you are ready, I will have a wife for you! You will eat biryani every day!"

He grinned. She knew about the men, but thought he would come to his senses.

Pulling into the driveway, he could hear her behind him. "Do not wait too long!"

There had been that one day at Jamal's house. Martin was fifteen. Everyone knew he was gay. He had sat stiffly, waiting to hear the worst, that his sanctuary among them was being taken from him. Auntie Zeb had sat him down and tried to counsel him, maybe on the instigation of his mother. But Auntie Zeb turned out to be nothing like her. There was no visceral disgust, no bodily rejection of her own child. She only heaped food on his plate and expressed her worry about his future.

"What will your life be without a wedding, wife, and children?"

"I can give you two of those, Auntie," he joked.

The look of confusion on her face was so sweetly innocent that the stiffening resentment he had carried into the conversation melted away.

"Auntie. A wedding someday. And babies."

"But how, beta?"

He reached over and took her hand, kissing it and bringing it to his forehead like he had seen her children do.

Since that day, whenever he joked to Jamal that his mother was pressuring him to find a wife again, Jamal would answer seriously, "You don't have to marry a woman. But give her babies. It's the babies she wants."

If they thought it was going to be Oliver, he hated to break it to them. It had all been a ploy. His leaving. His coming back.

"You sure can pick them," he told himself.

Maybe if he could get Jamal's mother to find him a man, it would stick and maybe there would be biryani made at home.

Dripping from the shower, Martin stood over the boxes in the living room, trying to remember which one held the printouts of their analysis. He opened the flaps, but could not find it. Had the intruders returned and gone through them? He felt violated all over again. Martin pulled a box down off the dining room table, emptying it onto the floor and kicked the papers around. They were not what he wanted. He threw down the next box, watching the papers scatter with satisfaction. And there they were. Martin fell to his knees, gathering them up, trying to get them back in order, but it was a mess. Why was he like this? No one deserved this. Even if Oliver was not working for Stone, how could he let anyone into his life when he could not control himself long enough to go through the boxes one at a time?

The phone rang. Conor's tone. He followed the sound to the kitchen.

"Where have you been?"

"Fuck, Conor. It's been hell."

He went to the fridge, found a beer, and pried off the cap with the bottle opener under the kitchen cabinet.

"I saw the news," Conor said.

"Did you see that board members might have been involved in forcing my termination?" Martin took a deep drink of the beer. It was early in the day, but it settled in nicely.

"It's just a list of names. It said 'possible' that's not even 'probable'. Don't react until we know something."

"You heard of those people?" Martin asked. "Do any of them have a connection to the Wellingtons?"

There was a pause. "No connection I am aware of."

His brother was a shit liar. "Sounds like you know some of them."

"Nothing that would amount to a connection with this case."

Martin withheld the story about going to the Wellingtons and his fight with Stone, let alone that there was a gun in his car, only saying, "The Wellingtons' security guy, Stone, he told me that Oliver was working for him."

Conor blurted, "No!" Then said, "Not Oliver. This man, Stone, could only be trying to get under your skin, isolate you from people you trust to make it easier to get at you."

"You don't know that."

"I know Oliver."

"From all the coffee you've bought from him?"

"You can trust him. Go see him now. He's at the counter today."

"How do you know?"

"I've been swinging by your house looking for you. Yesterday, and then this morning. When your car wasn't there again today, I stopped by the cafe on my way to the office."

"Fuck's sake, Conor. What did you say?"

"That I am rooting for him."

"If you're rooting for him, you shouldn't want me for him."

"Why would you say that?"

He nearly told him about the boxes, but was worried someone was listening. Besides, he knew what Conor would say. "So much has been taken from you. Your life was threatened. So you got frustrated and knocked over a box. Please."

Conor did not wait for him to answer, only repeated, "Go see Oliver. Then come to me."

Martin said his goodbyes and hung up. He would go see Oliver, but he would go to find out if he was working for Stone or not. He would ask him straight to his face. There had to be a tell. He couldn't be that good of a liar, or he was, and he had everyone fooled.

The cafe was busy and Martin hung back outside, just out of view of the counter, waiting for the line to clear. There'd be a break, then he could call Oliver outside to talk. He leaned against the wall next to Steady's, feeling hungry. He would get this conversation over with Oliver, then pick up some oxtail and go home, fill his belly and get good and drunk.

Two customers left with to-go cups. Martin stepped out onto the sidewalk far enough to see in. If the rest of the customers were seated, Oliver could come out for a moment. But there was a man at the counter. Martin swore. Despite having his back to him, he recognized Stone immediately. He was favouring his injured leg. Oliver was smiling, bantering with him, calling in someone sitting down into the conversation.

Gut punched, Martin ducked out of view, going past Steady's and straight home, head down, and muttering, "Stupid. Stupid. Stupid."

There, he found Frank James' contact information, including an address for the journal. He collected the loose papers of the work on Wellington Payday Loans and carried them out to the car. Checking the glove box to make sure the gun was still there, he left to deliver to *The Spanner* what they would need to take down every one of those fuckers.

26

Conor hung up the phone and sank heavily into his office chair. Maybe he should have told him. What good would it do? The brothers were not directly involved, but that would not stop Martin from storming into Vincent's law offices or charging up to Agape's home. When Martin had a bone in his mouth, he hunkered down and there was no prying it out. At least Vincent had called off Fort Security from following him or the graduate student.

It still rankled that Vincent represented the Wellingtons. Surely money such as that could not be cleansed through good works. Vincent paid the salaries of his firm out of that money. His partners ate from that money. Vincent himself. How could he not see?

And Agape? Could he truly have done nothing? Did he hold no influence with the university board, with the Wellingtons themselves?

Despite the Ritual's instruction to carry forward with trust, suspicion threatened his peace of mind.

What had they done?

Worse, what had he himself done without knowing?

He stared out into the stillness of the office, hearing Miss Henson and Marta chatting happily outside as if each stick of furniture and each mote of dust were not accusing him of complicity in his brother's downfall.

Doubt spiralled in on him, twisting down from the top of his head, winding its way around every muscle and tightening until he was bound and the eye of his mind was forced open to see into his past.

Through a darkened tunnel, he saw flashes of Mr. Bailey leaning on his porch railing, beads of sweat on his forehead from the deep summer heat, settling in on the stoop with a grunt, sharing secrets one at a time, each offered as an invitation to the next until Conor wanted to know them all. Another, over a cool drink in the kitchen, he was promised that he would be able to care for his mother and brother. The memories slipped into Bailey's office. Conor standing beside the old man at his desk, Mr. Bailey advising him on the responsibility of the elder brother now his father was gone.

Then, young Martin was beside him on the walk home from Mr. Bailey's, angry, as always, warning him. "He's kidnapping you."

"I'm right here!"

"He's kidnapping you while you're right here!"

"You're just jealous," he snapped, looking down at Martin. "He won't teach you."

"I don't want to learn from him."

"Why do you keep coming if you hate him so much? You don't care what mom thinks."

Martin turned on him. "If that old man touches you. I'll kill him."

The suggestion had horrified him. It was not like that and never became that.

Only now, bound by doubt, and forced to watch, did he realize that was when Martin began training in Tae Kwon Do.

He wept for Martin, doubled over in shuddering grief, and the binds loosened one by one, but not from around his own heart.

There they tightened, and a voice said, "You."

The tunnel opened onto a vista of the life that had gone on without him. He watched his friends kicking around a ball. Saw himself eating alone at lunch. Rejecting his feelings for a shy girl out of piety to Mr. Bailey's judgment. Later, a woman who delighted him, he turned away. Another ignored. His chance for a family taken from him. Worse, his mother's pride at his loneliness and calling him a real man, a provider, unlike his brother, hated for loving men and his constant, flailing anger. Anger, Conor understood now, at not being able to save him. He had been kidnapped and his family ruined.

Conor answered the voice, "Us."

The binds around his heart tightened, crushing his chest until he finally said, "Me, too."

He slipped out of his chair, crawling under the desk, holding himself, knees up, weeping and snotting for everything that had been taken from him, Martin, and his family.

A hand touched his shoulder.

"I'm here."

Agape.

With his touch, he felt the tendrils rise from the earth, soothing him, following the path of the bindings of doubt and healing where they had rubbed him raw.

"I know. I know." Agape sat beside him, releasing a straining sigh.

Conor muttered, "I'm sorry," wiping his face like a child with his suit jacket sleeve and lifting himself to crawl out from under the desk.

"No." He placed his hand on his shoulder. "Stay." Agape clucked like a mother. "It is a womb in there."

But Conor crawled out and helped Agape stand. The smaller man hugged Conor, resting his cheek on his chest and the tendrils bound the two of them. He fell into their comfort and belonging.

Agape let him go, but the tendrils remained.

He took off his jacket and laid it over the back of the desk chair. Agape led him to the couch.

"Each of us bears alone what the Lord has asked."

"Yes." They knew what each other bore. They knew what each had seen. But none knew the particulars, those of Agape especially. His work was secret. His voice cracked. "But why are you close with those people? The Wellingtons? I don't understand."

"When I was asked by Lady Magdalene to form our path, I was

told to seek out the filthy and they would be transformed. From dirt to soil, we prepare them for the spore. I did not understand, but I served."

"I never considered how this path hurt my family. You work in secret and my brother is now at risk. What have I lost in becoming one of you?"

Agape leaned in and took his hand. "You lost the possibility of a wife and children. You lost a certain intimacy with your brother because you could not share with him the womb and stalk of your being. That is your bearing. I was told to change my name, dissociate myself from my family, my brother's work. There could be no relationship with them. But you were allowed to keep what you had."

"No. It hurt my brother. It hurt me."

"And this is about your brother?"

"He wanted to protect me."

"From us?"

"Yes."

"You want to protect him now?"

He stood up from the couch, throwing off Agape's hand. "I must!"

"How do you know that I have not been protecting him?"

Conor dropped to his knees before him. "Tell me!"

"I cannot."

"Did you press the tribunal to terminate him?"

Agape looked straight into his eyes. "No."

"Do you know who did?"

"The chair of his department was manipulated by the Wellingtons."

"But how did the Wellingtons get to him?" He gripped Agape's hands tightly.

"Conor!" Agape jerked away.

"Who was it?"

"I do not know."

"How can you not know? You are right there with the Wellingtons." Conor pushed away and stood.

Agape got up and went to the door.

Conor followed, grabbing his arm. "Are you walking out on me?"

"Is that not what you want?"

Agape's frown no longer expressed disapproval, but betrayal and loss, no different from what lay behind Martin's eyes all these years.

"Stay."

"You were told when you came to us you would be tested."

He nodded slowly. "The doubt."

"Each of us has travelled through it."

Conor compared the searing binds of doubt to the healing tendrils. How could those tendrils be wrong? How could the burning be right?

"Has anyone ever left?"

"One. He returned to us eventually, but the Ritual rejected him."

It was a warning.

He panicked. The only absolute certainty he had known in life was the Ritual, the visions, the path given to him by the Lord. The Lord had not lied to him.

Agape opened the door, waiting to hear his response.

"I will see you at the next meeting," he reassured Agape, and walked him out.

He shut the office door behind him.

Alone again, he leaned against the door and begged the Lord for an answer.

The answer came as the afternoon light spilled through the window, transforming dust motes into gold. Conor wandered in it, as the office fell away around him into a world he could not yet make out except for the scent of animals, frankincense, and myrrh in the far distance. The shimmering light fell on the harsh earth underfoot, speck by glittering speck, until the evening light was accepted into the earth itself and night emerged on the horizon. He heard his own voice in the distance, "Go and prepare the passover for us to eat, Peter."

A voice like Agape's asked, "Where?"

"Go to the city. A man will meet you with a pitcher of water. Follow him into a house. Say to the householder, I asked for a room to eat passover with the brothers. He will show you a furnished upper room. Make ready and I will join you."

The shuffle of the man's sandals along the rough earth faded into the hush and click of olive and palm trees in the wind.

The gloom of night rose around him. The walls of the city fell away. A window appeared in the distance, glowing with lamplight. He approached it, walking on air as one does on water. The brothers from The Cluster sat at a table. He saw himself, too. Standing while they were seated. Conor moved closer, stepping higher and higher until his fingers brushed the delicate flowers of the date palms and their honeyed scent filled his belly and he was outside the window, sated, open to what would come.

The Conor within the room remained standing, crushing fresh red capped mushrooms in a wooden bowl. He raised his mushroom-flecked palms to the men. "One of you will betray me." He poured wine into the bowl, pressing the crushed mushrooms into the thick red liquid. He raised his stained palms to the men, the wine and mushroom liquor dripped down his arms through the sleeves of his rough linen robe, appearing again at his ankles, winding rivulets through his toes, and pooling at his feet.

The Conor within gathered the wine into his cupped palms and poured it into a goblet before him. He gathered again and again until each man would have his share and passed the cup around the table. "Swallow my flesh. Drink from my blood."

Each of the men sipped and allowed the crushed mushroom to lie reverently on their tongues, except Agape who watched him furtively.

"You eat and drink of me and I will be sacrificed for this Cluster." The Conor within trembled at his fate, lowering his eyes, then lifting them, fearfully, staring directly into Conor's eyes, and said to him, "Do not forsake me."

Conor retreated in horror, stepping back, and back again, on the heavy air as it thickened and turned to jelly under his feet until he stumbled and found himself in a garden. The hush and click of olive and palm trees in the wind returned and he heard the even breaths of his sleeping friends.

He woke them, shaking their shoulders, their linen wraps rough to his touch. They grumbled into awareness, only to fall asleep again and leave him in this garden to face what was coming alone.

A donkey brayed outside the walls as the regular footsteps of centurions marched by, stopping for a moment, then a moment longer of terrible silence, broken by a woman protesting and weeping as they took her son from her in chains.

He stood by, listening helplessly, and begged, "Lord, take this sacrifice from me."

He shook a friend again. "You could not stay awake with me for one hour?"

But his friend only raised his head and laid it back down again.

These friends, asleep. The other, his betrayer. He left them, crying out in anguish for the boy taken, for the family bereft, and the sacrifice to come, "My Lord, My Lord, why have you forsaken us?"

The garden fell away around him, the wind quieted, the sleeping friends dissolved into the trees and the office took shape around him. He found himself splayed across the carpet, his cheek on the rough wool and the carpet wet with his saliva. None of his spontaneous visions had been like this. He sat up, terrified, expecting to find he had soiled himself, but found he was clean and trembled at the betrayals and what he must bear.

When he could stand, he returned to his desk, opened his computer and began the process of transferring his wealth into offshore accounts.

27

"Meet me at the Loveless Cafe in one hour," Amina said.

She was waiting for Tomoko, sitting on a bench on the sidewalk patio, tote beside her, cup in hand. The black awning was pulled back and Amina was in full sunlight. The sharp lines of her face were softened by her loosely wrapped red saash and her warm expression, as if a laugh were bubbling to the surface. Instead of scrolling her phone, she was watching passersby. It was inexplicable she could be so at ease after the press release and choose such an exposed place to have a private conversation.

Tomoko kissed Amina's cheek and dropped onto the bench next to her. "Shouldn't we go inside?"

"I can easily listen to what others say in cafes, can't you? Out here, with the street traffic, it's more private."

Tomoko nodded. "I haven't opened the data. I've got an appointment to see Anthony."

"Don't worry about that press release. It was expected. And we've caught a break. Frank just texted that Martin Monaghan dropped off print-outs of the analysis this morning."

"The analysis? We have it? Please tell me it just needs writing up."

"Not quite." Amina took a sip of her coffee. "We have to source the data and verify the analysis."

"Okay, great. Maybe Anthony can trace the source?"

"None of this is happening tomorrow."

"But it feels like we have to have the piece ready tomorrow."

"Yeah. Frank screwed us, releasing that teaser. But there's a way." She put her cup down beside her. "Monaghan apparently pressed Frank to centre the story on his termination. All about him and the conspiracy to fire him, instead of what Wellington Payday Loans is doing to its customers."

Tomoko said with ire, "One of us should have been there."

"Yes." She raised an eyebrow. "And, of course, Frank loves that angle. It's part of the larger story, but it's not the story. Nevertheless, we can use it to our advantage. We can write a preliminary piece about Monaghan's termination for plagiarism. Just something Frank can publish that will keep him at bay while we prepare our real article. We quote Monaghan saying his termination appears to be the result of meddling by the board and its associates, one of whom has a relationship with the Wellingtons, but be clear we have no evidence for it at this time. We end by saying *The Spanner* is working on verifying not only that claim, but the data he says proves fraud."

"Okay." Tomoko leaned in.

"For now, we need a comment from Wellington's lawyer. Monaghan's interview. Comment from the board members, and that one, Agape. The chair. See if we can get the transcripts. Can we get Parisa on record? We need to know what she has to say about the tribunal. We need her to talk about her work on the data, especially her account of taking out loans herself and the threat she received. More, later."

"I don't know if she'll talk now that she feels safe," Tomoko said. "Safety is all she wanted from sharing the story. I mean, I don't think she's safe, but she does."

"But were Parisa or Monaghan ever in physical danger? The termination was a big move. They've been intimidated, but the government is not going to sweep an assault or murder under the rug for that family. The Wellingtons know that."

Tomoko was not so sure. It was no secret that governments cover up assaults and murder when it suits them, and the Wellingtons might expect it. Amina knew it. She was not making any sense.

Her skepticism obviously registered. Amina said, "I get it, but the government's first impulse would be to control the story and any public outcry in order to shore up trust in the financial sector. It's in their self-interest. My call is that they'll reach out to Monaghan and Parisa. The plan would be a consultation with OSFI, then everything gets swept under an ineffectual investigation, followed by recommendations."

"And the Wellingtons?"

"The virus gets cleared and explained away as a malicious attack. Customers are compensated. At worst, the government proves that the Wellingtons knew the virus was in their system and did not act immediately to remove it, all amounting to a hefty, but meaningless, fine. The Wellingtons don't need to go down for this if they play it right."

"But this assumes that the Wellingtons are willing to act rationally."

"Fair point."

"So, what do we need to do now?" Tomoko asked impatiently.

"Do you still think Parisa is hiding something?"

"Something's going on that I can't figure out."

A server came by and cleared Amina's cup and they stopped talking for a moment. Tomoko looked out at the traffic going by. Her back was up. This whole thing was heading somewhere she did not like, out of her control, but she did not know what to do about it.

"We need to interview Parisa no matter what, but let's push on what she might be hiding. I think with your prior relationship, though, I should be the one to talk to her."

There it was. Tomoko was not expecting Amina to take the interview from her and she hit back. "My prior relationship means I have an in. I've been talking to her all this time. I've got her backstory. I know where to press her to reveal what she's hiding."

Amina considered her silently, but there was an air of judgment about it. Finally, she said, "Tell me how you'll get her to talk if she's feeling safe, as you say."

"She is not safe and I'll tell her. Then she'll talk."

Amina looked at her quizzically, then said, "That's just as good as threatening her. There will be moments like this when the pressure of a story blurs ethical lines. When that happens, I try to clarify my intention. It helps me make the best decision."

"Clarify my intention?"

"It's an Islam thing. Ask yourself what you really want. If you don't like the answer, then try another direction. Mainly, the idea is not to become someone you hate to get a story."

The sermon was unwelcome. "It's your assumption that the government is going to be able to control the Wellingtons. Not mine. She's not safe."

"An assumption backed up by experience, but it's a fair point."

Fair. It was the second time Amina had used the word to concede, but now Tomoko understood that she was only conceding a battle, not the war, and she came right back at her. "It's not unethical for me to tell her that we do not know if she is safe or not, and talking to us might help."

Amina shook her head. "You twisted that nicely, and it works for now, but think about what I said about intentions and maybe go back and review your notes on journalistic ethics from college."

"My intention is that I want the story," she snapped.

"Nothing else?"

She finally got what Amina meant and unashamedly laid the pieces out in front of her. "Yeah, okay. Parisa came on the scene and I lost my boyfriend, but"—she pointed at Amina—"I got the story."

"Then you've got to watch yourself."

"In my family, the cause comes first. Sometimes people get burned."

A cold clarity came into Amina's eyes. "If that's what you want to build your career on as a journalist, it's on your head. But I'm no longer on this story with you."

"I—"

"Yes?"

She did not get the problem, and would not lie, so answered, "Fair," not openly disagreeing, and hoping it was enough to keep Amina with her. Parisa was at risk as far as she was concerned and if that helped her to get Parisa to talk, then fine. Amina did not need to know how she got it.

Amina held up her hands in mock submission. "Parisa approached you to tell this story. It's yours. But you invited me in as a senior journalist. Please keep in mind what I said."

"You'll stay on the story with me?"

"For now." She sighed, then said, "I hope whatever you get from her will shed more light on Monaghan. We're not going to write a martyr puff piece on the man, not even to put Frank off. Do you know who his brother is? Wake Financial. And he's associated with some shady religious group. I remember there was talk once about a man who tried to leave and spill its secrets, then he disappeared."

But she barely heard Amina. Tomoko's mind was racing, figuring out how to get Parisa into a position where she would have to talk. She would let Parisa know that she might be in danger and that Cyrus's place was exposed now that Parisa had turned her phone on while there. But Tomoko needed a place to take her, a place without distractions, so she could get what she needed.

The commie camp up north might do it.

Long before Tomoko had been born, her parents and other communist friends had pooled their money to buy land and build off-the-grid cottages on a small lake. The families went up every holiday; the kids helping in the communal garden or keeping the place up, but mainly playing in the lake or out in the snow all day. Sarah and Izzy were living there year round now and could get her family's place ready for them.

She could interview Parisa on the five hour drive north or at the cottage, whatever it took.

"Tomoko?"

"Yes?" She returned her attention to Amina and grasped at the few words she remembered. "I heard you. We can't make Monaghan out to be a martyr."

"First, we write up something we can dangle in front of Frank to publish in a week or so. That buys us time to finish our big story our way."

"What about Monaghan?"

"He's talking."

"When do we meet him?"

She gave Tomoko a jaded look. "Frank already interviewed him."

"Is that typical?"

"Typical of Frank. Don't worry. I'll make sure we can stand behind our work."

Tomoko got her first taste of what went on in the office. She was given her assignments and produced her analysis and sent it in. That was it. If Frank James regularly interfered with the journalists' work, why the hell did they stay on? The realization made her consider Amina in a different light, one she did not like.

"When do you think you can get the interview?"

What could she say? Not until I drive Parisa north and force it out of her? She settled on the fewest words. "Tomorrow."

"We'll get a draft done now." She pulled out her laptop.

While Tomoko went in to get them more coffee, Amina sent off emails to the Wellingtons' lawyer, the board, and Agape for comment and got Frank on the phone for what he had from Monaghan.

Taking the coffee from her, Amina said, "Frank sent over his notes and a demand to send him today's draft. We'll write the draft assuming Parisa won't talk and with gaps for the comments we'll get in the next few days. We'll change it if you get anything from her."

Tomoko walked home after they emailed their draft to Frank. Amina's facility in composing the piece was humbling. It would have taken her a week just to know what to use from the documents they had and Frank's notes, let alone write those five hundred words. She was pissed at herself for being such an amateur. But it made her even more determined to get that interview from Parisa, and she considered how she could get her north to the camp.

The main question was, who could drive her up there? She had to have a plan in place before Cyrus could offer.

DAY SIX

28

"What's wrong?" Bea asked.

Nick stared at the message from Agape on his screen.

> A hit is out on Parisa Soltani and Martin Monaghan. The teaser in The Spanner made them less safe. Fort Security's man Stone is taking on the job himself. How is your failsafe coming along?

He darkened his display and turned around to face her. She was sitting with her feet up on the couch, drinking her morning coffee, wrapped in the chunky throw blanket she had picked out.

"Nothing," he said, hoping his tone sounded even. He had been up all night working on the failsafe and getting nowhere. His hands were shaking from exhaustion and he sat on them so she would not see.

"I know you." She came to him, tenderly kissing his cheek, then turned him around and rubbed his shoulders. "I saw you stiffen."

The message had come through from an anonymous account, but it could only be Agape taunting him through Panopticon's system.

The tracking windows were open, showing Parisa's phone and its location.

Bea looked over his shoulder at the displays. "Do you think Parisa knows her phone is being tracked?"

"She thinks she's safe," he said.

"Is she?" Bea asked.

Nick did not know how to protect her.

"Please tell me, my love."

"If I can see her, anyone can see her."

Her hands stilled on his shoulders.

"I got word there is a hit out on her."

Her grip tightened. "You have to do something." She paused, having forgotten herself, loosened her grip, and stepped away from the chair. "Please."

Nick swung around. Bea was frozen, eyes wide, waiting to see what would come. But he only reminded her, enunciating each word. "Do not tell me what to do."

All the same, he understood her outburst. Bea had come to care about Parisa as much as he did. Nick shared everything he knew about her, even got her to follow Parisa on Instagram. But there was no telling him what to do and there could be no breaks in that protocol or she might think she could tell herself what to do.

"I know you worry about her." He stood, taking her hand and leading her to the couch to sit beside her. "I can hire security to follow her."

Bea squeezed his hand in thanks.

But he would not. He was going to put a hit out on Stone. "Her security detail will be with her every step," he lied. "She won't see them, but she'll be safe."

Her hand stiffened in his.

Nick had not meant to threaten Bea, but she heard it that way. Now she would fear invisible watchers, being observed by more than the AirTag and tracking on her phone.

"I have to get back to work." He pushed her long hair behind her ear. "Why don't you go upstairs and lie down? I'm fine."

She stood mechanically, as if he were going to hit her when she was not looking. He had never hit her. There was no need.

"Yes, I'll go rest now." She shut the door behind her, careful not to make any noise.

The computer pinged. Nick returned to the display. The Wellingtons were speaking to the press. He clicked through the link and a video window opened up.

Wellington stood to the side, sleeves rolled up again.

Did anyone fall for that?

The lawyer was speaking.

The private investigation has revealed that erroneous charges have been made and were collected against their clients, but at no fault of Wellington Payday Loans. These erroneous charges were the result of a virus introduced into their system. This virus was so expertly and nefariously designed that their own system checks did not detect it. After the virus had been working long enough to produce incriminating data, the criminals who designed and implemented it released the data to *The Spanner*.

While the Wellingtons appreciate the role of whistle-blower journalism as essential to a thriving and free nation, they would have preferred if the journal's editor and the two journalists reporting on the story had followed basic practices and reached out to us for comment. Perhaps the virus could have been addressed sooner and more effectively and they might have been the first with whom we shared the news we are in a position to report today. Having met with the appropriate government agencies, we can now say publicly that this is a case of cyber extortion.

Wellington Payday Loans were threatened in May of last year that if they did not pay twenty million dollars, their company would be destroyed. Mr. Wellington is a man of great character, a man representing the best of old Canada. He would not be moved by threats and refused. The virus is the threat made good.

The Wellington family is presently addressing the attack to its system as well as undertaking a full review. They are most concerned about branch management who did not report these charges up the chain of command when there were customer complaints. Forensic accountants are determining which of their valued clients were affected. Wellington Payday Loans will be reaching out to these clients when the investigation has reached a thorough conclusion.

We hope the public appreciates Mr. Wellington's strength in the face of these threats. Cyber-extortionists put at risk not only our hospitals, airports, and our trusted financial institutions but also the average person. Everyone has heard the horror stories. Some of you have lived them. We must not give in. Our institutions must lead with courage in the face of these attacks. If they do not, how can they expect you, at home, to brave yours? Wellington Payday Loans have donned the mantle and declare these criminals cannot win in the face of Canadian goodness and Canadian grit.

Nick slammed his fist on the desk, then punched the video feed shut, nearly breaking his keyboard with the force. None of it mattered. The virus was probably already out or would be soon. Those fuckers were going to come out on top. The government would find a way to make it go away, citing the need to maintain trust in all lending institutions. Management who had only been following orders would be fired, maybe even face criminal charges, paraded in front of governmental hearings, their lives ruined. Money would be returned and the Wellington Payday Loans would come out of this better than when they came in.

He saw himself standing over his mother's grave, admitting he had failed her. Nick bent over, moaning, rocking back and forth, willing himself to feel his mother's arms around him. Her touch came to him, a memory strong enough to carry him through, and he heard her whisper in his ear, "Get them for me."

The touch awakened a realization. There was no hit out on Parisa and Monaghan. There was no need. He knew the tactic well enough. Just as he had Bea so completely under his control that she had become her own security detail, the Wellingtons had no need to kill them. Parisa and Monaghan would retreat from the field willingly. So why would Agape send him a message saying otherwise?

That realization led to another, and his shame only deepened. In the tension of coding the failsafe, he had not thought to do even the most basic research on Agape. Nick got back onto his computer, searching Agape's name alongside the Wellingtons. There it was. Agape and Wellington standing next to each other, smiling at fundraisers. One social rag called them "old friends." Agape was setting him up and Panopticon was watching everything he did.

There were no cameras or microphones on this system. If they could see or hear him, it would only be what they got through the devices in the house and his phone, despite having the highest security loaded into it. He would be followed. That much was to be expected. That was fine.

Nick opened the Faraday box and took out a phone without Wi-Fi, Bluetooth, or a camera. Three packages with pre-paid sims lay beside it and wired headphones. He left his regular phone in the box, and left with the phone in the pocket of his wool overcoat, winding briskly through the desks towards the elevators.

His employees looked up to greet him, but seeing his expression, returned their attention immediately to their work.

"Sir!" Trang caught up with him at the elevators.

Nick spun around. "What the hell do you want?"

"Bea left a message." Trang paused, unsure if she should speak.

"Tell me!"

"She went to Reverend Lee's to help out in the kitchen."

What was she doing going out without asking him?

He spat out at Trang, "I'm going out without my phone. If

anything happens, get Samuel to put the problem in a holding pattern for twenty minutes. Do you think you can do that?"

The elevator opened behind him. It was crushed with office workers. He slid in, people making space for him with muttered sorries. The ride down, stopping at floor after floor, was smothering. At the lobby, he ran through the atrium and pushed against the automatic revolving doors. Nick burst out, sucking in the crisp air as if he had been suffocating. His breath finally slowed and his body calmed as he observed the angular fall light refining the lines of the buildings, the edges of the bodies walking along, even the movement of cars through the intersection, giving each a strange purpose and life to his own.

Nick crossed between the cars to a parkette dominated by an inane blob-like sculpture of concrete and several benches nestled in-between two tall buildings. He popped a new SIM into the phone, plugged in his headphones, and touched a contact.

"Who's this?" a male voice answered.

"Elliot."

"What can I do for you?"

He gave the password, one that changed each time a new request was made. "I've lost my ferret."

"You've come to the right place."

"I've actually lost two of them. One is new, you don't know him. I'm guessing he won't survive, but if you can tell me where the other one is, I'll get her."

"Send me all the information. We'll get right on it."

The line went dead.

Nick texted Bea and Agape's names. They already had on file the tracking on Bea's phone and her AirTag identity.

Within moments, he got the text on Bea's location. She was at the church. The question was whether to send a car for her or give her enough rope to hang herself. This is exactly how it happened with his other women; he would become too comfortable, let his guard slip for just a moment, and they would find a way out. This was the first time he had used deepfake porn as a threat, though. He told himself it had to be an innocent mistake. Bea only did not want to disturb him when he was so deep in the work. She did tell Trang, after all.

Nick sat on one of the cold benches without looking, glancing off a high protrusion meant to keep people from sleeping on them, and winced. He cursed the city for denying people on the street a place to sleep. But the pain softened his anger toward Bea. She only cared about what mattered to him, too, the forgotten, those taken advantage of by the rich. He would leave her to feed the hungry and decide what repercussions there would be once he had handled Agape.

Another text came through.

> First request is on hold for oversight review.

Nick looked away from his phone, furious again. Young professionals sat on benches for coffee, scrolling their phones. Secretaries clustered together in their running shoes, chatting. An unwashed man with a long filthy beard, a blanket drawn over his shoulders, wandered past the lifeless concrete sculpture, muttering. Most shrank from him. Nick could text back their locations and descriptions and have any of them killed.

"Oversight." Why did he keep this firm on retainer if they would not do what he said? If they would not go after Agape, he could only focus on taking down the Wellingtons another way. He got up off the bench and walked away from the office.

29

Turner, that twig of a lawyer, looked even more ridiculous perched on the wing-back chair. How could he ever stand up to her father?

She, her father, and Brandt clustered on the couch, her father glowering, but Cassandra's mother remained standing, stiff backed.

Francois walked into the room as if they had gathered to discuss the organization of a fundraiser and laid a tray with tea and bite-sized pastries on the coffee table.

Her mother did not make a move to serve it, instead she cast her eye disdainfully on the tray and moved to the other side of the room. It was on Cassandra. She knew how her father took it, but Brandt shook his head at her. Turner waved off the milk and sugar as he waited for Francois to leave before speaking.

"The good news is that the government is willing to work with you as long as the clients' trust can be restored with a full return of funds."

Her father stood abruptly, his tea cup clattering into its saucer. "What could be the bad news? These are matters to be negotiated, later, after the clients bring a class action suit."

"Typically, yes. But you can see how that would work against re-establishing trust with your client base as well as trust within the government."

"Remember Tylenol, father."

But he only glared at her, then turned his ire back on Turner. "First, you make us remove the virus. Then you tell us we cannot kill Monaghan even after he trespassed on our private home and threatened my family. My God, we cannot even report him to the police. Now this!"

Cassandra looked toward the hallway leading to the kitchen, wondering if Francois had heard him say it, or the cook. They were loyal, but who would be loyal enough to cover up a conspiracy to murder? She looked at Turner desperately, begging him to control her father.

Turner put his hands out, speaking loudly enough for anyone nearby to hear. "You should take care with such inflammatory language. While we understand that you are merely expressing the distress you feel at Wellington Payday Loans being so unfairly attacked, others may mistake it for literal intent."

"Literal intent?" Wellington charged him. Turner thrust himself as far back as he could in the chair without toppling over. "Of course it's literal intent! Bring me their heads!"

Brandt got up and put a hand on his father-in-law. Wellington threw his arm off, but it was enough. Turner slipped out of the chair and backed into the foyer. "If you continue to use this language, Mr. Wellington, the firm of Allen and Park will withdraw their relationship with your family and Wellington Payday Loans."

Finally, her mother spoke up. "Leave then. Tell Vincent we will only work with him."

Turner gaped, turned on his heel and left without a word.

Her mother said firmly. "We got enough from him. Our press conference worked. The government has made their first offer to us. That, obviously, can be negotiated, so stop blustering. You scared the poor man off."

Cassandra put down her teacup and stood, moving quietly to the adjoining dining room as if her parents had not just thrown their lawyer out of the house for refusing to go along with killing two people, one a young mother. Through the arched doorway, she slid up against the wall, out of view, and pressed her back against its smooth surface, focusing on the feel of something solid, as if her world were not crumbling around her.

Eyes closed, she became the pink-haired girl again, screaming at her parents, tearing at anyone and anything to have the upside down world around her turned right side up. But there was no right side up. If there was one thing she learned over the years, there was only this world that made no sense, and she was born to it. Brandt's comment when she had asked him what happened to them came back to her like a slap. "Nothing. We were always this way, only putting it off."

The lives of the children, as they had known them, were over. She saw it all slipping out of her hands and she watched it go, hearing herself whisper, "You do not have to be this way," and clapped her hand over her mouth to keep her from saying aloud, "You can turn them in. You can tell the truth."

The conversation in the other room carried on. She opened her eyes. Francois was standing in the opposite doorway, watching her. He put his finger to his mouth to encourage her silence, then disappeared. She hurried across the dining room after him and into the serving alcove.

"Watch yourself," he scolded.

"You've seen everything and done nothing. You cleaned up after Patricia. She died. What did you do?"

"It is on me, is it?" Francois looked down at her, as if she were the servant and he the master, and left her standing alone.

Cassandra snuck back into the dining room, remaining just out of view. She pulled out her phone, opened the voice note app and tapped on the record button.

"Leave her to me," Brandt said.

Her mother's voice cut in. "She's always been so emotional. We were never able to count on her like we could Patricia."

She waited for Brandt to say something in her defence. Instead, she only heard her father grumble in agreement, then say, "Just keep it from her."

"Of course," Brandt said soothingly.

The three were silent for a moment. Cassandra looked at the phone screen, the recording clicking away at the seconds and nothing of use to share with the authorities other than her parents' hatred of her and her husband's collusion.

"So we are in agreement?" Brandt asked.

"Why are you even asking this question!" Her father bellowed.

"I will call Stone and tell him to solve the problem of Monaghan and Soltani."

"Her son?" her mother asked.

"For God's sake," her father complained. "Have you gone soft on me?"

"Darling," she said, as if she had swallowed something luscious. "And the boy."

Cassandra held the phone out for only a moment longer, afraid of missing something, but more afraid of getting caught. She tapped the recording closed. Moving quietly into the kitchen, she put the phone in her back pocket and walked past the cook, who was rattling a pan on the stove.

The scent of sautéed onions and garlic in butter hit and bile came up in the back of her throat. She rushed through the kitchen back door to the patio and retched. One hand on the cold iron of the patio furniture, her knees grinding into the stones, her stomach spasmed again and again, but nothing came up but tea and congealed milk. Her stomach still spasming, she wiped her mouth on the back of her hand. The small woods beckoned her to hide among the trees as they did when she was young, but the sunlight cut through the evergreens, sending shards of light to the needle-covered earth, making it seem as if wolves and witches lay in wait. There was nothing left for her here.

A hand touched her shoulder and she jerked, yelping.

"You all right?" Brandt asked, holding out a hand to help her stand.

"I don't know what happened. It felt so claustrophobic in there. I came out for some air, then suddenly I felt nauseated." She looked up at him, took his hand, and stood. "Maybe the milk had turned?"

He shrugged.

"I feel better now." She held onto him, unsteady and unsure how to lie to him. "Did you all sort out what needs doing?"

"Yes, you don't need to worry about it."

"Thanks, Brandt. It's too much for me." She smiled weakly. "I wasn't made for this. I'll leave it to you and my parents."

"Good girl," he said and pulled her in for a quick hug.

"Can we go now, or is there business left to be done?"

"Some business. Some calls." He looked down at her tenderly.

"Do me a favour, then? Grab my purse? I'll go around the front from here and head home."

He disappeared inside, returning in a moment. "You got your phone?"

"Phone?" She tried to read his face, fearing he knew she had recorded them.

"It feels a bit light." He held up her small handbag, swinging it back and forth on his finger.

"Oh!" Cassandra tapped her back pocket. "Got it."

He bent down and kissed her on the cheek, lingering just a moment too long, and whispered, "Off now, you. I'll find my own way home."

She turned, eyes toward the woods, then hurried around the house to the front and into her car. The gate was taking forever and she had to back up and towards it again to get within the sensor's range. Finally, it rumbled open. She put her foot down, nearly clipping the edge of it as she roared into the street. Cassandra raced out of the neighbourhood and onto Leslie Street. The entrance to Wilket's Creek Park opened up to her right and she tore into it. Pedestrians stared as she went past. A dog walker with a crew of dogs yelled at her to slow down, but she did not stop until she was at the far end of the furthest parking lot.

Out of her car, she headed down the asphalt trail toward the West Don River. She stopped near a gap in the split-rail fence and followed a narrow path down to the river, pushing aside clumps of dying purple aster and browning yellow-disked tansy until she was at the gravel bank. The water was low and she continued on the stony river bed until she was at the water's edge, the river nothing more than a wash in some spots and pulled out her phone.

Cassandra opened the recording, saved it, naming it "listen now," sent it off via a text to Agape and waited. The wind had picked up and willow leaves rustled as they fell along the far bank. Her eye followed the flickering long brown leaves down to the water and a dead salmon caught in the rocks.

The phone vibrated. She rushed to answer it.

"Come to me," Agape said.

"You heard what they are going to do?"

"No one will touch that child."

"And her, the mother?"

"Not her. Not Monaghan."

"What about me? They have to know."

"Come to me. Now."

She clicked her phone off and ran back up the hill to the path, into her car and out of the lot, accelerating so quickly that her tires spun out for a moment. As she turned out of the park towards Agape's home, she looked behind her. A black car like an airport sedan was one back and over. Cassandra craned to get a better look, but the driver was out of view. The light turned. She faced forward, slapping her hand on the wheel, yelling at the car ahead. "Go!"

Cassandra made a right onto Eglinton instead of the left to Agape's, found an opening, and slipped ahead of the SUV on her left, hit the accelerator and popped ahead of a sedan on her right, then drove full on. The light ahead was hers, the pedestrian warning flashing 3, 2, 1, and she was through the yellow, clear. The cars behind her were caught at the red light. She finally slowed, checking behind her, turned south at the next intersection, then east to Agape.

30

———————

Tomoko banged on her neighbour's door. The listing Victorian mansion was divided into off-cut apartments; even closed, the door had a gap big enough for the scent of skunk to waft out with a mish-mash of traditional music set to dance beats.

Larry opened it and, seeing her, extended his arms. "Tomoko!"

She let him hug her, briefly. Tomoko could deal with white-dreads-man and hippie-universe-peace talk if he were sober enough to drive. "I need a ride."

"As always, my lady!"

"Do me a favour. Take the car out to the street behind us. I'll meet you there."

"This sounds like a clandestine mission."

Tomoko wished like hell she had learned how to drive. "Larry, are you sober enough for this?"

"If I were sober, I couldn't drive." He went back in the house and got his things.

"Meet you around the corner!" Tomoko ran back upstairs to her apartment and got what she needed, including a small digital tape recorder her parents had bought her when she first graduated from journalism school.

She watched Larry pull the beat-up Taurus wagon out of the rear parking lot, waiting until he got to the street out front. Then she climbed out the window and down the fire escape, slid through a gap in the fence, and ran through the small garden of the house behind them to the street where Larry was waiting for her, door open, Peruvian flutes set to trance beats shaking the car walls.

By the time they got to Cyrus's house, the Peruvian Flute Trance was growing on her. Larry had been babbling about some supplement he was taking to open his third eye. Thankfully, she had heard very little of it over the beats, but he was a solid driver, as he said.

"I'll be right back," she said, but she took her time walking up to Cyrus's house, not sure what she wanted to say to him or Parisa. Putting him out of his misery would be the right thing to do. No doubt he would be tied up in knots, not wanting to upset her while she was on her first story and not wanting to keep Parisa on a string. Cyrus was so obvious. Tomoko had meant it as mocking, to shore herself up for having to see the two of them together, but it only made her feel worse. She wanted to go back to the car and see if Larry had any of that weed on him. Instead, she pressed the doorbell rather than use her key. That would tell him all he needed to know.

He answered the door. "Tomoko. Why did you use the bell?" Cyrus gave a concerned glance at the car pounding music loud enough to be heard by all his neighbours. Mrs. Aquino must be peeking out the window and wondering when to call the police.

She ignored the look, asking, "Is she here?"

It took him only a moment to understand why she had not used her key. "No. She's out with Arash. They took my car." He held out his hand.

She took it, and he shut the door behind them, pulling her into his arms. Tomoko lay her head on his shoulder and to her surprise she shed some tears, making a mess of his shirt.

"I am sorry," he said.

"Romantic love is a capitalist manipulation," she joked, sniffing.

He held her more tightly. "We had perfect days, days I will never forget."

"How you say things!" She pulled back, gazing into his face one last time, drinking in his brown eyes shining with old feeling. His lashes made her dissolve like a teenage girl, and she ventured, "One last go?"

Cyrus bent down and kissed her lips lightly. "Just a kiss for farewell and in gratitude."

"Can we be friends?" she asked, wondering if she could do it and knowing she could not.

"My heart may not be able to manage it, but I'm willing to try."

"Let's see, then."

She stood apart from him. "I came about her."

"For the story."

"I need to interview her." Tomoko said carefully, imagining Amina next to her, listening. "We do not know if she is safe or not. Maybe the government can help her. But we agreed I should interview her and offer her a safe place out of town. You know, the commie camp."

"You're sure she'll be safe there?"

The intensity of the question made her stomach sour, but she managed to reply evenly, "Perfectly safe."

"What do you need?"

"A ride to my parents. When will she be back?"

"Soon. Wait for her."

"Okay, let me just tell Larry he can go."

Tomoko went out to the car, jealousy and grief fighting with her desire for the story, and welcomed the pounding bass against her body, wanting to open all the doors to Larry's wagon, releasing the sound onto the street, then drag Larry into the road so they could jump around together, arms in the air, and shake open their third eyes. Instead, she yelled over the music, "I'm good. Thanks for bringing me."

Larry nodded, head to the beat. "Glad to be of service, my lady!"

Now, she had to wait awkwardly with Cyrus for Parisa to return so she could tell her that her life was in danger, then isolate her into getting the story they needed. Amina would not have put it that way, but that was exactly what she was doing. She did not feel bad about it, even though she knew Amina would prefer if she did.

Tomoko was barely to the front door when Cyrus's car pulled up behind her.

Parisa got out, looking at her expectantly as she went to open the back door for Arash. He was holding a Happy Meal and ran up to her, beaming. "Tomoko!"

With one hand on Arash's shoulder, she said, "Good to see you, little buddy!"

He babbled on about whatever toy he had got with his Happy Meal and she pretended to pay attention, amazed that simply giving a kid a hamburger and fries on one occasion could inspire such devotion. All the while, she kept an eye on Parisa, who now stood behind her son, waiting.

Tomoko still did not understand Cyrus's attraction to her. She was wearing dumpy jeans, crap running shoes, and a shapeless green down vest that was far too long for her short body. She compared it to her own outfit of curated used clothing, a skimming denim shirt tucked into high-waisted black and tan plaid slacks under a long fitted suede coat straight out of the seventies. How was Cyrus ever going to make this work?

Parisa spoke over her son. "Is there some news about the story?"

"Arash, come on in," Cyrus called out.

The boy went to him, but did not like it.

Tomoko gave him a look of silent thanks.

"Yeah." Tomoko decided not to equivocate. "Despite the story coming out, you're not safe."

Parisa nodded, then walked to the edge of the driveway, making a call.

It was too quick for a conversation, but she had said something. Maybe she left a message?

Parisa returned, betrayal plain on her face. "I'm not safe. Meaning what?"

"I'll take you and Arash to a place up north until we know what to do."

She went back to the edge of the driveway and bent over, hands on her knees. Parisa straightened, then returned, walking past Tomoko without a word into the house and shut the door behind her.

The phone call deepened Tomoko's suspicions and she was now determined to get what she needed from Parisa, whatever it took. Leaning against the car, Tomoko texted her parents to say they were coming, and wondered how she and Parisa were going to get north.

Her phone pinged.

> How's it going with Soltani?

Frustrated by the intrusion, she replied to Amina with one word.

> Soon

But ten minutes passed, and Parisa had not come out. Cyrus knew she was standing out there alone in the cold and it pissed her off he did not come out in all that time, even to bring her some of his oh-so-special tea.

The door finally opened. Parisa was alone, carrying a tote.

"Where's Arash?"

"Cyrus is taking him to his mother. The two of them will stay with her until I'm safe."

Tomoko held up a finger and walked past her toward the house, but Cyrus was already coming out with Arash, carrying a backpack, waving the car keys. "To your parents."

"Just the subway." She tried to say it nicely, but he became disconcerted and glanced worryingly at Parisa.

She went to the car, getting in the front. There was no talk on the drive, except from Arash, who complained that his mother was leaving him. Once there, Tomoko guessed Cyrus was grateful for Arash's tears, as comforting the boy meant he did not have to decide which woman he should kiss goodbye.

Tomoko held out her hand for Parisa's phone. She gave it to her unwillingly and watched as Tomoko removed the SIM card and turned everything off before Parisa could object.

They stood in the crowded subway car, swaying as they held onto the poles, taking care not to touch each other as riders pushed past them in and out of the car. Cyrus hung in the air between them. It felt far from that first day when they sat together heading to Parisa's apartment, holding hands, comrades in what would come. Tomoko did not think they needed to talk. She traded her boyfriend for a story. As far as Parisa should be concerned, she got Cyrus and Tomoko was helping her escape danger.

Her mother was waiting in the doorway, sitting on her walker, eyebrow cocked, watching them as they came up the steps. She led them in, pushing her walker ahead of her. In the kitchen, she said to Parisa, "Have a seat. Isamu will take care of you."

He was already preparing the tea, and salted plums were on the table. His look was not as skeptical as her mother's, but he was wary as he welcomed Parisa to sit.

"You," Amale said, pointing at Tomoko. "Out back."

She followed her mother through the mudroom and down the ramp into their small backyard.

"Look," Tomoko began, already feeling defensive. "I need to put her up in the camp so she'll talk."

"Of course you use the cottage. It's yours, too," her mother touched her arm. "And anything for the story." But then she turned and stared into the distance, obviously holding back, only to give up a moment later, and faced Tomoko, pointing toward the house. "If that woman had an ounce of courage, she would speak here and now and not need to be bundled off."

"She has a child."

"We had you, and that never stopped us."

Her mother's righteousness fed her own, and she took an ugly pleasure in it, saying, "So she's a coward." But the spectre of Amina's threat to quit the story spoiled it, forcing her to say something Amina would accept. "Okay, that's not fair. She was in prison. In Iran. We don't know why she's making these choices."

"I'm worried about you."

"Oh, mom." There it was. How could she be so dense? She put her arm around her. "You who just said you were willing to sacrifice your young daughter for the cause are not willing to sacrifice your adult daughter?"

"We've gotten used to you over the years, that's all." She pushed her off, gesturing toward the brick row house behind them. "There's Abdi. Ask him if he'll take you."

Abdi was standing in a hoodie and his Somali ma'awiis, unlaced boots on his feet, examining his tulip bed. He was usually out in the yard, working on the small pond, changing out the plantings, and watching the frogs. But it was fall and he probably had a lot of land-scaping gigs lined up. "Isn't he working?"

"He'll take you. I would prefer it if you went with him."

"Okay." She faced her mother. "If Parisa talks on the way up, I can leave her at the camp or turn around and bring her back to the city."

"Back to the city?"

"To talk to the government."

"The government? Do you trust them with this?"

"Me? I'll put Parisa in contact with Amina. It's her idea. She can handle it."

"It'll be cold up there. Parisa'll need to know how to feed the fire. And take warm coats from the hall closet."

"Izzy and Sarah are there. They can help."

"Abdi!" Amale yelled.

Abdi looked up and waved, a restaurant-sized container of cayenne pepper in his hand, and came to meet them at the gap in the chain-link fence.

"Abdi, can your mother spare you? I need you to bring my daughter and her friend up to the camp."

"Sure. I haven't decided on my tulip placement yet. Otherwise, no," he joked. "I have a job tomorrow, but I can get to it if I come back early."

"Thank you," her mother said.

Abdi asked, "Who is the friend?"

"My source. You know the story I'm writing with Amina Warsame?"

"Of course." He beamed. "Lenin would be proud."

"Agh," her mother complained, grasping her arm with comic flourish. "That's it. Abdi will bore the life out of her with his doctrinaire crap on the ride up and she'll tell you anything after the first hour. You can turn right back around."

Tomoko smiled. "Ready to torture my source for information?"

"I'll just change and get the keys."

She followed her mother inside. Parisa was standing in the kitchen doorway, waiting for her, incensed. Tomoko gave her father a questioning glance.

He winced. "You two. Your voices carry."

"Take me to this camp if it will keep me safe for my son's sake," Parisa said. But I'm not telling you shit."

31

———————

Martin rolled over on his brother's couch, burying himself in throw blankets and the warm scent of leather. After dropping off the analysis with Frank James yesterday, he had gone straight to Conor and had taken another shower, this one to beat the pain of the last two days out of him. Six shower heads pummelled his body as he chanted, "Fuck Oliver. Fuck Bernard. Fuck the Wellingtons." But the pain was stuck in deep and he almost wished Stone would find him and end it. Hands against the tile, leaning in, the water streamed down his head and into his mouth. He let it in, willing himself to breathe it down, but could not and spit it out. Martin got out, dressed again, ignored the guest room for the couch and had not moved since except to eat.

The Spanner could tell the story now. Frank insisted on interviewing him, saying Warsame and Abrams were busy on another piece. He seemed to be pushing the termination angle over the data. But the termination only showed how much the data was a threat. It was not the story and he was afraid Frank would run with it, but he did not see any other options.

"You're awake." Conor peered over the back of the couch at him. "It's dark again and nearly time for dinner."

Martin pulled himself up, rubbing his head. "I need coffee." He got up and went around the massive island. "Where is that weird coffee thing?"

Conor waved him off, and pulled out a small bag of beans, the grinder, and the cylinder press, placing them on the island. "Get the water on the boil."

While Martin filled the kettle, he debated bringing up the board members Conor had acknowledged knowing. He had already gone over it with him, once on the phone yesterday, then again this morning. Both times it felt like Conor was holding something back. Martin wanted to push him, not just because something was there, but because the thought of his brother being among those who had betrayed him was too much.

Leaning against the counter behind him, Martin was grateful for the burr of the coffee grinder that kept him from speaking. He focused on the earthy scent of the freshly ground coffee, the rumbling of the water in the kettle, the warmth of the heated floors against his bare feet and told himself, *You can trust him.* He repeated it until it felt true enough that he was able to stand beside his brother at the island.

Conor bumped him playfully, then said, "Water."

His brother poured the water into the cylinder, then pressed the coffee into a cup. Conor handed it to him. Martin looked over the stupid handleless cup at him, his eyes pricking with tears.

Conor said, "Now. Food."

"You're going to cook? You don't want to call Oonagh from the coach house?"

"Who cooked when we were kids?"

"So a bologna and frosted flakes sandwich?"

Conor went to the fridge, retrieving a carton of eggs and a box of spinach. He got out the utensils, salt, and pepper from under the counter. Martin shook his head. Not even utensils could be out and ruin the modern lines of the house. Then Conor brought out an iron skillet to heat on the stove.

"You going to ruin one of Oonagh's pans?"

"I forgot the butter." He pointed to the fridge.

Martin handed it over. Soon it was sizzling in the pan and its creamy scent sent him looking for a loaf of bread.

"Freezer."

Conor broke six eggs into the pan, cut the yolks with the spatula, tossed the spinach on top and ground fresh black pepper.

Frozen loaf in hand, Martin asked, "Do you even have a toaster?"

"It's somewhere."

He gave up on the bread and got out the plates and forks. "Call Oonagh in. I want her soda bread fried in bacon fat."

The two leaned their backs against the island, plates in hand, and ate the scrambled eggs and spinach, shoulder to shoulder.

Dinner finished, plates set aside, Martin sipped the last of his coffee, now cold.

"I have something to show you." Conor smiled softly.

He led him out of the open living room and kitchen to his office. The space was like the rest of the house, modern and uncomfortable. Huge windows and minimalist furniture. Except for the pop of the bright red leather chair, everything was black, from the bookshelves to the lacquered desk. The office was dark, except for a pinpoint desk lamp. The landscape lighting outside sent shadows against the window coverings.

A single sheet of paper was positioned under the beam of the lamp.

"Sit down."

Martin shrugged nervously and sat in the red chair. He pulled the paper towards him. It was some kind of bank statement. The number was incredible, not something he could imagine beyond words. Although he should have expected his brother had this kind of money, it never entered his mind that he would have forty million dollars in cash in an account somewhere. "Why are you showing me this?"

"The number at the top. That's you."

"I don't understand." His chest tightened.

"Yesterday, I opened two numbered accounts. One for me, that goes to you on my death. This numbered account for you. No one can trace it. You can disappear. You can live well the rest of your life, wherever you want, however you want."

Martin pulled his hand back from the paper as if it were electrically charged. Fear drove the words out of his mouth before he could stop them. "Is this a bribe?"

"A bribe? What are you talking about? This is for you."

"For what?" Martin stood, hands on the table, leaning across it. "What do you want from me?"

He cried out, "For you to live!"

Martin came around the desk, grabbing his brother by the arms. "Tell me what you know."

"People are trying to kill you." He shook off his brother's grip and returned to the living room.

Martin came after him. "With *The Spanner* teaser out, I'm safe. What can they do?"

"Kill you!" Conor yelled, turning back to face him. "These people, they're like the mafia. You think they'll stop because of a paragraph in a far-left journal run by a man who deals in conspiracy theories? Are you so lost in your small academic world you think anyone outside, anyone in the business world, thinks your existence matters?"

"The news. Everyone's already picking the story up. Everyone would know it's them," he said, sounding smug but not feeling it.

Conor threw his hands out. "But no one will be able to prove it."

It was true. Fuck. Martin reached for the mantle to steady himself.

Conor saw he finally understood. "Take Oliver. Go somewhere. You can disappear."

"I can't just disappear. If they are what you say, they'll follow."

"I can get you a new identity. A British commonwealth passport would be best. Pick a name."

"I don't want to leave. I'd rather die."

"You won't be alone. Tell Oliver."

"Oliver?" Martin tucked his head back. "He's with them!"

"Impossible," Conor scoffed. "I refuse—"

"You refuse? Stone was at the cafe. I saw them. The two of them laughing."

Conor went around to the couch, tossing the throw blankets aside to sit. "There's some explanation. Stone's trying to get at you through him."

"How? Stone didn't know I'd seen them talking."

"I trust Oliver." He looked up at Martin. "How can you not?"

What could Martin say? He did not even know if he could trust his own brother anymore. He was utterly alone. The silence had gone on too long.

Conor stared at him, wide-eyed. "You don't trust me." His lip began to tremble, his voice cracked with fear like when they were boys, when he had been scared after their father died. Their mother had wailed and screamed for weeks and weeks. They ate because neighbours fed them and kept close to Auntie Zeb. At home, they crept around the house, hands touching the walls, afraid to make a sound and send her to wailing again. He begged, "Don't die, Martin."

The old tremor in his voice drew Martin back. Conor could not be lying, not about this, not about wanting him to be safe. Something else was going on, but the money was not a bribe, a cover up or anything else. Conor wanted him to live. He wanted Oliver to live. If he did know something, and Martin was sure he did, then the fact that he trusted Oliver meant Oliver was not involved. But that also meant Oliver was not safe.

He suddenly saw Stone's visit at the cafe as intimidation and Martin wanted to die all over again from the shame of suspecting him. Good Oliver, who had only ever cared for him, while he railed on about how his work was more important. As if he could not have made time for both and allowed himself to fall in love. He forced himself to admit it was not work that had driven off the men in his life. The thought of love terrified him. Everything he was afraid of he felt right then and he made himself face it. What if Oliver were hurt? What if Oliver died? He let the fear sit in him until he could hear himself say, *You love him.*

"Tell me." He sat next to Conor. "Is Oliver safe?"

"I don't know."

"I have to get him. Can I bring him here?"

"Of course." Conor squeezed his hand. "But I have to take care of something."

"Here?"

"No. A meeting. Colleagues. It can't be avoided." He got up and went to the office, nervously tugging his cream sweater straight over his grey trousers.

It was a self-consciously vague answer, but Martin hoped it was just confidentiality around his work and not to do with any of this. He pulled out his phone and called Oliver. The phone rang over and over, then went to voicemail. "I'm sorry. I need to come and get you. Don't ask me any questions. Just trust me. Call, okay?" He texted.

Call me. It's important. Please.

The cafe was closed for the evening and he felt like the shit he was because he did not know where to find him. The coffee and eggs soured in his gut. Martin went to the kitchen and pried off a slice of the thawing bread and forced pieces down to sop it up.

Conor returned with two file folders in his hand, tapping them nervously against his palm.

Martin probed. "What'd you say this meeting is about?"

"A mess I have to clean up."

There was more to it than that and Conor saw the thought on his face.

"It's not for you to worry about." He left, grabbing his keys from the foyer table.

Martin called after him, eating the last of the bread, "Oliver's not answering."

"Where does he live? I can stop by on my way to the office and tell him you're coming," Conor said, returning.

"I don't know. Somewhere around Church Street."

"How could you not know?"

"He always came to my place after work," he answered defensively.

"Hold on." Conor pulled out his phone, tapping, then held it up. "He's not at home. Out. Do you know the place?"

But the image had gone by the time Conor showed it to him. "How the hell does this thing work?" Conor got the Instagram story to play again. It was not any restaurant he had been to. Just Oliver with two men he did not know, smiling. He felt sick again.

Conor took the phone back. "He was tagged in it about thirty minutes ago. But he's not active at the moment." He tapped a bit more. "There. I've messaged him to call you. Why don't you have Instagram, for Lord's sake?"

"I don't spend my free time looking at images of modern architecture like you do."

"You can follow him."

"Is that how you know so much about Oliver?"

"We follow each other, you fool. Yes."

Martin was dumbfounded. He did feel like a fool, left out of Oliver's life, his brother's life.

"You call me and let me know when you've reached him. Then go get him. I would feel better if you two were here. I'll set the security code when I leave."

"I've got the number, don't worry," Martin said to his back.

The door shut, and the security system engaged.

Martin pulled back the edge of the covering from a window and watched as Conor pulled his car out of the drive. He went back into the office and began opening drawers. Conor got those files from some place. He was going to see what the mess was. He expected the drawers to be locked, but they were open. In Conor's lonely life, who was ever here but Oonagh rushing about in her work coat and sucking her teeth?

He rifled through the papers in the drawers, realizing he would not know how to tell if there was anything incriminating or not. Papers about transfers of money. Accounts. Some numbered, others with names. Then he saw it. A request from someone named 'Marlene Jordan' to invest one million dollars in Wellington Payday Loans. Underneath it was a cancellation of the request. Underneath that was a request to liquidate all her money into a numbered offshore account. Grief surged into furious purpose and turned him right back around. Conor was involved. And if he was telling him to trust Oliver, then Oliver was involved, too.

Martin ran to the foyer, grabbed his jacket and his keys. He could get to Conor's office, interrupt the meeting, and then he would know. They might kill him. But even if they killed him, before he died, he would know what was going on. More, he would know if the only person in this world whose love he could be sure of had betrayed him.

32

―――――

The papers handled, Conor locked his office door behind him. Martin was protected. His own affairs were in order. The Cluster was no longer among the beneficiaries of his wealth. Wake Financial would be dissolved after his death. He had begun the paperwork to establish a trust for Parisa and Arash. Conor had no idea who else's life had been turned upside down by Agape's actions, but he could do something for those within his grasp. If he only knew what Agape was doing, why he was involved with these people, why he would betray the path.

But he trusted the vision. While the other brothers had only slept through the night in the Garden of Gethsemane, one had betrayed him. The betrayer could only be Agape. That meant Vincent and the rest were the sleepers. Maybe they knew, like Vincent, maybe they did not, but they were not directly responsible for what would come, not like Agape, his Judas.

He pulled out of the parking lot and headed to the medical building. The traffic was heavy and he was grateful for it, using the few moments he had left to get his bearings.

At the light, he looked into the window of the car next to him. He could not see the passengers' faces, only the striking pattern of a woman's dress, like a Mondrian in silk, and the driver's hand holding hers. It seemed easy, the way their fingers intertwined, and he imagined the love they shared, an assurance and intimacy denied to him.

Bailey had kidnapped him. Bailey had manipulated him. He said the words aloud that he would never have permitted himself to think before. "Bailey groomed me."

The driver in the car next to him stroked the woman's hand with his thumb and his heart ached. The visions of the Lord had fed him, but he did not understand why it had come without the blessing of love in this world, and he hungered to hold a woman's hand just like that.

The light turned and the road opened up before him. Cars sped around him to take advantage of the momentary break in traffic. But a glance in the rearview mirror showed one car hanging back, maybe four car lengths behind him, too far to see the make or the driver, but it was a dark SUV pacing his speed. Agape had someone following him? For what? He was coming to him. There was no escape. Other cars came up from the light behind and filled the gaps and he drove on.

He stood before the medical building, accepting as the Lord accepted his fate. The door opened easily without its signature crack and scrape and he took it as a sign that his transition to another life was near. He could hear the sound of chairs moving and the men whispering.

Vincent said, "He will be here any moment."

Conor turned into their meeting room. "I am here now."

They all stood to face him, all except Pierre, whose skin looked even worse than the typical effect of the fluorescent light on his pale skin. He had not taken off his wool overcoat and wore a thick scarf wrapped around his neck.

Agape addressed him. "We are now even more concerned about your brother."

"Why don't you tell me about that?"

There was a metal crack outside, the sound of the outer door opening.

"Check that," Agape pointed to Conor.

But he did not move. "Probably the man you had following me."

"Following you?" Vincent glanced worriedly at Agape and ran out into the hallway, yelling, "Who's there?"

It was all Conor could do but accuse them of a performance. But he kept himself under control, like the others, listening in silence for Vincent. Marcus stood behind Pierre's chair, one hand on his shoulder, while Benjamin and Ipe kept their eye on Agape, waiting for his cue. They heard the crack again, then steps.

"There's no one there. It's windy outside." Vincent addressed Conor as he passed him to sit down. "You should have locked it when you came in."

"How was I to know I would be the last one?" He took a seat and crossed his legs, leaning with one arm slung over the back of the chair.

Agape looked at him like he had already had enough, but sat back down and the others followed.

"There's no need to be concerned about Martin," Conor said. "I have him under control."

"Word is that he has disappeared. We are concerned for his safety."

"He's safe, and he's dropped his interest in the Wellingtons."

"It would be wise," Vincent said. "I've had concerning reports from the attorney I asked to represent them when speaking to the press."

Conor stiffened. "What kind of reports?"

"Nothing that you need to know, as long as what you say is true. I can pass that information along. I can send assurances. And the woman and her son? Does your brother know about them?"

"She has gone completely underground. She wants nothing to do with any of it. It was all my brother's work." He sat forward, insisting. "Pass that on."

Agape frowned. "What are your brother's plans?"

"He's going to leave the country for a while. He's fallen in love."

"The one who owns the cafe," Agape said.

Of course, Agape knew about Oliver. Conor said, "The two of them are leaving together."

Vincent audibly sighed, and Ipe reached out to reassure him.

Ipe asked, "What about this piece in *The Spanner*?"

"Martin does not know how they got the data."

"Do you trust him?" Ipe followed up.

"It is his brother," Agape intervened. "He would know if he were lying."

"I'm telling you that Martin did not help them get the data."

Benjamin asked, "How did they get it, then?"

Ipe answered with his own question, "It is better to ask how the woman got it." He turned to Vincent. "What is her name?"

"Parisa Soltani."

Conor wanted to retort, "No, it is better to ask you are covering for them," but held back.

Ipe looked around the room. "How did Soltani get it?"

"We do not yet know," Agape answered.

Benjamin scoffed. "Agape, can you honestly tell me your brother has no idea?"

"Focus!" Agape snapped, losing his composure for the first time in all the years Conor had known him. "You know I keep my distance from him."

Pierre coughed, at first as if to satisfy a tickle in his throat, then it became rolling and wet. He doubled over, coughing into a tissue. Marcus crouched next to him, rubbing his back.

"What's wrong with him?" Conor asked.

They looked at him as if he had crossed a line, but Marcus stood, putting out a hand. "It's a complication of the COVID case he had. He's become susceptible to chest infections. It's under control."

Pierre looked up, smiling wanly. "The cough, it's good. It's clearing. Don't worry about me."

"May I?" Agape looked at the men, eyebrows raised.

Conor steeled himself, believing the attack was coming and not knowing now the moment had arrived if he would fight it or accept what was willed for him. "Lord," he whispered in prayer.

But the men did not attack. They merely indicated one by one that they agreed.

"It is time to tell you about Miss Henson," Benjamin said. "She should not have revealed herself to you. But, as you know, she is in the early stages of dementia. We held back the truth from you. You must trust us."

"Of course, I trust you," Conor lied, hoping his voice carried something of their past companionship.

The men looked at each other again and decided to carry on. Even Pierre raised a weak hand.

"It is more than the extraordinary breaking through," Benjamin explained. "She is The Cluster's emissary from Legion."

Conor stared.

"Please," Agape said, putting a hand out. "Listen."

"I am listening!"

"Legion recognized the Lord and demanded to know if he had come to torture them before the appointed time. You remember the scripture?" Agape signalled to Ipe.

Ipe stood, hands clasped, one hand over the other, creating a mushroom crown, and recited,

When he saw the Lord from far away, he recognized him and ran to him, falling at his feet, crying out, "What have I to do with you, Lord? You are the child of the Womb alone. O Glans-Crowned-White-Flecked Lord, the Lord of Womb and Staff, have you come to torment me before the appointed time?"

The Lord said, "Demon, come out of that man!" Then he demanded, "What is your name?"

"My name is Legion, for we are many."

Benjamin continued, "Since that day, a representative of Legion has always been with those who know the secret of the Mushroom and the Cross, watching for the appointed time, keeping the peace."

"The peace?" Conor's throat was tight.

"An agreement that until the appointed time, they would have their way with humanity. We would work within our sphere of influence and they theirs. When the Anointed One returns, then the battle begins again."

"And the appointed time has come?" Conor asked, wavering, wondering if what the Lord had asked him to accept was to fight these demons and if he misunderstood all of it, and the men, his brothers in The Cluster, were to fight with him.

"No. Her dementia and the present crisis have forced our hand to inform you of it," Agape said.

Conor leaned over, head in hands, praying, *Lord. Guide me. What do you want from me? You placed me in a den of liars. Protect my brother. Protect Parisa. Protect her son. Do what you will with me, but protect the innocents.*

Each man came and put a hand on him. Bile churned in his gut. He broke away, pushing their hands off, and ran to the washroom. But once there, free of them, the sickness passed.

He left the stall and stood in front of the bank of sinks, looking into the cracked mirror. Sparks flew around him, taking the shape of spores exploding into worlds of ever increasing depths. No sooner did he fall into the detail of one, another opened, and another, until there was the blackness of a moonless night. The scent of frankincense and myrrh. The sound of a woman screaming for her son dragged away in chains. Another voice, a sweet voice, the voice of his Lord, said, "Return to them. Assure them you are with them. This is your bearing tonight."

The exquisite darkness dissolved into the sickening blue of the medical office lights. He left to join them again, grasping the doorway, leaning into it. He took strength from his Lord and returned.

All but Pierre stood, waiting. He saw them so clearly. Every one of them was lying to him and everything depended on him lying to them now. He wept easily at the horror of it all and came to them, arms out. "My brothers. My brothers. By the Mushroom and the Cross, I am a bearer of the Lord. I am a servant of this Cluster."

Conor fell to his knees in their embrace.

The crack of the outer door sounded down the hallway.

33

Each revelation was worse than the next. Martin listened to Conor's weak protests, heard the men's control over him, his brother's rising panic, and then his dash to the washroom. Martin ducked out of sight, but could still hear the sickening oath. "I am a bearer of the Lord. I am a servant of this Cluster."

He crept down the hall, painstakingly threw the bolt and opened the door just enough to squeeze through without a sound, but the door betrayed him. He pushed through and ran to his car, got in and sunk down low, watching.

The men left one by one. Conor was in his Polestar and down the street before Agape finally came out with Vincent Allen. The two were speaking closely, then split up, walking in opposite directions. Allen found his car and left. Agape lingered at the door of his Corolla, searching for his keys, then finally got in. Martin gunned his car, pulling up next to Agape, trapping him. Agape ignored him for a moment, but when Martin's car did not move on, he glanced over and a look of resignation came over his face.

Martin took the gun from the glove box, put it into the pocket of his fleece jacket, came around to Agape's door, and opened it. "Get out."

"Monaghan, there is no need for this."

He showed him the gun. "Get into my car."

"As if you would use it."

"I can wring your neck, if that's what you want."

Agape sighed, turned off the car, and got out.

"In my car, now."

He did as he was told and Martin hurried around to the other side before he could escape, but when Martin got in the car, Agape asked in a bored tone, "Tell me what you want."

Martin pointed the gun awkwardly at him with his left hand.

"It has been a long day. If you are planning on killing me, I would like to get on with it."

Martin was not sure what to ask first, wanting more than anything to know if his brother was involved in his termination. What Agape's role was and why they were carrying water for the Wellingtons. Instead, he blurted out, "What the fuck is the mushroom and the cross?"

"That is your question?" Agape raised his eyebrows.

"Fuck you."

"That's not a question."

Martin pulled out, tearing down the street. "Why me?"

"You made your own bed, Martin. Your graduate students have been asking for you to be censured for some time. You made a mistake. An opportunity arose and you were caught in it."

Blood rushed up into his ears and he did not hear anything else Agape said and nearly went through a red light. "How. Why?"

"You did not cite Soltani. How are you confused by this?"

His hands began to shake. He shoved the gun in his pocket and gripped the steering wheel tightly to control them. "No! Why were they complaining? Before this!"

Agape said, "Why don't you pull over? You seem upset."

He wanted to drive straight into a building rather than do as he said. Instead, he turned down Queen, then Leslie, heading for the beach.

"What were the complaints?"

"They felt you took advantage of their successes to make yourself look good." He chuckled. "I think the term *en vogue* is that you 'centre yourself'."

He stopped sharply at a red light, the car jerking forward.

"You have a gun in your pocket. Do you want to be pulled over?"

He could not see any cars coming in his peripheral vision and slammed his foot down on the accelerator, jumping through the light.

Agape sunk into the back of the seat, pressing his hand against the door.

He sped towards Lakeshore Drive, wishing the light to turn green ahead of him. It did. He sped through the four lane road toward the back road to the beach. Then he swerved the car to the other side of the beach road and into the tall grasses, nearly up onto the disused train tracks. Martin got out and ran to the other side, opened the door, and dragged Agape to the ground. Rhythmic sounds came out of a drumming circle in the woods. He grabbed Agape's arm, pulling him up and over the tracks into the scrub woods leading to the beach and threw him down, shoving the gun in his face.

"What the fuck did you people do to my brother?"

Agape finally looked afraid. He tried to scramble back, but Martin stood up and planted a foot squarely on his arm, pinning it and holding the gun on him with both hands.

"Talk!"

"Bailey saw he had potential. He was right. Your brother bears a heavy weight."

"What the fuck does that even mean!"

"It's an old religion, before religion. It is the truth." Agape turned his head toward the sounds of the drums in the woods and suddenly softened. "I did not see my death this way, but perhaps this is the moment?"

Martin pulled the gun back, leaving it swinging in his hand. "Get up." He took a few steps back, giving him room. "Explain yourself."

"Your brother had a choice." Agape sat up, then stood, brushing himself off. "He chose to perform the Ritual and the Ritual chose him."

"Only after Bailey had worked on him year after year."

"From your perspective. From ours, he was refined."

Martin's voice broke. "He chose you and not me."

"Yes, because we have to choose the truth, even over family."

"He chose to support the Wellingtons over me. To let me be terminated over something I did not do, something that even if I had done it—" his voice rose, but Agape cut him off.

"Yes. Yes. As I said, you made your bed. Everyone jumped at the opportunity to rid themselves of you. From your graduate students to your colleagues and the board and their interests."

Martin wanted to think that Agape was lying to him, trying to get under his skin, and he held onto the thought like a drowning man. "Why the Wellingtons? What does that have to do with the truth?"

"Nothing." Agape faced him squarely. "Each of us has a bearing." He corrected himself. "Rather, a role to play. For my role, I keep the Wellingtons and many others under watch. I have failed at times. Important failures. Failures that haunt me. But I will not fail now."

"What?"

"Legion will consume them."

"More of your mushroom cult insanity!"

Agape smiled. "You wait and see. Maybe bring your gun."

Martin could not understand a fucking thing this piece of shit had to say.

"If you have no other questions, then take me back to my car."

"What about Oliver?"

"Your lover? I don't understand."

"What's his role in all this? He works for the Wellingtons?"

Agape trudged toward the car, saying as he left, "He's a bystander."

"What about Stone? Stone was talking to him!" Martin went after him.

"Oliver is a bystander. An innocent bystander. If all goes well, you two will be free to live as you like. If not, escape with him and live as you like."

Martin followed, unlocking the driver's side door, and got in, turning the ignition. Agape knocked on the window, gesturing for him to unlock it. But Martin stepped on the gas, leaving him there, and drove on to find a safe place to park for the night.

It was all too much. He had to bring it to his brother, hear what he had to say, hear his betrayal said out of his own mouth, but not yet. He needed to be alone to think, without the interference of Oliver, Jamal, any of them.

He drove like a drunk down the dark roads, consumed with his loss of his brother, the shame that he had suspected Oliver, and that he had been wronging his graduate students all these years.

DAY SEVEN

34

Bea had not come home last night. 'Elliot' had made the call for the security team to search for her as soon as it was dark. They had the AirTag identification and could track her phone. Both located her at the church, but the team said the doors were locked and the place seemed empty. They tried again in the morning and reported no one had seen her, but they could no longer track her. Nick had watched as the AirTag and phone went dark. One minute, the location pinpointed on the map, the next minute gone. The team knew her haunts, the dog park at Cherry Beach and the encampments on the far side in the scrub woods and were checking hotels, including cash payments under any name, shelters, everything. Nick was twisted up inside with worry for her, refusing to believe she had left him.

Every time they sent him an update, he demanded to know their answer on Agape, but they continued to say the decision had not yet come down. This morning, he finally accepted that no answer was their answer. And if they would not find Bea, he would look for her himself.

He took his regular phone and the one he used to call the security firm, despite the risk that Agapov's people might be listening and walked the city, silently cursing Agape, cursing the security firm, cursing each of the Wellingtons, even cursing Patricia in her grave. He went east out of downtown along Queen Street, examining the faces of everyone he passed, and cursing the day each one of them had been born.

As he crossed the bridge to the east side, his curses came fewer and far between, and the knot of code that would destroy the Wellingtons' system unravelled before him. By the time he walked north to St. John's cemetery and his mother's grave, he knew exactly what to do.

He took his time wandering through the small woods, stopping at the gravestones, marking lives gone for more than a hundred years. Who would know they existed if not for the them?

As she was losing herself to dementia, he and his mother had walked this cemetery so she could choose her spot herself. She looked at her son with a glint in her eye, pointing at an obelisk. "What'd it be like for a cleaner to be here, with a big headstone like that? You make sure and have 'cleaner' written on there. Let them know people like us deserve to be remembered, too."

Nick knelt before his mother's grave, the grand obelisk rising before him. ROSE BARNES, 1956-2005, and the one word, "CLEAN-ER," was chiseled in with the same noble lettering as the tombstones of great men. "I'm going to finish them," he told her. "I am going to bring the Wellingtons all the way down."

He stayed for a moment longer, wanting to tell her about Bea, his worry that something had happened to her, to ask her if he should call the police, if only to file a report, but left her only with news she would want to hear.

Nick called for a taxi, waiting beside the busy road, watching for the familiar orange and green sedan. His regular phone pinged. Bea's AirTag had come back on. She was there, at the church. Every bit of him came alive with triumph. She was alive. She was well. He would get her, take her home, make love, then sit down and write the code. They thought they could destroy his family, and he was the one who would destroy them and Bea would share it with him.

The taxi pulled up. "Unity Church."

There was a lineup at the kitchen door, but it was moving quickly. People came out the other side, food in hand. They were good people who had got the raw end of life: made a mistake, experienced a loss not recoverable, a land stolen from them, and those without a mother like his own. He smiled as he passed, greeting each one, and slipped into the kitchen. But Bea was not there with the other volunteers and staff. He ducked out and went around the side to the office. Reverend Lee was just coming out. The black sleeves of their fleece jacket were rolled up. Tattoos covered their arms and crawled up their neck from the white tab collar into their messy, cropped blond hair.

"Mr. Barnes!" They smiled, arms open for a hug.

Nick stepped back to escape the embrace.

"So glad to see you here! You just missed Bea."

"Missed her?" He opened his phone and held up the screen. "No, she's here."

Reverend Lee smiled. "She must have forgotten something and come back. That thing tell you exactly where she might be?"

He switched to "Find Nearby" and tracked the exact location of her AirTag.

Reverend Lee wondered at it as they used it to go around the building to the door where the clothes were sorted. "The government's got to be logged into all that, watching all of us."

"Too much data for them to process. Only if they are after someone in particular."

"I'll just pop in and get her."

Nick waited outside, watching shoppers pass the church on their way to the Eaton Centre and glad they had to see how people suffered in this city before spending their money, hoping it would sour their every penny spent.

"She's not here. Maybe that thing is wrong?"

He checked the phone again. "No. She's here." Nick's chest tightened as he strode past Reverend Lee into the building. Bags of clothes were neatly set up on one side of the room while volunteers sorted them onto tables on the other side. But Bea was not among them. He held the phone out, locked onto the AirTag and followed it across the room, his heart beating out of his chest. His phone screen flashed. There was Bea's purse, lying in a basket of tote bags and backpacks. He spun around. Reverend Lee was right behind him.

"Poor thing." They smiled, hand on Nick's shoulder. "She'll be back for it."

Nick swiped their hand off of him, opening the purse. Her phone was there, too. He turned it on. It had been turned back to factory settings and there was no SIM card. "Her wallet's gone. She always goes out with a lot of cash when she comes here."

"She gave out a lot of cash yesterday morning and put even more in the donation box." They looked around, shrugging. "I'd like to say no one would've taken the wallet, but these people are in dire circumstances."

"Take the wallet, but not the phone?"

"What use is a phone? It's a brick once it's been stolen."

"It's not bricked. It's at factory settings."

"Maybe she bought a new one and left that one for someone who needs it?"

"When did she leave?"

"Hey." Mouth half-cocked in a quizzical smile, she asked. "Why are you so worried? Go home. She'll call you."

"She did not come home last night," he said through gritted teeth. "I've been worried."

The reverend's face fell. "I'm sorry you had to go through that. I don't know where she was last night, but she was here just a bit ago. She's alive and well. Maybe she ducked into the Eaton Centre?"

Nick left, his mind swarming. She had not gone shopping. She would not be back. He turned out onto the narrow street behind the church. She had left him. Every single woman had walked out on him. But there had always been signs. Small rebellions. Not eating what was put before her. Wearing clothes not to his taste. There was nothing like that with Bea. They shared something. She had been rich, but understood the fate of the poor. Their relationship had become more than domination. Had he imagined it? No, he argued with himself; she was consistently loving and attentive to all of his needs. She chose her submission out of love. And the deepfake? If there had been a lie, one he did not detect, she knew what he could do to her if she escaped. He tried to conjure up for himself Reverend Lee's certainty, but could not. She was gone.

Breathlessly striding towards the building with his offices and his penthouse, he called ahead. "Is Bea there?"

"No, sir."

"Did she come back this morning?"

"Not since she left yesterday, as I said before."

He grimaced, realizing the question he had not asked yesterday. "What did she have with her?"

"With her?"

"Yes! Was she carrying anything?"

"Nothing, sir."

He hung up and put the phone deep in his pocket to muffle the mic, risking Panopticon hearing the call, and opened the other one. "This is Elliot. I was just at the church. Her AirTag came back on."

"It could have been on all that time, sir. There could have been a drop in signal. No other iPhones nearby. Weak battery."

"Are you searching or not?"

"Yes."

The thought hit him. She had not left him. She took nothing with her. She had killed herself. "Check the police, hospitals. Maybe she—"

"We understand. Our systems would let us know if a woman of her description, let alone by that name, showed up at any hospital or morgue in Canada. We've also got the police covered in case she was arrested."

Barely breathing, he veered into a laneway and then a loading dock, taking shallow breaths until his chest opened again. Then the tears came. He prayed to a god he did not believe in that she had not killed herself, that his men could find her and bring her home. There was an answer to whatever could have driven her to it and he would find it, make her happy again. A truck pulled into the dock and he hurried off, wiping his eyes, and rushed back to the office.

He made it back without breaking down again, eyes straight ahead, ignoring greetings, until he got his private office door shut behind him. After checking for Bea online again, he gave up and went back to work, knowing Bea would want him to finish what he started. His only goal could be the complete destruction of the Wellington's system, for his mother's sake, but for Bea, too. What he should have done from the start.

35

———

This time, Tomoko knocked on Anthony's door and waved to the camera. It wasn't long before he came out to get her. She held up her phone to show she had turned everything off.

He grinned. "I didn't think you would do it again."

As they walked past the velvet couches, she veered to sit on the deep blue one inset with odd cut sections of red.

"Work's over here," he gestured to the enormous desk and computer display.

"I blame you," she said, getting off the couch, "and my recently-exed-boyfriend."

He shook his head, not understanding.

"This couch has made me hate my perfectly serviceable futon."

"If it makes you feel better, I picked them up used and reupholstered them with remnants of microfibre velvet. You could have them and not have to give up your commie card."

She raised her eyebrows. "You must be the devil."

This time he laughed and she got up and joined him at the computer, handing over a USB drive of the data she had downloaded from her email.

"Okay, give me some time. Enjoy the couches. Go make yourself some coffee or something."

The last thing she needed was more coffee.

During the long drive north to the camp, Parisa had indeed not told her shit. She kept her mouth shut even withstanding over five hours of interminably bleak highways listening to Abdi's lecture on opportunism within the Communist Party. As an interrogation technique, Tomoko would have been willing to admit to just about anything to get him to stop. Abdi would give you the shirt off his back in the middle of winter, but there were limits.

They got there deep in the dark of a clear night. Abdi led Parisa away from the cottages and tree line to the lake for an unimpeded view of the Milky Way, stars, and planets unknown to those who lived in cities. Abdi called it a celestial dome. Or the Greeks did. She could not remember. Parisa's gasp carried in the stillness of the night.

Tomoko turned on a battery lamp in the cottage, got the fire going in the wood stove, made beds, and got a pot of coffee on. Izzy came by and brought food, apologizing that Sarah was stuck inside with her bad hip, assuring her they would make sure Parisa was looked after.

Despite the lecture, the grandeur of the celestial dome, and being plied with coffee late into the night, Parisa continued not telling her shit. In the end, Parisa fell asleep wrapped in blankets in a lumpy armchair in front of the wood stove. Tomoko left her there to have a sore neck in the morning and went to sleep.

She tried one last time before Abdi brought her back to Toronto. "You came to me with this. You wanted your story told. Now Amina and I are going to write this piece. Your story will be told by us without you. This is your chance."

"Fuck my chance," she said, settling deep into the armchair.

Out on the road, Abdi turned off the highway for more coffee.

"There's a local place not far," he said, driving down the shabby main street of a tiny town at first light. A lone brick shop front was open. "Tea for me. Bourgeois decadence coffee for you?" He jumped out, grabbing enormous travel mugs from the back, and returned with pastries and enough coffee for her to stay awake and reflect on how she had ruined her one opportunity to get information out of Parisa.

Tomoko wandered into Anthony's galley kitchen. It was spare, yet as richly designed as the living room. Open shelving on an exposed brick wall held mismatched plates, bowls, and cups in vibrant hues. The counter was made of that weird, impossible to ruin material used in restaurants. A canvas knife roll sat next to a beautifully cared-for cutting board. Spotlights were placed so there were no shadows wherever you stood. She got herself a glass of water and leaned against the counter.

The wall separating the kitchen from the living room was covered in family photographs. It reminded her of the wall in her parents' kitchen where there was no governing aesthetic but love. An elderly couple in djellabas stood with a very young Anthony in front of a Moroccan mosque. There was a shot of the Jamaican side of his family eating fried fish in front of a small shack, the cook waving from behind the counter, a bright blue ocean behind them. Children and more children, aunts and uncles, and parents at family events. Friends, arms draped over each other, half-drunk, grinning. Who were these beautiful people? She wondered if Anthony was single and began searching the photos for evidence of a girlfriend when he called her back into the room.

He was walking towards her, hand out, holding the USB drive.

"I can tell you one thing. You are being used."

She took the USB and dropped onto the couch. "Tell me."

"It's not raw data downloaded from the Wellington system. It's data laid out in such a way as to make an argument. Digital breadcrumbs to force a reading. This is not just some whistleblower leaking data, this is someone directing a point. You publish the analysis as pushed by this data, you are writing up someone else's agenda."

"Could you trace it?"

"That's just it." He sat across from her. "Whoever prepared it knows exactly what they are doing. I don't know if I can. If so, it's going to take me a while. But it's not just some whistleblower."

"Parisa says she got sent the data anonymously, but she won't answer any of my questions."

"You've got to wonder why. Put that together with her computer being too clean and that she never saved the data in a renamed file or even tried to hide it."

"Yeah."

"I know Frank is pressuring you to publish something, but I would hold off."

"He said something to you?"

"Uh huh." Anthony smirked. "But I don't work for him. I volunteer for the journalists I respect."

She paused for a moment, not sure if he meant her, then certain he meant her, said forcefully, "Parisa is part of this."

"It's a good assumption for now."

"Do you have a phone I could use?"

He got up and retrieved a phone from his office drawer.

Tomoko took it to the windows, looking out at the trees in fall colour bursting over the brick houses, bungalows, and low-rise buildings, then texted Cyrus letting him know it was her first so he would answer the call.

"It's about Parisa."

"Is she safe?" His voice held a note of panic.

His concern pissed her off, and she gave him an answer that would piss him off. "Our guy is looking at the data, and given everything, Parisa is involved with whoever sent it."

"How can you say that? She's on the run."

"That's down to the Wellingtons. Just know she's not just some innocent graduate student who got sent data for no reason at all. Be careful."

"I can't believe this."

"Just be careful, okay?"

There was noise, as if he had moved from a quiet room to one filled with people. "Sorry, just checking on Arash. He's with my nephews."

"Did she say anything to you about how she got the data?"

"Nothing that you don't already know." He paused, moving back into a quiet room. "But when we drove to the subway station, I thought we were being followed. It's Toronto traffic. How could I be certain? I was overthinking. I am overthinking. But you should know."

So whoever had followed him to the subway station had likely followed them to her parents, then north. Amina was wrong. The government was not able to pressure the Wellingtons. The next call would be to Izzy and Sarah.

"Hold on," he said. Someone was calling his name. There was some muffled sound, a definite, "Just there," then something in Persian. He got back on the line. "There's a black sedan parked in front of our house. A man is in it, looking at us. My mother has called the police."

Tomoko said to Anthony, "Someone may have followed me north with my source and it looks like someone else is watching her son. My ex is with her son at his family's house, says there is a sedan out front. They've called the cops."

Anthony stood. "The cops will just move the car on. Get me the address. I can arrange for someone to guard them round the clock."

"What's he saying?" Cyrus asked.

"It's Anthony. He's the one looking at the data for me. Hold on." She handed him the phone.

"Give me the address. I can arrange to have someone watch the house. My cousin, John, runs a bodyguard business. They're solid." Anthony went back to the desk and made a note. "No," he said over the phone, "we don't know if Parisa is behind it, only that she doesn't seem to be a passive player. There's enough to make us question her involvement, that's all."

Tomoko winced, wishing she had not said what she wanted him to hear, and got caught out.

There was another pause, then Anthony said, "I agree. It means her son could be in danger. Your family, too. You want to move him, for your own sake?" He shook his head at Tomoko, chuckling. "I get it. I have a mother like that. Here's Tomoko." Anthony picked up his own phone and got up to make a call.

"You going to stay there?"

"We'll be fine." His voice was no longer warm toward her and it was her own doing, but it made her angry that she was the one being punished when Parisa was the liar. "Hold on," he said. Again, there were muffled voices. "Sorry, my mother." Then another pause. "I just got a text from Anthony's cousin, John. He and another man will be here within the hour. And you, are you safe?"

She was glad he finally asked, but replied, "Don't worry about me."

The next call was to Izzy and Sarah, she explained, then said, "Don't intervene. Whatever happens, you stay hunkered down in your place like nothing."

She could hear Izzy say in the background, "There's no cars on the property. I'll let Stan up the road know to give us a heads up if someone comes through."

"You got that?" Sarah asked.

"Yeah, and listen. You don't need to save her."

"Honey, I can barely walk with this arthritis. You better hope she can save herself." There was a pause. "Izzy!" She returned her attention to the call. "Izzy's got the shotgun out."

"Sarah!"

"We'll know if someone is coming down the road from Stan. That's a good ten minutes to get her out of the cottage. We'll go up the back path to the main road. Let the old people have a little something. I've never seen Izzy so alive."

"But your hip."

Sarah hung up on her.

Tomoko could not help but love them and hoped she had fight in her when she was their age, bad hip and all, and that she stopped giving in to men with long eyelashes, that is, unless they were proper revolutionaries.

She opened the Signal app on the phone, found Amina, texted her, then made the call. "I'm with Anthony. He thinks we should hold off publishing." Tomoko gave her the rundown on the security detail, the data, and their suspicions about Parisa.

"It's not odd she would not want to talk, especially if she is being used. I'm not convinced she's guilty, but she sure does not sound uninvolved," Amina said.

Anthony called her over to the computer display. "You need to see this."

"Hold on, Anthony has something."

She leaned over his shoulder and looked. A video display was up of Parisa's apartment, the same as she saw before, but this one was different. Parisa opened the door to her apartment, unscrewed a heating vent, then pulled out a USB drive and a phone. He forwarded through the video until the moment when she pulled up a chair going directly to the camera and dug it out, killing the feed.

"I set the feed to download from Fort Security in the background. I forgot about it, sorry."

Tomoko squeezed Anthony's shoulder. They had her. "Amina," she said into the phone. "We've got proof Parisa is involved. We can't go forward with this story the way it is. Can you put some pressure on Frank? Anthony said—"

"Frank! You piece of shit!" Amina cut her off. "He rewrote our draft and published without our permission!"

Tomoko said to Anthony, "Pull up *The Spanner* site."

The website appeared. Anthony clicked on the headline.

POWERS CONSPIRE TO TERMINATE MONAGHAN IN PAYDAY LOAN FRAUD SCANDAL

No ring to it, but it made its point. It was based on the draft that she and Amina had sent to Frank just to get him to hold on. His name was first in the by-line, with theirs under "reporting by."

She barely recognized their work. He had rewritten and expanded it from his interview with Monaghan and his own analysis.

The focus of the piece was centred on Monaghan's termination as a conspiracy, listing the board members and mentioning Agape, in particular, an associate of the Wellingtons. He had all the details they had been able to find. In the story, Monaghan was a hero. Protector of women and the vulnerable. There were photos of Agape with the Wellingtons.

"Like I said," Anthony remarked. "I don't work for Frank James."

36

———————

"How can you not find her?" Nick demanded through clenched teeth. In less than thirty seconds, he had gone from soaring relief to rage.

The woman's voice on the call said, "Again, she is alive and well, out there, but analog."

"But you just said there was someone who saw her at Cherry Beach!"

"A dog owner recognized the photo yesterday, said she was standing at the gate to the dog-park. We got her on CCTV, taking transit from the neighbourhood of Unity Church to the beach. That's it."

"No one can simply disappear!"

"You said she may have had a lot of cash on her."

"We've been following her friends from the Cherry Beach dog-park, and those in contact with them. None of them are making calls or doing anything that would indicate they've been talking to Bea."

"Send me the video." He closed the call without another word.

In a moment, the video arrived. She was wearing clothes he did not recognize and was tapping a Presto card to get into the subway.

He called back the number.

The woman answered. "Yes, Elliot?"

"She's using a Presto card!"

"If you had not hung up on me, I would have explained that we tracked all the Presto cards used at that time. Everyone checks, except one, paid for with cash in a machine at Queen Station. $20 dollars was on it, but—"

The grainy video showed her exiting the subway at Union Station and getting on a bus. She was clinging to a post, swaying with the movement, and keeping a constant, fearful watch outside. Then her expression changed, as if she had been caught, and she slowly looked up at the bus's security camera. She frowned, took the Presto card out of her pocket, held it up for the camera to see, then bent down to speak to an elderly woman bounded in by a metal shopping cart and handed her the card.

"I saw it."

"There's no point in tracking the card unless you want to know where that old woman goes."

"Call me. Any hint you have."

The bus arrived at Cherry Beach. She exited and the video ended.

He stood, pacing the office. She had left him. Was their love a lie? Had every gentle touch, every gaze shared as they lay sleepily next to each other in the mornings, every sweet concern she showed for his needs, had they all been lies? He stopped, staring at the blanket on the couch, the pillows she had picked out. The scream came up from his toes. He grabbed the blanket, pulling and tearing at it until he was on the ground and the blanket, unharmed, lay twisted around him.

"Bea, why did you leave me?" He moaned, holding the blanket to his face, searching for her scent in it. The world opened up underneath him and he sobbed, clutching at the pillows and calling out to his mother. "Mum, she's gone. She's gone." He lay on the floor, his choking sobs easing until he finally fell into a deep, grieving sleep.

He jerked awake, sucking in air as if he had been smothered, and tore the blanket off him as if it were woven of writhing snakes. He opened the door to his office, threw the pillows and blanket into the hall.

The door shut behind him. He took a Red Bull from his fridge, sat at his desk and messaged Trang.

> There's garbage in the hall outside my door. Tell the housekeeper to take every single thing of Bea's in the apartment and get rid of them. I want nothing of hers in the house when I return.

Nick angrily turned back to the virus designed to take down Wellington Payday Loans' entire system. It was making frustratingly slow progress. Rather than code it from nothing, he had built it on the back of his original virus that introduced the fraud bug. It kept slamming into a wall, when it should have broken through already.

He went back to reread the piece in *The Spanner*. At least Parisa's name was not mentioned. She was an anonymous graduate student used by powers greater than herself to bring down Martin Monaghan. But his anger grew more precise with every word. The fraud had fallen into the background. Everything was about Monaghan. Martin Monaghan, the man who testified in the WBSN scandal, single-handedly bringing down the MP Gunnar Armitage. Martin Monaghan, the great man who had mentored a generation of activist-scholars. A conspiracy of wealthy board members, their associates, and their relationships with the Wellingtons, Agape especially. The same photos he had found online were reposted there.

He had already begun a deeper search of Agape. His money seemed to come from nowhere. Information on his brother, Agapov, was highly controlled, as he expected. The family was Russian. There was money and power. The mother served under the President of the United Russia Party. The father was listed simply as a businessman. But the obvious wealth displayed in the one photo he could find meant the man was not selling potatoes by the side of the road. It was a large grouping in a countryside setting. There was no date to it, but the parents were already elderly. Eight men and several women were lined up with a mess of children in front. Andrei Agapov was not indicated among them, but Agape was easy to spot. He was the short sibling, standing apart from the rest, but shared their family's powerful build. It was impossible to see which children belong to which parent. But a woman with long black hair stood next to Agape with her arm through his, leaning in as if they were in love. He did a facial recognition search of her, but it was not a good enough resolution photo.

Nick went into Canadian government records and quickly found their immigration papers. In 1978, he was listed as Piotr Agapov. The wife's name was Marya. No children. There were no tax returns for either Marya or Piotr Agapov. They may not have filed, but he wondered if they had been erased by Panopticon. A deed to a house in Piotr and Marya Agapov's name was amended in 1985 to read Peter Agape alone. Only then did tax records appear, and then for "Agape." He checked the census. There, he found them. The two lived at that address in 1981. But by the next census, five years later, she was gone and his name had changed. Marya had a driver's license in 1980, but it was never renewed.

All he could tell was that by 1985, Piotr Agapov had become Peter Agape and his wife Marya disappeared from all public records. Agape emerged in 1985 as an independently wealthy "businessman." From that point on, there were regular photos of him in the social pages, including the pictures he had already seen of Agape with the Wellingtons. Certain people kept showing up, though. The attorney Vincent Allen. Harold Bailey. A doctor, Marcus Fanhorn. Ipe Palakkadu, the head of a chain of private schools. Pierre Tremblay and Benjamin Cormier. He dug deeper into their relationships. A pattern emerged in comments in different corners of the web, a mention here, a snippet there, but all in relationship to a book called *The Sacred Mushroom and The Cross.*

He opened the Wikipedia entry.

"The book, written in 1970 by John Marco Allegro, relates the development of language to that of myths, religions, and cultic practices in world cultures. Allegro argues, through etymology, that the roots of Christianity, and many other religions, lay in fertility cults, and that cult practices, such as ingesting visionary plants to perceive the mind of God. Allegro argues that Jesus never existed as a historical figure, but was rather a mythological creation of early Christians under the influence of psychoactive mushroom extracts, such as psilocybin."

There were self-styled groups that tried to reprise the fertility cults, some arguing that Jesus did exist and others denying it, each claiming to be the true inheritor, all of it hilarious to Nick. Allegro's colleagues had harshly criticized him. His career ruined. Nick downloaded the book and skimmed it. It was a mass of citations. Nick snorted derisively as he scrolled through page after page. The man saw penises everywhere. He had no trouble with that. Maybe people did worship penises, but as for his argument, it looked like Allegro mistook correlation with causation, something no one working in tech could do and survive.

A message from Trang pinged through on his display.

All garbage has been removed.

Nick slapped his desk. If she crawled back to him, if he found her, she would find herself in a cage. He salivated, thinking of her coming up for digital air and finding herself a prisoner.

The names associated with Agape came up in a few comments about a possible cult in Toronto. He clicked on one link and smiled. The commenter claimed the cult had been formed in 1985. When Agape changed his name from Agapov to Agape and his wife had gone missing. The commenter claimed a member had left and had supposedly drowned, although others claim that member moved to Greece. No name or gender was mentioned. Maybe that was Agape's wife?

He had to assume that Panopticon was in his computer and knew he was researching Agape. They had to expect it, but he could not do more than that or risk reprisal. It was in their power to destroy him entirely.

But he could go after the Wellingtons.

Nick sent the team a picture of Wellington with the head of the Bank of China at a party. They were smiling, but their body language made it seem like they had been disturbed after being in a close discussion. The team was to ask why the Wellington family, accused of defrauding hard-working Canadians, were cozying up to Chinese interests in the banking industry. Every comment would come from innumerable sources through multiple countries. Articles would go up on news sites of their own creation. One way or another, they would go down.

Another message came through from Trang.

> The Tracey-Carlton account still needs your
> attention.

He was glad she was not in the room or he would have torn the old woman to pieces. As if anything mattered more. Instead, he punched the keys.

> Send it to Samuel. He has full authority.

Nick opened a message to Samuel directly.

> You are in charge. Trang is coming to you.
> But I want you to build the campaign on Bea
> as we discussed. Take it live.

He stood, pushing the chair back so forcefully it slammed into the couch behind it. Nick grabbed his jacket, phone, and wallet and left. Bea was out there. What could he do but walk her old haunts looking for her, drag her back to see what she had lost, and wait for the code to break through.

37

Cassandra paced, listening to Agape carefully and praying he could influence her father.

"It's unlikely whoever is trying to get into the system will be successful, but even if so, there should not be a break in service for longer than an hour," Agape said.

"Your brother should have been handling things from the start." Wellington stared meaningfully at Stone, who did not shrink under the reproach.

"Fort had weaknesses in this instance. It is true," Agape said. "But they remain in my trust."

"And your brother?"

"My brother trusts no one but himself."

"Once the government deal is done, let him know we want that virus back in the system."

"I told you, if you want the system to withstand the present attack and any in the future, it can never be reintroduced."

"If attacks are going to make us money, we should invite them!"

No amount of bluster was going to get the virus reintroduced to the system, but that still left the physical threats to Soltani and her child, as well as Monaghan. Agape promised this, too, was now under his control with Fort Security following the directives sent to them through Vincent, but she still feared her father could find a way around it.

As if he could read her mind, he demanded, "Where are we at on Soltani and Monaghan?"

Before Stone could speak, Agape stepped in. "Leave this to Vincent, please."

Wellington turned on him. "If I left this to Vincent, we'd be handing over our home to our clients!"

Agape gave Cassandra a reassuring glance. It touched a euphoric place within her, a perfect certainty.

"Soltani is still missing, but we've located her son," Stone said. "He is staying with a family in North York. We had a car out front. Unfortunately, the family noticed our car and had it moved on. We still have them under surveillance, less obtrusive, but still present. We can move on the child whenever you say."

Agape opened his mouth to speak, but Wellington cut him off. "When you take over leadership of this company, let me know." He addressed Stone. "And Monaghan?"

"He has not been home. His boyfriend hasn't seen him."

"Father! Leave them alone!" The words were out of her mouth before she could stop them. She got up and left the room before she let it all slip. Instead of shrinking away through the dining room, she boldly walked past him through the living room and out to the back.

It was cold and overcast, but she did not return for a coat, instead she opened her arms to the pleasing chill and went into the woods. Agape had transformed her. The woods did not frighten her, but welcomed her as a sanctuary again. The ugly world of her parents disappeared under the canopy of pines. The needles underfoot muffled the sounds of the neighbourhood and the breeze whistled above. Everything was alive. The trees, her childhood friends and protectors, held her. She found her tree and settled underneath it. From there, the house was barely visible.

She thought she could see Patricia winding her way through the pines, touching the bark on each one, but her ghost was only a trailing whisp, then gone.

Back then, Patricia would follow her out, begging Cassandra not to leave her with her parents and their friends. "If you're there, they'll leave me alone."

"It's your fault you go," she spat back.

Patricia would look out past the small woods to the fence beyond. "We could leave."

"You leave."

"Come with me?"

"Just tell them to fuck off. Works for me."

"I can't go alone."

What if she had left with Patricia when she had asked that time, or any of the other times? Those nights when Patricia would open her bedroom door, red-faced, in tears, begging, Cassandra had turned her away. If she had not, there would be no need to make the choice she had made now. But the momentary doubt melted away into the euphoric awareness of the life around her, that there was no death, only change.

When she had arrived at Agape's bungalow the day before, breathless with fear, having escaped the car that was following her, he sat her down in the small kitchen. The linoleum table was shining and clean. Everything in the house reassured her as if she had found herself in a black and white television show where parents cared about their children and troubles were solved with a few firm but loving chats, and all within half an hour.

"Take the money and go, Cassandra." He looked away. "I fear their intentions."

"Brandt can't be trusted. I will have to take the kids and go on my own."

"I know, but Brandt was never the man I hoped for you. That man is out there."

"Is he rich?" She asked, staring out at the weedy backyard through the dusty aluminum blinds. The money he had set aside for her would not last long. He had to understand that. If she turned in the family like she wanted to, she would lose their wealth. Further, she could not protect Brandt. He had tied himself up in it too tight.

"You see how it is now," he said. "I cannot control everything."

She turned back to him. "Could you ever?"

"Perhaps not. I tried to protect Patricia, but freedom was not for her to bear in this life."

"Not for her?" A spike of the old anger thrust through her.

Agape got up from the table and opened a bottle of wine, bringing back two glasses.

She picked up the bottle and looked at the label, a Rioja easily found on the shelves at grocery stores, and sniggered. "You even know the best cheap wine. Always something, but"—she put the bottle down—"never enough. You could afford better wine, but you don't buy it."

"You want more money."

"Of course I want more money," she said coldly. "Can you at least protect me, so when the government comes looking, they let me go with what I have?"

"The government already knows everything."

"Help me."

"They are open to your parents stepping down from their roles in the company. You could not take their place, though. They would require a new board, no family members, but you would retain your financial stakes." He poured her wine into a cheap glass. There was a thumbprint on it, near the lip. It had not been properly washed. She slid it closer out of politeness, but did not touch it.

"As if my parents would."

"I only want what's best for you." He looked at the wine glass sideways in the slanted light coming through the blinds. "My apologies." He took her glass and bottle to the counter. His back to her, he asked. "If your parents were to die, what then?"

"The virile Wellingtons?'

He handed her a new glass of red wine. This one was spotless and he handled the glass by the stem, placing it before her, then took a sip of his own. "It is a hypothetical. We are thinking of a new life for you. I am asking you to imagine it."

She held the glass and considered her parents' deaths. The freedom denied Patricia would be given to her. Her preference would be to sell the company. Brandt would be free of them, free to be her husband. The boys would not lose their father to divorce or a fraud case or public shame. "To their deaths, then," she said and took an ungraciously large sip at the thought of it, wincing slightly at the heavy tannin, but then found herself enjoying its odd, earthy mouth feel. "Is this from the same bottle?"

"Yes. You've had it before. You don't remember?" He held up his own glass and drank deeply, matching hers, and smiled. "Odd to wish death on anyone with a toast."

But saying it aloud made her feel free, and she took another long sip from her wine. It warmed her stomach and went straight to her head. Cassandra giggled at the idea that it might all be possible. She drank again, emptying her glass. "Do you have any crackers? The wine is hitting me."

"Let's go into the living room." He stood and led her into the small room with its uncomfortable furniture, couches and armchairs in the same old-fashioned yellow upholstery, the sort you would expect to be covered in plastic.

Her stomach turned. "I really need some crackers."

"Why don't you lie down on the couch? You've been through so much today."

Cassandra did as he suggested, but the couch was supremely uncomfortable. The hard arm under her head and the cushions gave her no more comfort than would lying on the sidewalk, but she closed her eyes and rested for what felt like a moment. She tried to get up, but felt strange. Everything seemed out of place and time, and she panicked, crying out to him, "You have so much money. Brandt and the kids. Give it to me, if you want to save—" Her head fell back against the arm and Agape approached, leaving a trail of ghosts with his every movement. The room shifted in shape, the beige walls transformed into a deep creamy jelly with purple waves of froth as they slid down on themselves and kept flowing. She managed, "Where's all that jelly?" then lay back and closed her eyes again.

"What if your parents died?" Agape asked soothingly, as if from far away.

She heard herself describe a life beyond her grasp, each word manifesting pulsating shapes and symbols as if she had come awake in a dream and suddenly saw how it was all done. Meaningless letters burst in on themselves, spelling out "PEACE." Ever-spiralling paisleys opened up into unknown shapes in tranquil blues and yellows, becoming a white sand beach meeting a turquoise ocean. She and her boys were resting on a covered lounge, Brandt smiling down on them, framed by gossamer curtains moving in the breeze. The water reached them, slaking their thirst for love.

"How would they die?"

The beach disappeared into swirling shapes that melted into stick figures like the kind they made in primary school. A chain of people cut from faded construction paper bounced between her small hands. The people left her hands, dancing in the air, their red bellies opening up as her small scissors snipped the paper into pieces and their purplish guts fell out onto the floor of the classroom. Her teacher clapped her hands. "Well done!"

"Will you do it?"

"Yes," she said, and trembled in ecstasy. Cassandra opened her eyes, expecting to find Agape watching over her, but she was alone.

She got up from the couch, her neck aching, but felt released into a new world. She wandered the house. Late afternoon light silently streaked through loosely woven curtains onto furniture standing so proudly they must have grown up from the earth. The drawers invited her, some more than others. But she could feel the invitation in her hand and held it out until she reached the bedroom. There, her hand took her to the bedside table in the simple room and pulled open the drawer. A gun. She took it out and embraced it, feeling its love and its promise of release. In the kitchen, a glass of water and a package of saltines were set out on the table. A note was beside it. The letters made no sense, but the meaning was clear. "I have left for the night. Drink. Eat. Rest. I will protect you."

The gun on the table, always within reach, she drank the water, astounded by its taste of clarity and light. She ate the saltines and the grains of salt became the sea. Taking the gun with her, she returned to Agape's spare bedroom, pulling back the neatly tucked yellowed sheets and worn coverlet, placed the gun beside her, and fell asleep dreaming of the reward to come.

Now, under her tree behind her parents' home, her fingers dug into the loose soil under the cushion of needles. Cassandra felt the tendrils moving beneath her, death returning to life, and planned how she would snip her parents' bellies open.

38

Izzy banged on the door of the cottage. "Parisa! Now! Someone's coming!"

She threw the lock and opened the door, grabbing her things and ran out into the dark, but Izzy held an arm out, directing her back inside.

"Stan called. He stopped them. A young woman and an older man. They're not armed. The woman wants to talk to you. She claims to know who sent the data."

"How did she find me?"

Izzy shook his head. "You can ask her. Stan and I will sit with you." He glanced down at the shotgun broken open over one arm. "Don't worry."

"Don't worry!" She turned around and went to the back bedroom, looking out the window for three people walking down the long road to the camp. A flashlight was moving towards them, nearly there. "You said we would have ten minutes," she called back to Izzy.

"I know," he said, stoking the fire back to life. "Stan took it on himself."

Tomoko and Abdi had left early that morning. Despite the cold, she had sat by the lake all day to escape the confining cottage, thinking about Arash and hoping she was safe. Now she stood back against the wall, waiting while Izzy closed the shotgun and pointed it toward the door.

Izzy and Parisa both jumped when the knock finally came.

"Come in. Slowly." Izzy called out.

Stan came in first. He must have been in his seventies, but looked like a man who had cut timber his whole life, and she hoped he was truly on her side.

"Now Izzy, no need to overreact." Stan held a hand out. "They aren't armed. I'm here. You're here. Nothing is happening unless they are trained killers."

A beautiful young woman in ill-fitting clothes stepped out from behind him. She had bow lips and a pointed chin, one of those heart shaped faces, but it was her eyes. Parisa knew those eyes, openly speaking of depths of pain and ready to fight back. An older man followed her into the room. He was large and bow-backed, looking as though life had broken him again and again, but he had designated himself as the woman's protector and Parisa was glad she had someone.

"I'm Beatrice, and this is my friend, George. He brought me to you."

"You had better explain," Parisa said.

"I've been"—she paused, looking at the man, who nodded, encouraging her to speak. "I've been held captive for over a year by the man who sent you the data on Wellington Payday Loans. Nick Barnes. I've been watching him watch you. I saw where you were. He's tracking you and your son." She took a step forward. "There's a hit out on you. I had to tell you."

"Captive?" Izzy scoffed. "You're here."

Her companion shot back, "Don't speak."

Izzy gestured at them with the gun. "You came here uninvited. Sit down."

The woman sat in an armchair, trembling, eyes on the gun, while her friend swaggered as best he could to stand behind her.

"Izzy let them talk," Stan said.

Her voice trembled. "He broke me down until I couldn't leave him. He had trackers on me."

Parisa sat up.

"I left everything behind at the church. I even changed my clothes there. Nothing to track."

"All right." Parisa said, but she was still on edge. "Tell me what you want me to know."

"He's using you to get back at the Wellingtons. He's using you like he uses all women."

"So why does he want me dead?"

"He doesn't. It's the Wellingtons who want you and Monaghan dead. Nick said he would have security follow you, but I know his every mood, his tones. I've had to. He was lying. You're on your own."

"Nick is tracking me? That's how you found me?"

"You turned your phone back on. I saw early yesterday morning, on his computer, that you were at someone's house in Etobicoke. I went to the church and left everything I had behind, then I met up with George. He drove me to the house and we waited outside. I followed you and the journalist on the subway and used someone's phone to text George that we got off in Kensington. He picked me up and we followed you here."

Parisa looked down, saying under her breath, "Amateurs."

"What? Me?" George asked.

"Not you, Tomoko and the driver. They never noticed we were being followed."

"Hey!" Izzy objected.

George threw his shoulders back. "They wouldn't have. I never stayed in the same lane and kept a few cars between us. Plenty of cars on the road the whole way."

Parisa refrained from suggesting George had done anything other than a professional job and addressed Beatrice. "I still don't understand why you're here telling me this. Other than knowing now where the data came from, I have the rest. I'm here, hiding, because I know there is a hit out on me. My son is hiding, because I was told I was not safe. Now it's possible that you led people to me."

Stan stepped in. "They've been with me since yesterday."

"Stan!" Izzy yelled.

"I watched them, I watched the road and trails. No one came up behind them."

"If there's no one following, what's there to warn about?"

"Are you so thick?" George asked, putting a hand on Beatrice's shoulder.

"I guess I am."

The pain behind her eyes flattened Beatrice's expression. "I couldn't save myself. I wanted to save you."

It hit like the truth, and Parisa understood it too well. She turned to Izzy. "I agree with Stan here. These two are safe. Whether or not they were followed, we'll find out. But why don't you leave us? We have a lot to talk about."

"No." Izzy said, the gun still pointed into the room.

Stan said, "Izzy, put the gun down, come outside. We'll start a fire in the pit. We can wait out there. If she screams, we'll be back in a second."

He wavered for a moment, then asked Parisa, "You sure?"

There was a pride in his eyes that he was able to stand up for her and she suddenly felt for him. Parisa stood and pushed the gun down so it pointed to the floor and kissed him on the cheek. "Stay nearby, okay?"

Izzy and Stan left, Izzy giving her one last look before he shut the door behind him.

"George. I'm good," Beatrice said. "Sit down."

She pulled her armchair closer to the wood stove.

"What did he do to you?"

Beatrice looked toward George for help, then said, shaking her head. "I don't even know. One day I was just stuck in his house and couldn't leave. He has videos."

She imagined sex tapes. But he did not seem the type who would ask her consent.

"He's probably already leaked them." She looked stricken and began trembling again. "My family. I can't even warn them."

George reached out. "I told you, I'll tell your parents. First, we get you out of town."

"You are out of town."

"Not this close," George said.

"Okay." Parisa got up and got a blanket from the other room and gave it to Beatrice. "Why me? Why did he send me the data?"

"I don't know, only that he thought Monaghan would be able to get it published and like that minister of parliament he took down, get a full investigation going."

"Who is this guy again?"

Beatrice seemed amazed she had not heard of him. "Nick Barnes, the founder of Cristo Solutions."

Parisa shook her head. "So this guy just found my email on the department website and sent me evidence that the Wellingtons had been defrauding their customers in order to expose them?"

"No." Beatrice's eyes widened. "He created the virus. Nick installed it in their system, it created the evidence to set them up."

All this. She was sitting in a musty cottage with no electricity, her son was terrified, everything taken from her because of some psycho with a plan straight out of a conspiracy thriller.

"He was really upset when Monaghan got terminated."

"We didn't expect it to happen," Parisa said. "Monaghan thinks he's everyone's hero. He does a lot of good, but it's always him out front. Even when he does everything he can to help one of his graduate students, somehow he's taking the credit. I was warned after I came into the program."

"Warned?" George asked.

"Told to do a project that he could not write about himself. That if there were any similarities, he would use my research in his own work. Not plagiarism, mind you. Monaghan would cite it, other graduate students told me, but he would use it before I would be able to make a name for myself with the findings." She looked away. "It's hard to explain. For instance, I give a paper at a conference, but the findings are not published, nothing that would make a paper trail proving I said it first. Even if I do publish it later, everyone cites him for the argument, not me. My work disappears under his."

"But none of that could get him terminated?" George asked.

"Not even the plagiarism should have gotten him terminated."

"So what happened?"

"When I got the data, he asked me to work on it with him. We corroborated the data, but could not verify the source. I didn't want him to cite me. It seemed dangerous, professionally and personally. But no matter what, I didn't want to be a stepping stone for him." Parisa almost said more, then stopped.

Beatrice waited.

She hesitated, glancing toward the door and Izzy outside, then Parisa said, lowering her voice, "The chair of the department asked me into his office. There was a man there, an associate to the university board. He asked me if I wanted to have Monaghan held responsible." She looked at them both. "Everyone in the department knew I was working on payday data and that I had told him not to cite me. No one thought anything of it."

"So what happened?" George asked.

"The chair and this man assured me if I supported them in going after Monaghan, he would be censured. We could use my case to make him understand what he had been doing. He'd learn. That's all. I knew I was being used. The chair hates him." She snorted. "He's another matter. What he does—"

"What does he do?" George demanded.

She waved his question off. "The point is, they were out to get him and they used me to do it. But I don't see how knowing Barnes set me up, too, makes me safe."

"The journalist. Tell her. If the story gets out, you'll be safe?"

"Tomoko," Parisa said in a flat tone. "I thought the same thing. But she screwed up what little I shared, now here I am. Did you see *The Spanner*?"

"Nick was really angry."

"I want to hear more about the chair of your department," George interjected heatedly. "You weren't saying something, and the way you looked, and what was the name of the man who spoke to you?" It all came out in a tumble. Beatrice put her hand on George's arm.

"You mean who did the chair have talk to me? His name is Agape."

Beatrice gasped. "I think he came to see Nick. His brother is Agapov. Agapov of Panopticon Security. They want to take down all the payday loan corporations. They wanted Nick's help."

"That's a name everyone knows." But Agape had not shared that bit of information with her.

Parisa got up, opened the door to the wood stove and poked at the fire, deadening the small flame instead of stirring it back to life. She grunted, angry at herself that something so basic to life was beyond her ability. What made her think she could get herself out of this mess without trusting somebody with everything? She thought of Cyrus, wishing she had held nothing back, feeling like she was betraying him by telling these people first.

"I know this man built himself up in your eyes, Beatrice. But do you really think that Panopticon needs Nick, whoever he is, to do their work for them?"

"What is going on?" George demanded.

"I don't know." She felt suddenly tired and went to the door, opened it, and found Izzy standing beside it, looking guilty. "We're fine. I got enough of their story."

Izzy looked at George and Beatrice suspiciously, but Parisa did not have the energy to deal with it. "I just want to sleep. Could you put some logs on? I don't know what I'm doing."

Stan said to Beatrice and George, "You ready to come back?"

"No." Parisa said. "They'll sleep here. We'll talk more in the morning."

39

"Tomoko," Sarah said, "two people are up here speaking to Parisa."

"Who!"

Amina looked up from her laptop, gesturing, "What?"

Tomoko answered Amina, "Parisa," then got up to pace *The Spanner*'s office.

"A young woman named Beatrice and an older man named George," Sarah said. "Izzy ran over to tell me. They're involved with someone named Nick Barnes, and Parisa is talking to them. I wish you were here."

"Does she know them?" Tomoko asked, writing the names down and handing it to Amina.

"Not according to Izzy."

Amina typed them into her laptop, then swung the computer around for her to see.

"Nick Barnes of Cristo Solutions. And Beatrice, or 'Bea', is Nick Barnes's girlfriend." A pause, then, "Wow."

"What is it?"

"His girlfriend is a porn star. Videos. Photos. She's on OnlyFans."

Tomoko got up, pacing *The Spanner*'s small office. "Why the hell is his girlfriend up there? Parisa's involved somehow. Parisa wouldn't talk to me in the car or up there. First she wants me to help her, so I go to her apartment with her, but she barely searches it with me and then all this other suspicious shit shows up." She huffed. "Sorry for swearing."

Sarah said, "You're not ten, and swearing is appropriate in this circumstance. But she seems to be talking now."

"Maybe they are in this together."

"I don't think so. Stan and Izzy say she escaped Barnes's control. She's here to warn Parisa."

"Where is Izzy? Can he report back?"

"He's stuck outside by the fire pit with Stan. Parisa made him leave."

"Tell him to put his ear up to the door."

"On it." She put the phone down to tell him, then returned a moment later. "He's trying, but those doors are thick."

"You're the best. Did she say if she wanted to leave?"

"Not so far."

"Thanks." Tomoko hung up. "You're not going to believe this."

Amina shut the laptop.

But once she had said it, Tomoko knew she was going to have to admit to Amina how she had screwed up with Parisa. She sat back down at the desk across from her and repeated what Sarah had said, ending defensively, "Parisa wouldn't talk to me."

"I think you need to consider she won't talk to you because of your former relationship with Cyrus."

The "I told you so" was about as welcome as her earlier sermon on ethics. "This is more important than feelings. She should understand that. Her child is at risk."

Amina said, "Okay," in that way that means the exact opposite.

But Tomoko was not going to give it to her. Nothing was taking her off this story. Instead, she focused on the papers that Martin had given to *The Spanner* laid out in neat piles on the long table. "I don't know what to take from any of this."

"We have their analysis, but, like Anthony said, we can't trust it.

We're doing someone's dirty work if we tell the story that Martin and Parisa outline here."

"How can we stop Frank from publishing the wrong story again?"

"All we can do is give him a story that tells it right."

"Maybe we need to go to a different journal?"

"Devil you know."

She disagreed, but left it. "I need to call Cyrus."

Amina stood, stretching her back. "Good luck with that."

"He's got to know about the video and the rest."

"We've all been there. Part of being a good journalist is examining your own prejudices in telling the story. We're working on this story together. So we can check each other. I'm checking you right now."

She grabbed her phone. "I'm stepping out for a call."

Cyrus's phone rang on the other end. "Tomoko!" He answered cheerfully, but there was worry in his voice and family noise in the background as he moved some place quieter.

She suddenly wanted to see him. "Can I come by? We need to talk."

"Certainly." He did not sound eager, but gave her the address and it hit her for the first time that he had never invited her there to meet his family. Well, now she would.

Returning to the office, she grabbed her bag and coat. "I'll be back straightaway."

Amina looked at her over her reading glasses. "I'll be here."

It felt like the taxi took forever, but at least the cab driver did not try to talk to her. She watched the lamplit streets pass one by one and was grateful for every red light as she rehearsed what she would say. They pulled off into a well-lit neighbourhood of large suburban homes that looked shabbier than she imagined they would be, expecting more of the money she saw in his neighbourhood in Etobicoke. She texted him.

> Pulling up in a sec.

By the time they turned the corner to his mother's house, Cyrus was standing outside and her stomach flipped. She got out, pausing for a moment to give herself a moment before speaking to him and to scan the cars on the street for the security Anthony sent to protect Parisa's son. Nothing seemed out of place, not even someone sitting in a car.

Cyrus was there before she could turn around.

"What's wrong?"

Not even a hello.

"Should we talk inside?" The front door was ajar, letting out the sounds of the kids laughing and a woman calling after them. It only made her feel worse. This could have been her family, too. What was she thinking, not fighting for him? Why could she not have the story and him both?

"No, out here. I don't want to upset Arash."

"How is he?"

"Not good. He's crying a lot. He's sleeping with me."

Jealousy got the better of her. "You said you never wanted children."

He nodded slowly, understanding, and took her hand. "I'm sorry."

"It's fine," she pulled her hand back. "But Parisa's not the person you think she is."

"Tomoko, are you sure you want to do this?"

"She hasn't told you everything."

"If she hasn't, she will."

Of course, he would answer this way. This was his character. Beautiful Cyrus. A desperate urge rose up within her. Every bit of her fought it, her body turned rigid, but the words came out all the same. "I love you."

Cyrus frowned and reached out to her.

Then from the house, "Tomoko!"

Arash was running towards them.

Cyrus bent down to catch him and send him back inside.

But a streak of a man in all black ran up from behind them, knocking Tomoko down, another behind him, shouldering Cyrus to the ground before he even saw them coming, and scooping up Arash.

Cyrus scrambled up to go after Arash, but the first man forced him back down, striking him in the face. Cyrus flailed, grabbing at anything he could and pulled off the man's balaclava, revealing a brutal, white face and a military buzz-cut. Tomoko got up and ran around them. Arash, thrown over the other man's shoulder, was screaming, but his abductor ran down the street like he was carrying nothing. She followed as fast as she could, but had nothing on his speed. He was already halfway up the long block.

She heard the heavy footsteps of someone behind her, bracing herself as he ran up, expecting to be knocked down, but the man who had been beating Cyrus only sprinted past her. Tomoko followed, redoubling her speed. Maybe, at least, she could see what car they got into, which direction they took off.

Out of nowhere, a third man, and then a fourth, passed her. They faces were not covered. They were black and wearing track suits. She hoped they were Anthony's cousins. The men who took Arash turned the corner onto a side street, closely followed by the other two men. Tomoko's breath was already tight in her chest as she lost sight of all four men, but she pushed on.

She rounded the corner, stopping short as one of Anthony's cousins rushed back toward her with Arash in his arms, nearly toppling her as he ran past. The other of Anthony's men had hauled Arash's abductor to the ground next to the passenger side of a dark Chevy Suburban. The one with the buzz-cut jumped out of the driver's side brandishing a night-stick and ran around. He clocked Anthony's man on the back of the head, then dragged him off his partner. He was aiming a second strike with the nightstick when Tomoko rushed at him, releasing a guttural, wordless scream.

The man stood still for a moment and smiled at her, curling his hand, begging her to come at him, then laughed. He pulled his partner up, helped him into the car, and the two sped away. Tomoko hurried to the man on the ground who was unsteadily regaining his feet.

"Are you okay?"

But he did not answer, instead he pulled out his phone and

walked away from her, touching the back of his head, checking for blood. He spoke into the phone, but Tomoko could not hear what he was saying.

He finally turned back, still speaking on the phone, then dropped his hand, done.

"I got the plate number," he said as he reached her.

"You call the cops?" she asked accusingly.

"Of course I called the cops. They tried to kidnap that child!"

She did not realize how she had sounded, and tried to joke it off. "You better get back to the house, then, so Cyrus's family can vouch for you before they get here."

"Who the fuck are you?" He gave her a look she would never forget and stormed past her. She followed, slowly, letting him get further and further ahead.

By the time she got to the house, it looked like Cyrus's whole family was in the yard. Arash was clinging to Cyrus's mother. She recognized them from the photographs. The humiliation of it all. Not only had he never invited her here, she had never been invited to his home when his family was over. And somehow she had allowed a declaration of love to come out of her mouth.

Cyrus saw her and limped over. "Thank goodness. You're all right."

"Not you."

Cyrus's lip was split and his clothes were torn. His eye was starting to swell. "He kicked my leg fairly hard. I couldn't follow. But I saw John and Mark go after him," he said. "They got Arash back."

"What now?"

"John says the police are coming. We have to wait for them. Give our statements."

"Me, too?"

He nodded, but looked at her quizzically. "They'll want to know everything you know."

This is not what she wanted at all. The story would explode before they could tell it.

"I have to call Amina."

"Maybe now they'll stop coming after Parisa with the police involved." He was angry. "We should have gone to the police immediately, but I held back."

She saw it; he had held back because of her politics and now he was angry with himself and even if he did not love Parisa, this one thing would have driven a wedge between them as it had all the other men of this class she had been stupid enough to fall for. She controlled her tone for his sake, but meant it as full-throated sarcasm. "I'm sure of it."

"You have to agree now, Parisa cannot be involved in this. Her own child!"

What was she supposed to say? That the attempted kidnapping of her child did not affect if she was involved in this mess in some other way? That it may actually confirm that she was involved, otherwise why go after her like this?

"We had already told the police about the threat to Parisa and Arash, the phone call, everything. They took a report but said there was nothing they could do, but now, certainly."

He was saying too much. She thought she saw it in his eyes; he did doubt Parisa.

"Tell me what you know," he said.

Instead of answering the demand, telling him what she came there for, she answered his earlier question. "If the cops can trace the car back to them, I guess they can do something."

"Tomoko, please. Tell me what you know about her."

She did, gratefully, as if it would get the taste of humiliation out of her mouth. "Two people followed us north to the camp. They're involved with the person who leaked her the data. But her apartment was being secretly filmed. Anthony tapped into the video and I saw her go into her apartment and pull out a hidden USB drive from a heating vent. Remember when she told us it had been stolen? Then she went up and dug the camera out. She knew exactly where it was. All that effort that first morning to avoid a possible tail and she knew there was none. She was lying to you the minute she walked through your door."

His face became strangely passive and he looked down the road, seemingly expecting the police car to turn the corner, but she knew it was just because he needed time. When he returned his attention to her, he had changed. His expression was distant. "What you said before."

She walked past him. "Forget I said it."

He joined her, limping. "Tomoko, don't talk like that."

"Don't tell me what to say." She snapped, then stopped. He did not want her and she did not want his apologies. "I'm sorry. It's all just been a lot. I was feeling a lot. I'm feeling a lot right now. But none of it means I think you and I should be together."

With that, they walked silently together to the crowd. The security man who had yelled at her approached, holding an ice pack to the back of his head.

"John." Cyrus said. "Is there anything else?"

"No. I want to apologize to her," he said, gesturing to Tomoko.

"What happened?" Cyrus looked between the two.

"I said something stupid." She said, addressing John.

"I get you. Don't worry about it. I shouldn't have sworn like that."

She put her hand on her heart, but, she hoped, her expression indicated that she was grateful because she was in the wrong. She was in the wrong about a lot of things. Then she turned to Cyrus. "I have to tell Amina I won't be back anytime soon."

DAY EIGHT

40

At dawn, Sarah hobbled over with Izzy, the two bringing a hot pot of coffee for Parisa, Beatrice and George. Parisa got Sarah seated and took over the coffee, serving everyone.

George took his to the door, standing by it like an old guard dog with nothing left in him but his obligation to his people. Beatrice smiled sweetly at him and sat near the wood stove.

"Breakfast at our cottage," Sarah said, then pointing at Beatrice and Parisa, "but only once you two tell us what's going on."

Stan and Izzy had been reluctant to leave them last night, but Parisa had finally got the two men out. After George insisted on sleeping in the armchair by the door, Beatrice came to her room and the two had spent the night talking.

She unravelled what Nick had done to her, and why it had been possible in the first place. She explained the videos, telling her about the deepfakes and the threat to use them if she left. Parisa wanted to strangle her father for his cruelty and Nick for using her brokenness to break her further. But Beatrice only marvelled at the kindness of her friends, at how they came together to help her escape.

In turn, Parisa told her about the protests, prison, the rapes, her ex, and his abuse. Then she recounted meeting Cyrus, the kind man he was then and now, and admitted that she had lied to him. She loved him and was afraid the lies had ruined it all.

They held each other, promising better days were to come. Beatrice fell asleep next to her and Parisa vowed come morning, she would tell the truth.

"Okay, you two," Parisa said. "Take notes. You tell Tomoko. I'm done talking to her."

Izzy sat forward, but Sarah got a protective look in her eye and it was not for Parisa.

She began, leaving Beatrice out of it. If she wanted to jump in, she could. "Nick Barnes created a virus that would defraud customers of Wellington Payday Loans. He installed it, suspecting the Wellingtons would let it run. The virus kicked back data to him proving the fraud. Barnes pulled the data together and packaged it so it was easy for us to read and making it seem like the Wellingtons installed it themselves."

"I came up here to tell her that," Beatrice said. "She needed to know."

"Izzy said you escaped this man?" Sarah asked.

"Yes." She glanced at George. "George is helping me get away for good, but I insisted we warn Parisa about the threats on her first."

Sarah put a hand out. "How do we know we can trust you?"

George gave her a hard look.

"Once we had your names, we called Tomoko to check them out. You're an actress. How do we know this is not a performance?"

"I don't understand." A look of panic came over her face.

"Your work in pornography."

She moaned, her already pale skin turning white. "The deepfakes. Oh God. He released them. My parents."

Parisa went to her, but George was there first, getting her up to take her outside.

Parisa grabbed their coats and tried to follow. "I promise you, we'll get news to them." But George pushed her off and Parisa let them go, returning to sit with Sarah and Izzy. "Tell Tomoko to call her parents and tell them it's all a lie."

"What do you mean?"

"Deepfakes."

"What is that?"

"He can make pornographic videos, even supposedly live videos, that look like her, photographs, anything he wants, but it's not her."

Izzy looked at Sarah. "People can do that?"

"Yes!" She stared them down. "Call Tomoko. It's fake. He did it to keep her from leaving. She lost everything coming up here."

"How can you be sure?"

"Did you see her face? Do you have no judge of character?"

Sarah nodded, slowly accepting it. "Okay. You're right." Then, she said, looking out the window, "Poor thing." She turned to Izzy, who looked stricken. "Please go call Tomoko. Now."

He got up and left the two of them alone.

"Now you, talk." Sarah's skepticism was back.

Parisa sat, repeating what she had told Beatrice and George last night. How she had helped produce the analysis, yet did not want to be cited. How the chair and Agape conspired to terminate Monaghan, despite Agape promising her it would only amount to censure. "Monaghan is not a bad man, but you don't have to be bad to do a lot of harm. He needed to know it and I needed to see him take responsibility for it."

"Anything else?"

"Agape not only offered to have Monaghan censured, he asked me if I wanted the chair, Bernard, to be taken down for raping students."

"What?" Sarah nearly jumped out of her chair, but her bad hip forced her back, wincing.

She explained, "Sex with students is not illegal or even against university policy. If they consent, nothing can be done."

"But can they consent?" Sarah retorted.

"Exactly. And the way Bernard went after them demonstrates he was grooming them. I found out about it when a student forwarded me email exchanges between him and her friend. Her friend had shared them, excited about the affair with her professor. But the student who sent the emails to me understood it was wrong and hoped I could do something. When I dug around, there was more, a lot more, but nothing the law could touch."

"I'm all for sexual freedom, but this is not that."

"No, it is not. Agape said he could get him another way. Bernard was being bribed by the Wellingtons to go after Monaghan and he had proof. That could take Bernard down. He gave me a burner phone, promising contact and news."

"And?"

"That's just it. I trusted him to do it, but all I've seen is Monaghan get terminated and our lives threatened. I was willing to ride it out for a bit, but he never called." She added angrily, "I lied to someone I love because of him, but all I got was one phone call from some woman representing Agape telling me there was a camera in my apartment, even where it was, and that the Wellingtons had put out a threat on my life. Arash and I got out of there fast. Before I left, I called another graduate student. Karine. I said I hated Monaghan and had no interest in the Payday Loan data. I was going to get out of town for a bit. I knew she'd tell everyone."

Izzy came back and took a seat next to Sarah. "I couldn't reach her, but I left a message. And I told those two outside we're trying."

Parisa nodded gratefully.

"You went to see Cyrus?" Sarah pulled her back to the conversation.

"Yes. That's where I met Tomoko. I felt she could tell my story. The threat of the press might get Agape to get everything under control, like he promised. And if he could not, then maybe public exposure might. I only told her enough to get the story going. I wanted to give Agape a chance, but all that's happened is that he used me for some end that I don't understand and I'm fucking tired of being used." Her voice broke. "I want my son!"

Sarah looked at Izzy, indicating him to speak.

"We got a call from Tomoko this morning. There was an attempted abduction of your son."

She was out of her seat and had a hold of Izzy's arms. "Is he—"

"He's fine. He's safe with Cyrus and his family. The police have a car out in front of the house and there is private security, too."

"I have to leave." She got up, throwing what little she had back into her tote. "You have to get me out of here."

Sarah suggested, "Maybe Stan? We don't have a car. Stan does everything for us."

But Parisa had another idea. She opened the door and looked back at Sarah. "If I can get George to take me to the city, can you protect Beatrice until he returns?"

They nodded.

"George!" Parisa called out as she left the cottage. "George!" She found them by the lake, watching the mist crawl through the stepped white pines and across the water. She took Beatrice's hand, explaining everything. "They'll watch you here. If George can take me to my son. It would be the world."

"Go," Beatrice insisted. "George, I'll be safe here. Come back to me and we'll head out."

He agreed reluctantly.

I'm going to a friend," she began.

"Stop!" George shouted.

"I can trust her," Beatrice assured him. Unable to stop her, George stalked back to the cottage. "She's in her hometown in Newfoundland. It's barely even a town, and she lives outside it, pretty much off the grid. She said people can disappear out there."

"I'm horrified he did this to you." The two held each other, then went back to the cottage, meeting Izzy and Sarah outside.

"You staying with us?"

Beatrice nodded.

"Then we'd prefer if you were in our daughter's room, where we can take better care of you."

George returned, giving Parisa a look that said he would come for her if she told anyone, then leaned down, whispering something to Beatrice, who said, "Don't worry."

Parisa and George began the walk up the road to Stan's house to get his car.

George was still steaming.

"I'm sorry to take you from her."

"She's a daughter to me and I'm going to bring down anyone who tries to hurt her."

"These men, always these men." But Parisa knew he meant her, too.

For her, "these men" were the prison guard, Andy, Agape, Bernard, and even Monaghan. Would any of them ever understand what they had done? There were good men, and she held onto them or she would have nothing left for love. She conjured up the images of her father and uncles. Cyrus. Beautiful-souled Cyrus. But there was a trickle of fear that he would change on her, become one of them. Then she realized the answer to trusting him was in her lies. Parisa would know him when she admitted it all. If he was not cruel, even if he left her, then she was not wrong to have loved him.

"I watched her get caught up with Nick," George said. "Nothing I said could get her away. I just told her every time I saw her, I would help when she was ready. Reverend Lee, too. All our friends. We were always ready. She called me and here I am." His voice turned cold. "Barnes is going to get it if it is the last thing I do."

Parisa got an idea. "I can't give you Barnes, but can I give you someone else who's done the same to young women, a lot of young women?"

"Who?"

She touched her backpack. "Remember the professor I mentioned last night? I have a USB drive in here of emails between him and three students he raped, including attachments of intimate photographs he took of them together."

"How do we get him?"

"I can't expose the students by going public with it. But I know where he lives. You get me to my son first, then I'll get you and all the emails and the images to this professor's wife."

41

Martin barged through his brother's front door, yelling, "Conor!"

Oonagh hurried to him, drying her hands. "Mother of God, you startled me! He's upstairs. Tell him to come down in time for breakfast before he goes."

"Sorry, Oonagh." He rushed past her and up the floating staircase, watching his feet, despising his brother's taste in architecture.

"You, too!" she called after him.

But Martin had no intention of sitting down for breakfast with his brother; he wanted answers and opened the black double doors to the bedroom suite without knocking.

Conor swung around, wearing only his underwear with a pair of trousers laid over his arm. He dropped them and went to his brother. "Martin! I was so worried!" Conor looked him up and down. "Did you sleep in your car again? You would have been safe here."

"And you would have known I was safe, how?" He broke free of his brother's grip.

"I don't understand."

"I followed you last night. I saw everything."

Conor blanched, stammering, "Followed me...where?"

"Where do you think? You set me up. You and the cult you belong to. You did this to me."

"Martin." He took a step forward, hands out.

"Back off."

"I lied to them."

"You lied to me!"

"No. I didn't know what Agape has done. I still don't know the whole story. They're dangerous. I lied to them last night to protect you."

He examined his brother's face, wishing he could be certain. "What is this fucking mushroom thing? You never said anything about that back in the day. You've been lying to me about it from the beginning."

Conor flushed with guilt. "I couldn't. You wouldn't have believed me. You would have fought me even harder." He turned away from Martin, picked up his trousers and hung them up on the suit caddy, and disappeared into his dressing room.

Martin wanted to follow him there, watch his face, see if he was finding a way to lie to him without him observing.

He returned in a pair of sweats that looked as though Oonagh had pressed them, but his face was a mess. "I'll tell you, as best I can, although it won't make sense."

"Whatever it is. You tell me the truth, I won't turn on you."

"You don't know that." Conor pushed him away and sat on the edge of the bed.

Martin sat across from him, perched on a black leather chair. "Let's try."

"You were right. When you told me all those years ago that Bailey had kidnapped me. He worked on me little by little. You saw it. You tried to save me." He looked at him desperately. "There was nothing you could have done. They had me."

"Mom didn't help."

He raised his head, stricken. "I don't want to speak ill of her. Lord rest her soul."

Martin frowned. "I will. She pushed you into it, wanting you to take our father's place. She was a wreck, I get it. Bailey was giving her money."

"He what?"

"Yeah, Mom told me before she died." He sniggered. "She sat there beaming, telling me how Bailey had protected us. He had paid all the bills for years, payment he said for all the work you did, cutting grass and then at the office, right up until you graduated and he officially hired you on."

"That means I was the one who paid, then and after."

"What choice did anyone ever give you?"

"You warned me," he said. "I didn't listen."

"They made it so you didn't have a choice."

"No. You remember. I told you. If I did not join them, I could not inherit the business. But it was not entirely about that. I wanted to know Mr. Bailey's secret. I don't know. I think, too, when I heard about the Ritual, that the Ritual had to accept me, I wanted to be accepted."

"That's how they did it. They tied you up in it, told you everything you'd worked for, the man you looked up to, all of it depended on some ritual. They gave you no choice, Conor." Martin shook his head. "Tell me about it."

"It's mushrooms, like you used to do, but different." He gave him an uneasy smile.

"What?" Martin leaned back.

"It's an old religion. Maybe the oldest."

Agape had said that, and now his brother, too.

"Think of it like this: all religions are misunderstandings of fertility religions, putting names of prophets and the word 'god' to what we know is the Lord of all creation. The stem of heaven impregnates the womb of the earth. When we take our communion, our sacred mushroom wine, we see that truth. But there are as many manifestations of the truth as there are spores. We are connected by the hyphae, the filaments that allow us to know each other as one." His voice rose with excitement, his cheeks flushed. "We only know what we have been asked to bear. Our manifestation carries it through the vision of our Lord in the form of Jesus."

None of it made any sense. He clung to something that fit into his head somewhere, asking, "Form of Jesus?"

"Yes, Jesus never lived. This is the form The Lord takes for us. Over time, people mistook the visions for something material, cheapening the truth, leading everyone astray. The churches are nothing but lies. Look what they did to—"

Martin cut him off, horrified. "So you believe this despite what they did to you?"

"I believe Agape has led The Cluster astray."

"'Cluster', like a cluster of mushrooms?"

"I know it sounds stupid, but that night I took the communion. Our Lord, in the form of Jesus, came to me and asked me to bear the burden of cleansing the temple of the moneychangers."

He wanted to shake Conor into some semblance of sanity. All the old arguments came back, taking on new meaning. Conor saying small, private acts mattered most, while Martin wanted to take down the rotten system itself. What was this other than wealthy people creating a whole religion about why they did not have to change a damn thing? This is what the rich do. Fucking rich people will always serve their own interests and exploit the vulnerable; now, he saw, turning some of the vulnerable into themselves, to keep it going, like they did with his brother.

No wonder they thought Jesus wasn't real. That would screw up their game. He had heard preaching at protests that Jesus was a social radical. Jesus was a real person who sided with the poor. He would not side with people like Agape; he went after whole systems, not handing out charity to the rich and changing nothing. Martin only hoped this mushroom Jesus of theirs saw the vulnerability in his brother and would save him because Martin had no idea how to bring him back.

Martin prodded, "How does all that work if your cluster has a relationship with the Wellingtons?"

Conor answered, embarrassed. "I didn't know. Vincent's firm

represents many people we would not approve of, but the firm uses the income to support the true mission, their *pro bono* work. Agape only just told me he had acted as advisor to the Wellingtons. But it was a vision, one of our visions, that told me Agape had betrayed me. The path is true and they are the ones who have been corrupted."

Martin let it stand. He knew that voice and knew his brother believed what he was saying. "Tell me more about Agape, then."

"Last night, after I got back, I went through Agape's account, going back decades, to the founding of the firm. There have been large lump-sum payments to women over the years."

"I can only imagine what he is covering up. Where does he get his money?"

"There was only ever one deposit into our financial records. At the founding. One hundred million dollars. Back then, in the late eighties. Probably family money. His brother is Agapov from Panopticon Security. They are estranged, so maybe it was a onetime gift, a goodbye?"

Martin's eyes widened. "You sure they are estranged?"

"Yes, it was part of his bearing for The Cluster. We all had to be celibate, but he had to break ties with his family. You can see why. His brother's security firm is, to put it lightly, ethically compromised. The payments to women, though, may have to do with his role as a servant to Mary Magdalene."

"For services rendered? She was Jesus's disciple. A sex worker."

"No. I cannot imagine that!" He looked aside, but was obviously doubting. "I don't know. We don't tell each other. Only my role is transparent to all the members as I control the finances."

"So, what's your relationship to the Wellingtons?"

Conor stood, protesting. "I don't have one. Not one that I know of, honestly."

"Agape said I made my own bed."

"When did you talk to Agape?"

"That night, I questioned him after you left. He says the Wellingtons bribed Bernard. He had nothing to do with my termination."

Conor paced. "He told me he tried to protect you, but failed."

"The man has a lot of failures, it seems."

"What is that?" He stared. "Tell me."

"Just something he said. I saw the papers in your office. Who is Marlene Jordan?"

Conor approached him, intent. "Answer me first, the failures."

But Conor was in no position to direct the conversation, and Martin stared at him silently until he answered.

"A client." Conor gave in. "I've never met her. Agape set up her account. There was a request to buy stock in Wellington Payday Loans. I refused. Then"—he paused, a strange look came over him—"the request changed to liquidate her funds and put it in an untraceable account in Singapore. I did that, happy to get her out of my business."

"You don't think that was odd?" Martin pushed, trying to get at whatever it was he saw behind his eyes. "Right when all this is happening?"

"Yes, now I do." He took a deep breath. "I don't know how to explain the rest. But Miss Henson insisted I buy the stock, then, uh, showed her true colours."

"What does that mean?"

"She's got dementia, but that's not it. She is the administrative assistant of The Cluster, but more, she is an emissary." He looked at Martin apologetically. "She is an emissary of Legion."

Martin rubbed his face with his hand. "I heard that night at your meeting. Agape used that word about her."

"A representative of the forces of evil." He looked away. "With us until the final battle".

"So crazy Miss Henson insisting on you buying that stock for Jordan was part of that?"

"I don't know. I guess. But whoever Jordan is, she's not my concern anymore."

"But Legion is?"

"Always will be. Something is coming." His voice became quiet. "I had a vision. I observed the Last Supper, then I was in the Garden of Gethsemane. Remember? Jesus' night before his trial and execution.

He is warned of Judas's betrayal. He is told he will have to offer the greatest sacrifice. During that night, his friends slept rather than stand beside him because he must do it alone."

Martin remembered the scene, one of the nights that came before the crucifixion. The youth worker who had them in Sunday school must have wanted to be an actor because he did it like Jesus was a character in a soap opera, lots of clutching at his chest, and looking desperately up to the heavens, begging God and when God did not answer, screaming, "Why have You forsaken me!" They could barely hold back their laughter and when it burst out, they got hit with a ruler and every smack was worth it. "So you watched Jesus go through that?"

"No. I was Jesus."

Martin saw it all. They had manipulated some sort of magic mushroom vision so that they could kill his brother and Conor would let them, thinking he was Jesus Fucking Christ. Agape's cryptic message came back to him. He said he keeps the Wellingtons and others under his watch. He said Legion would consume them. He was going to kill the Wellingtons, too. No, he rethought it. Agape and those men were not going to kill Conor. They were going to set him up for the murder of the Wellingtons. He was going to be the sacrifice to bring the Wellingtons down. How the fuck did any of this make any sense? They could have just let the data go through, kept him from being terminated. He would have been able to take the Wellingtons down and none of this would be happening.

But Martin could protect his brother. He stood and went over to him, kneeling. "Conor, listen. Promise me you'll stay home. They are going to try to set you up. I need you to invite someone over. Keep Oonagh here tonight. You're going to need an alibi."

42

"You know where she went!" Nick screamed at Reverend Lee.

They stood in the doorway of the church kitchen, chest out, tattooed arms holding either side of the frame, a woman stood just behind them, arms crossed. Reverend Lee was small, easy enough for him to push aside, but the woman behind them had the build of a tank.

"You're disturbing our people. Leave. Now."

A rail-thin man came up beside him, shrugging a ratty blanket off his shoulders. "Go," he said in a voice ruined by drink and a life on the streets.

Nick turned around to see nearly a dozen more. One man was as big a mountain, with a face that had seen the worst of life. All were dressed in layers of clothes that Nick himself had surely paid for, and all were ready to act for Reverend Lee's sake. Hands up in surrender, he said to the reverend before he left, "You'll answer for this."

He faced down the crowd, expecting them to part as he walked toward them, but they held firm, forcing him to walk along the wall of them instead and cross through a bed of plantings. A small bush pulled at his pants and seeds from dried up flowers littered around him. Out onto the main path, he waited until he was out of Unity Square to brush them off.

His driver held open the car door and he slid inside. "Cherry Beach Dog Park."

He pulled out a phone and made a call.

"This is Elliot. You must have something. I've just been to the church. They're lying. They helped her escape."

"Yes, we know you were there. We've just had a call from one of our men at the church."

"You have someone there?"

"The one who threatened you to leave."

Nick pricked with embarrassment that he had not seen through the man's disguise and punched back. "Then why hasn't he found anything out?"

"He has, but nothing of use. When people ask after her, the reverend just shrugs. Anyone who was there that day reports that she left on her own."

"I know they were involved."

"We don't know that."

"You need to put pressure on the reverend." He hung up without waiting for an answer.

Nick scoured the streets for any sign of Bea as they drove. The driver slowed in the dirt parking lot, but the car still lurched as he navigated through the deep potholes. Nick got out and hurried to one of the gates.

A lean, sun-burnished dog walker in an old down vest opened the back of a van and one dog after another jumped out. She took a long look at Nick as he walked by, and commanded the dogs to stick beside her.

He opened the gate wide for them, but inside, a white spotted cattle dog ran for the gate. The dog walker reached her hand out and yanked it shut, just in time, and scolded him. "Watch it."

"Barney!" A slim woman dressed in expensive work clothes ran towards them.

"Fucking people with dogs they can't handle," the dog walker muttered, opening the gate again now that Barney was under control. Her dogs tumbled through and Nick went in with them, the woman shutting the gate behind him.

"Where's your dog?" She came up next to him.

"I'm looking for a friend," he turned, giving her one of his smiles.

"I don't know any friends," she said and strode after the dogs.

He caught up with her. "That's an odd answer. I wasn't asking you."

"Fuck off. If you don't have a dog, leave."

She called after one of the dogs and hurried ahead, but he saw her pull out her phone, texting.

Three dog walkers ahead who had been talking to each other while the dogs ran through the woods, pulled out their phones, then looked at him. There was no point in asking questions, they were not going to answer.

Turning back out of the park, he called the same number, angry. "This is Elliot. Did you question the dog walkers at Cherry Beach again? They all know who I am. They warned each other off from speaking to me."

"Yes, we've sent someone down there with dogs to listen and talk, but like with the church, there is nothing. She will come back online at some point. We suggest you wait."

"I can't wait!" He hung up the phone, shoving it into his jacket pocket and unlatched the gate, leaving it open.

A scrawny woman who looked like one of Reverend Lee's people ran up to shut it, yelling, "Hey!" Then, with a meaningful look, said quietly, "Meet me up the road."

Nick climbed back into the waiting car. "Drive up past the lot, out of view of the park, and wait there."

The driver pulled up and Nick opened the door, standing just within it, and looked across the spread of the beach to the spot where his mother and friends would meet. A biting breeze blew off the water, but people were still out walking along the shore, kayaking and paddling on the lake. He watched a kite surfer catch the wind and take off. The woman caught up, dragging an ancient short-legged dog.

The dog walker looked up and down the street, then said, "George took her. But no one knows where."

"What is George's last name?" He gripped the door.

She shrugged. "George took Beatrice. We haven't seen him since."

Jealousy burned through him, imagining him as her secret lover all this time. "Why would he help her?"

"A big dog pulled George's back out. He lost all his clients, but Beatrice took care of him," she said bitterly, as if no one had ever cared for her when she was down.

He demanded, "Who was he to her?"

She tucked her head back, realizing what he meant and snorted. "Not that. No. George's an old guy, more like her dad or something."

But that only burned more deeply.

The woman held out her hand for money.

Nick ignored it. "None of them would talk to me. Why you?"

She tapped her hand.

"They need money in there, but they didn't give Bea up."

"Because when George came back, he moved in on my territory, stole all my dogs."

With her gaunt face, ragged hair, and threadbare clothes, he guessed George had no trouble taking her clients. "Where was your territory?"

"Distillery." Her face lit up. "George's got posters up there with his phone number."

"Thanks." Nick turned to get into the car

"Hey, what about me? Pay me!"

With a glance at her hand, he smiled. "Who carries cash?"

"Fuck you, man!" She turned away, dragging the ancient dog along.

Nick looked out down the beach toward the small woods where his mother took him and sighed, going after her. He peeled off a hundred dollars from his billfold and held it out. She snatched it from him, then spit on the ground, carrying on, this time slow enough for the dog to keep up.

Back inside the car, he told the driver, "Go to the Distillery District, drive down Mill Street, slowly." They had only gone one block when he saw a light pole covered with flyers. He got out and found George's poster among the offers for bitcoin, piano lessons, and a meeting to protest for more affordable housing in the condos going up around the area.

The poster showed a picture of a giant man in a denim shirt, surrounded by dogs sitting at attention. "Cherry Beach Walks. Exhausted Dogs Guaranteed." And a phone number.

He dialled again. "This is Elliot, doing your job for you. A dog walker named 'George' left with Bea. Here's his number. Track that." He hung up and said to the driver. "Back to the office."

Nick tapped his finger on the back of his phone, eager to return and see how the trolling and bots were doing. Bea's online ravaging was taking perfect shape. The Cristo Team had gone above and beyond. The OnlyFans deepfake "live" streams had taken off. They created a string of porn subscribers and fans who commented and shared her content, pushing her up in popularity on the site, bringing in real fans, pushing her up even further. They leaked images and comments on social media, tagging her rich family and old friends, created accounts calling her a slut, some slathering over her, while others gave a feminist take on sexual freedom. Then they pushed the feminist posts in front of traditionally minded women and toxic men. It took off perfectly. Bea was both hailed and reviled.

For the Wellingtons, the team built on *The Spanner* story, ignoring Martin entirely and pushing the fraud narrative in leftist accounts, a government collusion narrative in both left and right wing accounts, kept the China angle going, and then had bots set to nitpicking each other until real people piled on, then his team inflamed them further. Samuel had called him in, tearing up with laughter, to show him a web of blogs, posts, and connections made by creating a storyline about the Wellingtons privately funding male sterility drugs introduced into vaccines. They used photos of Wellington sitting at a dinner with the head of the largest pharmaceutical manufacturer of COVID vaccines in Canada. Quotes were planted in stories of the liberal elite's plan to sterilize good, virile men.

His fury ignited. The bonfire was beautiful.

43

Conor promised Martin he would stay home and call Oonagh in to give him an alibi. For what, Martin would not say. He was adamant, so Conor reassured him, but the moment Martin left, he called an emergency meeting of The Cluster. One would betray him. It was time for the confrontation and, perhaps, through it, in the garden of his own Gethsemane, he would better understand the nature of his sacrifice.

The medical building was still locked when he arrived. He turned the key, having to jiggle it, and shoved the door open. Despite the fall sun, the windows let in little of the late afternoon light. He flicked on the lights one by one and went to their meeting space, taking Agape's chair, facing the door to observe the men.

The door scraped. Pierre and Marcus were speaking. Pierre coughed and when they came around the corner, he was dressed in a toque, scarf, but a deep winter coat this time. Marcus was supporting him.

Conor stood. "How are you?" Then he asked Marcus. "That cough?"

"I have him on antibiotics." Marcus gave Conor a scolding look. "He should not be here, but you called an emergency meeting."

There was no response to that. If one of them called a meeting, they had to come unless they were physically restricted, in which case, the meeting could not go forward. It was an absurd rule he had suggested amending any number of times, but Agape refused. He only now realized why. It had less to do with making sure all the members were included, than Agape making sure no meeting could go forward without him.

Marcus was easing Pierre into his seat as Ipe and Benjamin came in together. Benjamin said, "Agape is behind us and he's brought Miss Henson."

Conor asked, "Did he inform any of you she was coming!"

"No." Pierre's face, already grey, now blanched with fear.

Agape came in, Miss Henson on his arm.

Benjamin pulled up another chair for her, but Agape waved him off. "Only The Cluster sits."

But he placed the extra chair by the wall anyway, glancing at Agape in apology as he did so.

Agape sat in Conor's chair without remark and opened the meeting, laying a hand over a fist and saying, "By the Mushroom and the Cross. I am a bearer of the Lord. I am a servant of The Cluster."

They repeated after him in unison.

Conor steeled himself, then began. "There are secrets among us that must be revealed."

Except for Pierre, the men gazed at Conor with simple curiosity, as if he were about to ask about a cookie sale, while Miss Henson kept her attention on Agape.

"Agape," Conor said, "you have not been honest about your involvement in my brother's case."

He frowned. "I do not understand. I explained to you I tried to protect your brother, it was not possible. The chair of the department had taken a bribe from the Wellingtons. There was nothing I could do at that point."

"But what is missing from your account?"

Agape leaned forward, clasping his hands. "Miss Henson even called Parisa and warned her and her child to leave their apartment.

She went to your brother's house to warn him as well. My involvement is purely an act of protection."

Conor glanced at Miss Henson, who was nodding in agreement, then addressed Agape. "Why is a representative of Legion assisting you?"

Ipe intervened. "I feel uncomfortable with this line of questioning."

"Yes," Benjamin agreed, while Vincent gave Conor a look of reproach.

"No, brothers, he must ask. I must answer," said Agape. "She is here to watch, but also to assist when those who are against us must be opposed together. The enemy of our enemy is our friend."

"And who is the shared enemy here?" Conor asked, knowing it to be himself.

"The Wellingtons, of course. I cannot speak to Legion's interest in their destruction, but the Wellingtons are beyond my help. Miss Henson, do you care to comment?"

Everyone turned to her, except Pierre, who seemed afraid, but the old woman simply tightened her lips.

Conor pressed, asking her, "Why did you insist I purchase Wellington Payday Loan stock for Marlene Jordan? Did Agape ask you to do that?"

Vincent said, "Truly, Conor. This is enough."

"I did ask her to do that," Agape interjected, hand out to Ipe.

Ipe said, "You had better explain."

"Marlene Jordan is not her real name. She is Cassandra Wellington."

"Agape!" Ipe exclaimed.

"I made the initial investment in her name. I wanted her to have what she needed to escape her family, but she never used it." He said with contempt, "The investment in her family's business was, shall we say, a warning to her that if she did not leave, she would be forever tied to their concerns, tainted by their filth through her mere inaction."

"Why do you care about her?" Conor asked.

"It is my bearing to care about all of those who are within my scope of influence. But I knew her from the time she was a girl. The family was hard on her. She rebelled. I had high hopes she would leave them, but she seems to have fallen in line with their ways. It turns out she cares more for money than her conscience."

Benjamin said, "But you just said you gave her money."

"Hardly anything in comparison. Nothing like what she gains by taking over the family business. Her husband is bound to the wealth, her children benefit from it. She cannot or will not give it up. I admit, I asked her to make a sacrifice."

"I checked your account. You've been making payments to women over the years. Explain that."

Conor had expected Agape to be affronted, instead he bowed his head in modesty. "I tried to help many women, including the Wellingtons' daughter, Patricia."

It made sense on the surface, but something about it was a lie. The men seemed to have accepted his explanation, except perhaps Pierre.

Marcus stood, his hand on Pierre's shoulder. "I propose the Ritual. Pierre needs the cleansing, and you two need it to trust each other."

"We will set the Intention," Agape said.

That was the last thing Conor wanted. He trusted his vision and feared that the betrayal might come while he was away in the world of the extraordinary, and before he understood the nature of his sacrifice. He imagined his brother, Parisa, her child, all those who had been harmed by Agape in ways he did not know. If he failed, if the betrayal came before he was ready, he could not save them. He choked on a half-spoken objection. But there was no avenue of refusal once the words of Intention had been said.

Agape stood and crossed the room to Miss Henson. "I will have to ask you to leave."

She unclenched long enough to get up to go, but not before she delivered a matronly stare of disapproval, then walked in an uneven line toward Conor. She clawed at his jacket, pulling him close and hissed in his ear, "See? The brother knows everything. Ask Agape about his wife." She released him and carried on.

Ipe followed her out.

"What was that?" Agape took a step towards him. "I heard my name."

"She told me to trust you."

Miss Henson's footsteps disappeared, and the outer door shut. Ipe returned. "The door is locked."

Benjamin began the preparations for the Ritual. He brought out the leather case that carried their sacramental objects, removing the wooden bowl, the ladle and cups, then finally, the dried mushroom powder in its leather sack and the wine. Reverently, he laid them out on a small table. His back to them, they sat in silence as he whispered the prayers.

As Benjamin recited, Conor swayed, drawn into a vision before even tasting the communion, pulling him from the room and back to Jerusalem. His hands were in a wooden bowl before him, crushing fresh red capped mushrooms. His hands raised, their stained palms facing the men, and said, "One of you will betray me." His hands poured wine from a jug into the bowl, pressing the crushed mushrooms into the thick red liquid. His hands raised, their stained palms to the men. The wine and mushroom blood dripped down his arms.

"Conor, brother."

He returned to them with a start.

Benjamin handed him his cup.

"Forgive me."

They held the cups out, saying as one,

"Under the shade of the Mushroom Cap, we meet our Lord, Ukushtigila, The Key to the Kingdom. We eat our Lord. Ukushtigila, The Key to the Kingdom. We drink our Lord. Ukushtigila, The Key to the Kingdom. We serve our Lord."

They drank. The woody mushroom wine warmed him.

Pierre stifled a cough, then the cough overtook him. Marcus gave his cup to Benjamin and kneeled beside Pierre until the coughing subsided. Despite seeming too ill, Pierre gestured they should continue. Conor only prayed the communion would heal him.

Benjamin took their cups and they pulled their chairs into a circle, knees touching, bringing their hands together into the shape of a vulva, saying the words,

"The earth produces first a womb, the Mushroom in the womb."

Then they raised their hands, the vulva becoming the glans-headed mushroom. As they recited the rest, the scent of frankincense and myrrh enveloped him, delivering Conor to the garden of Gethsemane.

As before, the donkey in the garden brayed. The centurions marched. The woman protested, weeping. Her son was dragged away in chains. This time, the sacrifice was before him.

The Lord held out a cup. He knew the truth would be proven through it and drank. The pain of the sacrifice burned down his throat and into his belly. He begged, "Lord, take this from me." But the Lord only held out the cup for him to drink again. The Lord's face gleamed from a gentle light within. His luxuriant brown beard shone, its waves smooth like an ocean on a steady wind. His brown eyes glistened, his tears a gentle rain. He said, "Your Lord has not forsaken you."

Conor sipped again from the cup of the Lord and fell into the abyss. A white-flecked red crowned mushroom emerged in the featureless black cosmos. Small mushrooms grew from its stalk. A red snake slithered around and through it, entwining itself around each of the smaller mushrooms, until its head was shaded by the crown. It opened its mouth and its severed tongue lolled, saying, "Legion."

Conor returned from the horror of the vision to the room slowly, first feeling the hard seat, the firmness of the floor, then the chill of the room, and, finally, heard the men whispering. Conor opened his eyes.

Pierre waved him over.

Marcus was leaning into the shoulder of Vincent, sitting next to him. The two caught up in private conversation.

Conor crossed to Pierre as if he were walking through another dimension, and sat at his feet, taking his hands. "I saw. Did you see?"

"Legion is closer than we think." Pierre looked in Agape's direction, then doubled over, coughing.

Conor whispered in his ear, "A snake. I saw a snake. It said that Legion has come."

Marcus jerked him back. "Let me tend to him. This is not for you."

44

────────

Martin leaned against the trunk of a cedar outside the Wellingtons' iron fence, his feet out. It had been hours since he left Conor. He had texted his brother, wanting to be sure he was at home with Oonagh, securing an alibi, but there was no response. He could not be sure that the Wellingtons were going to be attacked tonight or that Conor was going to be framed for it, but his gut told him it was true. All he could do was hope Conor listened to him.

The sun set. The street lights came on. Headlights rushed past in either direction. In the house, outlines of people illumined by lamplight moved from room to room. He caught the immense figure of Wellington striding, and a woman circling him when he stopped. Then they would disappear and return into view.

Lights turned on in a sunken room on the far side of the house. Wellington and the woman moved in that direction. Martin was going to have to climb the fence again. He touched the gun, zipped up in his fleece pocket, then checked his phone one last time for Conor's reply. He stood, ready to climb the fence, but then the gate rattled open.

A small beat up sedan drew up next to the Wellingtons' Jaguar. The gate closed behind it. He recognized crazy Miss Henson through the passenger window. She got out and walked like a drunk to the house, turning once towards the trees. Even from there, he could see the wild look in her eyes.

It was happening tonight. She was an emissary of Legion. And what had Agape said about the Wellingtons? "Legion will consume them."

She knocked. An elderly servant opened the door immediately. Martin was up and over the fence the moment it shut, his footing more prepared this time. The outdoor lights were on, but he hoped no one was watching the security cameras. He snuck across the driveway towards the room with the sunken windows.

The windows were clouded and dripping from humidity, but he could see the pool below just fine. Wellington and his wife were wearing bathrobes. She removed her robe and waved him off angrily as she slipped into the pool to make swift laps. He could hear Wellington yelling at her as she swam. His words were unintelligible, but the tone was clear enough. Martin moved to another window so he could see the door, wondering why Miss Henson had not joined them.

The gate opened again. He scrambled away from the exposed windows into the nearby shrubs. A small BMW arrived, pulling alongside Miss Henson's car. It was Cassandra. She slammed the door shut and rushed into the house.

He crawled on hands and knees back to a window and peered inside. Miss Henson had come in. Wellington was now yelling at the old woman. His wife bobbed in the water, listening, then swam over to the ladder to join her husband, dripping beside the pool.

Miss Henson's head turned strangely on her neck and she looked directly at Martin through the window and grinned. He dropped down, fished his phone out of his back pocket, fumbled opening the camera, and switched it to video. There was a scream. He popped his head up, video on.

Wellington was holding her off, his hands on her shoulders, while she swiped at him with a knife in her gloved hand. Then he saw it. It was not a knife. It was Bailey's ivory-handled letter opener. But it was not Bailey's letter opener anymore. It was Conor's.

Agape was setting his brother up. For what, though? This woman could not kill Wellington. He was holding her off as if she were a child. Martin kept the video running. At least, it would prove to Conor who these people were and what this religion of his was. It was this, this bloodthirsty insanity.

Then Mrs. Wellington began screaming at Miss Henson. Her muffled voice became suddenly clear, as if a window had been opened on the other side of the poolroom. "Get away from him!" Then, "Francois! Call the police!"

Mrs. Wellington grasped her husband's arm. What could she be thinking? One distraction and he would lose his focus.

Miss Henson was wildly slashing at the air with the letter opener.

Wellington turned slightly, ordering his wife, "Back off!"

As he turned, the blade came up and sliced his neck. Martin dropped without thinking, then raised the camera back up to the window. The screams of Wellington's wife could have shattered the glass. Then her screams stopped and there was a terrible stillness. All Martin could hear was his own ragged breath and his blood beating in his ears.

Then, another scream.

He got up again, peaking over the edge of the window, still filming.

Cassandra was near the door. Her parents lay beside the pool; her mother was face up, draped over her father. Blood was pulsing from her mother's neck and Miss Henson was on top of her, lapping it up like a rabid dog trying to quench its thirst.

She raised her bloody face and turned to Cassandra, grasping for the stiletto beside the bodies, then got up to come at Cassandra, too.

But Cassandra backed up, then turned and rushed to the glass door. Instead of escaping, she threw the bolt. Their servant arrived and pounded on it. Martin could not hear his voice, but the sound of his fists on the glass was enough.

She ignored him and turned to face Miss Henson. "Everyone takes everything from me!"

Miss Henson stopped. Her head cocked, and her hand with the stiletto fell beside her.

"This was for me!" Cassandra reached into her bag and pulled out a gun, pointing it at Miss Henson. There was no sense she had registered a weapon was aimed at her.

Martin crawled along the walls of the house, looking for the open window to see and hear better, holding up the camera to the windows as he went along.

He turned the corner. There was Stone, crouching, watching through the open window. Martin sprang up, hands out, dropping his phone, and leapt onto Stone, who crawled back out of his way, but not far enough. Martin took hold of his arms and trapped his legs underneath with his knees. But he did not fight back, only stared at Martin, then tipped his head toward the window. "Listen."

"I wanted to kill them!" Cassandra moaned.

Martin rolled off of Stone, releasing his legs and arms, and joined him at the window. "Call the police," Martin hissed, then searched around him for his dropped phone.

"I did."

From inside, Cassandra shrieked, "They whored out Patricia to their friends." Martin stopped searching and looked through the window, straining to catch every word. "They gave her to the bankers and their filthy sons in exchange for what?"

Miss Henson was walking toward her, speaking, but her voice was more of a whining dog than human. "Agape tried to save you, but you would not be saved."

"He gave me money. To go where? It was nothing. Not enough."

"You want too much!"

"I was a child! Patricia was a child!"

Miss Henson walked toward Cassandra slowly. "Agape tried to save her. She would not be saved. You would not be saved."

Cassandra looked past Miss Henson at the bodies of her parents. "It was for me," she cried.

"You can, still." Miss Henson continued to walk slowly toward her. "I did it for you."

She pulled back, focusing on Miss Henson again, and pointed the gun at her.

But Miss Henson kept coming.

Muffled screams came from behind the door. The servant had returned, trying to get in. Someone else was behind him.

Finally, sirens sounded in the distance.

The women moved closer to one another.

"Why aren't you in there?" Martin accused Stone.

"I'm not being paid for this."

"You tried to kill us!"

"Threatened. Not tried. Wellington wanted it, but he wasn't our boss."

The sirens got closer.

Martin stared through the window.

"You can be saved. Save yourself." Miss Henson said. Her voice, only just shrieking, lowered to a strange hum. "Run."

For a moment, Cassandra seemed entranced. The gun in her hand wavered.

"Go," Miss Henson said in the same voice, reaching out to her.

Cassandra watched as Miss Henson tried to take her arm. "Free yourself."

A shot cracked. Miss Henson crumpled to the ground.

Martin turned around on his knees, searching for his phone, found it, and tried to shove it into his closed pocket, but felt the gun through the fleece. He had forgotten about it. He shoved the phone in his other pocket, then unzipped the pocket with the gun, pulled it out, and pointed it at Stone.

Stone had been kneeling, transfixed at the window, then turned, saw the gun, and scrambled back.

He got up slowly, hands out.

Martin followed, the gun still pointed at him.

"Listen to me," Stone said. "We answered to Agape, not the

Wellingtons. He controlled everything. He ordered the intimidation. Kidnapping. Everything. You know who his brother is?"

The sirens were only blocks away. Martin stepped back, wanting to run.

Stone answered his own question. "Agapov. Panopticon. I got sent the key to the virus out of nowhere right at the start. We never could have figured it out. We knew it was from Nick Barnes, but Agape had us keep it a secret." He pointed to the window. "That old woman. She worked for Agape." Then Stone gave him one nod and tore past him and was gone.

Martin followed, running straight for the fence, shoving the gun into his pocket and zippering it. There were no trees along the fence this side of the house, but somehow he leapt high enough to grab the top, hauled himself up, got a foot on the rail and threw himself over, landing hard on his side. He was up and across the street and into his car just as the police were turning the corner.

One police car after another arrived, lights flashing. He pulled out slowly and past the cars, turning onto the next street, then another and another, then pulled over. He opened his phone. The video was still recording. He stopped it, then called it up to play. It was blurry and shaking, hard to see, but if he had to, he had everything he needed to protect Conor.

45

———————

The wait to call Cyrus was agonizing.

"Not until we're back in Toronto," George insisted. "Maybe Nick has figured out I took her. I'm not putting my SIM card back into my phone until no one can guess we've been north."

George would not even let her get a burner, saying he would leave her by the side of the road if she did. But when they had pulled in for gas, she checked the convenience store. Infuriatingly, they did not even sell prepaid sims. Parisa had put a hundred dollar bill on the counter, begging the clerk to let her use the store phone, but it had only scared him and he demanded she leave.

Finally, the blinking lights of Wonderland's roller coasters rose in the distance. A few more kilometres and they would make it into the city, then she could call him. It was late. George needed to nap before he could drive her down and then would not leave until he was certain Bea was safe. Parisa pulled out Cyrus's card from her wallet, touching the edges, praying Arash was safe, but knowing even if he were, he was afraid and she had not been there to protect him. Worse, she was the one who had put him at risk. Parisa watched the cars rush past them and wanted to scream at George to go faster. Her muscles twitched. By turns she wanted to vomit or open the car door and throw herself out as if she could land running to her son.

Wonderland was beside them now. The lights of the city were just ahead. Parisa could not stand it anymore and demanded, "Give me the phone!"

To his word, George stared straight ahead until they had turned off the 400 onto the 401, then handed it over. "SIM is in the back cover."

Parisa tore the back cover off, nearly dropping the tiny card and the pin. She placed the SIM card frantically, telling herself to slow down so she would not break the paper-bound sliver of metal, ruining her chances, but she could not control her hands. Once in, it seemed like minutes before the bars appeared. She called and it rang and rang, but he did not pick it up. Of course, an unknown number. She texted him.

> It's Parisa. I'm calling on someone else's phone.

Then she redialled.

He picked up immediately and began speaking before she could say a word. "Arash is safe. He misses you. But he's fine."

"I heard. Tomoko got the news to me. I came back as soon as I could."

George threw her a dirty look and whispered, "Don't say where we were!"

"Where are you?"

Parisa nodded, answering Cyrus as if others were listening, "Coming east. From London. She has some friends there at the university."

"What?"

She cut him off before he could mention Tomoko's cottage. "I'm coming to you now. Are you at your mother's?"

"Yes." He gave her the address.

"Get off at Yonge and go north," she said to George, then to Cyrus, "Tell me how he is."

"It was frightening, of course. He had been sleeping with me anyway, but during the day he was playing with my nephews, and enjoying my mother's attention, the whole family. Then this happened. If he's not clinging to me, he has my mother's hand."

"I did this to him."

"You thought you were protecting him by leaving. How could anyone know they would come for him?"

There was something different in his voice. Was it fear? Resentment that she had brought violence to his mother's home? She asked, "And your family? I am so sorry."

"We'll talk when you get here. Just come and hold your son."

She hung up, near tears. There was undeniable distance in his voice.

"What's wrong?" George asked.

"I need to see my son."

"It's more than that, but if you don't want to tell me, fine."

She gave him a hard look, but answered, "The man I left my son with, to keep him safe while I hid out, he's judging me for it."

"Fuck him."

But Parisa did not agree. Cyrus had a right to be upset.

George turned off the 401 and threaded into traffic on Yonge Street. "We all have to learn to trust our instincts the hard way, I guess."

"I love him."

"That makes it more complicated."

"It does."

"Maybe I misread him," she added reluctantly.

"I guess you'll see."

They turned off onto a suburban street of aging split-levels with big front lawns. Parisa craned her neck, watching the house numbers go by, then finally she saw it. "There!"

She was out of the car before it came fully to a stop. Cyrus must have been waiting by a window. The front door was open and Arash was in her arms before she could get a few steps up the path.

"Qorboonesh beram." She held him deep in her arms, cupping

his head, feeling the softness of his hair, breathing in the sweetness of her baby boy. "I'm here now."

But Arash struggled in her arms as if he were trying to break free. She did not let go, only whispered again and again, "I'm here," until he returned her embrace and cried.

Cyrus stood above them, but she refused to look up, not wanting to think or feel anything about him, only wanting her son to fill her senses. Little by little, Arash's tears passed from exhaustion, his body going limp in her arms until she sat on the path and held him like a baby; his long legs stretched out and his arms and face curled up against her. Only then did she look up at Cyrus, seeing his injuries and what she feared.

It was not judgment in his eyes, instead a veil had been drawn across the openness between them. She frowned at the loss of it, the loss of him, not knowing if she had the energy to fight for him. Parisa wanted open fighting. Hurled accusations. Honesty, not this distance meaning the depth of his love was not what it seemed.

"Come inside," he said. He reached down and touched Arash's shoulder.

She let Cyrus pull Arash up, but once she stood, she drew her son close to her again.

George stuck his hand out. "I'm the driver."

"Cyrus, this is George. I owe him a lot."

"Then we owe you more," he said warmly, and gestured for them to come inside.

Parisa sparked with hope. It was the warmth she had wanted, not simple Iranian politesse. Maybe she had misread him? Or maybe it was only for George?

The house was quiet. The living room was richly furnished, so much like back home. Italianate chairs with gold leaf touches and a long couch upholstered in gold and white jacquard were placed around a matching coffee table holding several small crystal bowls filled with wrapped candy and nuts. All of it on a richly patterned Persian rug that must have cost thousands. Another carpet, small, and certainly silk, hung on the wall. But the centrepiece, hanging on the eastern wall of the home, was a devotional portrait of Imam Ali. It could have been Cyrus. Nobly handsome. His dark eyes and perfectly arched eyebrows, thick auburn beard, and dominant nose, were all softened by gentle cheeks. She dared not look at Cyrus, but then his mother came through the dining room.

"Salam." The simple greeting without a smile was the equivalent of cursing her from her home. Here was the judgment she had heard in Cyrus's voice. If she thought she and Cyrus had a future, this woman's stern face told her that would not be the case.

Cyrus took Arash's hand to lead him away. "My nephew is in the backyard."

But he did not want to go, and Parisa did not push him, preferring him next to her.

"I don't want to impose on you more than necessary. I am only here to pick up Arash." She glanced meaningfully at George. "My friend does not have much time."

George caught it, but said too brusquely for any Iranian. "I have to leave."

Cyrus's mother frowned deeply. Parisa grasped the problem. She did not want them to stay, but also could not accept them leaving too quickly.

"May I get Arash's things?"

His mother stepped closer. "Where will you take him?"

"Mother," Cyrus intervened.

"Home."

"Have you seen the news?"

"What news?" She looked between them.

Cyrus asked Arash, "Would you go to the kitchen? We have to speak privately."

He did not release his grip on Parisa, but buried his face in her waist.

"It's okay," she said, giving him a reassuring squeeze. "I'll be there in a minute. That's all."

Arash let go reluctantly, looking back at her once before he finally disappeared.

"The Wellingtons have been killed," Cyrus said.

She grunted as if someone had punched her in the stomach and dropped to her knees.

Cyrus squatted down, taking her hands, touching her cheek, then looked up at his mother. "Could you get her some juice? Water?"

He put an arm around her and brought her to the couch while George hovered.

Parisa's head felt loose on her neck, and she held it in her hands. "Who?"

"We saw the daughter being walked out in handcuffs by the police on the news. But there was another woman there who died. A secretary who worked at Wake Financial."

She looked up. "Wake Financial, Monaghan?"

"Yes," Cyrus said. "You know them?"

"Conor Monaghan. My graduate advisor's brother."

"What could be the connection?" he asked.

George sat next to her.

How could she know? She took slow breaths. A glass of orange juice was set down before her. Parisa drank it in small sips until she was able to face them and say what she hoped was true, no matter who killed the Wellingtons. "We're safe, then?"

"You cannot know it," his mother insisted. "Arash stays here."

What was this woman saying?

His mother continued, her tone becoming sharper. "You put your son in danger. If not for the security team, you would have lost him. You are not capable of protecting your son. We will, until you are prepared."

But she said it as if that day would never come. She looked at Cyrus to disagree with his mother.

"It's safe here. Let him stay with us. You stay with us, too."

He had disagreed with his mother in the only way an Iranian son could, by coming at it obliquely. It gave her hope. But his mother coughed her disapproval all the same. Parisa understood her. How were they any different? Both wanted their sons to be safe, and she was grateful Mrs. Dadashi's maternal ferocity had extended to Arash.

Cyrus continued, his eyes pleading, "We don't know if it means you are safe. There are men outside. Stay."

She looked toward the window.

"The police have been here, but they left. We have the security Tomoko arranged."

Parisa turned to George. "I have to stay."

"You do that. I can take care of the thing we discussed. Just get me the emails and photos."

Parisa put her hand over George's. "No. I have to do it."

"What do you have to do?" Cyrus asked.

"It concerns the chair of my department." She refused to say more, certainly not now, and she did not even know if she should do it at all. "We wanted to give him documents about some problems in the department. Nothing to do with this. It can wait. It should wait."

"Let me do it." George insisted.

Parisa searched George's face as if the answer were there. She considered if he presented Bernard's wife with the evidence he had cheated on her with his students, it would not be tied back to her. George could say he was an uncle of one of the undergraduates. Bernard would be held to account. She would have done right by those young women. She could live with it. "Only if you go straight back for Beatrice."

"I can't drive back tonight. Let me do this, then I'll get her tomorrow. Maybe Nick will give her up now the Wellingtons are dead?"

"Who is Nick?" Cyrus asked.

His mother paced behind him, then turned on her. "Both of you, leave. Let us care for Arash. We are afraid, do you see? What if you bring more trouble with you?"

"The people after me are the ones who came for Arash. They have to have been hired by the Wellingtons. They already know where you live." She stood, shaky on her feet, but after that, what choice did she have? "Hopefully, it is over now they are dead. But it's better if we leave together. You'll be safe then."

Cyrus gestured for her to sit back down and tried to lead his mother away, whispering, "Please—"

Parisa could not hear the rest.

But his mother threw off his arm and turned on Parisa. "Tomoko told us. You are involved. You are behind it."

"Me!" She stood.

He tried to stop his mother, but then she saw something in his face. Was he suspicious, too? That was the veil between them and she begged him to tear it away, accuse her, so they could fight it out. "Get me a computer I can use." She pulled out the USB. "I need to transfer some files to George's phone." She said, determined to fight for them, "I'm staying right here, with my son." Then she addressed his mother. "If you want me to leave, I'm taking him with me. It is your choice."

DAY NINE

46

"Why are you calling if you don't have Bea?"

Nick stood at the penthouse window, staring out at the lake. Dawn had just broken on the horizon. It had been a fitful night of sleep. The Wellingtons' murder was not what he wanted, and he was furious. He did not care that it had been brutal or even that their own daughter had done it, because he had not done it.

At least, the digital attacks were doing damage. The approach to the Wellington family changed tack, tying the murder to the scandals they had already laid down. All the same, he could not go to his mother's grave and tell her he had destroyed them and the shame was unbearable.

Now these fools.

"She's not with George, but we're tapped into his phone. He dropped off Parisa Soltani at a house in North York, then went offline again. His phone just turned back on. He's made a few calls, but only leaving messages for his dog walking clients."

"What was he doing with Parisa? Maybe she knows where Bea is!"

"Our focus is George. We can be sure he knows."

"I want to get the answer out of him myself."

"We found out she is in London. It won't be hard to get the rest. Citizens are not trained to withstand questioning."

"Get a car to me."

"Do you want to compromise your ability to distance yourself from what we are about to do?"

"If you do your job, it won't be a problem."

"We have someone outside his apartment. There are other people there, so we cannot approach him now. We'll send a car for you when he is on the move, alone."

He messaged Trang and Samuel to confirm that he would not be in the office today. He could not completely trust them, but he was going to get Bea back, even if it took his business down.

He paced the penthouse, ate breakfast only because Étienne insisted, and looked out at the lake. His phone finally pinged. A car was waiting for him downstairs.

Nick grabbed his jacket, leaving his primary phone behind, and went down to the lobby. Despite the elevator's stomach turning speed, it took forever. He pushed the doors aside as they opened and rushed to the street. A black Chevrolet Suburban was waiting out front. A driver stood outside, dressed in comfortable black clothes made for fighting. He only gave his own clothes a thought at that point. His pants, dress shirt, and cashmere sweater were comfortable enough to question George, but nothing else. But surely he would not have to physically restrain the man?

The driver opened the door and he slid into the back.

As they moved into traffic, the driver spoke over his shoulder. "I've got his location live. He's heading toward the Annex. We should have eyeballs on him soon."

"The other car is with him?"

"Yes, sir. They are following him and expect us to meet them. If necessary, we'll apprehend George ourselves."

The Suburban moved slowly through the morning traffic. He sat forward, impatiently watching their progress on the street ahead, but also the moving dot on the small screen marking George's location.

"We won't lose him, sir."

Nick was paying them enough, they had better not.

"He has stopped. We're a block away." He touched his ear. "He's gone up to a house. A woman has opened the door. The woman has stepped out onto the path and is arguing with him."

They turned the corner onto the street. Nick sat forward, watching through the windshield. George was a stooping, grizzled man who had seen a hard life. Nick imagined Bea caring for him and searched his memory for any story she might have shared about those days. What other intimacies had she denied him? Jealousy drove fury through every muscle and into his hands. Nick would get Bea's location, then he would crush him.

"They are asking us to stay back and observe. We are not taking him here."

He pulled into a driveway two houses up.

Nick watched from the side window.

A beautiful young woman in form-fitting yoga clothes was standing on the stoop of a Victorian mansion, pointing George to the street. But he did not move and held out his phone.

"I can't hear! Lower the window!"

The driver did, but only a bit.

"You'll be visible to witnesses, sir. That's it."

Nick could hear her raised voice, but nothing specific. A teenage boy came out and stood beside her. He was tall, with long, dark hair. They looked alike, a younger brother, perhaps. He grabbed the phone out of George's hands and went out onto the lawn. The woman came after him, pleading, trying to take the phone from him. But he jerked his arm away and stalked off down to the sidewalk. She froze, hand to her mouth. The young man turned back and threw the phone at George, yelling, "You got what you wanted. Leave!" An older man with longish silver hair appeared in the door and ran to them, but the young man pushed him aside, put his arm around the woman and led her back into the house.

George stooped to pick up the phone, hand on his knee to help himself back up, then returned to his car. The other black Suburban drove past George and stopped. His own driver pulled out of the driveway and came up just behind George's car. The door of the Suburban ahead of them opened. A man jumped out, all in black, wearing a balaclava, and grabbed George before he could get into his own car, expertly twisting his arm and pushing his head down with his other hand. George swivelled his body towards him, his free arm swinging out, and broke the grip long enough to scramble away onto the sidewalk. He was no match for the younger man, who quickly got him under control. The driver's side opened, a second man jumped out, also wearing a balaclava. He quickly scanned the street before helping drag George into the back, kicking the entire way. The car tore off and Nick's driver followed.

Gripping the front seat, Nick said, "I thought they weren't taking him here!'

The driver touched his ear. "They are driving to a laneway nearby. Get ready to join them."

The Suburban turned down the laneway at the end of the street, then went north at the next street, then west two blocks, then south again down another laneway. They stopped abruptly in front of a two story laneway house offering good coverage from the surrounding homes. Nick jumped out. A man in the car ahead opened the back door, got out, and directed Nick to get in.

George was pushed up against the other side, bound with black plastic ties. His eyes were wide with terror, but he continued to struggle. Nick slid in, the door shut behind him. But it was tight and George's feet were against him. He kicked, grunting, but Nick felt nothing other than the desire for George's flesh in his hands.

"You know who I am?"

George nodded slowly.

"Tell me where to find Bea."

He shook his head, but there was no defiance in his fear and would not hold out for long.

The driver handed him a stun gun from the front seat. "Feel free to use this, sir."

George watched, a moan escaping him. His chest heaved, but he showed some fight and kicked Nick's leg in earnest. There would be some bruises. Nick hoped the old man would hold out so he could stun him more than once.

"Is it on?"

"Charged and ready to go."

Nick had to twist himself to place the stun gun against George's thigh.

"Need help?"

He answered by making contact. George kicked him again, but from the full body spasm of the electric shock. It was going to be a deep bruise, and Nick's anger deepened.

When George's eyes opened again, Nick demanded, "Where is Bea?"

George only shook his head like a trapped animal.

Nick hit him with the stun gun one more time. George's body jerked. But this time, Nick lifted his legs out of the way and missed getting kicked.

George's eyes opened, but they had rolled into the back of his head.

"Where!" Nick yelled.

But his eyes did not return to focus.

"Fuck." Nick opened the door and got out, pulling on George's feet, but could not budge him. He turned to the man standing just outside. "Help me!"

The man crawled in, said something to the driver, then pulled George out. Still unconscious, George's head fell from the back seat and hit the car door threshold, then the broken asphalt below. Nick went to kick him, but the knot in his leg had weakened him. So he jumped on him instead, putting a knee into his gut.

"Tell me!"

Nick grabbed his face, but his eyes were lolling and glazed, his face slack. He slammed his head over and over against the asphalt until blood seeped into the dirt and blackened grit. "Where! Where! Where!"

Hands grabbed him and pulled him off. He fought them, but the men forced back into the car. Nick tried to get upright and outside, but the back doors were locked and the car was speeding away.

"Get me back there!"

"He's dead, sir."

"You can't know that!" He grasped the front seat, then turned around, looking through the rear window just as the car made it around the corner. The laneway was empty except for George's body.

47

Frank James had changed their story, misrepresented what they sent him. He went to publication without the facts. Now the Wellingtons and a woman were dead.

"It's not your fault," Tomoko's father said gently.

"I didn't say it was," Tomoko snapped.

"These people made their own bed," her mother remarked. "Who killed them? That old woman? Their daughter? These people were not even being covered in your article."

"But we pushed the family into crisis with our reporting."

"Did you do your work responsibly?"

She had not, she knew it now, but said instead, "You know Frank misused what we wrote."

"Then hold Frank responsible for his part."

"The work you do will always come with risks and, it seems, one is working under a man who is professionally and ethically unreliable."

Her father handed her a salmon onigiri for a late breakfast, but she could not eat it. The implications were clear before she had walked in the door of her parents' home. She and Sky had discussed it earlier that morning. She wanted to quit *The Spanner*, but Amina had said, "Devil you know." Tomoko hoped she would not say the same now. She doubted Amina's principles, and doubting her was pissing her off.

If only Amina would return her calls and texts. After she had heard Parisa's story from Sarah and how Nick Barnes set up the Wellingtons, she had been calling and texting without response. Then the news broke that the Wellingtons had been murdered. She could not have been the only one trying to reach Amina.

Tomoko's phone had never stopped pinging since the news broke. Friends texted her links to talking heads being interviewed on local and national news, and endless Twitter and Telegram posts. Tomoko and Sky watched the news coverage on her laptop. The two roommates sat, heads together, on the futon couch, taking turns pausing the video to bitch out the commentators.

One round table took the side of the family's lawyer, spicing it up with a devil's advocate whose actual job was reinforcing the lawyer's point of view by giving the rest of the panel stupid arguments to counter. All the coverage criticized *The Spanner* for not bringing the story to the appropriate oversight agencies, threatening the stability of Canada's banking systems. Interviews were variations on: Yes. Fraud is wrong, but it was called out in the wrong way and now three people were dead.

Then Frank shows up on the national news, turning the story back to how Martin Monaghan was a victim. How whistleblowers are hounded in this country rather than heralded. The fraud was played as just another scandal in an industry of scandals.

Sky jumped up, complaining bitterly, "Of course, Frank is looking out for the harm done to a white cis-het man of privilege and, of course, they are letting him do it."

"Where is the call for the abolition of predatory loans?" Tomoko had countered. "What about the working poor? He's only worried about Monaghan!"

But even if they had published the truth—that Nick Barnes had inserted the virus into the payday loans system—the plight of the working poor would be forgotten in a frantic news cycle about viruses undermining the stability of banking, followed by reassurances from the office of the Minister of Finance.

She toyed with her onigiri under her father's watchful eye. Her phone rang. She flipped it over on the table, expecting it to be anyone but Amina, but there was her name on the Signal app. Tomoko pushed back her chair to take the call in the hallway. She answered, short-tempered. "I've been trying you nonstop."

"I needed to talk to Frank first."

She wanted to retort, "Even yesterday evening, before the news broke?" But instead, she directed her ire at Frank. "What did that misogynist, self-centred shit have to say?"

"He apologized."

"He was on the news not talking like an apology."

"Tomoko, listen to me. He did not apologize for what he did to our story. He apologized for not putting us out in front of the media."

"Oh, and that satisfies you?"

"I understand you're upset, but if you would give me a moment."

"I can't do this."

She paced up and down the hallway. Each time she passed the kitchen, she could feel her mother's stare.

"Tomoko," Amina said sharply. "I called to say the same thing."

"You did?" She stopped, looking at her parents, who sat forward expectantly.

"There is nothing we can do about what he wrote, but we can take our story and publish it our way elsewhere."

"Then we pull our work," Tomoko looked meaningfully at her parents, who sat back, sharing a relieved look. "But where?"

"I don't have that answer right now. Let's just keep writing the story until we have it where we want it."

"You make it sound like we have all the time in the world."

Amina laughed. "Uh, no. Can you bring Parisa in for an interview?"

She doubted it, but said, "Maybe."

"I called Anthony. He wants to work on the story with us. We can research and write it there, with him."

She leaned in the kitchen doorway. "So, how does the resignation work?"

"A letter and I drop off the key to the office."

"We'll write it together?"

"I had hoped we would. I want it to detail exactly why."

"Can we make the letter public?"

"Yes."

"Isn't there some omertà with journalists and editors that calling them out ends careers?"

"I want to be careful how I say this, but what Frank did may have put the Wellingtons at risk. None of us could know that their family was at the brink of murder or why that other woman was involved. We don't know why this happened yet. They could have been killed for an unrelated reason. But when a story goes out, one has to be able to stand behind it, no matter the blowback. That did not happen here."

Tomoko swallowed hard. Amina was not just talking about Frank. She was talking about how she let her feelings for Cyrus drive the way she handled Parisa as a source. Tomoko turned to the wall, leaning her forehead against it. She did not want to say it to her parents. They would defend her, as always, but she did not want a defence. She wanted to face that it was by luck alone nothing she had done ended up with Parisa and her son being killed.

She asked Amina, "Has this happened to you before?"

"Not this. But when I have exposed a crime, people have gone to jail and families were affected."

"They deserved it?"

"I'm not going to put it that way. But I did not put their families at risk, they did. Then they got caught."

"You sure of that?"

"I carry some guilt, always, but this is why we have to constantly check ourselves."

Tomoko took a long breath, grateful that Amina stood by her. "I get it," she said. "I know what I did." But she would not linger on it. Carrying that emotion past the moment of its usefulness would be wasteful. *Admit it. Change. Move on*, she told herself. Tomoko turned around, straight-backed, ready to return her focus to the story, and saw her parents looking at her with pride.

"Good," Amina said. "Now, let's get to that letter."

"First, there's more to this story than you know."

"I'm sure."

"I mean, I found out yesterday that Nick Barnes of Cristo Solutions created the virus and installed it in the Wellingtons' system and had it kick back data to him, which he sent to Parisa and Monaghan."

"Who's the source for this!"

"Beatrice. She told Parisa and Parisa told Sarah. I got it from her."

"Can Beatrice be trusted?"

"She's not his girlfriend. More like his captive. It's a long story."

"How did she find Parisa?"

"Nick was obsessed with Parisa and kept track of her. Beatrice saw. When she escaped Nick, Beatrice found Parisa using the tracking on Nick's computer and told her everything."

"We need to get her on record."

Tomoko paused. "If she's still at the camp, we could drive up there."

"Bring her back down here."

"Beatrice can't come back. This is Cristo Solutions. She's running off-grid. She's not coming back to Toronto where Barnes can find her."

"Where's Parisa now?"

"She's in town. The dog walker who drove Beatrice up there brought Parisa back after she heard about the attempted kidnapping of her son."

"Tomoko. What's the name of the dog walker?"

She asked it in a way that gave Tomoko a sinking feeling. "George something. Older guy."

"Hold on."

Her phone pinged. She clicked the link.

BREAKING NEWS: LOCAL DOG WALKER GEORGE HAMMOND FOUND DEAD IN APPARENT HOMICIDE

Tomoko grasped the door frame.

The article was just a few lines:

Homicide detectives are investigating the death of a local dog walker, George Hammond. Hammond's body was found badly beaten by the resident of a laneway house in the Annex neighbourhood of Toronto. The laneway house was equipped with security cameras and the footage has been shared with the police. An investigation is underway.

"What is it?" Her father was beside her.

Tomoko ignored him, saying to Amina, "Nick did this. He could have been involved with the murder of the Wellingtons, too. He was trying to destroy them."

"The police have security footage. Hopefully, they got something."

But her father would not budge, and her mother had raised herself into her walker.

"Hold on," she said to Amina. Then, to her parents, "It's bad, but let me finish."

Her father nodded, and retreated into the kitchen with her mother, who sat reluctantly, keeping her eye on Tomoko.

She moved out of view into the hall, but nearby so they could overhear. "Nick was probably trying to get Beatrice's location off George. Barnes had someone question George and it went too far? As for the Wellingtons, maybe he hired the older woman?"

"Is Beatrice safe?"

"She was waiting for George to come back and get her, take her wherever she was going."

"You need to call her now and tell her to run. Can you contact her via Signal? George might have talked."

"They've only got a pay-as-you-go flip phone there. We'll have to take the chance Nick's listening."

"But Tomoko, see if she'll agree to go on record about Barnes creating the virus. She can record a voice note and send it to us. Anything she can give us, any background would be great."

"I'll try."

"I'll write up a first draft of our resignation letter and send it to you. I'll also tell Anthony about Barnes. Maybe that will help him get us proof it came from him."

"One last thing. You know the porn you saw when you searched her name? He came after Beatrice with his troll farm, created deep-fake porn of her and released it when she escaped. I had to call her mother when I got back and tell her."

"Poor Beatrice. It looked real. How did her mother react?"

"She was grateful to know, grieving more than angry, and wanted to see her daughter."

Amina grunted. "I can imagine." She paused. "I've been tracking the trolling of the Wellingtons on social media. Maybe it's Nick Barnes, then, his troll farm?"

"I've seen it and that fits. Anthony can look into it." Tomoko hung up, then went back to the kitchen, wanting a cup of tea to steady her. Her father was already pouring it. She put her hands flat on either side of the cup and breathed in the roasted scent of the genmaicha to get a hold of herself. Then said, "George. The man who drove Beatrice up, the one who brought Parisa down here. He's been murdered."

She never expected her parents to be truly afraid for her, but their expressions told it all. Her father's fear was touched with uncharacteristic anger, while her mother already had a sword out and was storming down the street at her enemies. Tomoko tried to pick up the cup, but her hand was trembling.

Her mother said in a commanding voice she had not heard directed at her since her teen years, "There is no time for fear, Tomoko. Is Beatrice safe? Are Sarah, Izzy, and Stan safe?"

"I'll call Sarah and Izzy."

"No, you drink that tea," her father said, giving her mother a look. "You call."

"Mom, I have to talk to Beatrice if she's there."

Her mother made the call, placed the phone on the table and pressed it to speaker.

Sarah answered, but her mother barrelled through without a hello. "Are you all okay?"

"Yes. Yes. Stan walked down and gave us the news. Poor George."

"What about Beatrice?"

"She's gone. Stan packed her up and they left."

Tomoko was relieved despite needing to interview her, but maybe Sarah could remember more of what Beatrice said. She intruded on the call. "Sarah, do you remember what she said about Nick Barnes? I need it for the piece I'm writing. Just background."

"Of course. You want it now?"

Her mother barked, "She can call you later. Listen, where did they go?"

Tomoko thrust a hand out. "No, mom!"

But Sarah was already answering. "Stan only said that she had a place to go and he knew how to get her there safely."

"What about you?"

"Does this man after Beatrice know where we are?"

"We don't know."

Tomoko asked, "Sarah, can you and Izzy go into town for the night, maybe longer?"

"Do you think he's listening in on our phones?" her mother asked.

"Maybe," Tomoko said. "Throw out your phone, Sarah. Get another one with a new number. Pay cash. Pay cash for everything."

"How will we know when we're safe?"

"Call mom in a couple of days from your new phone. If you aren't safe, then we'll sort out a new plan."

"Don't worry."

I'll know more soon, I hope. Mom will tell you what to do when you call."

"I'm going to pack. What about you all? Are you safe?"

Tomoko did not have an answer. She had to go see Parisa, tell her about George, and ask her for an interview. She had to do that, but first she had to right one of her wrongs.

48

"They're trying to set you up." Martin held the phone out to him.

Conor leaned in to get a better look, but Martin had filmed through windows dripping with humidity. As the shapes moved and the screams came, though, it was clear what had happened. "I can't see it, Martin. Make me see it."

"I'll cast it up to the TV." Martin walked past him to the room next to Conor's office, dominated by a seventy-inch television and a black leather couch. He found the controls and in a moment, the sounds and scene of the murder surrounded them, but it was still hard to make out. "I could see it much better in person."

"The camera's fighting focus on the window and what's beyond."

"There." Martin pointed. "That's Miss Henson."

Her arm was swinging, and Wellington was holding her off.

"I can't see the letter opener."

"It's yours."

"I believe you." He grasped his brother's arm.

Wellington fell. The camera dropped, then reappeared, held at an odd angle. Then his wife fell. Another scream.

Oonagh ran into the room.

Conor took her by the arm. "It's a horror film, Oonagh. Quite life-like. I'm sorry it disturbed you."

She looked back disapprovingly as he ushered her out. "Are ye sure?"

"Yes," he said, shutting the door. Then returned to the paused video. "What's she doing?" He pointed at Miss Henson.

Martin did not answer immediately, then said, "She's licking the blood."

"Lord protect us," he said. "She is Legion."

"I guess a representative of evil would drink blood?"

"She watched over us as children!"

"That's who these people are, Conor. Don't look away." Martin started the video again. "Listen."

"I can't hear it."

"I get closer to the open window soon." Martin turned up the volume, glancing back at the door, worried Oonagh would come in again. But they could hear Cassandra now.

"This was for me!" Cassandra screamed.

Martin moved around to the other side of the pool house. The images shook, then the camera fell to the ground and he could hear a struggle.

"That's where I found Stone. I don't pick up the camera again until I leave."

"What's going on?"

"Cassandra has a gun."

"She kills her?"

"Yes. But listen. It's what she says."

Conor interjected. "Stone did nothing to stop the killing."

Martin shook his head. "Just listen."

It was difficult to hear, but it was enough and he felt sick.

"They whored out Patricia to their friends." Cassandra was moaning. "They gave her to the bankers and their filthy sons in exchange for what?"

"They trafficked her!" Conor exclaimed.

Miss Henson said, "Agape tried to save you, but you would not be saved."

"He gave me money. To go where? It was nothing. Not enough."

"You want too much!"

"I was a child! Patricia was so young!"

"Agape tried to save her. She would not be saved. You would not be saved."

Conor stopped the video. "I asked Agape about the payments to women. They were to help girls like Patricia escape. But he did not say why they needed to get out."

"He gives them money? He doesn't go to the police and help them catch these people? No better than one of Epstein's cronies. He was on the inside and could have gathered evidence."

"You? Suggesting the police?" Conor felt unaccountably defensive.

Martin's cheeks flushed. "I'm going to the police with this video. To protect you."

"You don't know they were trying to set me up. It's idiotic. Miss Henson had access to the letter opener and there she is! Someone is watching from the door."

Martin huffed and turned the video back on. Sirens were getting closer.

"It was for me," Cassandra cried.

"You can, still." Miss Henson continued to walk slowly toward her. "I did it for you."

"Why would Legion kill for her?"

Martin shrugged angrily, then they heard Miss Henson saying, "Run."

"What's happening with her voice?"

Martin said, "I don't know, but it hypnotized Cassandra. Scared the shit out of me."

"Free yourself."

Then the shot came. The sirens were close.

"Miss Henson died." Martin paused the video. "Listen. Stone will tell you. Agape's brother is Agapov of Panopticon."

"Martin, I know that."

"You don't know this. Agape hired Fort Security for the Wellingtons and controlled everything they did, including the intimidations. He got his brother to supply them with the identity of the man who made the virus, Nick Barnes. The head of Cristo Solutions."

"Why is Barnes after the Wellingtons?"

"I don't know."

"And Agape? Is he trying to punish the Wellingtons for Patricia?"

Martin pressed play again and Conor listened to Stone's speech, then took the controller out of his brother's hand and turned it off. "If you won't accept they were trying to set you up, you better believe that Agape planned on this murder. He got Miss Henson to do this. He said about the Wellingtons, 'Legion will consume them'."

So Legion was in Agape's employ. *One will betray you.*

"I believe it," Conor said as he sat on the couch. "Don't take it to the police. They won't suspect me. The murderers are right there. Again, the servant at the door saw everything. But you were outside that window. Stone, too. If they find out you were there, you'll need it to protect yourself as a witness."

"Would Stone volunteer to go to them? He'd mention me. Maybe it's better if I go in first with a lawyer?" He paused. "And not one of Vincent's."

"No. Do not go in. I'll hire the best criminal lawyer I can find."

Conor's phone pinged. It was Pierre.

> I'm in Michael Garron Hospital. Alone now.
> Come before Marcus returns.

"It's Pierre, one of the brothers," Conor's head shot up. "He knows something, but Marcus was keeping him from speaking. He's in the hospital. I think they've made him ill, tried to silence him. Come with me?"

"No more secrets?"

Conor agreed, but was unsure if he could promise it. How much could Martin understand about his visions? But the visions were leading him to expose Agape. Pierre's visions, too. If Martin understood, saw their value, maybe he would see that there was something true in this path. He barely allowed himself to think that Martin might join him. But maybe when the sacrifice was made, Martin would himself be convinced of the truth of the Lord.

Once out on the road, Martin said, "Fill me in."

"Pierre told me at the last Ritual that Legion was closer than we think."

"He meant Miss Henson?"

"I think he means Agape. I told you. One of them will betray me."

Martin did not reply, and Conor took the silence as disapproval.

"I know this makes no sense to you, now, at least, but—"

"By betrayal," Martin jumped in, brushing his explanation off, "you mean that Agape got Miss Henson to kill the Wellingtons? I know you don't want to hear it, but the betrayal is setting you up for this murder, even if it did not work out as planned. You are in the way of something."

Conor would not argue with him. He could not understand that the betrayal was the betrayal of their path.

"I think Agape was coming after me, too. He called me out. His game is protecting women? He told me my graduate students, especially my female graduate students, resent me."

The idea of Agape accusing his brother of anything inflamed Conor. He sped up and made a tight turn. The Polestar silently rushed through the narrow residential streets. Martin wisely kept his mouth shut and grasped the handle over the door. Conor found a space on a side street, turned the car off and faced his brother. "I will not have it, Martin."

He got out and ran into the hospital, Martin following close behind, and was at the first bank of elevators before he realized Pierre had not given him a room number. "I don't know where he is." Conor headed towards the information booth, leaving Martin by the elevators. He stopped short, seeing Marcus stalking to the front entrance as if leaning into the wind. Conor spun around to avoid being seen, but Marcus was already out the revolving door and gone.

"Pierre Tremblay, please." He took the slip given to him by the volunteer, then went back to Martin. "Marcus just left."

"One of the others?"

"Yes. He's a doctor. He said Pierre had a chest infection, but it did not feel right to me."

"Why?"

"He was smothering Pierre, dominating him."

The elevator door opened and they stood in the corner, whispering.

"There was something sinister about it."

"I can believe that," Martin said.

They found the room easily enough. It was a large, bright single. Pierre was resting under neatly folded sheets and a warm blanket, an oxygen cannula in his nose. How bad could it be? His colour was better, and he was not coughing.

"Pierre," he whispered, taking his hand.

His eyes fluttered open and Conor realized just how sick he was. They were red and pus was gathering in the corners. "You came."

"I saw Marcus leaving. He was angry."

"My doctors won't allow him in," he said with what little breath he could manage. "I took a cab here yesterday. I showed them what he had me take."

Martin stood beside him.

"Your brother." He half-smiled. "Good. Someone you can trust."

"What was it?"

A doctor came in behind him. "Who is this?"

Pierre waved his hand, coughing, then said, "My friends. Please. Tell them everything."

The man was coldly furious. "We reported Dr. Fanhorn's actions to our regulatory body. But when I questioned him directly just a few minutes ago, it was clear his mistreatment of Mr. Tremblay was intentional, not malpractice. I was on my way to call the police when I saw you come into the room."

"What did he do?"

"Dr. Fanhorn admitted to giving him capsules to suppress his immune system and an inhaler containing the fungus aspergillus. It's common enough. In a healthy person, it causes little trouble. But because Fanhorn had been weakening his immune system over the past several months, I'm afraid his case has become more serious."

Pierre squeezed Conor's hand.

"He has Subacute Invasive Aspergillosis. The fungal masses in his lungs are causing internal bleeding. We are giving him antifungal medication, but surgery will be required to remove them."

"Will he recover?"

"The outlook is good, but not absolute." He glanced at Pierre, giving him a look of assurance. "His age is a complication, but our goal now is to get the fungus under control and strengthen him for the surgery. We are moving him to a ward without access to visitors, even doctors, without my express permission."

"Now do you believe me?" Martin whispered.

"What was that?" The doctor asked.

Conor jumped in, not letting Martin answer. "He warned me about Dr. Fanhorn."

"I'm sure that the police will want to speak to you. I consider this a criminal case."

Martin huffed with satisfaction.

"Thank you, doctor," Pierre said. He coughed and held a tissue up to his mouth; bloody sputum stained the tissue. Conor comforted him while the doctor came around to the other side of the bed. When the coughing subsided, Pierre said to him, "Let me speak to them alone, before you lock me away."

The doctor nodded and left him, but not before staring at the two in warning.

"You are in excellent hands," Conor said.

But Pierre could not rest. "Marcus tried to kill me. They will try to kill you, too."

The sacrifice was coming for him, but why Pierre? "Do you know why he was making you ill?"

"Their arrogance. My vision of the snake," he paused, struggling to breathe, then continued, "a snake crawling up the stalk of a multi-headed mushroom. It is Agape. Legion is their arrogance. They have left the bearing of the Lord for their own desires."

"Yes. Remember, I saw it, too." Conor stood back.

Pierre said, "I should have known."

"Why?"

"Agape sent me a patient. Her family had abused her."

Martin finished it. "They made her have sex with business partners?"

"You know?"

"It happened to someone else," Conor said. "Why did Agape want you to see her?"

"She wanted to leave the family, go live with her aunt in Vancouver. But Agape wanted me to convince her to stay until she accepted his help instead."

Martin rolled back and forth on his feet, wanting to speak, but Conor held his arm out.

"What happened?"

"I sat with her while she booked her ticket to fly to her aunt." He struggled for breath.

"And Agape was angry."

He nodded, holding the tissue to his mouth, then dropped it. "I came down with COVID, you remember? It was just after that. Marcus started me on the capsules. Then, the inhaler. I kept getting worse." He began coughing again, raising himself up, wracked with pain.

Conor helped him up and put a hand on his back.

Martin ran out of the room and returned with a nurse, who pushed them out.

He knew his brother wanted him to say that he believed him now, but he could not, not in the way he wanted.

49

———————

Arash's breathing was even and quiet. He had not been able to sleep until the early hours of the morning. Parisa comforted him and read aloud from *Sadiq and The Desert Star* until he finally drifted off without jerking awake again to see if she was still there. But she felt safe, finally, knowing John and his men were outside, Cyrus, ever watchful, was within, and her boy was in her arms.

Last night, Cyrus had invited Anthony's cousin, John, to meet her. He introduced himself and his team, explained they were watching the place, front and back and not to worry. They even had battery-run cameras at the end of the street at the stop signs, so they could anticipate who was coming. He opened his phone and showed her the feed.

As Cyrus's mother handed John containers of rice, fesenjun, and carefully prepared chopped salads, she glared at Parisa, saving her warmth for John and the bodyguards. As he left, she got up on her toes to kiss his cheek.

Parisa did not blame her, but she was reluctant to leave the bedroom this morning and face his mother, let alone Cyrus and the inevitable, telling him the truth.

There was a light rapping at the door before it opened slightly.

Cyrus whispered from the other side. "If you are awake, Tomoko is here, and would like to speak to you."

"What time is it?"

"Nearly lunch."

She slipped out of bed without disturbing Arash. All her clothes but the dress chosen to meet his mother were dirty, stinking from her fear. But she pulled on her jeans and a t-shirt anyway, hoping his mother would not try to kiss her cheeks.

When she opened the door, she did not expect Cyrus to be waiting for her. But he was, and took her hand, looking down, unsure of what to say. Here it was. He would tell her that her troubles were too much for one night of surprising love.

But when he raised his eyes to meet hers, he was near tears and pulled her into an embrace, his whole body against hers. Her cheek rested against his chest. He bent his head down to hers. "I thought I had lost you again. Having Arash with me, to have a part of you, your perfect son, saved me."

She unwound into his arms, her body becoming so heavy she thought she was fainting, but her senses were heightened and she wanted him. The scent of sandalwood and rose enveloped her. His breath was quick, and his body, at first softly pressed against her, became aroused, meeting her own desire. She wanted to lift her head and kiss him deeply. Instead, she pulled away, holding him at a distance and memorized his features, worrying over his bruised eye, his cut lip, wondering if this was the last time he would love her freely, before she told him the truth.

"What is it?"

She admitted, "I was afraid you suspected me, like Tomoko."

"Of being behind all this? I only suspected that you had not told me everything and that hurt."

"I lied to you."

"I understand. It's done."

"You don't want to know?"

"I know why. I know enough."

"How?"

"Tomoko is on your side now," he said. "After hearing everything from the woman up north, Sarah, she believes you. She told me what you said. Then, she asked to speak to my mother alone, to set things right."

Parisa considered what it meant for Tomoko to vouch for her, and said, "I was wrong about her, too." Then asked, "You still love me?"

"I never stopped loving you."

"I brought all this on your family."

"You brought your love to me when you came to me for help. You brought me Arash."

"Can you love him?"

"I already love him. My mother does, too. You saw how she loves him."

"She would be glad to have him and not me." She frowned. "But I love how fiercely she wants to protect him."

"I told her before you returned, you are family now. I told her—" He paused, searching her eyes.

What she saw in his face made her want to beg him to say it, but she would not ask.

Finally, he said, "I told her I want you to be my wife and for Arash to be my son."

His eyes were expectant, but not certain, and she could not understand how he could doubt it. "I am your wife. He is your son."

He bent down and kissed her lightly on the lips, then more fully, his hand pressing against the flat of her back, and she savoured the first taste of the life they would have together. The world fell away, his mother's voice becoming more distant even as she drew near. Then Tomoko's voice carried through the closed hallway door. They reluctantly let go of the moment, sharing a guilty smile.

He held up a finger, asking her to wait, then disappeared down the hall into another room, returning with a beautiful blouse, obviously his mother's.

"I smell," she said with a crooked smile.

"Not you, the shirt." He kissed her again.

She stepped back, keeping his eye, and pulled the t-shirt off over her head.

He handed her the blouse, taking her in with pleasure. "They are waiting for us."

Dressed, she mussed her short hair, then went ahead of him down the hallway, opening the door to the living room. There were his mother and Tomoko, seated next to each other, tea glasses in hand. Parisa could not be sure, but Cyrus's mother did not seem as distrustful as she had been.

Tomoko stood. "Parisa. It's good to see you."

"I'm glad to see you, too," she said, and meant it.

"I'm on my way to Anthony's to work on the story, but I wanted Mrs. Dadashi and Cyrus to hear what we know so far."

Cyrus prompted, "And you are not with *The Spanner* any longer?"

"We're submitting a resignation, going to go public with it."

"Where will you publish the piece?" Parisa asked.

"We don't know yet. We'll get there when we get there. Parisa, do you mind if I ask you a few questions?"

Parisa pulled up one of the chairs and sat, wary again.

Tomoko got out her phone.

"You want to record me? Can I correct what I say before you print?" She could see Tomoko hesitate, but she would not speak without it.

Tomoko sat across from her. "You can clarify and correct."

"That works."

She pressed record and put the phone between them.

They went over old ground, everything she had told Sarah. Tomoko asked good questions, teasing out the details. Parisa glanced at Cyrus as she explained, worried he would change his mind about her, but only found him encouraging.

Tomoko said, "I want to turn back to Agape."

"I trusted he would do what I asked, make sure Monaghan was only censured and Bernard was exposed for raping his students."

Cyrus's mother stared at her in shock, but did not interrupt.

Parisa acknowledged her, understanding. "It's an awful story. I can explain it later."

Tomoko asked, "To your mind, was he sincerely interested in holding the chair accountable?"

"He seemed like he wanted to expose Bernard. In fact, it seemed like Bernard was his primary concern and he was going to use the case against Monaghan to do it."

"Did he say why?"

"No."

"Did you know that Agape is an associate of the Wellingtons?"

"That explains why he did not intervene to keep Monaghan from being terminated. I guess he knew about the bribe from the Wellingtons and helped get rid of Monaghan for them. Bernard was nothing to him then."

"Or he wanted both? If he knew Bernard raped his students, maybe he was trying to get rid of him, too."

"Your guess is as good as mine." Parisa took a moment. "I believed Agape wanted to protect me. None of it felt like a lie."

Tomoko lit up. "I think he imagines himself as a protector of women."

"Maybe there is something to that?"

"And that was the last you heard from Agape?"

"Yes, except for the woman."

"The older woman called to warn you and your son to leave?"

"Yes. She said Agape asked her to call, told me where I could find the camera in my apartment and to get out of there."

"I saw the video of your apartment. When you were there last, you took a USB drive and a phone out of a heating duct."

Parisa grew hot. "I couldn't tell you when we were at the apartment together. I'm sorry."

"Tell me now."

"The phone was from Agape, to keep me updated, ask me questions. I only got the call from the woman on it."

"And the USB?"

She looked at Cyrus. "It's the USB I had yesterday. I transferred the contents to your computer to send to George's phone. Can you get my backpack out of the guest room?"

He went to retrieve it.

She said to Tomoko, "It's the proof that Bernard raped his students. Since Agape did nothing, I wanted to expose him to his wife. She would know what she was seeing. She had been one of his students. I gave it all to George, and he was supposed to confront Bernard and his family before going back up for Beatrice."

Tomoko glanced worriedly at Cyrus as he came back into the room with Parisa's backpack. "Tell her about George."

His expression fell as he crossed to her. "George was killed early this morning."

She shot up, looking among them. "How?"

"He was beaten in a laneway in the Annex," Cyrus said. "There's security footage, so the police may be able to identify who did it."

"The Annex," she sat heavily. "I sent him there to confront Bernard, to show his wife the evidence and expose him. I did this. It's my fault."

Cyrus pulled a chair close and sat next to her. "No, Parisa."

Tomoko watched. A hint of jealousy crossed her face, but she said evenly, "You'll want to tell the police. But we suspect Nick Barnes, more like someone he hired, was trying to force George to give up Beatrice's location."

"I gave up George's location," she said to Cyrus, then turned back to Tomoko. "I made him turn on his phone to call Cyrus on the drive here. They must have tracked him. My God. George. He gave everything for her. For me, too." Her stomach turned over, thinking how she tried to get him to turn his phone on earlier and how she nearly exposed Beatrice, too. Then she became afraid Nick Barnes was listening in now. "Give me a pen and some paper."

Mrs. Dadashi got up to get it. Returning, she placed it on the coffee table between Parisa and Tomoko, then sat next to Tomoko again.

Parisa wrote:

IF THEY WERE TRACKING GEORGE'S PHONE,
LISTENING, THEN THEY THINK BEATRICE HAS
GONE TO LONDON. I LIED, SAYING THAT INTO
THE PHONE WHEN I CALLED CYRUS ON MY WAY
HERE.

Cyrus nodded vigorously to Tomoko.

Relief washed over Tomoko's face. She wrote:

THAT MEANS MY PEOPLE UP NORTH ARE SAFE.

Cyrus' mother put a hand on Tomoko's back. "Good."

Tomoko pushed the pen back, gesturing to see if Parisa had more, but she shook her head. Tomoko said aloud, "I don't have any proof, but I'm wondering if the woman who contacted you was the same woman who was killed at the Wellingtons? She works for Monaghan's brother."

"I wouldn't know."

"Did you know that Monaghan's brother has a relationship with Agape?"

She sat forward.

"More than that. They belong to some religious group, small, just a few wealthy men."

Parisa dropped her head, holding back tears, and staring at the Persian carpet. Rumi's story of the ant crawling through a thicket of wool threads in a richly designed carpet, unable to discern the pattern, made bitter sense to her. "I don't know anything about that. You need to speak to Monaghan."

"Are you ready for me to talk to him?"

Parisa looked up, wishing the interview was over. "I couldn't let you talk to him before. Like I told Sarah, I don't trust him and I was waiting for Agape to do as he promised."

"Did Agape ever mention Nick Barnes to you?"

"No. I didn't know he had created the virus and sent me the data until Beatrice told me."

"Do you know why Nick was after the Wellingtons?"

She jerked out of her grief, remembering her late night conversation with Beatrice before they fell asleep. "Beatrice said Agape came to Nick, pretending to be the brother of Agapov, you know, Agapov of Panopticon, saying they wanted his help taking down all the payday loan companies."

"Even I have heard of the Panopticon," Mrs. Dadashi said. "Are they related?"

"Yes," Tomoko said, looking at them. "But the question is why Panopticon would need Nick Barnes to do anything for them."

She needed her boy in her arms, fearing such powerful people could reach him anywhere.

"Let's go back to Agape acting like he wants to protect women." Tomoko asked, "Maybe he knew about Beatrice and wanted to help her? Maybe that's why he went to Nick?"

"But it makes no sense. If he wanted to protect women, he would have exposed Bernard. He would have done what I asked about Monaghan. As for Beatrice, Agape did not help her," she said, her voice rising. "Beatrice freed herself. George helped. Reverend Lee. Not Agape."

Cyrus leaned in towards her and she wished she could take his hand, but not in front of Tomoko.

"The USB?" Tomoko asked.

"Of course." She opened the backpack and handed the thumb drive to Tomoko, still incensed. "Maybe you can use it for a story on why universities should make it illegal for instructors to have sexual relationships with students as long as they are enrolled."

Tomoko stood. "Amina and I may want to interview you together, but it can wait a day or two."

"Okay," she said, but wanted to run back to her son and shut the door and never talk about it again.

"Will you contact Monaghan and urge him to speak to us? He's only been talking to Frank James and we need him."

She wrote his number down on the paper between them and pushed it toward Tomoko. "I'd rather not call him."

Tomoko took the paper, then turned to Cyrus's mother, who stood alongside her. "Thank you for welcoming me into your home."

Cyrus's mother took her hands, then looked at Cyrus accusingly.

"I will not forgive him for not bringing you before. But now that you know us, you are family, you must come."

Tomoko kissed her on her cheeks three times, then Cyrus walked her to the door.

Parisa hung back, letting them have a moment.

His mother waited with her, then once the door was shut, faced her, speaking loud enough for Cyrus to hear, "I understand you are family, too. But you understand why this is difficult for me. You, too, are a mother. God willing, we will know each other in the better times. I welcome you." She took a breath, let it out, then said, "Daughter," and retreated hastily to the kitchen.

Cyrus returned to her, arms open, mouthing the word, "Daughter."

Tears welled in her eyes for George, for Beatrice, for Arash, their suffering, all mixed with the beauty of this man and this moment, their beginning.

50

―――――

"It's a shame we can't talk to Beatrice, but it's enough to go on," Anthony said, swivelling his chair around from his desk and the large displays. "Barnes was good. My judgement of the man aside, it's a great design. The virus does not just create a problem for the Wellingtons and kick back the data that the problem existed and how they responded to it, but the data came back in a form that would be easy for Parisa and Monaghan to analyze. There was nothing raw to it. That data came to them fully cooked."

"If only he weren't the bad guy in this story," Tomoko said. "We could use more of that on the side of the revolution."

Anthony chuckled.

"So in the story," she said, "we outline how he did it, how he set them up. But we still can't trace it to him. All we have is Beatrice's word, and not directly. It's not enough."

"It's not enough even if we had her word on the record," Amina said, without looking up from her laptop.

"Barnes was good, but not as good as me." He slapped his chest comically. "There's a deep signature here. I can't say it was him, but right now I can prove it was his system. Maybe more, with time."

"Yes!" Tomoko nearly leapt off the couch.

Amina grabbed her hand. "We've got him!"

Tomoko got up and paced. "So why was he after them? The puff pieces on him all detail his poor upbringing. Self-taught. Mother had dementia and died in his last year of high school. Couldn't get into the Computer Science program at Simcoe University, but now funds them." She stopped and looked between them. "I'd like to think it's a class war thing, but he's one of them now, so how does that work?"

"Wait a sec," Amina said. "Funding Simcoe when that program didn't accept him?"

Anthony said, "Sticking it to them."

"I don't get it," Tomoko responded.

Amina answered for him, "They didn't take him, now he's shoving his wealth in their faces."

"Not trying to be accepted by them?" Tomoko suggested. "He doesn't give to any of the other colleges and universities."

"Maybe," Anthony said, obviously disagreeing.

"What other donations does he make?" Amina asked.

"That's just it," Tomoko said. "Nothing other than a few thousand to Toronto Unity Church downtown."

"You'd expect donations placing him with the charitable gala crowd." Amina scrolled through her laptop. "No pictures of him at events. Not like Agape."

"So, how does he show up?"

"Nothing but the biographies. There are the bits that came out when he first began seeing Beatrice." She turned her computer around. "She looks like a deer in the headlights."

Tomoko leaned in. "Nick is good looking, if you like that Ryan Gosling sort of thing."

"You can see how he drew her in."

"Amina, look." Tomoko pointed to a photo. "Beatrice has blond curly hair in all those. Later pictures all have her with straight auburn hair."

Anthony said, "She changed her style. I don't get it."

"I saw chatter about him and strange relationships with women. You know, that he did to them what he did to Beatrice." Tomoko sat back down, clicked on a tab, then turned her computer around, showing an array of women with Nick Barnes.

"So he's got a type," Anthony said.

"Hold on." She went into their social media history. They all existed right up until they began seeing Nick. Photos were up at the beginning of their relationships, like with Beatrice, then they fell off the map. "Anthony, I'm sending you a list of names. All rich girls who were associated with Nick. Can you check what's up with these women now?"

Anthony's display pinged. "Got it." It did not take him long. "They're all alive, but no social media. Some working, some not. Only old photos. Hannah Irwin is married and runs a florist shop in Vaughn. The shop doesn't even have an Instagram, but I've got a new picture of her."

"Vaughn? That's not quite money."

"They've got money there, but yeah, not the Bridle Path."

"But they are all staying low online, not drawing Nick's attention."

"Reasonable call," Amina said.

"Wait. Here's a picture of her."

Tomoko got up to see his screen. Hannah Irwin was a white woman with short red hair, grinning and holding hands with a Korean woman. "The white one?"

"Yup."

"Here's a picture of Louise O'Neill," he said. "Another white woman."

Amina asked from the couch, "Louise. Does she have auburn hair? Looks brown from here."

"Light brown."

"All the women, when they were with Nick, have long, straight auburn hair. You know what else?" Tomoko went back to the couch and picked up her laptop, showing them the screen. "They all have the same bow lips and sharp chin."

"I know what you're thinking," Amina said.

Tomoko sat and typed into her search bar, then turned the screen around to them. Long, straight auburn hair, bow lips, sharp chin. "That's Patricia Wellington."

Anthony whistled. "So did Patricia reject him?"

"What year is that? What year did she die?" Amina asked.

"2004." Tomoko replied.

"He was just graduating high school downtown. She went to a private school uptown. How could they have met?"

Anthony turned back around to his own computer.

Tomoko got up again and looked over his shoulder. He was searching high school records, athletic meets, school theatre, anything where Patricia's circles and his own might have crossed. She left Anthony and headed for the kitchen. "Anyone need coffee?"

"Yes!" Amina called out. But before Tomoko could disappear into the kitchen, she said, "His mother died in 2005."

Tomoko returned to the couch, leaning over the back. "In the interviews, he talks about how hard her decline was, how they struggled. His mother was a cleaner."

Anthony pointed at his display. "Look at this."

"Did they know each other?"

"No, I can't find that." He thumbed toward his screen. "That's a picture of his mother's grave."

He made the photo fill his large screen. An obelisk rose up in St. James cemetery with her name and the one word, "CLEANER."

"Anthony, you were right." She put a hand on his shoulder and felt the muscle even under his down vest. "If that's not trying to stick it to all those rich people, what is?"

"Maybe it is like you said, a class war?" Anthony's long-lashed eyes glinted with the pleasure of the search.

Tomoko's cheeks grew hot, and she turned away, so he would not see and went back to her computer, sitting cross-legged on the couch, away from him. But once seated, she snuck a look. He was watching her curiously, then turned back to his computer.

"Okay," Anthony said. "Here we have it. His mother's credit history."

"I thought those things didn't go back more than seven years?" Amina asked.

"Yeah, but the records don't disappear, at least not from where I can find them." A moment later, he yelled, "Oh yes!"

"What?" Amina asked.

"She took out a payday loan in December of 2002."

"Wellington?"

"Wellington," he said.

"December. Probably for Christmas," Tomoko said.

"She ever pay it back?" Amina asked.

"Guess."

Amina said with satisfaction, "After photos of Patricia Wellington vomiting on the hood of her red Porsche show up in the tabloids."

"They say she killed herself because of those photos."

"He as good as killed her. Then he went after women like her, over and over, getting his revenge. But that wasn't enough."

"It's not a class war," Tomoko said. "He doesn't give a shit about the working poor. He gives a shit about his mother."

Amina said, "Okay, let's get a sketch out of everything we know. Get our evidence lined up. Interviews. Maybe one of those women will talk to us? We have to go to Nick for comment."

"He won't answer."

"No, but we stand behind the evidence we have, suggest what we can suggest, and report that he refused to comment."

"We still don't know where we are going to publish it," Tomoko said, still angry with Frank.

"Let's get it as far as we can take it first."

Anthony turned back to them. "There's something weird about the women Nick used."

Tomoko gestured, turning her hand like she was opening a door knob.

"Who taught you how to gesture 'what' like that?" Anthony asked, head tucked back.

"Moroccan friend." This time she gave him her best smile, the one she brought out when she knew exactly what she wanted, and he felt it.

If she thought she could fluster Anthony, she was wrong. He relaxed back into his chair, throwing an arm back, opening himself up to her in invitation.

She gave out a deep sigh of pleasure. The story. This man.

Amina killed the moment. "Don't shit where you eat."

Anthony nodded, taking the correction as if Amina were his elder aunt, but Tomoko bit her tongue to keep from clapping back. Then she closed her eyes for a moment, calling herself to account. *The story is more important. The work is more important.*

"I'd like to know what Anthony found," Amina said.

"Guess whose name is associated with getting those women away from Barnes?"

"I don't want to guess, Anthony," Amina said, now sounding exactly like an elder aunt.

"Peter Agape."

"Agape," Tomoko said. "The man who talks like he wants to save women, but goes after Nick without protecting Beatrice and lets down Parisa, has helped some women, after all?"

Anthony asked, "Maybe Agape was trying to save Patricia from something?"

"And he's involved in some weird church," Amina added. "The mushroom thing."

"Yeah, you want me to dig more into that? All the members, their pasts, money, anything."

"Please."

Anthony turned back to his display.

"I'll reach out to Parisa," Amina said to Tomoko. "You talk to the Monaghan brothers?"

"On it," Tomoko said, relieved she did not have to go back to Parisa with more questions. She found Conor's contact information and sent him an email requesting an interview. Then got up to call Martin.

DAY TEN

51

———

"This is Elliot."

"I'm sorry. No one here recognizes that name."

"Elliot dammit! You recognize my money!"

"I'm sorry. No one here recognizes that name."

The phone cut off.

Nick opened the bitcoin wallet he used only for this purpose. Every penny he had paid them had been returned. It made no sense. This is what they do for a living. They kill people. They find people. They take hostages. His head swarmed, remembering. As they followed the first car, there was no license plate. In the laneway, he was the only one with his face visible. They did not need to answer his call. The security footage must have captured him, and they were erasing their relationship.

A cold wash of fear seeped through him. He turned around to grab the throw blanket off the couch, then remembered he had rid himself of it. Bea was out of his reach and the police would be coming. Nick got out of his chair and stomped up and down the office, forcing his blood to warm and to think, to think of what he needed to do next, and ended up with his head in the wastebasket, vomiting.

With the last heave, he rolled over and sat against the wall, his feet out. Then he crawled to the refrigerator and pulled out a glass bottle of water, taking small sips.

His display pinged.

He pushed himself up and back into his chair.

Trang messaged.

> A call waiting from Tomoko Abrams. Take a
> message or take the call?

Tomoko. She had something, something about the data for him to confirm. The article would go forward. It was something. His stomach lurched again. She should not know who he is or his connection to the data.

He threw the water bottle against the door, shattering the glass and spraying water everywhere.

> Take a message.

Only Agape could have told her. Or Bea.

Nick pushed back the chair and stood dizzily, waiting for the message to come through. When it did, he leaned in, gripping the edge of the desk.

We request comment or confirmation on the following:

> 1. The claim that the virus infecting
> Wellington Payday Loans was authored by
> Cristo Solutions.
>
> 2. That the virus was designed to produce
> data making it appear as if Wellington Payday
> Loans was intentionally defrauding its clients.
>
> 3. That Nick Barnes sent data of the fraud he
> manufactured to Martin Monaghan through
> Parisa Soltani with the intention of publishing
> proof of fraud.

> 4. That Nick Barnes was responsible for the photographs taken of Patricia Wellington in 2004 which were sold to the tabloids and led to her death.

> 5. That Nick Barnes has consistently cultivated relationships with women who bear a resemblance to Patricia Wellington, and who come from her social class, and that these relationships were controlling and abusive.

> 6. That the photos of Patricia Wellington and the sabotage of Wellington Payday Loans' system was part of a long-standing plot of revenge for the debt incurred by Nick Barnes's mother, Rose Barnes to Wellington Payday Loans.

Shaking, he took several unsure steps back until he hit the couch and fell back on it.

The display pinged again.

> Mr. Agape is waiting in your office.

He rose, as if drunk, and went to the door, the glass crunching underfoot.

The main office, spreading out in a perfect spiral, was in disarray. No whispered questions passed between cubicles, spreading the news. Employees were packing up their things and leaving. Agape stood at the centre of it all, smiling.

Nick waved at him, then gave him the finger.

Trang waited nearby, standing firm, Samuel just behind her.

She frowned deeply and held a large envelope against her chest. "I have called your lawyer." Trang handed Nick the envelope. "Our deal to stay."

He took it and ripped it in half, sneering. "Deal?"

Samuel said, "I asked the employees to leave for the day. They trust me. I instruct them, not you from behind your security glass. We will take over Cristo Solutions, but only if you sign over ownership to Trang and I. We agree to an annual percentage payout to you. You won't have to sell your penthouse or change your lifestyle, that is, unless your lawyer cannot find a way out of the evidence of that video. The company is saved by its disassociation with you. The work carries on."

"Why would I give you my life's work?" He watched the office empty.

"How can you not understand the position you are in? BTV got the security video. It's all over social media, the news. The murder," Samuel said, coolly. "We all saw you."

He rushed at them. Samuel pulled Trang back and came around in front of her, grabbing a fist full of Nick's sweater, whispering, "You killed a man."

"I was after Bea!"

Samuel let go of him, pushing him back. He stumbled to right himself.

"There is another copy of our deal on Trang's desk and an electronic copy has been sent to your lawyer. She will help you understand."

Nick screamed after them as they returned to their offices, "You think what you did never killed anyone? You think you didn't ruin any lives? You loved it!"

Wiping the spittle from his face, he walked in between the cubicles to meet Agape, his dizzy stumble turning into a swagger. If they thought he had lost it all, they were mistaken.

"You here to gloat?" Nick fell back into an Eames chair.

"I guess we do not need the frequency jammers." Agape smiled wryly and sat across from him. "I saw the news reports. The police will be here any moment, so I wanted to reach you first. I know what you did to Patricia Wellington."

Nick laughed from deep within his belly until he was bent over on himself and in pain. Finally, he sat up, tears streaming, snot running onto his lip. He smeared it away with his sleeve. "You know? They all know. Those cunts at *The Spanner* just asked me about it."

"The other women, too."

"Yeah, them, too. Too late, old man."

Agape's expression turned hard. "Did you know I saved them?"

The laugh died. "You?"

"Their parents were referred to me. I arranged their escape." He leaned forward. "Each one of them, mine. Not yours."

Nick imagined kneeing Agape in the gut like he did George. "This is your hobby. Saving women?"

"It is my bearing. The bearing bestowed on me."

"By your mushroom god."

"What do you know about the Lord's mission?"

"Nothing," Nick said, wanting to know exactly what this man thought he was so he could take it from him and use it to destroy him. "I did background on you."

Agape's eyes widened slightly.

"Nothing Agapov doesn't want out there. Don't worry. But I did wonder how you went from being a married man named Piotr Agapov to a man without a wife named Peter Agape."

He did not answer immediately, but Nick could see him wanting to, wanting someone to know. Had he not been the same with Bea, wanting her to know that it was him taking down the Wellingtons and why? Everyone wants to be seen. He came at him with a prod. "Did the mushroom god make you change your name?"

"My 'mushroom god' saved me."

"Just how does a mushroom save a man?"

Agape huffed. "You mock me, but we are not so different. I have killed. But I was saved."

Nick raised an eyebrow. That's what happened to his wife.

"Do you want to be saved?"

He wondered which response would make Agape talk and chose, "Convince me, then."

"My wife had been used by a man like you. He took her from me and he ruined her. I offered her a way back, but she would not take it."

"Way back?"

"I brought her to the beach and told her what it would take for her purity to be restored to her, but she did not want to save herself." He seemed incredulous. "She said she would rather die a whore, if you can imagine. I took her throat in these hands. It was harder than I imagined." He looked at Nick with avid interest. "Do you know how long it takes to strangle a person?"

He had read about it once and wished he had done that with George, and in the car, or simply tased him a few more times until his heart stopped. Nick looked toward the entrance of the office, wondering when the police would arrive.

"I put her in a canoe left by the shore and took her far out on the lake, and threw her in." He placed his right hand over his left fist and closed his eyes for a moment, mumbling something, then said, "I did not know that the currents would wash her up, but the Lord protected me, she had been well-eaten by fish when she eventually appeared. I knew it was her, but there was nothing left for the police to identify."

"Can we get to the part where you were saved?"

"I came back to shore and heard the drumming in the woods. I wandered into the hippie camp. One of them, a man who would become my brother, Vincent, came to me. I ate their sacred mushrooms. The Lord came to me. He brought Lady Magdalene with him. It was she who gave me my bearing, my mission, to protect women, like my wife would not be protected. Divine love demands it."

"So you were saved."

"Only by saving others. You, too, can be saved. All of this can go away."

Nick sat up. Maybe this delusional old man could save him after all. "Will your brother wipe it all away, like he did for you?"

An ugly cast came over his face. "The Lord directed him."

"Is he one of yours?"

"A brother of The Cluster? No."

Nick said desperately, "I'll eat your mushrooms, if your brother will make it go away."

"If the Lord directs him," he said in that smug way that meant no help was coming.

"What good are you to me, then?"

Agape dismissed him. "You are no better than a woman."

"Tell me what you want before the cops get here, if you can't do anything for me."

"Where is Beatrice Young? I will return her to her parents."

Nick crossed his leg and leaned back, eyeing the door again.

The gesture infuriated him. "Bring me Beatrice Young!"

"She's gone."

"What do you mean?"

"She left. Your brother tells you so much, but he doesn't tell you that?"

"He tells me what I ask."

Agape said it confidently, but there was something there, an opening. "Does he do what you ask or not?"

"I asked him how to ruin you. He gave me everything on your virus. I guided Soltani. I trapped Monaghan. I—"

"I— What was that?" Nick grinned. "A plan fall through?"

"Take down the porn. Call off your dogs."

Nick threw an arm back, gesturing to the office. "The dogs are gone, didn't you see?"

"Take. It. Down."

"No," Nick said. "Even if I took it down, turned off all our bots, closed her porn accounts, she's out there, downloaded on someone's computer. It's out of my hands."

Agape turned red, sputtering, "Take down all the porn! Erase it all!"

"Call your brother. He could do it, maybe even the downloads."

Agape stood, shaking. "You must do it! It is on your head!"

"So your brother doesn't do what you want." Nick looked up at him, unmoved. "When he looked into me, why did he tell you about the virus? It wasn't part of your hobby."

"It was part of ending you for good!"

"He could have ruined me with a few keystrokes, wiped my

systems, created deepfakes, reams of evidence demonstrating I committed whatever crime they chose. This is all a bit complicated, isn't it? Maybe he's just mocking you, laughing at you as you run in circles. Maybe he's tired of you and your mushroom piety saving the women of the world from monsters like me." Nick sat forward, knowing exactly how to get at him. "Did it ever occur to you that he might be a monster like me?"

"What are you saying?" His face turned a blustering red.

Nick pointed toward his desk. "Why don't you search 'Epstein and Agapov' and see what comes up, or maybe he's got his own Epstein game in Russia. Maybe a sideline in trafficking? Who are his friends?"

"The Lord will judge you!" he sputtered, pointing at him.

Nick ran his fingers through his hair. "I killed Patricia Wellington with just a few photographs. Then I killed her again and again by grinding the life out of every one of those women. Bea's gone, but I'm going to find her and I'm going to destroy her, too. You know how long it will take this case to go through the courts? No one is taking this company from me. No one can touch me. I wish I killed the Wellingtons, but maybe, looking at you now, maybe I killed them by setting it all in motion, just like I killed Patricia."

"You did not kill them!" Agape screamed, approaching him. "That was the Lord's execution!"

Nick remained seated. "I'm curious. How did you get the old woman to do it?"

"The Lord intervened!"

"That explains it. Listen, I know why I wanted them dead. Why you?"

"Do you know what they did to Patricia? Do you know why she was a drunk? They made her have sex with men for business deals. Her mother, Mary Wellington, too, if they liked older women, but she wanted it. Not Patricia." Quiet tears streamed down his face. "I was trying to save her when you took those photographs. She wouldn't go, she wouldn't go without her sister." He screamed. "She chose her end by refusing me!"

"Oh, please." Nick stood. "I did it all for my mother. The Wellingtons ruined her. All these wealthy people. All these people, just like you. I ruined you all. Look at you drooling and screaming. You couldn't save Bea, either. You loser. You and your fucking mushrooms." He looked him up and down. "I ruined you!"

Agape lurched at Nick, toppling him over and against the wall. Nick's head struck the metal edge of the door frame and he slid down, landing on his side, his arm trapped beneath him. The room faded to black as he watched Agape's thick old man shoes tread past him on the deep blue carpet.

———

"Mr. Barnes." A light flashed over his eyes. He tried to squint to protect himself from it, but a blue hand was holding his eye open. He was lying on something soft and there was rumbling underneath him. He heard voices.

"Is he conscious?"

"Not enough for you to arrest him."

52

Conor placed another carafe of coffee in front of Tomoko Abrams and Martin. He continued to admire her. She was a beautiful woman, tall and elegant. The clothes she wore were carefully chosen, a perfected look that was her own. But it was the fire in her eyes and her intelligence that lifted her into the sublime. Conor's eyes stung with tears of longing that he might never know the arc of such a woman's life in his own. The sacrifice tonight would free him into death or a new life, but he did not know what the Lord had planned.

"Take this cup from me," he said under his breath.

"How is Parisa?" Martin asked her.

"She'll be fine. I know she wants to go back to her graduate work, if she feels safe."

"Is she safe?"

"She's got people taking care of her. I trust them."

Vague answers. Martin had told him this morning he hoped to see Parisa to apologize, but Tomoko was not giving him anything.

She politely waved off the coffee. "It's getting late."

"Before you go," Martin said, "I have to say something."

Conor frowned. He would give her the apology; maybe she would take it to Parisa. But after Martin explained it all to him, he did not believe Martin fully understood what he had done wrong or why he had done it. An apology given without understanding was better than none, but his brother would continue to carry his pain, and pain others, unless he accepted it. Poor Martin had spent his life trying to save everyone else because he could not save his own brother, even though the failure of losing him to Bailey and, then, The Cluster, was not on him.

"I understand my graduate students, including Parisa, say I've promoted their work in ways that take advantage of them and I want to apologize to all of them, especially Parisa. I want to apologize." He looked away. "I mean, whatever it was I did, I can't do any more so I guess that's done, but—"

"Let me stop you. I can't pass on any messages to Parisa. I appreciate how open you both have been with us." Tomoko nodded to Conor. "What you shared with me about The Cluster must have been difficult for you. Making available all their financials, everything you have. I know we'll have more questions as we go along."

"There may be more to share with you after tonight," he said, hoping they could not hear the grief he carried. But Martin did, opened his mouth, then shut it.

"And you, Dr. Monaghan. It would be helpful if we could meet again with the data and the analysis before us. We're also eager to get a better read on Agape's role in your termination and its relationship to the work he considered his bearing in The Cluster."

"That's just it. That's what I wanted to discuss with you, pass on to Parisa."

"Maybe bringing it all to us for the story will be a way for you to make things right. You could make a public apology."

Conor wanted to object, but chose to wait to discuss the matter of a public apology with him alone. He had no doubt Tomoko would make him see what he had done wrong. That was all to the good, and he prayed for it, but Martin could not withstand the inevitable social media onslaught a public apology would bring. How could he ever heal?

She stood to go and he joined her. "Let me walk you to your car."

"I don't drive. I'll call a cab."

"Nonsense. I can ask my gardener, Tom, to drive you home in my car."

Tomoko answered him by taking out her phone, saying, "Journalistic independence," but there was something else to her objection.

Conor could sense Tomoko bristling as Martin followed them to the door like a sad dog.

"You wait here, Martin," he said. "I'll take her outside."

He acquiesced, unhappily.

Conor waited until the app showed the cab on its way, then made his point. "I will withdraw my cooperation in your piece if it includes a quote of public apology from my brother. He is not on social media and does not understand what it means to be dragged. I support you in holding his feet to the fire so he understands. But understanding what one has done wrong is only the beginning of lasting change, and I intend to protect him in that process."

She tucked her head back. "Are you threatening me?"

"By the Mushroom and the Cross, no! I am saying my cooperation is conditional."

"If his apology is part of the story, I'm reporting it." She paused, watching the cab come around the corner on the app, then faced him. "We can discuss how it is reported as long as the reporting is not compromised."

"I accept." He had confidence in her and held out his hand. They shook on it. Now he needed to sort out how to ensure the agreement would hold if he died tonight.

The taxi arrived, and Conor held the door open for her.

"Talk soon," she said.

It came to him as he returned to the house. He opened the front door, calling out, "Martin, I have an idea."

His brother was splayed out on the couch in the media room, a hockey game on.

"Turn that off."

Instead, he muted the sound. "What?"

"I have an idea for the money I set aside for you."

"I'm not taking it, I told you." He unmuted the game and increased the volume of the scrape of the skates and sticks against ice and play-by-play commentary.

Conor went to the speakers and turned them off. "Listen to me."

"What?" Martin sat up sullenly.

"They've resigned from *The Spanner*, yes?"

"So?"

"So, they do not have a journal yet for the piece. Why don't you start your own, take up the causes you believe in?"

Martin's eyes lit up.

"Hire them, make Amina Warsame the managing editor."

He fell back against the couch. "It's a conflict of interest. I'm part of the story."

"I am sure you can work something out that would satisfy their journalistic integrity."

Martin got up, pacing.

This would do it. Conor watched his brother come alive. He would start the journal, he could see it. Martin would have purpose, and be protected. Tomoko could hardly ruin the man who paid her.

Martin walked past him into the office, and Conor followed. He took the document with the banking account number on it and folded it, putting it in his wallet. "You can't do anything with this money now? You can't take it from me?"

"Why would you ask me that? But no, I cannot. Your name is on it, not mine. Despite it being offshore, you will have to prove your identity to use it."

"Then I will do it. I'll put the money in a trust for the journal's use and remove myself from any involvement."

"Martin! You are to own the journal. That was my idea!"

"Oh, so that whole conversation about me taking responsibility for what I did to my students, that's to end in a simple apology? Words? Nothing else? Well, it's my money. Recompense is in action, not words." He went past him, back to the media room. The sounds of the game resumed.

So Martin had understood what he had done, after all. He was torn between relief for him and fear that he could not protect him from what would come. Conor stood a moment longer in the office and listened to his breath, trying to gain control of himself.

A voice deep within him said gently, "Do not compromise your soul." He felt a hand between his shoulder blades and the tendrils touched him, calming him. The voice spoke again. "Prepare yourself."

The tendrils withdrew and he ascended the stairs, trembling, to dress for the evening; but what to wear to a sacrifice?

53

The men were already seated when Conor arrived, except Pierre, who was safely protected in the hospital. The soft flannel of Martin's shirt under his sweater comforted him. The lights were flickering, as always, and, for the first time, he found himself impatient with it rather than unnerved. Finally, he understood it was not humility or frugality that kept the brothers from renovating the building. It was manipulation.

He stood in the doorway, seeing the old men with new eyes. Their white hair, sagging cheeks, and lined faces holding onto a path gone astray. Each frowned silently from their assigned chairs, peeling laminate tiles underfoot, surrounded by walls of sickening grey and swollen plaster. He was always meant to be a little afraid, a little fascinated, invited into a secret brotherhood and its privileged piety. Had it always been like this? Had they never respected the truth?

Marcus glared, standing abruptly, breaking the strange silence. "You have meddled in our bearings! I cannot reach Pierre because of you!"

"What do I have to do with it?" Conor took his seat, back to the door. "You admitted your treatment was killing him."

"That doctor reported me to the College of Physicians and

Surgeons, even to the police! They came to my home today and interviewed me. I set them straight! But the crime is that Pierre is now beyond the reach of the Lord."

Vincent assured him. "Sit, Marcus. Please. My legal team is on it."

But Conor pushed. "Why did you give him medication that would weaken his immune system, then introduce a deadly fungal infection?"

"Conor, you too, please," Vincent said. "Must we?"

Ipe turned to Agape. "Did you know this?"

"Was it for you to know?"

But Marcus answered them both, "To purify him, you fools."

"With respect," Ipe ventured, "This seems, I mean, I admit, it—"

Conor cut him off. "I am curious, Marcus. How would it purify him?"

"With respect"—Benjamin gave Conor a scolding glance before turning to Marcus—"your bearing is to heal."

"Lord giving, it was to populate his every cell until nothing of his filth remained."

Benjamin and Ipe looked at one another, Ipe saying, "What filth? Pierre?"

"Doubt!" Marcus spat out, then turned on Conor. "The same filth that inhabits you!"

Ipe nearly turned over in his chair from the force of the declaration, and Benjamin grasped his arm.

"Forgive me, Conor. I shared your admission of doubt with our brothers." Agape inclined his head. "You, hiding under Bailey's desk so pitifully, it pained me and I shared it so I might better carry the burden of supporting you."

He was meant to be humiliated, but Agape did not know about the vision that followed. Crushing the mushrooms into the wine at the Last Supper, feeding them his blood and body, the night in the Garden of Gethsemane, knowing one would betray him while the others slept, allowing it to happen. "I do not doubt the Lord."

"You doubt this path, brother," Benjamin said.

"On the contrary, I do not doubt the path." And if it took the sacrifice of his blood and body to purify this path, he would sacrifice himself.

"No?" Marcus threw his hand out. "Yet you have put it at risk."

"You put Pierre's life at risk. I refuse to believe that a bearing given to us by the Lord would require killing our brother, yet you believe it was. Perhaps you misunderstood the visions given to you?"

"Oh, the condescension. How dare you, a mere child?"

Vincent rolled his eyes, but Agape added a sage nod of the head to Marcus's retort. Benjamin saw and dutifully looked down. Ipe wanted to speak, sitting forward. But with one glance from Agape, Ipe gave up.

Conor watched Benjamin, knowing he would have been instructed to add the poison meant for his cup, and wondered if he would refuse. "Marcus tried to kill our brother." He pointed at Agape. "This one has a secret. Tell us about your wife."

Agape's face hardened.

But Vincent dropped his expression of impatience, saying to Agape, "Let me handle him."

Putting a hand out to Vincent, Agape said to Conor, "Vincent wants to protect me. But I have the protection of the Lord."

But Vincent's expression had changed, his eyes became glassy, his pupils widened, as if he had come under the influence of a spontaneous communion and was entering into a visionary state. The others did not seem to notice, but Conor had tasted it himself. Vincent held out both hands to Conor, as if to be cuffed.

Agape stood beside him and took one of his hands, but instead of holding it, he wrapped his hands around Vincent's wrist as if he were strangling it and Conor knew what he had done.

"You killed her."

Vincent tore his hand away from Agape and stood awkwardly, wobbling on his arthritic knees, stuck both hands out again, and spoke from deep within his chest. "If you doubt his hands, you doubt our path."

Agape went after him and took his arm. "Stop. I demand you return."

"Let him tell it and let's be done with it." Marcus looked over at Ipe and Benjamin. "You should have known. I told them you all should have known. How can we protect this path otherwise? This filthy doubt comes from not knowing."

Benjamin and Ipe stared wide-eyed as Vincent took permission from Marcus and pushed Agape aside, but Agape righted himself, grabbing Vincent around the waist, as if to wrestle him to the ground. Marcus got up and pried Agape off. Vincent broke free, his eyes lost in the middle distance, and whispered to himself. The elderly men struggling was pathetically comical, and Conor laughed nervously at the absurdity of it.

"Help me!" Agape begged the others, but Benjamin and Ipe stood to aid Marcus, each taking an arm and forcing Agape back into his chair and held him there.

Conor prayed aloud. "Let the truth be revealed."

"He took her down to the water. I followed," Vincent said, swaying, eyes wandering as if to the heavens. "I followed her beautiful hair, so long and black against the night, it switched like the tail of a wild horse. She was a whore. A demon in the form of a woman in the form of an animal. He said words to her. Words of purity. She nipped at him. She pranced. She reared, refusing the bridle. He took her throat in his hands and he tamed her. He held the reins.

Conor put a hand to his own throat. Miss Henson had said the day she attacked, "The women bridle and he pulls the reins."

"I watched as he took her out into the lake and came back alone. He was glorious. I mistook him for an angel, not yet knowing him to be my prophet."

Conor gasped.

"Prophet?" Benjamin looked at Ipe.

But Marcus was exultant. Agape relaxed in their hold, as if hearing his secret, his prophethood, finally proclaimed, was a fulfilment rather than a damning.

"His face shone brighter than the fires lit in our camp. His heart beat louder than our drums. He came to me. His feet not touching the ground. I held the mushrooms out to him. An offering. My prophet ate them, joining us around the fires, dancing with us to the drums. A woman saw his power and circled him, hands flicking, feet stomping, head rolling on her neck. She disrobed for him. Her breasts swayed, loose. The firelight played on the ecstasy of her lips and tongue. He proclaimed she was a whore from the ages of whores."

Marcus explained with satisfaction. "Elizabeth. Miss Henson."

"The broken twigs and leaves under our feet became a carpet of dust, the scrub trees swaying palms, and we saw ourselves together before the Lord. And our prophet said to the Lord, 'Have you come to torment me before the appointed time?'"

Agape said this? Conor felt sick. This was the voice of Legion.

"The Lord asked him his name and Agape answered, 'My name is Legion, for we are many'."

Ipe turned on him. "You are Legion!"

Marcus shook his head and finished what Vincent had begun. "No, you fool. How many times have we recited this passage! He was the one who wandered, possessed. Our Lord cast Legion out of the prophet and into the swine, the whore of the ages, Henson. She has been with us ever since and filled with their madness."

Hearing the revelation admitted should have been a triumph, but it only stabbed at his gut. He pressed his hand against the pain.

"Masked, she taunted Pierre when he turned astray. She taunted Conor. Our prophet is pure." Marcus let go of Agape and joined Vincent, embracing him, and the two men circled each other, their limbs bent and swinging in a sickening dance to unheard drums.

Agape stood. "I am pure. I am your prophet. Do you doubt? Do any of you doubt?"

Conor stood to confront him. "Did Mary Magdalene come to you with the Lord?" Agape ignored him, approaching the dancing men, trying to lead them to their seats, but Conor kept at him. "Is our path founded on the murder of your wife?"

He turned on him, "Lady Magdalene came to me! She begged me to choose love! The Lord cast the demons out of me and into that whore-swine Henson. And I vowed to save women from whoredom!

To protect them, just as the Lord saved the Lady. I watched as the Lord put his blessed hands around Lady Magdalene's neck and told me to save all those who would be saved. I am the bearer of love and I have given you all my love, the women my love, the love of the Lord."

Taking careful steps backwards, Ipe and Benjamin retreated to the table at the side of the room. Once there, Benjamin took the leather case containing the sacraments and held it to his chest. Ipe placed a hand on the case, as if they could protect the path from what they were hearing, but they had given their life to a false prophecy.

Conor fell to his knees. Agape's visions of the Lord and Lady Magdalene were delusions. That meant that so were his own, even those that brought him to this moment. There was no truth or path to be saved. The path itself was poisoned. He cried out, "My Lord, why have you forsaken me?"

Taking the leather case from Benjamin's arms, Agape returned it to the table, then embraced them both, saying, "Do not doubt the path of my prophecy. It is not for you to understand, but for me to bear." He put a hand on the case. "Set the Intention as we discussed. Prepare the vessel of truth. I will drink of it. Conor will drink of it. The one who lies will die."

Benjamin nodded uncomfortably and turned to withdraw the wooden bowl, the ladle, the wine, and two wooden cups, then finally a small leather sack different from the one they used for communion.

Conor watched from where he kneeled on the floor. He lifted the collar of his brother's shirt to his face and felt him near as he watched Benjamin prepare the wine. Every movement was made with reverence, Ipe whispering prayers beside him.

Seeing, Marcus turned Vincent from the dance. The two joined the men at the table, whispering the prayer, until their whispers were a single voice. "By the Mushroom and the Cross. If the womb is poison, it must die. If the womb is truth, the stalk will arise."

A shadow appeared beside Conor. Agape held out a hand. "Come, brother."

Conor took his hand, and stood beside him, but he drew Agape away from the others, towards the door.

"No one can hear us," Conor said. "I will not say a word and drink. I beg you, let me die with the truth."

Triumph ate away at the mask of piety. "Ask me."

"Did you order Miss Henson to kill the Wellingtons?"

He scoffed. "She was trying to protect Cassandra from her punishment. Cassandra would not be saved and Legion would do anything for her."

"You ordered Cassandra to kill them?"

"I gave her wine with our sacred mushrooms. Then I gave her a word, from a distance. They would never stop. The Wellingtons wanted a pure woman killed, Parisa and her innocent child. Stone would not kill except by my word, but they would have found another way." He moaned lightly, his eyes shining with tears. "They were my failures. But I purified them. The Wellingtons. Their daughters, Patricia and Cassandra. Nick Barnes."

"Why Nick Barnes?"

"Do you not know? I saved the women he held hostage over the years. Their parents were referred to me, never knowing me by name, only knowing a man from among them could free young women who wanted to be pure again. I saved one after another, but Nick would never stop. Then he brewed the virus."

Conor glanced behind him, then asked, "How did you know the virus was his?"

"Miss Henson," he frowned viciously. "My brother, Andrei, sent an underling to cover over Piotr, the man I was, the man who had murdered his wife, to reveal to the man who was a prophet. He approached Miss Henson."

"Your brother is one of us!"

"Filth! He denied me, but he protected me all the same. A brother's love. Sometimes the Lord sends the faithless to lay the foundation of his paths."

"But Miss Henson—"

"You heard. She was there that night. She remained with Vincent and I in those early years, long before Marcus, Bailey, and the rest joined us. She was mad, possessed by Legion. But my brother had bound her to report to him as a condition of enshrouding my past life. He lifted her family out of poverty and into wealth. If she denied him, they would fall. But she would have done it for pleasure. The two-faced game came easily to Legion. She did my bidding, yet told him everything. He said that if I purified with these hands again, he would know. She would inform him." Agape said with deep anger, "'The brother knows all', she reminded me, endlessly."

Conor remembered the day she attacked him. She had said just that: "The brother knows all." But he assumed she was imagining speaking to Bailey's spirit. He asked, "And Nick?"

"I was forced to ask Miss Henson to go to my brother. He gave Nick to me, through her."

"Why did you never kill her?"

"My brother would know. I would die." He touched Conor's arm lightly. "But see what the Lord arranged! Cassandra killed her for me, without my asking! I am freed of my brother. Now the purifications can begin. The whores will die. The Cluster is freed. My prophecy is revealed. We may begin. My bearing is the bearing of you all." He paused, laughter in his eyes. "Not you, Conor. You will not be among us."

"My brothers," Marcus called.

Conor clutched at the collar of the flannel shirt as he followed Agape and sat beside him.

Benjamin held out the wooden cups.

"What do we say?" asked Conor.

"As usual, with one difference."

The brothers knew what to do without Agape telling them. And Conor knew what had happened to the one brother who tried to leave years ago.

Together they recited,

"Under the shade of the Mushroom Cap, we meet our Lord, Ukushtigila, The Key to the Kingdom. We eat our Lord. Ukushtigila, The Key to the Kingdom. We drink our Lord. Ukushtigila, The Key to the Kingdom. We serve our Lord."

Conor felt the words on his tongue one last time, but words that had once been a revelation to him were now a devastation. He wept like a child whose mother is torn from him. The visions he believed were true, and had acted on with sincerity, were nothing but hallucinations. His sacrifice would be for nothing. There was no path to purify. There was no life to give for the truth. His life had already been taken from him as a boy, manipulated by forces beyond him, handed over by his mother, beyond the reach of his younger brother. For nothing. His life was built on lies and he would never know how to trust what was true again. There was no sacrifice to be made. There was no point in living.

Agape added, "I accept the vessel of truth. I accept its verdict. I accept its purification."

"I accept the vessel of truth." Conor repeated. "I accept its verdict. I accept its purification."

They sipped together, and he welcomed the scent of bitter almonds in the wine.

Knowing the poison would be slipped into his cup alone, he had promised Martin he would not drink it, that he would pretend, find some way to pour it out. His brother was standing behind the wall in the hallway, recording everything, gathering all the evidence to expose Agape. But he could not see from there if Conor drank or not, and he prayed Martin would not intervene.

The men sat across from him in the circle, chanting, as they waited for the truth to be proven.

He imagined holding the hand of the woman in the silk Mondrian dress, stroking her fingers, bringing her home, hearing her quiet, even breaths as they slept. He followed her as she wandered through his home, now their home, her dress sweeping the floor behind her, touching his things, smiling, finding Oonagh in the kitchen and kissing her cheek. The old woman blushed, bending her head, honoured by her. His wife was exquisite, lithe, green-eyed and laugh-lined. Her long nose was elegantly set on a narrow face set off by a jutting chin. Her red hair fell loose down her back. She was out of a storybook, a woman meant for a castle, and she held her hand out to him.

The nausea came, little by little. It was not what he thought, and he believed he could ride out death easily, if this is what it was, until cramps arose from the sickness, clawing at his gut. He moaned, doubling over as they ripped him open. He screamed, falling onto the floor.

Agape stood over him. "The verdict is given!"

Vomit came up and he choked on it, struggling for breath. Screams erupted around him. The sound of the brothers rejoicing. He coughed, trying to spit out the vomit as the claws came at him again.

Hands were under his arms, dragging him along the floor. The brothers retreated, backing up against the wall, hands out. Vomit dribbled out of his mouth. He shut his eyes and waited for the moment, praying there was a God to meet him. Then he was up in the air, and thrown over something. Was it Martin? His arms swaying, his legs loose. This was death.

Martin yelled, "Back!" Then a deafening shot. Then, "I said back!"

His stomach was pressed against Martin's shoulder, pounding against him, forcing more vomit out and up his nose. He was unable to breathe, and the sounds of the world faded around him.

A man appeared outlined by blinding light and lifted him from his brother and lay him down on the soft, sun-warmed earth. His scent was frankincense and myrrh. Conor knew him and placed his cheek on his sandal. The man lifted him up and took his face in his hands. In the shade of that glorious face, Conor gazed on eyes that shone like a thousand stars.

He asked the man, "Are you God?"

"Who do people say I am?" He answered with a slight smile. "You served God with purity of intention. I was with you as a child, I was with you as a man, and I will be with you now. Return. Live in service of my love and be loved."

TWO WEEKS LATER

EPILOGUE

Martin wheeled Conor into the chapel at St. James cemetery, positioning the wheelchair at the back. Although gothic architecture was not to his taste, Conor admired the small church. The dark oak pews faced a small sanctuary inset into a pointed arch with three horizontal purple and orange stained-glass windows cut in a complimentary design. A small dais had been placed before the purple draped altar. It held two arrangements of yellow, red, and orange sunflowers. The rows were filled with George's friends and dozens of dogs. The dogs' nails scratched against the stone floor, and yips and snuffles could be heard here and there, but the animals were strangely patient and quiet, as if they knew why they had come and respected the memory of the man who had given his life for another.

Conor was grateful to be there at all. He had been in intensive care for several days, then a regular room, then home again, with Oonagh and Martin fussing over him. Oliver had come once and made him a proper cup of coffee, just when he thought he could not stand another cup of Oonagh's tea. As Oliver prepared the brew, Martin moved around him, the two taking any excuse to brush against each other. Jamal and his family visited, and to Oonagh's displeasure, his mother bore richly scented tubs of Conor's favourites.

His lawyers had come, one by one, advising him on the sale and dissolution of Wake Financial, he and Martin on the distribution of the recordings to the journalists Warsame and Abrams, Cassandra's lawyer, and the police, and, finally, drawing up the paperwork for the creation of a new journal. Conor had finally convinced Martin to publish it himself, but he agreed only if he could remain anonymous and sign away all editorial control.

The day after, Martin met with Amina Warsame and returned, bouncing with a freedom he had not seen in him since before their father had died. Warsame had accepted the job of editor-in-chief and her first act was to hire Tomoko Abrams and Anthony El Buhali. Then she suggested Martin might have a role as an analyst, if he were interested. But in all his news, Parisa's name never came up, and Conor did not pry.

Martin came to attention beside him and Conor turned to see what had caught his eye. A short woman with cropped hair, wearing a wide-belted camel coat and beautiful cream leather boots, joined them. She could only be Parisa. Some might call her beauty unre-markable, but her eyes held depths and Conor understood her, wishing he could stand to embrace her or that she might allow him to kiss her hand.

"I'm so glad to see you, I—" Martin stumbled over his words.

"Stop," Parisa said, obviously uncomfortable. "I heard about what you've done from Tomoko. There's no need to say anything. I wanted you to know Arash and I are good and I'll be going back to my studies next year. I'll take the rest of this year off for the sake of my son."

"He's not with you?"

"No," she said brusquely, then relented. "He's been through enough. We appreciate you getting the rabbit to us."

Only then did Conor notice the substantial diamond on her left hand. He was glad for her.

She turned her attention to him. "You must be Dr. Monaghan's brother. I was sorry to hear what you went through, but we're all relieved you're going to recover."

"Nothing compared to what others have endured. We can only hope that justice will be served."

She gave him a skeptical look, but nodded politely and asked, "What about Beatrice?"

What could Conor say aloud? His lawyers had reached out to Panopticon to see what they could do. There was no response, but the OnlyFans account, videos, and the rest had disappeared from the web. Then came the sudden announcement that Nick would plead guilty. Conor's lawyers suspected a threat from Panopticon was behind it, and they hoped Nick was under Agapov's watch for good. But all Conor could do for certain was set up an income for Beatrice. Stan had contacted her mother, and the two drove out to take care of it. So, he said what he could. "She's safe."

"That's something," she answered, gave Martin an unreadable look, and walked away without a goodbye.

"You all right?" he asked Martin.

"They're safe. That's all I wanted."

More than safe, he wagered, given the ring, but he would point it out to his brother later.

Reverend Lee came in holding a sweet-faced golden lab puppy and crouched next to his chair. The puppy squirmed and Conor held out his hands to take her. She landed floppy-legged onto his lap, but settled down immediately, looking up at him with pool-black eyes before laying down her head. Conor placed a hand on her warm back and felt the rise and fall of her breath, his own finding a rooted peace with the touch. The puppy sighed loudly. Eyes wide with delight, he and Reverend Lee stifled their laughs.

"I guess Faro wants to stay with you for the service."

"It would be my pleasure," he said and felt Martin's hand on his shoulder.

"Thank you for this," they said. "And don't worry, no one knows it was you who paid for it. We're eager to see you downtown whenever you're ready. No hurry, though."

Conor nodded, and they leaned in to embrace him. Martin had brought Reverend Lee to him while he was in the hospital and he had told them everything, including the final vision. The reverend did not judge what he saw nor offer platitudes about repentance, suffering, and God's will, only saying, "The Jesus I know would have said what your Jesus said, especially, I think for you, he would stress the 'be loved' part." Conor had kissed their hands and held them to his face, but they pulled them away and playfully nudged his arm. "None of that with us. You just come and visit and we'll find a job for you."

Conor looked out at the pews and finally found Tomoko sitting with a man and woman he assumed to be El Buhali and Warsame, and an older couple that must be her parents. Conor caught her eye. She smiled and waved, said something to the couple, then got up to come over. But when she neared, she was no longer smiling. Something had happened, something beyond the grief of the funeral.

"Have you seen the news?" She scrolled through her phone and showed it to them.

MUTILATED BODY FOUND WASHED UP ON
LESLIE SPIT.

Martin took the phone from her and read through it quickly. "Is it Agape? No face, teeth, fingers or toes. But it's his body size and age."

Conor's breathing became shallow. His skin prickled and turned numb. He could not feel the puppy under his hand. Martin crouched beside him. "Slow breaths. I'm right here." He went into the bag hanging off the chair and brought out a water bottle. As soon as he could feel his fingers again, he took it from him.

"There's more," Tomoko said, but gestured to Martin that they should speak elsewhere.

"No," Conor said with what breath he had. "Here."

She seemed worried, but continued. "I called the police this morning, following up on the recordings of Agape and the murder. They told me no one by the name of Peter Agape with the address we gave them exists, let alone Piotr Agapov. I checked with Anthony. The house is up for sale. Anthony said ownership is now in the name of a

Marina Volkov. But that's not what we found before. Anthony's got copies of the previous ownership and the rest saved on an external drive and printed out. It has to be Agapov. We think Panopticon has digitally erased him, and now with this, well, also erasing him literally."

"Dead?" Conor asked, needing to hear it again.

"It has to be him. We're sending Cassandra's lawyer what we have to prove he existed, so she can use it to be declared not criminally responsible. We think Agapov won't try to get rid of the evidence to help Cassandra. She's one of Agape's victims. Anthony says he cannot imagine Panopticon would have given him the chance to print it out, if not."

She carried on, filling in Martin on the details, but Conor could not hear her. Agape was dead. He had said his brother, Andrei, would erase him if he used his hands to purify again. Cassandra, the Wellingtons, Miss Henson. He was behind it all. Conor would have expected to feel relief, some sense of justice, but it was grief redoubled.

Martin crouched again, wiping away Conor's tears.

He would tell Reverend Lee, then Martin, when he knew what words to use. For now, he understood he did not grieve the man, but all the harm Agape had done to so many. He grieved, knowing not even the death of their prophet would be enough to inspire the brothers to release themselves, even when he, himself, had nearly died proving the lies. Conor ran his fingers across Faro's soft fur, lightly tugging at her ears, and calling himself to the warmth and weight of the puppy in his lap.

Reverend Lee took their place on the podium. The chatter died down. Four dog walkers entered from the rear with George's cremated remains, each holding a corner of a carved walnut box in one hand and a dog on a lead in the other. Faro looked up, watching as the hounds kept solemn pace with the walkers until they reached the dais. As the walkers put the box down between the flowers, one, a lean brown dog, jumped up, putting both paws on the table and whined. The mourners gasped, letting out small cries here and there.

The walker holding his lead bent down, kissed him on the head, and brought the dog to a pew.

Reverend Lee waited a moment, then said, "I will share only a brief word to say that God places saints among us. They are not the high and mighty. They are not the perfect or even the pious. They are those with everything to lose who give to their last. They give their love, their friendship, their nourishment, and, sometimes, their lives. George was among them. May those who can testify to his life come forward and share their memories."

One by one they came up: his sister, dog walkers, and friends. Some were strong, others broken. His sister spoke of the joys of their childhood on a small farm up north, their parents' death, the loss of the farm, his life on the streets of Toronto, and his addictions, ending only when he found the dog walkers. She cried and thanked them for doing what she could not. The others shared what he meant to them, a few breaking down and unable to speak, some telling tales better left for the wake that would follow, but all mourning the loss of a good man who had lived a hard life. The last was a small woman, one of the broken ones. Her clothes were ragged, but she had made an attempt to tidy herself. Her hair was brushed hard and pulled back, exposing a gaunt face married by drugs and a grief unlike the others. She mumbled something that sounded like, "I did this to him," then shuffled out a side door, followed by whispers.

Conor looked up at Martin. "What could she mean?"

He shook his head.

A man got up and went after her.

Reverend Lee watched them go with a worried look, then held their hands out for quiet. "There is one who would have been here if she could, his life given in sacrifice for hers, and we, who know her, know that she wishes it had been the other way."

Then, they stepped down from the pulpit and took the lead of a black dog, an odd husky mix with short legs and a too-long tail. The dog followed the reverend up, tail wagging, looking to please.

They crouched down beside the dog, saying, "Billie Girl, will you lead us in our final prayer?"

Head high, the dog dutifully howled to the rafters.

One by one, the other dogs in the chapel barked and howled in answer. The mourners laughed at first, looking at each other, then one joined in, others following, all giving in to the prayerful abandon of the dogs until their prayers threatened to bring the chapel down. Thinking himself too weak to pray for George himself, he took his brother's hand, and Martin prayed for the both of them, raising his head to the roof, and Faro, her small mouth rounded, let out a "haroo," until Conor shook from the pain releasing and found his own prayer deep within him and howled.

AFTERWORD

While the action takes place in Toronto, I have changed the names of any locations that might be wrongly implicated by the ill intentions of my characters. This novel is not a roman-à-clef. I did not intend any associations with people, living or dead, news outlets, or institutions.

I adapted short passages and elements from John Marco Allegro's *The Sacred Mushroom and the Cross* and *The New Testament, King James Version*, to create The Cluster and Conor's visions. Megan Goodwin's sensitive analysis of "cults" in *Abusing Religion* guided my depiction of The Cluster and Conor's experience.

I do not know if the artist, Adrian Hayles, does private commissions, but we love his work so much here in Toronto, I had to include one in Anthony's apartment.

I did not intend to lead anyone astray on the uses of *amanita muscaria*, a sacred communion for some, a therapeutic tool for many, and a good time for others. I do not believe there is any evidence it can be used to entice people to kill, except in fiction, and that's what this is.

On research, I did very little. For instance, my account of the journalists and their methods did not go beyond searching "ethics of journalism" and relying on everything I know from watching journalism thrillers. Please understand. I had just given up writing painstakingly detailed historical fiction. The relief is still palpable and I am enjoying not minding being wrong for once. But if you want to see what I can pull off with thirty years of specialization in medieval Islam, a love of murder mysteries, romance, and mystical melodrama, check out *The Sufi Mysteries Quartet*. Those books are so accurate, they are used as university textbooks.

Aspects of the messy, good folk in the novel were inspired by the delightful personalities of friends with their permission, some of whom will go unnamed. You can find the real "Oliver," James Oliver, at Oliver Coffee Bar in East York for some coffee and craic. Reverend Lee is based on an old friend, and the final scene is exactly how they might lead a funeral. Abdi, The Leninist, is fellow author and gardening friend, Ahmed Salah. He approved his depiction and agrees his political discourses could be used as an interrogation technique. Check out his darkly satiric romance, *Man's Best Friend*. Tomoko's parents are inspired by the stories of a Jewish friend and the communist camp they belonged to up north. The Billie Girl who leads the prayer is our recently departed, much loved, Husky-Kelpie mix to whom I dedicate this novel.

———

Finally, thank you to all my friends and writing-comrades who answered questions, shared their expertise, and read drafts, and without whom I would be a complete mess.

Most especially, I would like to thank Michael Quinsey, Karen Heenan, and J. Austin Yoshino who gave me detailed notes on every chapter. Austin Yoshino made sure I got all the hacking and computer scenes right, as well as advised me on Japanese culture. He and Ahmed Salah advised me on my depiction of communist characters. Salah also advised me on Somali culture. Cyrus Zargar, Nasrin Mostafavi-Pak and Khaterah Majlesi, advised me on Persian culture and language. James Oliver advised me on Martin's character and offered lots of coffee and craic. I wrote and edited a lot of the book at Oliver Coffee Bar. Any errors are my own.

Two people urged me to write a badly researched contemporary thriller in which everything gets weirder and weirder. Cyrus Zargar, writing buddy and fellow scholar of Sufism, is hilarious and irresponsible and urged me to be the same. Karen Heenan ordered me to write this book as I binged a completely absurd thriller and thought, "Maybe I can do that." Heenan is the author of *The Tudor Court Series* and a series of novels set during the Great Depression *Ava and Claire*.

I want to thank Omid Safi for his translation of Rumi's poem. Domenico Ingenito shared his English translation of Forugh Farrokhzad's "The Gift." Check out Ingenito's other translations of Persian poetry in English and Italian (Forugh Farrokhzad, *Io parlo dai confini della notte. Tutte le poesie*).

Other friends kindly answered questions, found inconsistencies, or cheered, including Vernon Schubel, Cathal Keegan, Kathleen Self, Ausma Zehanat Khan, reneé mercuri, Leilehua Yuen, Jennie Jones, Amy Taylor-Mitropoulos, Janice Brown, and Ben Shakinovsky. If I have forgotten to mention anyone else, please forgive me.

———

As always, independent authors need your support. We do not have the promotional tools enjoyed by authors who are traditionally published. We cannot even get our books reviewed by big media or go up for significant awards. We need you, the reader, to help us out by leaving reviews on your favourite online platforms. Even just a few words are a tremendous help. Also, word-of-mouth matters. If you enjoy our books, tell a friend, make a post on social media. Thank you!

IDEOLOGICALLY PURE

No, that's—

ideologically pure.

If you would like the t-shirt "ideologically pure" (all lowercase, more hip) for yourself, you can buy them at Fresh Pulp's Redbubble store. A portion of the proceeds will support Fresh Pulp Magazine: a cooperatively run, and soon, cooperatively owned science fiction magazine that promotes STEM literacy within Black, Indigenous, People of Color, and Women through STEM-based storytelling.

(On RedBubble sizing: Make sure and measure a shirt of yours against the measurements of their shirts.)

ABOUT THE AUTHOR

Laury Silvers writes contemporary thrillers under the name, "Jayne Green." Under her birth name, Silvers writes historical mysteries set in medieval Muslim lands, including *The Sufi Mysteries Quartet* and *Rat City* in the collection *Revenge in Three*.

Who is Jayne Green?

Jane Green is Silvers' great-great-great grandmother. She was a single mother who raised three girls working cattle camps in old Florida and was known to throw a punch, maybe when you were not looking.

Laury Silvers was raised in the United States but is finally at home in Canada. Her research and publications as a historian of religion focused on early Islam, early Sufism, and early pious and Sufi women. She taught at Skidmore College and the University of Toronto. Silvers also published work engaging Islam and Gender in North America in academic journals and popular venues, was actively involved in the woman-led prayer movement in Islam, and co-founded the Toronto Unity Mosque. She has since retired from academia and activism and hopes her novels continue her scholarship and activism in their own way. She lives in Toronto with her family under Treaty 13.

A SMALL TOWN

A TORONTO THRILLER

From Jayne Green

Denora Dunne has a secret no one knows, not even her estranged daughter. When hints arrive on scribbled bits of paper through her mailbox, Denora wants to know who sent it and how they found out. A retired life of spy novels, trips to the local coffee shop, and losing the fight with her messy garden did not prepare her for neighbours turned into secret police, peering through doorbell cameras and sharing tips on the Small Town app. But if she's learned anything from all the novels she's read, it's how to isolate an enemy spy and plug a leak, even if that means murder.

SMALL JUSTICE
A GHAZI AMMAR MEDIEVAL MYSTERY

From Laury Silvers

Your favourite characters
from The Sufi Mysteries Quartet
return in a new series

The police have written off the death of a beloved father as an accident. His family refuses to believe it and begs Ammar to investigate, if only for answers. Problem is, they cannot pay, money Ammar sorely needs. When Ammar talks to the police as a courtesy, they stonewall him, whetting his appetite for the case, paid or not, and leading him to uncover a secret better left dead.

ALSO BY LAURY SILVERS

THE SUFI MYSTERIES QUARTET

THE LOVER • THE JEALOUS • THE UNSEEN • THE PEACE

Enter into the world of medieval Baghdad as Zaytuna and Tein solve mysteries and come to terms with the legacy of their mother and the violence that has consigned them to lives without love. Widely used in university courses, each mystery uncovers a different aspect of medieval Islamic history.

"Completely engrossing and richly atmospheric. Tenth century Baghdad comes alive through the eyes of a dazzling cast of characters." —Ausma Zehanat Khan, critically acclaimed author of Blackwater Falls, A Deadly Divide from The Getty-Khattak Mysteries, and The Khorasan Archivess

RAT CITY in REVENGE IN THREE

Love, money, power, betrayal... revenge. The Count of Monte Cristo has enthralled generations of readers the world over. Now three Muslim authors offer their interpretations of this classic tale.

From the seedy underbelly of a medieval plague fortress, to the lawless borderlands of the Wild West, to the darkest depths of outer space, each novella delivers a full dose of adventure and excitement while exploring different aspects of society, politics and religion.

Rat City • Alt-Medieval Noir • Laury Silvers

In the walled city of Aman Kala, the grisly murder of a sacred Rat Keeper pulls Detective Derya Mack into an investigation that threatens to expose the power struggles that guarantee the very safety the fortress offers from the plague world.

The Pasha of Texas • Western • Jibril Stevenson

A botched robbery lands Eddie Dawson in a Mexican prison. His friendship with a Muslim prisoner opens the door to repentance and faith, if he could only let go of the ghosts of his past.

The Spatial Condition • Science Fiction • J. Austin Yoshino

Mohsin Dawoud, 3rd mate on the interstellar cargo freighter "Nightshade", has been preparing for life in space with his betrothed, Solmaz. When the Nightshade is attacked, it draws him into a conspiracy of jealousy and greed among Earth's most powerful that could destroy the life he spent years building.

———

All books can be accessed for sale through www.llsilvers.com, through Amazon, Bookshop, or your local Bookseller.